TEX

BOOK TWO
BURNOUT SERIES
DAHLIA WEST

TABLE OF CONTENTS

CHAPTER ONE

Twenty two year old Abby Raines was cruising at 65 miles per hour in her six year old Toyota and singing happily along with the radio when the car started acting sluggish. She released the accelerator, tamped it down again. She got no significant response. She frowned at the dashboard where the Check Engine light had not come on. She put on her turn signal, changed lanes, and then pulled onto the shoulder of Interstate 90 just eleven miles outside Rapid City, South Dakota. She killed the radio, but left the car idling. She yanked on the parking brake, got out and strode to the front of her car, her boots leaving tracks in the damp earth.

It was cold, in the mid forties, and March in South Dakota was a hell of a lot more damp than she was used to. But the scenery was downright breathtaking. Highway 90 skirted the Black Forest from the minute she'd crossed the border from Wyoming. The weather would take some getting used to, but she already loved the view.

She popped the car's hood and leaned in, listening intently. She heard the telltale crackling noise and heaved a sigh. She stalked back to the driver's side door, reached in, and killed the engine. She continued on down to the trunk where she opened it and took out a folded white rag tucked into the corner.

She was on the last leg of her trip and had risen at 6 am to check out of her hotel in order to get on the road and get to her final destination at a decent hour. It was now going on 2 pm. It was her own fault though, that she was stuck out here, so far from her old home yet so close to her new one. She leaned down and pulled a spark plug out.

She was making up lists in her head for all the things she needed to buy for her new place when she heard a low rumble. She peeked around the side of the hood and saw a man pulling up behind her on a black Harley Davidson. He took off his helmet and hooked it to the handlebar and swung his leg over the back. He was tall, she could tell that just by how low the Harley was in comparison.

He had medium length blonde hair and was fairly intimidating in his black leather jacket and dark blue jeans. His boots were black, too, and rounded at the toe. As he headed toward her, Abby's heart knocked in her chest. She wasn't afraid. She was on a busy highway and if push came to shove she could handle herself. But damn this man was fine. She had seen few men this good looking close up and she was from a town where beautiful people reigned supreme.

He stalked up the length of the car and rounded the front. "So," he said. "Flat tire, huh?"

And she laughed. She had expected a man who looked this rough to be all growls and grunts. "I wish," she replied. "Wouldn't take nearly as long." She held up a disconnected spark plug. "I really should have gone for that tune up before I made the trip."

He nodded and his eyes raked over the rest of the car's engine. "It's important to keep up with your maintenance."

She sighed and continued to clean the inside with the rag. "I know. But lately it just seems like there's too much to do and not enough me to do it. You know what I mean?"

"Definitely. I'm Tex, from Texas. And you're coming from Vegas? Says your license plate. You actually live there?"

She nodded. "My whole life. I'm Abby."

His eyes glittered with interest. "I never met anyone who actually *lives* in Vegas. I mean...aside from people who work there."

She frowned at him. He was not asking if she was a stripper. She glanced down. Her jeans were not tight at all, her t-shirt wasn't either, and it showed no cleavage. "Well, I did work there. In a hotel," she told him quickly. "But I was born there, too. So were both my parents."

He nodded. "You here for a visit?"

"No. I just graduated from UNLV and got my first job offer at a hotel in Rapid City."

He studied her. "Aren't graduations usually in May?"

"Usually," she said, replacing the plug, "But I graduated a semester early. Just ready to get out of Vegas and start my life, you know?"

"I can relate. I wanted to get off the farm so badly I joined the Army at 18."

Abby's eyes widened. "Really?"

He grinned. "Yeah, but I had to quit after a while because the food's so bad."

She laughed again. She'd met all kinds of people in Las Vegas. Bikers weren't new, but funny bikers were few and far between.

"You would think it would have been the people shooting at you," she teased.

"Nah. They missed. Usually. But heartburn from the powdered eggs? That's a sure thing."

Her eyes widened again, but she couldn't tell if he was teasing her or not about being shot.

"So how did you end up here?" she asked. "Or are *you* just visiting?"

"No. I live in Rapid City now. My old lieutenant set up shop in town and the boys from the unit just...kind of fell in line, I guess. We'd spent so many years together at that point that it seemed odd not to just keep doing it."

"Well, he must be a really great guy for all of you to follow him up here," Abby remarked.

Tex nodded. "He is. He's the best man I know. And since I wasn't sure what I wanted to do after the army, I figured why not do whatever Shooter wants to do?"

Abby grinned. "And you all have nicknames?"

He chuckled. "No way around it. You get them when you enlist and they sort of stick. I've always thought mine was unimaginative, but now that I've met you, I couldn't see calling you anything but 'Vegas' especially since, like I said, I've never met anyone *from* Vegas."

She laughed. "I'm not even to the city limits yet and I already have a nickname. This might be a good sign. What's Rapid City like?"

"It's a good town. A working town."

She nodded thoughtfully. "Vegas is a working town, too, underneath the glitter."

"You should fit right in. There for damn sure aren't many pretty girls like you in town. It'll improve the scenery."

Abby blushed and quickly looked away, shoving the last spark plug into place. She dug her keys out of her pocket, but Tex brought his hand up quickly, capturing her own. "Now that you've done all the hard work, let me at least contribute."

He slipped the keys out and she swore he held onto her hand a little longer than necessary. She turned back to the engine. "Thanks," she told him, in a clipped tone.

He headed to the driver's side door and leaned in, turning the keys in the ignition. The engine caught and she leaned in to listen to it. Hearing no more crackle and not noticing anything wrong with the idle speed, she nodded to herself and stood up.

"Looks good," said Tex and she turned around.

He'd come up behind her and for a moment she wasn't sure if he was referring to her or the engine. Then she shook herself. Of course he meant the engine. Guys like Tex didn't go for girls like her. He'd said she was pretty, but he was just being polite. Tex was all man. More man than she'd ever dared to look at in the way her mind was turning.

She glanced back at the engine. "Yeah, I think we got it. Thanks for all your help."

He laughed as she brought down the hood.

"Well, always nice to help a damsel in distress," said Tex, grinning at her.

She couldn't help but smile back.

"There aren't a lot of bars in town," Tex told her as she wiped her hands. "Maria's is the best local watering hole. It's on the south edge of town. If you're thirsty, head on over."

She nodded. "Nice meeting you," was all she could think to say.

"You too, Vegas." He touched his head like he was tipping a

cowboy hat.

Abby tossed the dirty rag onto the floorboard of the passenger side and signaled before she pulled out into a lull between cars. Tex followed her into town, which wasn't unusual, she thought, since he said he lived there. But she did sigh a teeny tiny bit in relief when at the end of the exit ramp for Rapid City, he turned right and she turned left.

He gave her a wave, which she caught in her window and she beeped her horn once in acknowledgement. She threaded her way through the streets of Rapid City, amazed at its relative quiet compared to home. She was tired. Tired from the road and tired of the glitter of her hometown. Her GPS showed her the last three turns to a new condo development in the western part of town and she drove slowly down the street, looking for the one that was hers.

She'd chosen it over the internet and only paid for a six month lease, not being at all familiar with Rapid City and its various neighborhoods. She finally found hers and pulled into the narrow driveway. The bushes were well trimmed and there was no yard to speak of. Which was fine with her not having ever had a yard and not knowing quite what to do with one if she did.

She parked the car and killed the engine. She gathered her GPS, her purse, and her small overnight bag out of the front seat and headed toward the front door. The movers had arrived ahead of her, dropped off her small amount of belongings, and left the spare key she had given them on the kitchen counter. She walked through the condo, which smelled of new paint and the carpets appeared new, as well. Her only piece of furniture, her bed, which she had bought and given over immediately to the movers, was in the condo's only bedroom.

She tossed her purse and suitcase inside the bedroom and opened the box marked "bedding." She pulled out a pillow and a sheet set that had never been used and just managed to make the bed before collapsing on top of it. She closed her eyes and drifted to sleep. "Home, Sweet, Home," she whispered to herself just before darkness overtook her.

She woke the next morning, Saturday, or at least she thought it was morning, not having unpacked her alarm clock. She showered and changed clothes from her overnight bag and set about opening boxes. She cut the manufacturer's packing tape on a small set of pots and pans, not that she had any idea how to use them, and a six piece dinnerware set, not that she had friends.

She hung her clothes in the bedroom closet and set up the bathroom with her toiletry items. She checked the time on her cell phone and found it was nearly noon at this point. She opened her laptop and googled the local grocery and headed out with a list that she'd made and hung on her refrigerator.

On the way to the store, she caught a glimpse of a sign that said Maria's and slowed to check the place out. It looked like any restaurant/bar with a large gravel lot in front. There were a few cars and motorcycles for this early on a Saturday and she wondered what kind of food they had.

She shook off the thought and headed to the store, stocking up based on a suggested list downloaded from the internet. Back at her condo, she stored the items, but couldn't bring herself to actually use any of them. Instead she picked up her purse again and headed back out to her car.

Maria's was dark inside, but not a dive she realized as her eyes adjusted from the late afternoon light. She picked a stool at the bar, slung her purse on the counter and had a seat. She was still going to need another decent night's sleep before she was over this moving thing.

The tall blonde behind the bar gave her a chin raise. "Menu?" Abby asked politely. The blonde handed it to her. Abby flipped through it. The only thing remotely healthy was a cobb salad. The bacon cheeseburgers sounded delicious, but Abby was a size twelve and had been almost since she hit puberty at fourteen. Thank God she'd inherited her mother's height, 5'7" without the heels. But still, if she wanted to continue to indulge in her desire for French lingerie, she had to stay within the standard size range.

"Can I get a cobb salad?" she asked the blond. "And a martini?"

The blonde eyed her over the menu Abby was handing back. "Cobb salad, yes. But we don't serve Cosmos here, darlin'."

Although Abby had had a rough couple of days driving 1,070 miles in her cramped, piece of crap Toyota, she smiled at the woman. "You have Death's Door?"

"Yeah."

"Can you put it in a glass and I'll pretend there's vermouth and an olive in it?"

The blonde cracked a smile. "Can do, Red. Can do."

Abby waited for her salad, sipped her gin, and tried to pretend she wasn't waiting on someone. It was an odd time of day. Just before 5 pm. He wouldn't be here now anyway. She was just checking out RC's best watering hole, that's all. It's not like if he walked through the door she'd suddenly become a wittier, prettier, more dazzling version of herself. Talking to men at work, about work, because of work was one thing. Talking to them on a personal level was not a thing she was good at.

A thin, beautiful brunette wearing jeans and a blue t-shirt came out of the kitchen carrying Abby's salad. Abby guessed the girl wasn't too much older than herself, if at all. "Hey!" the brunette said brightly. "Here you go." As Abby picked up her glass to make room for the salad, the girl looked at her. "I haven't seen you in here before."

"Just got into town last night," Abby replied and gestured to her food. "Taking a break from unpacking. I heard a rumor this was the best place to go for a drink."

The brunette grinned. "Oh, yeah," she agreed. "I'm Slick."

Abby laughed and smiled back. "Interestingly enough...I'm Vegas." The girl laughed, too. "Does everyone have a nickname in this town?" Abby asked.

Slick snorted. "Just about. Except Maria," she said, nodding to the blonde who was washing glasses. "She's just Maria and I wouldn't recommend trying to call her anything else."

"Gotcha. Thanks for the tip."

Slick headed out to the main floor and checked on the few people there.

"Did you say you were from Vegas?"

Abby's head swiveled and a somewhat elderly man was sitting at the corner of the bar nursing a beer.

She nodded. "Yes, Sir. Born and raised."

The man rubbed his chin. "I went to Vegas in '66. With my wife."

"Win big or lose big?" Abby asked.

"Well, like I said, I went with my wife."

Abby laughed.

"I'm Milo."

"I'm Abby."

"Did you go by Vegas when you lived in Vegas? Wasn't that confusing?"

Abby shook her head. "Nope. Met a guy yesterday who called me 'Vegas'. I kind of liked it. I don't want to live in Vegas, but it's my hometown and I still love it." Abby sipped her gin. "Speaking of this guy," she said casually. "I was wondering if someone here knew him. I had a thing I wanted to ask him about."

"Got a name?" Milo asked.

Abby shrugged. "Not really. Tex. Just Tex. Ex-army, lives around her somewhere, but he didn't say where and I didn't think to ask."

Mile rubbed his chin again. "Might know him. What do you want with him?"

Abby shook her head. "Don't want anything with him. He was on a Harley, and I wanted to ask him a question about a Harley. So I was just wondering."

Milo looked at Maria who had moved further down the bar and was restocking the clean glasses. "Maria!" he called out. She looked up from her task. "Red's looking for Tex."

Maria's eyes narrowed on Abby and she felt herself actually shrink into the stool. "Why?" Maria demanded.

"Got a question about a Harley," Milo replied, but his voice was teasing.

Abby scowled. "I do," she insisted. "Have a question about a Harley. And he seemed like maybe the man to ask."

Maria stared at her for a few minutes then she thumped on the swinging door. Moments later Slick appeared. "Red wants Tex," Maria announced.

Abby felt her face flush. She did not *want* Tex. Women like her didn't want men like Tex. Oh, they *thought* about men like Tex. Maybe *fantasized* about men like Tex. But *wanting* Tex? It would be like being handed the reins to a 2,000 pound stallion and being told to hold on.

"You know Tex?" Slick asked. "I thought you said you just got into town last night?"

"I did. I had some car trouble and he stopped. And I forgot to get his name is all. I just wanted to ask him some questions, being as I'm new in town. That's it."

Slick studied her thoughtfully. Jesus, Abby thought. She hadn't meant to alert the whole town. She picked up her purse. "Look, I'm not a stalker," she said, pulling out one of the business cards she'd had printed as soon as she'd gotten the job. It had made everything feel more official. She put it on the bar and slid it toward the two women. "I just want to talk business with him. So since you obviously know him, maybe you could give him my card the next time you see him. If he wants to call me and help me out, great. If not, I'll find someone else. It's not a huge deal."

Slick picked up the card and read it. "You're the Assistant Manager at the Custer Hotel?"

"Yes. Well, officially I am. Though I don't start 'til Monday."

Slick was still bouncing her gaze back from the card to Abby. "Listen," Abby finally said, "If he's your boyfriend or something, I'm really not trying to chase after him. I'm new in town, I had a question about a bike, he *had* a bike. I thought he might be able to help me out. That's the truth."

"He's not my boyfriend. I'm married," Slick replied. "To Tex's old lieutenant when he was in the army."

"Shooter," Abby said without thinking. Slick looked surprised. "He mentioned it."

Maria put her hand on her hip. "Must've been an awful long conversation."

Abby shrugged and tried to appear nonchalant. "My car was acting funny so I pulled over. I was cleaning spark plugs and he happened along. We got to talking while I was fixing my car."

"Tex made you fix your own car?" Slick asked.

Abby's eyebrows furrowed. "Made me? No. I was already fixing it when he pulled up behind me. It's *my* car."

Slick pocketed the card. "I'll tell him you're looking for him."

Abby was momentarily stunned that everyone had made this such a big deal. "Okay. Well...thanks." She poured the rest of her gin directly down her throat, and left a twenty for the bill. "Good night," she said to them and quickly left the building.

Jeez, she thought as she headed to her car. They'd all acted like she was trying to track him down for alimony or something. She slid behind the wheel and cranked the engine. Thankfully the idle was still the right speed though she did need to have the plugs replaced. She pulled out of the lot and headed back to the condo.

Rapid City sure wasn't anything like Vegas.

CHAPTER TWO

On Sunday night, Tex pulled his Harley in behind Hawk's and killed the engine. He pocketed his keys and headed across the lawn and up the steps of the two story log cabin. He entered without knocking. He was the last to arrive and he shucked his leather jacket, hanging it up in the entryway next to the others.

"Something smells good," he called, heading into the living room.

Hawk was on the couch with a beer. "Slick's making pot roast."

"Nice," Tex replied. He rounded the corner of the hallway and headed into the kitchen where the 5'3" woman was stabbing potatoes to see if they were done. He leaned down and kissed her on the top of the head. "Smells good, Slick."

"Thanks," she said.

"Stop mauling my woman," said a voice from behind him. Tex turned and saw Chris 'Shooter' Sullivan ambling into the kitchen.

Tex grinned at his former lieutenant. "I can't. She smells like meat and potatoes. It's primal instinct." Tex reached out to snag a piece of meat and Slick slapped him with her hand. He jerked it back. "Damn woman!"

"Wash your hands."

"Yes, Ma'am," Tex said, teasingly and headed to the sink. As he dried them off, Slick looked back at him over her shoulder.

"Tex? Do you know a girl named Abby Raines?"

Tex frowned. "I'm not- wait- I met an Abby on Friday afternoon. Tall, redhead, amazing green eyes."

Slick's own eyes widened. "Really? She's looking for you."

A slow grin spread on his face. He couldn't get exactly what he wanted from that hot little recently-ex-co-ed, but she'd sure be fun to tumble around with in the sack.

"Not like that," Slick admonished and his grin faltered a bit. "She wanted to ask you something. About your bike. She didn't really say." He grinned again. Yeah, okay. That was a cover story he could deal with. Sure. She wanted to ask about his Harley. Slick rolled her eyes at him. "She really did say it was just a question." Slick pulled out a card and handed it to him.

Tex examined it. "She said she worked at a hotel. Didn't say it was that posh one off Main Street. Very nice." He pocketed it.

"Who works at a hotel off main street?" Hawk asked, coming in to wash his own hands.

"Cute redhead I met the other day. I helped her with her spark plugs."

"Is that what we're calling it now?" Hawk asked, drying his hands.

"You can after I give her a call and meet her for drinks," Tex told his friend.

"Take her someplace she can get a martini," Slick told him. "She had to settle for straight gin at the bar."

Tex considered this. "Hmm, I can do that. In fact, we can meet up at that hotel she works at. Get our drinks downstairs and then head *upstairs* for-"

"Stop!" Slick demanded. "No scary stories."

Tex laughed. "Relax, Slick. Even vanilla sex with Vegas would be a hell of a good time."

"Vegas?" Hawk asked.

"She's from there. Grew up there," Tex replied.

"Vegas is a weird town," Hawk said. "Maybe you don't want to get mixed up with a woman who might be freakier than you, cowboy."

Tex frowned. "I would *love* to get mixed up with a girl who was freakier than me. Especially one who looks like Vegas. But I don't think there are any." Tex opened the utensil drawer and grabbed a handful of spoons, forks, and knives and went to set Slick and Shooter's table for dinner.

He waited until Friday to give Vegas a call, not wanting to come on too strong and not wanting to give her too much lead time to talk herself out of going for a drink with him. She seemed pretty locked down sexually when he'd tried to flirt with her and got nowhere. He would've thought she wasn't interested except she'd had her hair pulled up off her neck and he could see her pulse in her throat, banging away when he'd complimented her and touched her hand.

She had gorgeous red hair, deep green eyes, ripe, full lips, a rack to die for and an ass to match. Surely he hadn't been the only person to ever compliment her on her looks. She was up for an award for worst-dressed woman in South Dakota, though, with those loose jeans and ill-fitting t-shirt. But then she'd been on a road trip 1,000 miles from Vegas to Rapid City and he knew he'd rather be comfortable than fashionable in a similar situation.

Surely she didn't dress that way for work. He imagined Vegas in a tailored business suit that accentuated those breasts and that lovely round bottom and smiled. Hot. Add a pair of killer heels and he'd get o n *his* knees and beg her to go out with him. He got out his cell phone and dialed the cell number printed on the card. She answered on the second ring.

"Abigail Raines."

"Hey there, Vegas. It's Tex."

She was quiet on the other end and he almost checked his phone to see if the call had gotten dropped. "Hi," she finally said. "Thanks for calling."

"No problem, honey. Sorry I didn't call sooner. Been a busy week." Teeny tiny lie. So worth it, though.

"I just needed to talk to someone about something and since I don't know anyone in town, you seemed like a good starting point."

Tex almost laughed at the lack of effort she put into her cover story. "Okay, sweetheart. Let me just finish up here at the garage and we can-"

Abby cut him off. "You work at a garage?"

He paused. "Yeah. We do car repair and custom bike builds."

"You're kidding," she said, sounding shocked.

"Nope," Tex said, wondering why she was so interested. "The place is called Burnout on the South Side, just a few blocks from Maria's."

"How long are you going to be there?" she asked. "I could come by..."

"Well, now the garage is closing in about 15 minutes," he told her.

"Oh. I can't get off work that fast. Maybe..." She thought for a minute. "Maybe you could come by my place? In about an hour?"

Tex was both shocked and pleased she'd jumped the gun on him so fast. He grinned widely. "Absolutely. Just give me your address." She did and he committed it to memory immediately, whistling as he put his phone away and then his tools.

"Why so happy, cowboy?" Hawk asked, coming into the bay area from the office.

"Vegas wants me at her place in an hour. To talk."

Hawk laughed. "Oh, the poor, poor girl. Has no idea what she's getting into."

Tex scoffed. "Hey, I can do nice! I can do nice very, very well thank you."

Hawk shook his head and walked away.

Tex closed and locked the bay doors and headed to his Harley. He threaded his way through the streets of Rapid City until he turned into her neighborhood. It was all condos, all exactly alike. They didn't have any personality at all. He cruised past the postage stamp lawns and stark white mailbox posts until he found the one he was looking for. Vegas' Toyota was in the driveway already.

He got off his bike and headed to the front door, intending to knock, but she swung it open and came out to meet him. She was wearing a business suit, and it showed off her T and A a little better than the jeans and tee, but almost by default. It wasn't tailored and it didn't look sexy at all. If you looked up androgyny in the dictionary, that suit would be pictured. He glanced down. The shoes were nice, though. High heels. He approved.

"Thanks for coming," she said. "I just got home."

"Pretty late for a Friday," he replied.

She nodded. "Pretty late every night, just trying to figure out the ins and outs of the hotel." She walked past him and flipped up the cover on the keypad for the single car garage. He watched as she dialed in a code and the door started to rise.

"So, I saw you had a Harley," she declared, gesturing to his bike. "And I thought maybe you could help me out. But then you said you work at a garage, which is really even better."

The door reached its full height and Tex saw why the Toyota was in the driveway and not in the garage. Sitting in the center was a gleaming black 1963 Harley panhead. He laughed in surprise. He gave a low whistle stepped inside, circling it.

"It was my dad's," she told him. "He passed away last year. I've held on to it. I just wasn't ready to sell. I take it out, though, and keep up with the maintenance."

Tex looked up at her in surprise. "*You* take it out?"

"Yeah. But...it's not mine. It's *his*, you know? And no matter how long I own it, it'll always be his. I don't even know why I brought it up here, except that I just wasn't ready. But then you showed up and you had a Harley and you work at a garage. Maybe that's a sign that's it time to let go of it. So, if you know anyone, or hear of anyone who might be interested in it, could you give them my card? I'd put an ad in the paper or online, but I'm too busy at work and moving in to deal with anyone who isn't serious about making an offer. I'll cut you in, as the facilitator. Say 15%?"

Tex tore his gaze away from the bike. "That's too much."

She shook her head. "Not to me. I just don't want to waste my time. It's worth it to me. And it's not costing me anything sitting here. So, I can wait until the right buyer comes along."

Tex tried to hide his disappointment that she hadn't asked him over for a booty call. On the other hand, it was a god damn gorgeous bike and if she needed help unloading it, he was her man. Plus, he'd at least have an excuse, a real excuse it seemed, to talk to her. He took out his phone. "You mind if I take some photos?"

Abby shook her head and he took several shots of the bike at all angles, the re-pocketed the phone. "I know a few people," he told her. "Up in Sturgis, Spearfish. I'll make some calls."

Abby extended her hand and he took it in his for a handshake. It was small and soft. Her nails were short, but neatly manicured. He imagined them wrapped around the handlebars of the panhead. Which then led to him imagining them wrapped around other things. He grinned at her and squeezed gently.

"Thanks, Tex," she told him.

"No problem, Vegas. My real name's Mark, by the way. Mark Marsten."

Tex got back on his Dyna-Glide and fired up the engine. Abby waved and he nodded to her as he backed out of her driveway and headed out to the main road. Well, that had been damn disappointing. But a lot of things were worth waiting for and he had a feeling Abigail Raines might be one of them.

In the morning, he got to the garage earlier than anyone else and let himself into the office. He emailed the photos from his phone to the garage's email address and turned on the computer to download them.

Shooter was the next person to arrive. "You're here early," he said, entering the office. "How'd it go with the redhead?"

Tex grinned. "Not terrible."

"What are you doing?"

"Downloading photos I took at her house."

Shooter frowned. "Tex, I don't even want *regular* porn on that computer, let alone your personal stash. Put them on your laptop. Be a pervert in private."

Tex chuckled and turned the monitor toward his boss. Shooter glanced at the screen. Then he moved closer. "Oh, sweet."

"It's hers," Tex told him. "Dad died, left it to her. She's been holding onto it a while, not ready to sell, but now she thinks she might let it go. Makes sense. New job, new city, new life."

Hawk ambled in. "What's up? What are we looking at?"

"Photos I took last night," Tex replied.

Hawk scoffed. "Cowboy, is it a good idea to document your crimes against the fairer sex?"

Tex shook his head. "Alas, there were no crimes. Not even misdemeanors. She's got a Harley she wants to sell and she's cutting the garage in 15% to find a buyer."

Shooter frowned. "Fifteen percent feels like we're ripping her off."

Tex nodded. "I said as much, but she doesn't want to deal with a bunch of mouth breathers showing up at her place. She said it's worth it to her to keep the hassle to a minimum."

"Alright," said Shooter. "Call Kenzie up in Spearfish."

"Yeah. I was thinking Harper in Sturgis, too."

"Good idea. No one's going to pass up a '63 panhead in that condition."

A lazy grin spread over Tex's face.

"What?" Shooter asked.

"She takes it out sometimes."

Shooter rolled his eyes. "Well, don't go falling in love with her. You don't even know if she's one of yours."

"I'm probably not lucky enough for that, but damn, one night with her would be sweet."

CHAPTER THREE

Abby leaned back in her chair and closed her eyes, pinching the bridge of her nose. She was on her fourth hour straight of analyzing the hotel's operational costs for the previous quarter and her eyes were beginning to cross. She stood up and shook out her limbs and decided it was time for a much needed break.

She shrugged into her black blazer and buttoned it up. Today she was wearing a cream silk blouse underneath and a just-below-the-knee black skirt. She had on her usual heels. She stopped behind the counter at the main desk, smiled at the girl working the counter, and tapped a key on the computer's keyboard to kill the screen saver and bring up the hotel's reservation software. She looked for three rooms chosen at random and collected key cards for them.

The job itself was beginning to look like a Herculean task. Her immediate boss, Steve Kessler, seemed to be the least organized person she'd ever met. He also seemed a little too grateful for Abby's presence. He'd started heaping piles and piles of work on her right after her formal tour. Financials, work orders for repairs, and a stack of customer surveys that needed to be reviewed and responded to as needed.

None of this was outside her purview as the hotel's Assistant Manager, but it was a lot to take on all at once and Steve kept throwing more at her under the guise of "getting to know the Custer." It made matters worse that she had no idea what Steve himself was actually doing all day. He seemed content to spend most of his days in his office with the door closed or didn't even come in to work at all.

Abby glided through the well-appointed lobby with its stone fireplace, gleaming, polished tables, and comfortable black leather chairs. Her heels clicked on the marble floors. The hotel was an art deco masterpiece, built on a whim by a retired New York City shipping magnate who had come to South Dakota in the mid-thirties to visit Mount Rushmore with his family and, sensing, an opportunity for a second career, he stayed and built the hotel in 1939.

Abby may not have liked Steve Kessler, but she liked the Custer. Definitely. The ground floor featured a newly renovated fitness room, but still kept the vintage feel with clean white tile floors and botanical green pinstriped white walls. Just off the lounge was a small, but well-stocked bar. Abby appreciated its elegance and though she could get a martini there, drinking in front of guests and her employees was not a good idea, especially since she had just started the job. She smiled a bit at the idea of *her* guests and *her* employees.

There was a grand, carpeted staircase that led to a ballroom that hosted weddings on the second floor, as well. Abby climbed the stairs and breezed past the ballroom, entering the long hallway that led to the guest suites on the second floor. She used a keycard on the door and did a spot check of the unoccupied room. The housekeeping staff seemed to be doing a fair job despite what appeared to be lack of any actual management by Steve.

The Custer Hotel had 150 rooms including a Princess, Presidential, and Honeymoon suite on the top two floors. The Princess was occupied, the Presidential was booked for the following weekend, but the Honeymoon suite was not reserved for another six weeks. They really needed to find a way to keep that room booked more consistently. Abby had a few ideas, but it was too early to pitch them.

She spot-checked the other two rooms and questioned the housekeeping staff about whether or not they felt the supplies were adequately stocked in the services storeroom. It was on her list to double check the supplies next week, but it wouldn't hurt to have some feedback now. She eventually decided that she'd had enough of a break and headed back downstairs to her office. Steve was waiting in her office when she got there. She hid her frown.

"Where were you?" he asked.

Abby smiled. "I was spot-checking some rooms upstairs. Just keeping up with housekeeping."

The corner of his mouth twitched. "Well, did you finish going over the quarterlies?"

"Nearly."

"Best get on that then and not running around upstairs," he said curtly and walked away.

Abby felt her heart sink. So far this was less the dream job than she'd hoped. Oh, she'd understood exactly what she was getting into with office work and daily management tasks. She hadn't lived in an 800 room hotel in the entertainment capital of the world her entire life and not learned a thing or two (or everything under the sun) about the day-to-day operations of a hotel.

But she didn't have the decades of camaraderie at the Custer that she'd had with the staff at the Coral Canyon in Vegas. And though the Custer was beautiful and definitely a luxury hotel, it lacked a few modern amenities. Most notably, to Abby, it didn't have a restaurant. Abby had gotten an extra certification in restaurant management and was disappointed not to be able to use it in her first job. Not that she didn't have more than enough to do, but it was a little disappointing.

She went over the books for nearly two more hours until it was officially quitting time. The hotel seemed to be doing well financially, according to the books, even though in the short time she'd been there it hadn't been booked anywhere near capacity. Of course it was the last week in March and peak season didn't start until May.

She marked her place in the binder and decided to call it a day. She'd stayed late every day her first week, but was now putting herself on a strictly normal working schedule. No sense in getting burnt out in the first month. She knew from the experience of working part time and taking one extra class every semester since freshman year in order to graduate a semester early, that she needed to get some air.

She drove home, shed her suit, and pulled on a pair of 501's, boot cut to accommodate her Icon El Bajo's. She pulled her hair back, fastening it at the base of her neck, and shrugged on her brown cowhide leather jacket.

The panhead's engine caught immediately and she tweaked the gas to warm it up. Paying for school out of pocket, she'd been making do with a Toyota for the last five years. It was cheap, required little maintenance, which between work and school she rarely had had time for. But now that she had her first post-grad job plus the money from her father's life insurance, she'd have to look into a new set of wheels. A nicer car, definitely, and after that, maybe a bike of her own.

It was chilly now, in the evening. The sun was just setting. But Abby, ever a desert dweller, had on a tank top and a long-sleeved henley and a t-shirt under her jacket. Nights in Nevada could get downright cold, as many a Florida snowbird unhappily discovered when they'd checked in to the Coral Canyon with only warm weather clothes. She took the ramp onto the highway and put the panhead through all five gears smoothly as she opened up the engine. She relaxed down into the seat and flexed her fingers through her leather gloves. Despite the chill, it was worth it to go for one final ride on her father's Harley.

Just a few days later, Abby's cell phone rang. She smiled at the screen before hitting the button. "Tex," she drawled, mimicking his on again off again accent.

"Vegas," he replied. "I've got a guy up in Spearfish who wants to come down and take a look at the panhead."

Abby wrote down the date and time and assured Tex that she didn't need anyone to help her get the bike to the garage.

Abby left work on time for once on Friday and suited up into a pair of jeans, boots, and her leather jacket. She tucked a check into her front pocket and snagged the keys to the Harley off the kitchen counter. She ran her thumb over the smooth metal of the keychain and for a moment considered keeping it, but thought better of it when she realized she already had boxes of photos. She used her remote to open the garage door and straddled the panhead one final time.

The drive to the garage was a bit longer given the hour, but she was still on time as she turned into the gravel lot of Burnout. It seemed the men were already waiting for her. Sullivan, whom Tex called 'Shooter' and Tex were talking to a man just outside the large bay doors. All three of them turned to watch her as she pulled up to them. She killed the engine and swung her leg over the bike.

Given the warm weather she hadn't worn gloves and so she simply extended her hand to the only man she hadn't met yet. "Hi. I'm Abby Raines."

He grunted as he took her hand. He looked her over first, then the Harley. "Nice ride," he finally declared.

"Yes, Sir," she merely agreed, not wanting to steamroll him.

"Your father's, they said."

Abby nodded. "Yep. My old man won it in '85 in a poker game with Dean Martin's chauffeur."

The grizzled man raised an eyebrow. "Dean Martin?"

"Yes, Sir."

"Martin ride this bike?"

"Not that I'm aware of. Martin didn't much care for motorcycles beyond the occasional movie role or publicity shoot. His only love was a '62 Chrysler Ghia. Which my father did *not* win a poker game, but he said it was just as well because it constantly popped out of fourth whenever he drove it."

All three men stared at her.

Abby blushed, forgetting herself momentarily. "Vegas is a small town, Mr. Hale."

Hale chewed on this. "Where apparently anyone can drive Dean Martin's car," he replied dubiously.

"Just the mechanics, Sir. My grandfather was a mechanic. So was my father." She gestured to the Harley. "My father rebuilt it from the ground up. Every part is original, no reproductions."

Hale grunted again and swept past her to inspect the classic motorcycle. Abby remained silent while he took his time perusing. When he was finished, he gave a low whistle. "Asking price is a little low," he countered.

Abby smiled. "Not in the mood to haggle."

Hale turned his attention to the bike again and Abby watched his shrewd eyes going over the chrome finish. She felt another pang of nostalgia as Hale ran his hand over the seat. She'd spent hours polishing the leather on Sunday afternoons, even when she was younger. His fingers brushed over a scratch that she'd accidentally put on it sneaking it out at 17. She'd frantically buffed it out upon return and had it quickly painted before her father had noticed. Or so she'd hoped. The next time her father took off the all-weather cover to tune it up and take it out for the "first" ride of the spring season, she sworn he'd paused over the spot she'd painstakingly fixed. If her father had noticed anything out of the ordinary, he hadn't commented on it, though.

Hale didn't notice it now, because there wasn't really anything to see. Only Abby's father appeared to have had a sixth sense about that bike. He stood up and took out his checkbook. Abby felt a heady mix of relief and anxiety and something a tiny bit like disappointment as he signed his name with a flourish and handed it to her. She was surprised to notice she was reluctant to take it from him, and even more reluctant to hand over the keys. The idea of selling the most precious thing her father ever owned was one thing. The reality of it was proving to be far more difficult.

After giving Abby a smile and handshake, Hale nodded to someone across the lot and she followed his gaze as a disinterested, younger version of the motorcycle enthusiast fired up a Chevy truck, gave the group a wave, and rolled out of the lot. Hale straddled the bike and bounced in the seat a little, feeling out the frame. Abby's jaw twitched.

He fired up the engine, revved it a few times and saluted the group before pulling out of the lot to follow the truck. Abby fisted the check in her hand for a brief moment before taking a deep breath and folding it up meticulously.

"Well, thanks," she said aloud to Tex and Shooter who were nearby. She dug out her own check, also folded neatly, and handed it to the owner of the garage.

"It's still too much," Shooter declared.

Abby shook her head, as much to quell any arguments as to will away any tears that were threatening to fall. "It's worth it," was all she managed to tell him. She pulled her cell phone out of her jacket pocket and turned away from them. "Have a good one," she called out in a chipper tone. Her thumb swept over the screen and she was about to begin dialing a cab when the phone was taken from her.

She turned and looked up into Tex's blue eyes. His blonde hair highlighted his tan. "I'll take you home," he told her.

Abby shook her head. "I can call a cab. It's not-"

"I'm taking you home," he said in a firmer tone. She realized he was holding her phone hostage as he guided her across the lot and toward a large, black Hummer. He opened the passenger side door for her and it wasn't until she was safely ensconced inside that he handed her the phone back.

Abby sighed and resigned herself to being given a ride. As Tex pulled out of the garage's lot, she leaned her head back on the leather head rest and looked out the passenger window.

"You okay?" Tex asked, glancing at her.

"Yeah," she assured him. She sighed. "Maybe I wasn't really ready."

He turned the wheel and took the cross street. "You're never ready."

"He had cancer," she declared. "It went on a long time. It's not like I didn't have time to prepare."

"My old man had a stroke," Tex confided. "He lingered a while, too. It doesn't make it easier when you see the train coming, Abby. All you can do is make decisions and stick to them. No matter how strong the impulse is to change your mind."

Abby turned to him, surprised. "How- how did you...?"

"The last thing I sold was my old man's rodeo saddle. Never fit me right, but that might've been in my head. It seemed like the right thing to do. It was the right thing to do. But at the last minute it took everything I had not to back out of the deal."

"Our relationship was....complicated," she replied.

Tex smiled. "I think you just described everyone's relationship with their father."

He pulled up in front of the condo and parked. "Wait there," he commanded.

Abby complied.

He came around the front of the Hummer and opened her door. He took hold of her elbow and helped her down from the rig. She smiled at him.

"I've got my boots on," she reminded him. "I can get down."

Tex was standing close, very close, and her body brushed up against his as she slid down to the pavement. His sparkling blue eyes met hers. "I didn't ask."

Abby's stomach fluttered. Tex reached out and pushed back a strand of her hair that had come loose from its tie.

"I will ask you if you want to go out for a beer, though," he said. "Rough day and all."

Abby sighed inwardly. Of course a guy like Tex wouldn't be interested in someone like her. He was just being nice.

"Well, thanks," she replied in a steady voice that covered her disappointment. "But tonight's a drinking alone night."

"Some other time, then," he said, in a tone that made it clear he wasn't asking about that, either.

Tex was a nice guy, Abby thought. It was disappointing to just be friends with him, but she couldn't complain.

"Some other time," she agreed.

In her condo, she unzipped her jacket and hung it up. She left her boots by the door and mixed herself a martini. On the stereo Frank crooned that he'd left his heart in San Francisco.

"I know the feeling, Frank," she said out loud. "I left something in Vegas. I'm not sure what, but it was big."

The next day, Abby was torn between going out for lunch and staying in her office. She chose the latter and kicked the computer out of sleep mode to begin surfing the internet. She was clicking through pages when the door to her office opened. Kessler stood in her doorway, taking up the space. "What's this maintenance request?" he demanded, jiggling a work order at her.

Abby tore her eyes away from the screen. "Pardon?"

She was more than a little irritated that he hadn't knocked.

He sneered at her. "Looking at porn?" he asked. He flashed a crooked grin that he probably thought made him look cute. It only succeeded in making him look like a creep.

"No!" Abby retorted, disgusted.

Kessler just shook his head at her. "Maintenance request. What gives?"

"Among other things the carpet in the elevator vestibule on the second floor needs replacing," she began, but Kessler only continued to shake his head.

"There's nothing wrong with it," he insisted.

"It's ripped near the elevator bank," Abby informed him.

"Whatever. I've never noticed it. It's not a big deal."

"It'll become a big deal if we don't-"

"Forget it," Kessler insisted. "I'm not signing off on it. Burton doesn't want any big repairs." He crumpled the form and tossed it onto her desk.

Abby swept it into the trash can after he walked away. She shook her own head at his trailing form. Kessler clearly had no interest in managing a hotel. She wasn't certain, though, that Burton wasn't interested in maintaining his multi-million dollar property.

Resolving to take up the state of affairs of the Custer with the owner himself at her next opportunity, she went back to surfing the web. She found a promising lead and picked up her cell phone. A groggy voice answered the phone on the other end. Abby frowned at the clock on the wall. Who slept at one o'clock in the afternoon?

" 'Lo?" the voice on the other end rasped.

"Hi," said Abby politely. "I'm calling about your ad online." The caller perked up and Abby thought she may have found a winner.

She woke up late, for her, on Saturday at around 9 am, showered and threw on some jeans and an old t-shirt. She counted through the 4,500 dollars she'd gotten when she cashed the check for the panhead, stuffed it in an envelope, and put it in her purse. The she pulled out her Smith and Wesson Small Frame .38 loaded with .357 rounds and double checked the safety. She slung her purse onto her shoulder and headed out to the cab that had just pulled up on the curb.

It was a bright sunny day, if still a little chilly, and Abby thought that boded well. The cab turned into Burnout and she paid and tipped the driver appropriately and swung out of the back seat. The cab had barely left the turnaround before Shooter Sullivan came up next to her.

"Well, hey there, Vegas," he said.

She turned to him and shielded her eyes from the sun. "Hey!"

He eyed the cab. "Car trouble?"

"No. I hope you don't mind if I borrow your place," said Abby. Shooter looked puzzled. "I talked to this guy over the phone, but I don't know him, and I'd rather meet up on neutral ground. I guess I should have asked before I told him to come here. But I didn't think you'd mind."

"What-" he began to say, but then he was drowned out by the loud sound of a motor rumbling toward them. They both turned to see a 1969 Chevy Camaro, or what used to be a 1969 Chevy Camaro, swinging into the turnaround. It was impossibly loud and Abby wasn't sure it boded well that the owner hadn't mentioned that it needed muffler work, too. She hoped the car would be the right fit.

It stopped in front of them and the door opened. A young kid, about 18 maybe 19, wearing cowboy boots and a pair of ripped jeans got out. He grinned when he saw Abby. Abby smiled back.

"Well, I guess you're Abby, then," the kid drawled.

"You must be Dave."

"I sure am." Then he scowled at Shooter. "Bring your boyfriend?"

"Nah," Abby assured him. "He owns the place. Why don't you pop the hood and let's take a look?"

The kid hesitated then headed back to the car and released the hood latch. Abby lifted it up and rested it on the metal arm.

Yikes. It was a mess. Carburetor appeared to be jury rigged and the distributor cap had a small crack in it. It was a wonder the kid managed to put 111,000 miles on it because it looked like it had never had a tune up.

The kid came up beside her. "I'm asking 5,000," he said.

Abby hid her smirk. "Uh huh. Except I'm only offering 2,500," she replied, opening up negotiations. Everyone heard the crunch of gravel and looked over as Tex strode up, stopping beside his boss.

"Hi!" Abby said to him, and couldn't help but smile.

"Vegas," Tex said, eyeing the car.

The kid looked at Shooter and then back at Abby. "This here's a classic car," he told her.

Abby stood up and looked at him. "This here is a classic car that needs, for starters, a new clutch assembly, a new air intake system, a new muffler, which you didn't mention over the phone, and I know you think I didn't hear that grinding when you hit the brakes, but I sure as shit did and that means it needs new discs, too. And that's just what I've been able to suss out in the 30 seconds you've been here. So, I'm offering 2,500."

The kid stared at Abby and scratched his head. She leaned forward. "This is the part where you make me a counter offer," she stage-whispered.

His eyebrows knitted together. "4,000."

Abby tried very hard not to roll her eyes. "3,000."

"3,800," the kid snapped.

Shooter groaned, but Abby didn't look at him. "3200. Cash. Right now," she said.

At that the kid perked up considerably. "Yeah, okay, deal!" Abby took out the cash that she had bundled into stacks of a thousand each and handed him three of them. He pulled the title and the keys out of his pocket and handed them over.

Then he grinned at Abby. "I could use a ride home," he said to her.

Tex answered from behind her. "Then take your 3,200 dollars in cash and get yourself a cab."

The kid startled for a moment and nodded, tucking the stacks into his pants and pulling his shirt down over it. He took off for the sidewalk out front.

"A fool and his money are soon parted," Tex said in a gravel tone.

Abby saw him looking right at her. "This is a classic car!" she insisted.

Shooter frowned. "Vegas, this is a classic piece of shit. And you overpaid by at least three hundred dollars."

She laughed. "Some women waste their money on manicures. I

really want this car. You lack vision, Sir. And I'm sorry for you."

Shooter and Tex exchanged a look as Abby dug a list out of her purse and handed it to Shooter. "Do you think you could order me the parts on that list? That'll get me started," she asked, then took out the remaining thousand dollar stack and the leftover three hundred. "This should cover it."

Shooter examined the list and the money in his hand. "Yeah, sure, Vegas. Whatever you need."

"Thanks!" she said looking down at the keys. Attached was a skull with red paint that looked like blood on it. "Ugh." She took it off the chain and handed it to Tex. "Here."

She lowered the hood and headed to the driver's side. She pushed in the clutch, noting it definitely needed a new one, at the kid hadn't lied about that. She cranked the engine and eight cylinders of Detroit steel roared to life, extra loudly since the muffler was shot. She made a face at the faint smell of gas and noted that she needed a new fuel system, too. She waved goodbye to Tex and Shooter and rolled her version of a mani-pedi toward her condo.

CHAPTER FOUR

Tex watched Vegas take her piece of classic shit home and shook his head at the skull he was holding in his hands. Shooter grinned. "We just made 1,300 dollars without actually doing anything," he laughed. Then he glanced down at the list. "Does she know what to with all this?"

Tex grinned. "I sure hope not."

Shooter shook his head. "I don't think she's one of yours, Tex. She put that kid down *hard*. I'd say she doesn't have a submissive bone in her body."

Tex still smiled. "You'd be surprised."

Shooter raised his eyebrows. "How can you tell?"

Tex shrugged. "I can't, but just because she wouldn't let a pissant take advantage of her doesn't necessarily mean she wouldn't submit to the right man. If he asked her to." Tex pocketed the skull and headed back toward the garage, taking a final note of the oil stain on the gravel. He shook his head, smiling. "Let me know when those parts come in," he called over his shoulder. "Before you call *her*."

Three days later, on Wednesday, Tex pulled his Hummer up outside Abby's condo at a little after 6 pm. He picked up one of the boxes and headed to her garage, the door of which was one-third of the way up. He heard the faint sounds of Tom Petty.

"Vegas?" He ducked down and entered the garage.

"Tex?"

"Yeah, babe. Got a special delivery," he replied. Then he kicked himself for sounding like every porno movie ever made. But Abby didn't seem to notice. It gave him pause. Slick would have laughed. Maybe Abby was too young for him. She was just out of college and couldn't be older than 23 or 24. Slick wasn't much older than that, but still. For all of Abby's professional suits, she was still just a young woman.

"Oh, thanks!" she said, taking the box from him. "You didn't have to do this. I could have come by the garage."

He smiled at her. "Delivery's free." He looked around the garage. "Whoa," he said, as he looked off to his left and saw that Abby had laid out a tarp and had parts lined up in rows. He went over to investigate.

"Be careful," she warned, setting the box down on the concrete in the corner. "I have a system."

Tex eyed the tarp carefully. It wasn't laid out in a typical 3-D pattern. "Yeah," he said slowly. "I'm...not seeing it."

She laughed and came up beside him. "It's alphabetical."

He stared at it again. "Oh, shit, okay. Now I've got it. But, Vegas, no one does it that way."

"I do!" she insisted. "That's just how my brain works."

He chuckled. "You got all this done in just a few days?" he asked, impressed. "By yourself?" He was really hoping she hadn't been in town long enough to meet anyone.

"Yeah. I work on it in the evenings. It's kind of nice to just shut my brain off and work with my hands." She drew in a sharp breath. "Oh, I didn't mean that you were...stupid...or anything. I'm sorry. I just meant-"

He laughed. "It's okay. I didn't take it that way."

"I just meant that I know this stuff so well, I can do it without having to focus too much. Especially when it's just taking apart the engine."

"What are you working on right now?"

"Fuel line."

"Want some help?"

She glanced at him. "Are you sure?" she asked. "I mean you do this all day. Don't you want to go home and relax?"

He shook his head. "Not really. I mostly work on bikes at the shop while Hawk does the cars and trucks. It'll be a nice change of pace."

"Yeah, great," she said smiling and Tex was pretty sure he'd do just about anything to keep that smile. She helped get the rest of the boxes out of the Hummer and then they set to work removing the fuel line. She was methodical and efficient, if not a little slow. But then Tex figured he was always used to working on a deadline and if you were going to this thing as a hobby you might as well take the time to enjoy it as much as she obviously did.

"So, where'd you learn to work on cars?" he asked, watching her set down the connecter in what he figured was the "F" column.

"My dad was the head mechanic for the fleet of cars and limos the Coral Canyon uses. When I was young I used to go to work with him after school. When I turned sixteen I officially made it to the payroll for about four years. Then I was in college and I turned 21. Casino Hosts make a lot more money than mechanics and I had books and tuition to pay for, so I did that for the last two years."

Tex nodded. "What exactly is a Casino Host?"

She picked up a socket wrench and changed the head. "Well, it's like a private concierge. A whale, sorry, a big spender, comes into town and he wants concert tickets, a 7 o'clock tee time at Aliante, his wife needs a spa day. I make all that happen for a fee plus a tip when they leave. I'm like their personal assistant slash entertainment director for their stay."

"Have you ever done anything besides work at a hotel?" he asked.

Abby shook her head. "Nope. I've only ever worked at the Canyon. I love it. It's like home to me, but my dad's gone now, and things are just...different. I thought I'd check out life away from the Strip."

They had finished up taking the fuel line apart and she invited him in to wash his hands. Tex looked around the empty apartment. "You unpacked fast," he observed.

"I didn't have much to unpack."

He noted the different dispensers of soap at the kitchen sink. Antibacterial Dial and some kind of Orange Blossom stuff. "Vegas, do you have anything-"

She reached under the sink and handed him a Lava Bar. "Ah, thanks, babe." When he put it back he noticed her cleaning supplies were in neat little rows. She caught him looking. "Control freak, huh?" he asked her.

She gave him a sharp look. "I prefer the term 'Vigilantly Organized'. I arrange people's schedules, including my own, for a living. I have to be organized."

"Nothing wrong with being organized," he told her, drying his hands on the towel. Suddenly, her microwave beeped.

He watched her put on an oven glove and pull a metal tray out of the oven. He moved closer for inspection. "What is that?" he asked with distaste as she attempted to peel the steaming hot plastic off a small rectangle of frozen dinner lasagna. "That is not food."

"Yes, it is," she told him. "And frankly I consider it a miracle that I'm using the oven. I've lived in a hotel my whole life, Tex. Room service? I have no idea how to cook. I'd order take-out, but I'm new in town and I don't know what's good here. Plus, I'm trying not to shop in the lumberjack section of department stores. Flannel is not a good look for me. This is a healthy alternative. Says so right on the box."

"Uh huh," said Tex. He took the oven mitt from her, scooped up the box, stepped on the pedal of the trash container in the corner and dumped it in.

"Hey! That's my dinner!" she protested.

"Vegas, that is garbage and that's where it belongs." He got out his cell phone and hit a number on speed dial. He ordered a massive amount of Chinese food and gave Abby's address. "Real food will be here in 20 minutes."

Abby tried to protest when the delivery boy arrived and Tex insisted on paying for the food. He silenced her with a look and told her to go get a towel. She did and came back with it. They spread it on her living room carpet and set out the food.

"I'm sorry I don't have any furniture. It's on my list," she told him while he gathered napkins from her kitchen.

He chuckled. "From what I've seen, there's probably an actual list."

Abby was chewing a dumpling and pointed to the fridge. He turned to see a shopping list pad stuck to it with a magnet. He moved closer to examine it. "What are Jimmy Choos?" he asked.

Abby swallowed. "Shoes. Like the Harley Davidson of shoes."

He picked up the utensils and carried them over. "So, you don't have furniture or a TV, but you're buying fifteen hundred dollars worth of car parts?" He settled down on the other side of towel, facing her.

"A girl's gotta have priorities," Abby insisted. "Besides, I need the stress relief. I was really excited about this job, but so far, it's been shit. My boss is kind of a dick."

Tex considered this. "Hmm. Well, my boss was my L.T. so I knew what to expect going in. Why's your boss a dick?"

She glowered. "Because I'm supposed to be the Assistant Manager. Emphasis on *assistant*. But I'm doing way more than my fair share of the work. Plus, I'm not getting paid extra for it or getting kudos from the owner."

Tex frowned. He didn't like the idea of her being used. "You gonna do anything about that?"

Abby shook her head. "No. Not right now. I just got hired. I can't go around bitching about the job nanoseconds after I started. Something will give. Plus, I don't want to make waves at the moment. My boss gives off kind of a weirdo vibe and until I know why, I'm just going to fly under the radar."

Tex's mouth twitched. "Weirdo vibe?"

She nodded. "I'm from Vegas. My weirdo vibe is finely tuned and something about that guy isn't kosher. I just don't know what it is."

Tex grinned. "I could be a weirdo."

Abby looked up at him, unconcerned. "My neighbor likes the Price is Right. And Days of our Lives. And the News at Eleven."

"Ah," he said with understanding. "Thin walls."

"Yep. So, if I scream for help..."

"Neighbor will come running," he finished.

"Well, no. She's 75 and uses a walker. But I'm sure she'll hobble right over."

Tex smiled. "A lot could happen in the time it takes an old lady to hobble over here."

She surprised him by muttering, "Yeah, but not the fun stuff."

They ate and talked about Abby's plan of attack for the Camaro and she came back from the kitchen with a new list of parts. "Have your boss call me and I'll give him my credit card number," she said. "And... you don't have to deliver them next time. I mean...if you're busy or whatever. I could come in. Save you the trouble."

Tex smiled. She was being polite, but the look in her eyes told him everything he needed to know. He took the list from her and pocketed it. "Told you, Vegas, delivery's free."

True to his word her part order came in early at the beginning of the following week and he pulled outside her condo again after work. Her garage door was slightly ajar again. He handed her some boxes and immediately picked up a wrench.

"So what does your mom do?" he asked.

Abby paused for a second. "She's not around anymore, but she was a showgirl."

"No shit?"

"No shit."

"Huh. I can see where you get it from, then." He, watched, pleased, as she blushed a little but kept her eyes on the electrical line she was disconnecting. He took pity on her and changed the subject. "My dad was on the rodeo circuit for most of his life."

Abby glanced at him. "Really? Rodeo's pretty tough."

Tex nodded. "My mom ran the farm when he was on the road or injured. Which was a lot of the time. She's retired now. My sisters didn't want the farm and neither did I, so they sold it, and divided it equally among all of us, plus a little something for them to live on."

"How many sisters do you have?" she asked.

He grinned. "Four. All of them older."

She laughed. "I bet they tortured you a lot."

"Well, thankfully they tended to just take swipes at each other and leave me alone for the most part. But my mama does have a fair number of pictures of me at about three years old wearing a cowboy hat and a hoop skirt."

Abby laughed so hard she had to a wipe a tear from her eye.

He laughed, too. "I'm pretty sure it didn't do any permanent damage."

When it started getting late they headed inside to wash up and Tex asked if she wanted to order Chinese again.

"Yeah, but I'm paying this time," she demanded.

"Okay, sounds fair."

She headed off to the bedroom to change out of her dirty t-shirt and the doorbell rang.

"Could you get it?" she called out from behind the closed door. "My purse is on the counter."

"No problem," he called out, picking up her purse. He opened it and reached in, but didn't come up with her wallet on the first try. Instead he found a snub nose .38. He turned it over and examined it. The doorbell rang again. "Just a second!" he called loudly. He put it back, opened her wallet, and took out some cash.

He paid the boy and set the food and the change on the counter. Abby came back out in a new, slightly better fitting shirt. "What did we get this time?" she asked. "It smells awesome!" She laid out a towel on the floor.

Tex brought over the bags. "What do you need a gun for?"

Abby looked up at him. "You didn't rob the delivery boy with it, did you? Because I love that place and I'm pretty sure they won't deliver here anymore if you point a gun at them."

"Nah. I put it back. But why do you need it?"

"I probably don't here. But Vegas is Vegas and I'm used to carrying it around."

"You take a class?"

She gave him a pointed look. "Yes, Dad. And I practice every month at a range. And I keep the safety on. And I don't talk to strangers even when they have candy or puppies, which are two of my really big weaknesses, I'll have you know. So if a guy has both, I'm fucked."

Tex laughed and took a bite of Kung Pao. "There's a good range off Catron Boulevard."

She nodded. "Thanks for the tip. I'll check it out over the weekend."

"Do you have a bed?" he asked her suddenly. Her eyes widened in surprised. "I mean, you don't have anything else and I don't know if you sleeping on the floor to feed your classic car addiction is going to be a great idea long term." Frankly, he did find it a little odd that she'd choose a project car over, well, anything.

"Yeah," she said, shifting a little uncomfortably. "I'm not that crazy. The bedroom's actually totally done," she said, sounding a little defensive. "It's the room I spend the most time in so I started with that one. I just want to finish one room at a time."

He nodded remembering she was 'vigilantly organized.' "Are you gonna paint?"

"No. It's just a rental. Only for six months. I wanted to get a feel for the city before I chose a permanent neighborhood."

"Good thinking," he told her, and it was. It was exactly what he would do. Choose a short term place and look around.

"I don't want to go crazy buying a bunch of stuff for this place just to move it all out again. Especially since I don't know the layout of whatever place I might get in the future. I'm just sticking to the basics, here. I only need a bed, a dresser, a couch, and a garage for my car."

He grinned. "Girl's gotta have priorities."

"Exactly."

Tex dug into his Kung Pao. Abby seemed a little young sometimes, but she was smart and independent and knew exactly what she wanted and how to go about getting it. And she'd been working her ass off for damn near ten years to make it happen. She had a plan for everything and he wondered if she had an idea about bringing a man into her life. She hadn't mentioned it. He figured she was probably too focused on her career and her hobby.

She was a little too well hidden in her non-descript clothes and he wondered if it was her size that made her self conscious. She wasn't stick-thin, that was for sure, but she wasn't fat by any means. She was tall, too, and maybe that intimidated a lot of men. Tex himself was 6'2" so it didn't bother him. He could tell she had a very decent sized chest and a nice ass, but she never called attention to either of them. He wondered what was underneath all that fabric.

"You should come to Maria's on Friday night," he said. "The guys will be there. Slick'll be there, too, but she'll be working. You should get out of here once in a while."

She looked like she was actually considering it. "I might. Thanks."

"It can get a little rowdy on the weekends," he told her. "But then again, you're from Vegas, so somehow I'm pretty confident you can handle it."

"Yeah," she said smiling into her House Special Fried Rice. "After the Strip, Friday nights at Maria's sounds like a day care."

He smiled. He loved her sense of humor.

CHAPTER FIVE

Friday should have been a work day to look forward to, but Abby was frowning at the check-in screen in front of her. She'd only been at the Custer for a few weeks and she couldn't possibly have increased its overall performance in such a short amount of time, but neither had she been made aware that the hotel was in such dire straights. Even at off-peak season, this week's bookings were dismally low. As were last week's and the week's before that, according to the reports she'd generated onscreen.

She'd checked the totals for last summer's peak season and the recorded bookings weren't nearly as high as a hotel of this caliber should be. She tapped the keyboard and generated a report for books on this same week for the last five years and waited patiently for the printer below the counter to finish.

Back in her office, she spread the sheets across her empty desk and picked up a highlighter. According to the reports, three years ago, the Custer's bookings for this same week in May began declining and still had not tapered off. She knew that the current owner, Burton Jr., had inherited the hotel from his father upon his death three years ago and it seemed the Custer had been in a steady downfall ever since. At this rate they would only be able to keep the doors open for a few short years.

Abby gathered the troubling reports and stacked them neatly together. She headed out of her office and down the hall toward

Kessler's office. Lord knew if the man would even be at work today. Or if he even knew what work was. As she neared the door, she heard the sound of two men laughing. She barely paused as she knocked sharply on the door and grasped the handle. Grudgingly Kessler acknowledged his visitor.

Abby swung open the door and came face to face with Burton Jr. himself, who was sitting in a chair. Kessler was rummaging through one of his own desk drawers.

"Mr. Burton," Abby exclaimed, caught off guard that her boss' boss was not only on the premises, but apparently having an impromptu meeting that she hadn't been invited to. Abby's blood boiled. Kessler knew damn well Abby wanted a sit-down with the hotel's owner and he hadn't bothered to let her know Burton was coming. The two of them looked like annoyingly useless frat brothers in polo shirts and khakis. Both men used hair care products and cologne in equally alarming amounts.

Burton looked her over and dismissed her by turning away. But Abby was undeterred. She breezed through the opened door and rounded the other empty chair in the room, though she didn't take a seat.

"Mr. Burton," she began. "I'm Abby Raines. Your new Assistant Manager." Burton merely nodded. "Mr. Burton, I have some concerns that we should-"

"Kessler, you concerned?" Burton Jr. drawled to the man who was his own age.

"Nope," Kessler replied, standing up. "Let's go."

Abby moved to block the door. She lifted the stack of reports. "Among other things, Mr. Burton, are you aware that the bookings have fallen well below an acceptable threshold for-"

"Bad economy," Burton replied, standing up as well.

"Mr. Burton if we don't-"

"Angie, we're late," Kessler announced. "We've got a noon tee time."

Abby flushed scarlet. "These reports-"

Kessler stopped in front of her and narrowed his eyes at her. All hint of his earlier frivolity vanished. "If I have to read reports, then what did I hire *you* for? If there's a problem, fix it, as long as you stay within budget. You came highly recommended from one of the largest hotel/casinos in Nevada. Are you saying you can't handle a hotel as small as the Custer?"

Abby's mouth dropped open. "No. I mean, yes I can. If-"

But Kessler was already waving her away as though she were a troublesome gnat. "Then do that," he demanded.

Abby felt instantly deflated as she watched both men swagger down the hall and through the doors that led into the hotel's lobby. She gripped the sheaf of reports that heralded the fact that they were on a sinking ship and stormed back to her own office. She slammed them down on her desk and sank into the chair.

The budget was ridiculous. She couldn't market or make any decent repairs. They'd switched to substandard linens, towels, and toiletries before Abby had even been hired, which she supposed was necessary when the hotel was losing money at this rate. But why was she trying to bail out the Custer with a teacup when the owner and the manager didn't seem to care at all? Within a few years Kessler would be out of a job and Burton would lose the only thing of importance that he owned. How could they *not* care?

Abby was so irritated at the two of them she could scream. She could quit the job, but that would look bad on her resume. She could ride it out until the Custer finally closed down, but that would make her look like an incompetent manager. She glared at the reports that were scattered on her desk. At a loss for anything else to do, she opened the bottom drawer and hauled out her purse. She opened the inside zippered pocket and located her Smith and Wesson .38.

"God damn it!"

Tex glanced across the garage at Hawk who was nursing a bloody thumb. "Aren't you done yet?" he said, just to irritate the large Sioux. Hawk glared at him. "I'm just saying, once you are, you gonna take it for a test drive?"

That earned Tex a slight twitch of Hawk's jaw. "Don't even," Hawk snarled.

Easy laughed. "An Indian on an Indian."

Shooter merely shook his head at both of them. "Tex. Quit being an asshole and head to Pearson's to pick up those parts for that chopper."

Tex gave his former lieutenant a half salute and his former squadmate a shit-eating grin. Hawk rolled his eyes, but grinned back.

Mid-town traffic wasn't heavy, but just enough to be annoying. It was Friday, though, and it would only get worse. He didn't care, though, since he usually stuck around Burnout until the 5 o'clock traffic thinned out and didn't head out again until it was time to go to the bar in the evening. His thoughts turned to Vegas.

It hadn't been a good time to push her too hard for a drink just after she'd sold her father's Harley, but she seemed to be in a better place now. He'd brought up the idea again and was pleased at her acceptance. Getting her into a more relaxed atmosphere might be the key to opening her up.

His cock stiffened slightly at the idea of Vegas letting her hair down, literally, with him. He'd only ever seen her with her hair pulled up and in baggy, unflattering clothes. Surely the woman understood that she couldn't dress like that in a bar.

As he swung onto Catron to get back to Burnout, he spotted a silver sedan out of the corner of his eye. Taking a closer look, he confirmed to himself that he recognized the little Toyota parked in front of the shooting range. Without a second thought, he turned sharply into the lot and pulled his Hummer into a space just three spots from the entrance. He reached under the driver's seat and pulled out a large black holster. He had been planning on waiting until tonight to increase the pressure on his little redhead, but there was no way he would miss any opportunity to spend even just a little time with her.

He swung out of the SUV, closed the door, and locked it with the key fob. He tucked the large semi-automatic under his arm and strode to the doors of the range.

Abby looked down the shortened barrel and squeezed off another round. It probably wasn't healthy to pretend the paper target was her boss but...whatever. Her ear plugs were holding up well and so she didn't notice anyone was behind her until she turned to the side to get some more ammo. She followed the long shadow across the floor until she saw Tex standing behind her, watching her.

She took out her ear plugs and let them dangle. She pursed her lips at him. "Are you stalking me?" she asked.

"Obviously."

She gasped. "I should get a gun!" She looked down. "Oh, wait." She gave him a sardonic grin.

He smiled and shook his head. "You're not bad." he said, nodding to the target.

She smirked at him. "I was just getting warmed up."

"Is that so?"

"That's a fact, Jack," she replied, teasingly.

As she set her handgun down on the small shelf, he came up beside her and set down of his own. She glanced at the large piece of hardware.

"Is that yours?"

"Yep."

She giggled. "Wow. Hummer, Harley, Desert Eagle. You know what people would say."

"That I'm surrounded by things I wish were as big as my dick?"

She let out a surprised laugh as she felt her cheeks pinken. Tex was definitely too confident and too cocky not to have a big- Well, she wasn't going to think about that. He slapped a clip into the grip and drew the slide back. "Mind if I take a turn?" he asked.

She nodded. Tex took a casual stance at the bar and brought up the gun. He made three shots in relatively quick succession hitting both shoulders and the head. "You're not bad yourself," she told him. "But really, what are you doing here?"

"I was picking up some stuff for the garage and I saw your car in the lot. Thought I'd stop in."

"So you're playing hooky from work?"

He grinned. "Maybe."

"Bad."

He stepped back from the bar. "Your turn," he said.

She finished loading the slugs and took her time, gazing at the target. She fired the first time, hitting the head, below where Tex had hit it. Then the throat, the chest, and finally the balls. She grinned at him.

Tex gave a low whistle. "Remind me not to piss you off," he said. She set her gun back on the shelf and reached for the box. His hand came down on hers and she nearly jumped. "Try mine," he said.

She gave him a smirk. "Oh, no. It's way too much for me."

"How do you know unless you give a try?"

"Mark, that gun is huge. My hands wouldn't even fit around the grip."

He opened her hand, sliding his thumb across her palm, and then placed the .44 in it. She instinctively tightened her fingers around it. He turned her hand first one way, then the other, inspecting it. His hands were large and warm. "Looks fine to me," he declared. "Go to the bar."

She hesitated for a moment then stepped over to it. She gripped it firmly because she knew the kick would be fierce. She raised it and waited a full two beats before squeezing the trigger. It didn't take much and the gun felt like it exploded in her hands. The shot hit the paper target, but not the black silhouette.

"Okay," he said. "You know what to expect now. Try again."

She re-set her feet and took a second shot. It hit just barely on the right shoulder. She felt Tex come up behind her. "Better," he said. He ran his hands down the length of her bare arms and took hold of her wrists, raising the gun level a third time. She felt his body pressed up against hers and it was hard not to lean back into that solid frame.

"Just relax," he said quietly into her ear, and she could do anything but. "Breathe normally," he told her. "Squeeze the trigger. You already know this. Just focus."

Abby licked her lips nervously, and steadied her aim. Before she could fire, Tex's hand slid around her throat. She froze. He wasn't hurting her. In fact his large hand only felt like a delicate brush of skin. Her heart started pounding. She tried to turn to him but he exerted the tiniest amount of pressure, and she stilled. His other hand had felt warm on her arms, but the one on her neck was downright scorching. She fought the urge to hyperventilate.

"What are you doing?" she managed to get out.

"Relax. Breathe, and squeeze. In between heartbeats."

"Yeah, I know. But what-"

"I'm feeling your pulse," he told her. "Otherwise how do I know you're doing it right?"

Abby tried to glance down, but couldn't. Ultimately she was probably glad she couldn't because she was dead certain her nipples were visible through her lacy bra. She would die if Tex saw that. What would he do?

Oh, God, she thought. Please don't touch me here in the shooting range. Oh, God, she thought, *please* touch me here in the shooting range. Knowing that there was another person in the booth next to them made it all seem so fucking wrong. And yet...

"Fire the gun, Abby," he said firmly, jolting her back to reality.

She aimed, waited, then squeezed. She hit closer to the heart.

"Very good," he said in a soft voice. He brought his arms around her again and took the gun from her. He released the clip and then stepped away from her. "Don't forget about Maria's tonight." And with that, he walked out.

Abby leaned against the bar to catch her breath. What the hell had just happened? she wondered. And then she wondered if it would happen again.

CHAPTER SIX

Tex held the Eagle and the clip in his hand and nodded to Cappy at the front desk as he opened the front door and headed out into the daylight. He had to get out of there before he bent Abby over and fucked the hell out of her. Her hair smelled deliciously sweet and the rapid beat of the pulse in her throat had given him a raging hard-on. Was she scared or turned on or both? She couldn't have been as turned on as he was.

Mark. She'd called him Mark and damn if that didn't do all kinds of things to him as he thought about Abby underneath him, legs spread wide for him by his chains, whispering his name, begging him to take her. He took a deep breath and swung up into the cab of the Hummer. Slow. Slow was the name of the game. He had to take it slow with her. But she was like a ripe little plum sitting on a windowsill and he damn if he didn't want to devour her one bite at a time.

He stopped at the garage and dropped off the supplies he'd picked up at the store before he'd spotted her car and impulsively driven into the lot of Cappy's range. After their little interlude, he'd left the garage early and headed home, taking a hot shower and fucking his fist relentlessly as he pictured a curvy, beautiful red head kneeling in front of him. He dried off and dressed in a pair of dark blue jeans, black motorcycle boots, and a fitted blue t-shirt. He grabbed his keys and his wallet and drove his Hummer straight to

Maria's.

It was almost nine on a Friday night and the place was starting to fill up. He spotted Hawk and Shooter by the pool tables. After scanning the place for Abby and not seeing her, he headed toward his friends. He grabbed a chair across from Hawk and sat down facing the front door, watching it intently.

Shooter laughed. "I'm surprised you didn't just order her to show up."

Tex took a sip of the beer Slick had brought him. "I pretty much did."

"Then relax, cowboy. If she's one of yours, she'll show up," Shooter replied.

Tex rolled his eyes. On the one hand he was grateful that his former lieutenant was cool about Tex's sexual proclivities. At one time, Tex had thought Shooter might be more than interested when Tex'd seen the man come on strong to a tiny brunette at a bar in London once. After that, Tex had taken his lieutenant to a club he'd heard about while they had a layover in Tokyo, but Shooter hadn't been into it. Apparently Chris Sullivan was just an alpha male.

But Shooter hadn't judged Tex after Tex had explained that everything was consensual and he had no interest in seriously hurting women. Encouraged by Shooter's acceptance, Tex had become more open about his interests with Hawk and Doc and neither of them had shown any real concerns over it. They hadn't shown any interest, either, and Tex was fine with that.

But it was sometimes hard to get them to understand what BDSM actually was and how it fit into Tex's life. Asking Abby to come tonight wasn't the same as ordering her when she was wearing his collar. It was her choice and she could always choose not to come. Which would be disappointing to Tex because he'd decided that he needed to at least have a taste of her.

He was on his second beer when she finally showed. She stepped in through the front door wearing a little black dress and high heels, all that red hair loose and flowing about her shoulders. A slow grin spread over his face.

Hawk gave a low whistle. "I'll admit you do know how to pick 'em, cowboy." All the men at the table watched as Abby headed straight for the bar. She ordered a drink from Maria. She took it, nodded appreciatively, and said something to Slick as she came back to get a round of drinks for a table.

Abby and Maria were talking when a guy in a Stetson and Tony Llama boots came up behind her. He leaned in, spoke to Abby, and she turned to him. She smiled, but shook her head. She started to turn back and he tried again. Abby again shook her head. When she turned back to Maria, the wannabe cowboy slapped her ass with his hand. Tex saw red.

He bolted out of his chair and headed across the main floor at a breakneck pace, but before he got there, Abby sent her left elbow flying into the man's face. She turned on her heel and punched him in the nose with a right hook. He fell back and landed on his ass just as Tex made it to the two of them.

Abby looked down at the cowboy with disdain. "If you get up again, I'm just gonna put you down harder, and then I'm gonna stomp a new hole in your ass with my motherfucking Jimmy Choos," she told him calmly.

"What the fuck is your pro-" the man started to say, but Tex had him up and was shoving him out the front door before he could finish his question.

"You don't ever put your hands on what's mine," Tex growled quietly into the asshole's ear and threw him out the front door.

As he turned back to the bar Maria said, "Vegas, are you gonna beat the shit outta every man in my bar?"

Abby turned to the older woman. "Well, hell, Maria, seeing as how I can't get a goddamn martini in this place I just figured we were so far off the beaten path that we no longer had to follow the rules of polite society."

Maria grinned and refilled Abby's gin. "Smartass," said the blonde to the redhead.

Abby picked up her drink and Tex put a hand on her shoulder. "Are you alright?" he asked.

Abby smirked at him. "Well, I wasn't the one on the floor so I'd say yeah."

"Come on," he said, grabbing her hand and tugging her behind him.

"Where are we going?"

"To my table where I can keep an eye on you."

Abby took a seat next to him at the table with Easy on her other side. Tex looked down at her feet. "So those are the infamous Jimmy Choos, huh?"

Abby followed his gaze. "Well, last season is the only way I can afford a pair, but yeah."

Tex smiled. "Last season or not, they make your ass look amazing."

Abby's mouth dropped open, but before she could say anything Slick came hurrying over. "Oh, my God! Abby are you okay?"

Abby turned to the slightly older but shorter woman and laughed. "Yeah, Slick, I'm fine."

"Are you sure? You punched out a guy!"

Abby smiled and shook her head. "It's fine, Slick. I'm not just Vegas. I'm Old Vegas. Third generation. Where people go for a ride into the desert and don't come back."

Slick's eyes widened. "Really?"

"Yes, now tell Maria to buy some goddamn vermouth and some olives so I can have a proper drink before I shoot up the place."

Slick grinned at her. "Will do."

Abby settled back into her chair.

"Are you in the mafia?" Easy asked her and Tex rolled his eyes.

Abby gave him a sidelong glance. "Yes, because the mafia, unlike the Army Rangers, promotes women into their ranks and lets them wear high heels while they pack revolvers in their designer handbags."

Hawk and Shooter laughed.

"Was your dad in the mafia?" Easy persisted.

"My dad was a mechanic."

"That's another word for hitman," Easy pointed out.

Abby sighed. "Jesus, I thought *I* watched too many movies."

Tex smiled. "You don't have a TV, Vegas."

She shrugged. "Well, when I get one, I'm buying a lot of movies. Casablanca, The Maltese Falcon, Gilda, Chinatown. All the classics. But right now I need a kitchen table and crank shaft."

Easy perked up. "I've got a shaft-"

"Stow it," Tex commanded and Easy sank back down in his

chair.

Abby took a slug of her gin. "Please tell me I wasn't the highlight of this evening's entertainment. Is there a band or something?"

"No band," said Hawk. "Just a jukebox."

Abby eyed it skeptically. "Any Frank?"

"Frank?" Easy asked.

"She means Sinatra," Tex declared.

"I don't think so," Easy told her.

Abby sighed. "No martinis, no Frank, no band. I'm beginning to miss the Strip."

"What?" asked Easy. "You miss strippers?"

Abby laughed. "Strip. The Strip."

"Oh. You know any strippers?"

Abby sipped her gin. "I know a lot of everybody."

Slick arrived with a glass and set it down in front of Abby. "Here you go, Vegas," she said proudly.

Abby looked down and gasped. "Olives!"

"I snagged them from the kitchen. I don't know what a good substitute for Vermouth is, though."

Abby wrinkled her nose. "Ugh, don't try. I got desperate once and used white wine. Disaster. Thanks, Slick."

"No problem, hon."

"You drink a lot," Easy observed.

"Don't judge me," Abby replied.

"I'm just saying."

"Whatever, how many beers are you on?" she asked. When he didn't reply she said, "Mmm hmm. Gotcha. You and your hollow leg can leave me alone."

The table got silent until Easy shoved his chair back and stormed away. Abby watched him go, shocked. She turned to Tex. "What happened? Did I-"

"It's not your fault, Abby," Tex said gently.

"But what did I do?"

"I'll go talk to him," said Doc, standing up.

Abby looked stricken. "I don't understand."

Tex stood up and took her hand. "Come on. Come dance with me, I'll explain."

TEX

Tex led Abby to the dance floor during a slow song and slid his hands around her waist, pulling her in close. "It's nothing you did on purpose," he assured her. "And Jimmy knows that. He'll be alright. He's got a prosthetic leg, Abby." Abby gasped. "It was an IED on our last tour. Jimmy and Chris got hit. Jimmy lost his right leg below the knee."

He watched tears brim around her eyes. He pulled her in and laid her head on his shoulder. "It's not your fault. You didn't know. It's no one's fault."

"I should apologize," she said in a shaky voice.

"No, no. Like I said, you didn't do anything wrong and he knows that. Once the sting goes away, he'll be fine."

He danced with Abby and calmed her down a little more and when the song was over they rejoined the men at the table. Abby opened her mouth to say something to Easy but Tex shook his head. She closed her mouth and picked up her drink.

A few minutes later, Slick came by. "You need another one, hon?" she asked Abby.

"No," Tex answered for her. "She's done for the night."

"Don't judge me," Abby insisted. "I can take a cab home. And I'm not even drunk yet."

"You're not getting drunk," Tex informed her while handing her empty glass to Slick. "And I'm taking you home."

"Yes, Sir," Abby grumbled. Hawk, Doc, and Shooter laughed uproariously. Even Easy chuckled slightly. "What?" she asked them.

"Nothing," Tex assured her while glaring at the men. "We're just, you know, ex-army. 'Sir', and all that," he replied while glaring daggers at his brothers.

Tex declined a final beer as well while listening to Abby tell the guys about the strange goings on in Las Vegas hotels. Men running naked, covered only by a pillow, to the ice machines and rooms accidentally being listed as vacant causing Ozzie and Harriet on their very first trip to Sin City to walk in on an all-male threesome.

He waited for her to finish her story and then picked up her purse from the back of the chair. "It's time to go, Abby," he told her.

Thankfully, she didn't argue. She said goodbye to the guys, took her purse from Tex, and allowed him to guide her toward the door.

51

He held the door to the Hummer open and helped her inside. He crossed the front to swung in beside her.

"I really can call a cab," she told him as he turned the engine over.

"Yes, you could," he replied and rolled out of the lot.

Minutes later he nosed into her driveway and pulled the parking brake. "Stay," he told her and got out. He held her door open and took hold of her arm, helping her down onto the concrete. She fished her keys out of her purse and unlocked the front door. He followed her inside.

She tossed her purse on the kitchen counter. "I have some leftover Chinese in the fridge."

She moved toward the refrigerator, but Tex reached out and gathered a large handful of her hair, pulling her back gently. She gasped. He put his lips next to her ear. "I'm here to fuck you, Abby, and we both know it." He felt her shudder against him. "Tell me you want it."

Abby hesitated, breathing hard.

"Say it," he prodded, keeping his voice low and gentle.

He felt her take a deep breath. "I- I want it," she whispered.

"Good girl," he replied and turned her around. He took her mouth, invading her with his tongue. She made the most lovely noise of surprise in her throat.

When she had gotten over her initial shock and started to kiss him back, he released her hair and slid his hands down to her ass and squeezed. She made another cute little noise. Keeping his mouth on hers, he turned her and walked her backwards, slowly, toward her closed bedroom door. He opened it with one hand and pushed her through.

He turned her around and bent her over the bed, holding her shoulders down with the palm of his hand. With his other hand he lifted her dress up over her hips. He got a very pleasant surprise. Her ass was round and gorgeous and framed by a lovely pair of black lace panties that sat mid-cheek, revealing the smooth curve of her rounded bottom.

He swept his hand over it slowly and then delved down between her thighs. "Spread your legs, Abby," he said gently. He was pleased it only took her a few moments to decide to comply. She spread her feet apart just a little more. His cock surged behind his zipper. Such a good girl.

He used both hands to tug her panties down to her knees and then returned one hand onto her back, gently holding her down, and started his right hand at the top of her ass, middle finger nestled into the top of the crack. He slowly slid it down. She gasped and surged forward, trying to get away from his hand.

"D-don't do that," she begged.

Tex wondered why that was off limits, but it was too early to ask. "Stay just like that," he ordered and started to unbuckle his belt. He pulled it free of the loops and took hold of the middle. He brought it in front of her face. "Bite this."

She tensed and tried to look over her shoulder at him. "W-what? Why?"

"Thin walls, Abby."

Abby didn't move and so he brought his other hand down sharply on her ass. It wasn't hard enough to hurt, but the smack echoed loudly enough in the room. As she opened her mouth to gasp, he pushed the belt in. Before she had time to spit it out or argue, he began delivering a series of slaps to her bared ass.

Erotic spankings were pretty mild on the kink factor and, in fact, a lot vanilla couples enjoyed them regularly. But the way his gorgeous little red head began panting and making soft, startled noises from behind the belt, he was fairly certain she herself had never been spanked before. After he'd warmed up her cheeks nicely, he delivered a slightly more stinging blow. He watched her fist her hands in the comforter. He rubbed her pussy from behind. She was starting to cream for him.

"Getting there, aren't we baby?" he crooned, rubbing her back with his other hand. "Just a few more to get you ready."

He slapped her three more times, alternating cheeks. When he was done, they were rosy red, but no prints appeared on them. He had been careful.

He unzipped his jeans and took out his hard cock. He took out a condom from his back pocket, ripped it open, and tossed the package on the bed where she could see it. He rolled it on and slid his fingers over her cunt. Nice and wet. He slid in a finger, checking how tight she was. She clamped down on it. It was pretty snug. No tearing into her tonight or he might accidentally tear her for real.

He held her pussy lips apart and guided the head in. He could feel how hot she was through the latex. He pushed in a little at time, letting her first contract then expand for him. "Almost there baby. You're so tight. It feels so good."

When he'd seated himself fully in her snatch, he reached around and rubbed her clit. She pushed back against him and he took the cue to start fucking her. He slid out and then back in gently, enjoying the feel of her pussy grasping at him. Surely she couldn't be close to orgasm already? But she was. She was squeezing and squirming. That spanking had really set her off. He also knew that every time her reddened bottom brushed against his pelvis as he sank into her, he was adding extra stimulation.

"Gonna come, baby? That's alright. Come on my cock, honey. Squeeze me tight. Just like this." He pinched her clit lightly and she squealed from behind the belt. Her inner walls tightened down on him like a vise. He let her ride it out then started fucking into her harder. "Just stay with me, honey. I'm nowhere near done yet. Just open that pussy back up for me again and let me have it."

She started to relax and he bottomed out against her cervix. "There you go. Good girl. Give me that pussy, Abby." With one hand he unzipped the back of her dress, letting it fall open and he slid a hand inside her bra, cupping her right breast. "So nice and soft," he told her, gently squeezing the supple mound of flesh. His fingers grazed her nipple and she moaned. "Except for this part," he said. "This part right here is tight and hard for me." He gave it a very slight pinch. She whimpered behind the belt.

He could feel his own climax start to build and he rubbed her clit harder with his left hand and squeezed her nipple with his right. "Come for me again, Abby. One more time. Come with me."

He felt her walls massaging his shaft again and he smiled. She had one more in her. "Come on, baby," he encouraged. "Give it to me. I'm giving it to you." He felt her start to go over, bearing down on him, and he gave her nipple a hard pinch. She screamed through her orgasm, muffled by the leather strap in her mouth, and his cock erupted into the condom separating them.

When they were finished, he pulled the belt out of her mouth and turned her head, giving her a long, slow kiss. "Beautiful, baby," he told her and took his belt and the used condom and its wrapper to the bathroom. He washed his hands in the sink and re-dressed himself.

God, she was a dream. First time out and she'd come twice for him, hadn't fought it, or him at all. If his cock hadn't been drained, he'd go back in and ravage her senseless for her good behavior. He turned off the light and headed back to her room.

She'd taken her dress and shoes off and put on a bathrobe. She was sitting on the edge of the bed, looking a little bewildered. He smiled and sat down next to her, putting his arm around her shoulders. "That was really good, Abby," he assured her.

She stopped biting her bottom lip. "I- I'm tired. I think I just want to sleep. Can- can you go?"

He paused for a moment. On the one hand he wanted to talk to her about what had just happened, on the other hand, he wanted to give her time and space to think about it. In the end, he decided it was best to respect her wishes. "Okay, Vegas. I'll let you rest." He kissed her on the side of the head. "I'll call you tomorrow," he told her and let himself out.

CHAPTER SEVEN

Abby managed to avoid thoughts of Mark for the last few days. Well, mostly avoid. Except when he called. Which she didn't answer. He'd left a message the first time. "Please, call me," was all he'd said. But Abby didn't know what she would say. Or what *he* would say. And so she didn't. He'd called again two more times, not leaving a message either time. She thought she'd escaped embarrassment by Wednesday when the whole day passed without hearing from him. Then there'd been a knock on her front door after work.

"So," he said, standing casually in her living room. "Nothing like having sex with a beautiful woman who won't return your calls afterward."

"I've been busy this week. With work," she said hastily. "I- I didn't think it really mattered."

"It mattered to me," he told her. "I guess I'm pretty disappointed it didn't matter to you."

Abby felt her face flush. He was making her sound like a slut. "I just meant that it was...you know...one of those things."

"One of what things?" he pressed.

"I just had too much to drink and-"

"I stopped you from having too much to drink, Abby. Remember? Try again."

She swallowed hard. "Okay. We're just friends and it shouldn't have happened. We'll just go back to being friends and pretend-"

"Pretend it didn't happen? Yeah, that's not gonna work for me Abby."

Suddenly anger erupted inside her. "Well, what *did* happen? I don't even know!" she snapped. "You didn't even look at me!"

In the wake of her sudden outburst, Mark remained calm. "Yes, I did. I may not have been looking at your face, but I saw your curvy little bottom wiggle. I felt your pussy cream for me after I spanked you. I heard your little moans."

"Stop," she demanded.

"You know exactly what happened, Abby. You were right there with me. What you really want to know is why you liked it so much."

Abby shook her head, not accepting his words.

"Oh, you're telling yourself you didn't like it? Then why did you do it? Did I hold you down? Tie up up? Pull my gun on you? If you didn't like it, why did you spread your legs when I told you to, Abby?"

"Stop," she whispered again.

His voice got lower and darker as he continued. "Why take the belt in your mouth when I asked you to do it? You could've taken it out."

Abby licked her lips nervously.

"You opened up your pussy for my use, just like I told you to."

Abby's clit jumped to attention and she gasped.

"You loved it, Abby," Mark assured her. "You want to know why? Because you're a sexual submissive."

Abby felt her mouth drop open.

He smiled. "I'm guessing that means you have at least a basic idea of what that is."

She frowned. "I've gotten tickets for guests at the hotel," she told him barely above a whisper. "Fetish balls and stuff. It means whips and chains."

"Well, that's...a little *too* basic," he replied.

"I don't do that," she added quickly.

"I didn't say you did," he clarified. "It's not about what you've done up to now. It's about what you want now that I've given you a tiny taste of it."

Abby shook her head vehemently. "I don't want any of it. No

whips, no chains, none of that. I don't want that." His face was kind and gentle and completely at odds with the pictures in her head of screaming women and bloodied flesh.

"Abby, like I said, that's a very basic stereotype. And you don't know what you want if you've never done anything beyond straight vanilla sex. Though I tend to agree that if you were really interested in serious pain, you would've experimented with it long before now.

"I'm not interested in heavy pain, either," Mark told her. "I don't enjoy hurting women like that. I've released more than one sub because she was too much of a masochist for me. But, Abby, there's so much more out there than just pain and suffering. It's different for everyone, what they like, what they don't, what they will and won't do. It's a constant negotiation and it changes all the time as people find out more about themselves." He paused. "What do you know about yourself, Abby?"

She pursed her lips. "Nothing. I don't know. I don't do anything, not like that, so there's nothing to know."

He smiled. "I bet there's a lot to know. Let me take a few shots. Do you ever initiate sex?"

Abby glared at him.

"Rarely, if ever, am I right?"

"I'm not a slut!" she snapped.

"Is that important to you? Not being a slut?"

"Of course!"

"How many sexual partners have you had?" he asked.

Abby's eyes widened. "What does that have to do with anything?"

"I bet you can count them on one hand," he replied.

Her belly lurched. How the hell did he know all this? "Four," she said cautiously. "Including you."

He nodded. "And you like them on top?" he added.

Abby took a step back. This was getting strange. Mark took a step closer to her. "Stop," she commanded, but he didn't. He took another step closer. She retreated instinctively until her lower back pressed against the kitchen counter.

Mark stopped right in front of her. "You're in total control in the bedroom," he said. "Am I right?"

"W-what?"

"You have a lot of rules. Things you won't do or let be done to you, right?"

Abby was now more angry than nervous. She crossed her arms in front of her chest. "Yes. Fine. I have rules. Tons of them. So there. I can't possibly be submissive. I don't let men walk all over me like I'm some kind of slutty toy they can use and throw away. I bet you think all women are submissive, or should be, especially to men. Well, I'm not."

He surprised her by shaking his head. "Not all women are submissive. Some are very, very dominant. Some people are just born wired one way or the other, regardless of gender."

That made her feel a little better. "Well, I'm not anything. I'm just-"

He closed the tiny gap between them and she put her hands to his chest to ward him off. He grabbed both of her wrists, forcing her arms to her sides.

"What are you doing?" she gasped. She struggled to get free but he wouldn't let go. His grip wasn't painful, but it was as unyielding as steel. He leaned down and took her mouth in a searing kiss. His tongue forced its way in. She made a noise of protest and moved to bring her knee up to his nuts.

He countered swiftly, shoving his own leg between hers and pressing into her. He nipped her bottom lip with his teeth as if to punish her for trying to hurt him. Her senses were overloaded. He tasted like he had before, like spices, rich and dark. And his scent enveloped her, woods and musk. She stopped trying to pull away. After a few long moments he leaned back a little.

"Stop," she begged. "Let me go. I- I don't like this."

"Really? You don't like it? Is that why your cheeks are flushed and your pupils are dilated and you're having trouble breathing normally? Because you don't like it?" He slid his hand around her left wrist until his fingers settled over her pulse. "Your heart's racing."

"Because I'm scared!" she lied.

"Abby. Your nipples are rock hard, your tongue was in my mouth, and you were rubbing your pussy on my thigh."

She looked down. Her face turned scarlet. "I was not," she

whispered.

He leaned in, his mouth so near she could feel his breath. He bit her earlobe. She yelped at the surprise pinch. "Don't lie, Abby," he murmured. "Not to me. Ever. I'll know and I won't like it."

She drew in a sharp breath.

"You like them on top, Abby. You like the feel of their weight on you, pressing you into the mattress, restricting your movements. You also like it because they cover you. If you're on top you feel too exposed, too much like you're on display."

She let out a breath. "How do you *know*?" she couldn't stop herself from whispering.

"Because I know what you are, Abby. And it doesn't make you a slut. It just makes you a passionate woman with very specific needs, that's all."

Abby nearly scoffed. Passionate. She'd been called a lot of things. That had never been one of them. She sighed heavily. "Mark, I'm not-"

"Tomorrow night," he said interrupting her. "Come to my house at 8 o'clock. I promise you I will give you a safe environment to learn more about yourself. Nothing out there, nothing too frightening. Just a chance to explore."

He let her go, took a business card out of his pocket, and pressed it into her hand. "Tomorrow, 8 o'clock. Please come." When he was gone, Abby inspected the card. It had his home address handwritten on the back.

She let out a breath and leaned back against the counter, turning the card nervously in her hand. Then she stuffed it into her purse.

Abby had managed not to give Mark's offer much thought through most of the next morning, but when it was time for lunch, she pulled her purse out of her desk and reached into it to get her keys, finding the card instead. She frowned at it. Then checked her watch, stuffed the card back inside, and headed out the door. She told Susan, the desk clerk, that she was out for an hour and hopped in her car. She started it up and turned left instead of right out of the garage, heading for the south end of town.

Maria's had a few afternoon customers but not much. The old man Milo was there and grinned at her as she headed toward the bar.

"Afternoon, Vegas," he sang brightly.

Abby smiled back. "Milo."

Without any fanfare, Maria set down a martini glass in front of Abby and poured some Death's Door and a splash of vermouth into a shaker. Abby's face broke into a grin. Normally she'd hold off on the liquor before five, but Maria had apparently gone to some trouble.

"Thanks," Abby said, picking up the glass. She took a sip and nodded at Maria. "Ah," she said. "Civilization."

Maria laughed. "Get you anything else?"

Abby hesitated. "Slick here, by any chance?" she asked casually.

The blonde's eyes narrowed shrewdly, but she reached back and pounded on the swinging door. Moments later the tiny brunette came through. "Abby!" Slick called out.

"Hey," Abby replied, smiling. "I'm on lunch and I was wondering if we could hang out. Do you have a break or something coming up any time soon?"

Slick looked at her watch. "Um, sure, I could take a lunch now."

"Great," replied Abby. She glanced around. "Maybe...some place else?"

The other woman looked a little surprised, but nodded again. "Let me clock out."

Abby drained the martini and set the glass down on the bar. "Thanks, Maria." She dug a twenty out of her purse and slid it across the bar. Maria eyed the huge tip. "To offset the cost of the glasses and the shaker and the vermouth," Abby told her.

The blonde nodded and took the cash.

Slick appeared and Abby re-shouldered her purse, following the woman out the door.

"There's a cafe a block down," she told Abby. "We can eat outside since it's so nice."

"Sounds perfect."

Five minutes later the two women were seated at a black wrought iron patio table outside. Abby ordered a salad and Slick ordered a sandwich. When the waiter left, Slick said, "I'm Sarah, by the way. Sarah Sullivan."

Abby nodded. "Have you lived here all your life?"

"No. I just moved here about a year ago. I've lived all over actually. Spent a few weeks in Vegas, too, a long time ago."

Abby raised her eyebrows in surprise. "Oh yeah?"

Sarah wrinkled her nose. "Yeah, but it wasn't for me. Too many people and too many lights. You can't see the stars at night in Vegas."

"No, you definitely can't."

"Plus," Sarah said, shifting a little in her chair, "I cheated some casinos."

Abby laughed. "No! You? You seem so...upstanding, for a chick who works in a biker bar."

Sarah laughed, too. "I needed the money. I think I'm on a watch list."

"So, what brought you here?" Abby asked.

Sarah rubbed the back of her neck. "The cover of a travel guide. Seemed like a beautiful place."

Abby sensed she was wading into waters with a pretty deep undertow. "It is that," she said, lightly, sipping the water the waiter had left. "So, you met Chris, and you got married," Abby observed. "That's nice. You two seem great together."

Sarah nodded. "He was my landlord."

Abby sat back in the chair. "Um..."

The tiny brunette laughed. "It's not as bad as it sounds. He didn't like me at first," she admitted. "That's why I'm called 'Slick'. He thought I was a con artist playing Maria for a job. And on some level I kind of was. Chris offered me a place to stay to keep an eye on me. Then we kind of ended up falling for each other. I moved in right after that, because he said it wasn't right to take my money."

Abby smiled. "Well, that's a hell of a story. People meet each other in all kinds of ways." *On the side of the road,* she thought, but kept to herself.

As if Sarah had heard her she suddenly said, "You want to know about Tex."

Abby took a sip of water. "Is it that obvious?"

"No. I mean, we could be friends. That could be why you're here. In fact, I really hope we get to be. But, yeah, if I were you, in your shoes, I'd want to know about Tex, too."

"So, you know," Abby said, letting it hang in the air in case she was wrong.

Sarah nodded. "He's pretty open about it. I mean, I don't know details or anything. But he was always honest with me about...how he is."

"So, everyone else knows, too? Your husband, the guys at the garage?"

"Yeah. Chris says Mark's a brother, part of the unit, and so whether he's gay or straight or...kinky....we just deal with it because we love him."

"So, you and Chris aren't..." Abby let the question hang in the air.

"No!" Sarah said immediately. "I mean, no, we aren't. I could never do that." Abby frowned at Sarah's words. "I didn't mean it like that," Sarah said quietly. "I meant, I can't ever do anything like that."

Sarah picked up a napkin and fiddled with it. "I...well, I don't like to talk about it, but most people around here know because it was on the news. I was attacked."

Abby felt her gut twist. "Oh, Sarah."

"It was years ago. Well, the *first* time was years ago. I got away, but my boyfriend at the time, he didn't make it. And I was afraid the man who'd taken us would find me again, so I ran. That's why I lived in all those places. To stay hidden. And, like I said, I went into a bookstore in Denver and picked up a travel guide with a photo of the Black Hills on the cover and then I bought a bus ticket.

"I met Maria, who gave me a job. And then Chris, who gave me a place to live. And he didn't like me at first, but then after a while he could see there was something wrong with me. The more we spent time together, the more he figured out on his own. He swore he'd keep me safe, and he did, for a long time. But the man who...raped me...found me again here in Rapid City."

"Oh, no," Abby said quietly, reaching for Sarah's hand. The other woman took it and squeezed, gratefully. "That's how people here know about it," Sarah told Abby. "Because he came to Chris' house when I was alone and kidnapped me again. I had to kill him," she whispered.

"Sarah, I'm so sorry. I hadn't heard any of this. I would never have asked you.

"It's okay. It's not your fault. But I told you that so you'd understand me when I tell you that when I first came here, besides Chris, Mark was the only other man I bonded with. I mean I got along with Hawk and Caleb. Jimmy and I had a rough start, but we figured it out. But I really liked Mark. He was honest with me about who he was and that he was disappointed that I wasn't his type of girl." Sarah smiled. "He likes my cooking."

Abby made a face. "I can't cook."

"No, but you work on cars and believe me, he's fascinated by it."

"Really?"

Sarah nodded. "They have Thursday night poker at our place every week, and Tex is always talking about your car and how much you've done to it already. Anyway, whatever Tex is into, I was always comfortable around him. And when things got really bad for me and my situation, Chris told Tex if anything happened to him, Tex was supposed to take me out of South Dakota and hide me. He told Tex that out of all the guys, Tex was the one he trusted with me the most. So that means a lot to me, that Chris would trust him that much."

"I could never be tied up or anything," Sarah admitted. "I sometimes still have nightmares. So, that's the only reason I could never do anything kinky. Not because I think it's wrong or anything. Chris would never, ever, allow one of his brothers to hurt a woman. But I know Tex would never do it anyway, whether Chris was around or not. He's just not like that. He never scared me or made me feel uncomfortable. Not once. Some of that's because he's Tex and he's a good guy. And of course a lot of it is because he's got a degree in psychology."

Abby sat forward in her seat. "He does? I thought he was in the Army."

Sarah nodded. "They all have degrees. The higher up in the army you go, the more common it is. In Special Operations like the Rangers, it's required. Chris has two. Business and Poly Sci. Mark has two, also. Psychology and Communications. Hawk's degree is in Computer Science. Caleb has a degree in Criminal Justice and Jimmy's is in Mechanical Engineering. They all enlisted, then took classes when they weren't deployed."

"Wow," Abby said, impressed.

Sarah grinned. "You thought he was a dumb mechanic?"

Abby grinned back. "Watch it, girlie. There's nothing dumb about mechanics. My dad was a mechanic."

Sarah laughed. "Well, there's not a dumb one in the bunch." She rolled her eyes, "Although, Tex, with that accent..."

"Yeah, what's the deal with that?" Abby asked. "It comes and goes. I don't get it."

"It's bullshit. You ever pick up on the fact that it only really comes out around Hawk?"

Abby thought about it. "Now that you mention it. At the bar, yeah, it does get a lot more noticeable."

Sarah nodded. "That's because Hawk and Tex have been doing this Cowboy versus Indian shtick since they enlisted together. Hawk was pissed about being in the army and he called Tex a dumb redneck and Tex asked him if he was going to put down the M16 and just throw tomahawks at the enemy."

"Oh, my God!" Abby gasped.

"And they traded insults for about a year until they got really wasted one night and dared each other to sign up for Ranger school. Which Chris told me one time is so hard that sometimes people die. *During the training part.*"

"Jesus Christ, seriously?"

Sarah nodded. "They starve or freeze to death. Not a lot, but it's happened."

"Well, damn," Abby said. "What's a spanking compared to that?" she wondered out loud. Then she blushed and looked at Sarah. "Oh. Sorry. Um..."

"It's fine," she said. "I kind of figured out that part at least. But yeah, their...worldview...I guess you'd call it?...is a little different than other people's. Because they've seen so much and done so much."

Abby cringed. "Jimmy has a prosthetic leg and I didn't know."

"IED," Sarah confirmed. "It killed almost half their unit. Four of the nine men. Chris has scars on his side from the shrapnel. The ones that lived, Chris, Hawk, Tex, Doc, and Easy decided to settle down together. Since Chris and Hawk are both from here, I guess this seemed like a logical place. They're hard men, Abby. They've gone through a lot together. But they're good men, too. The best men.

"I can't tell you if you and Tex are right for each other. Only the two of you can figure that out. But I can tell you without a doubt that he'd never hurt you. In fact, he'd die to protect you. Right now. Even though you don't really know each other all that well. Any one of those men would give his life if it meant saving yours. That's what they do, Abby. They just...ride black Harleys instead of white horses."

CHAPTER EIGHT

Abby pulled her car up to Mark's house and parked it. She stared at the house. It was a normal ranch style, one floor but large with an attached garage. The neighboring houses were spaced fairly far away, or maybe she thought that because she lived in a condo. She sat for a few moments, considering. She knew Mark. He wasn't a stranger. She'd had dinner with him on her living room floor. He'd helped her take the Camaro apart.

She wasn't going to come, though, until she came. In the shower. After a lackluster orgasm by her own hand, she'd kept going, rubbing her clit furiously and fingering herself until she finally gave in and pinched her nipple. She'd come a second time, screaming. Mrs. Fassnacht next door complained and Abby said the shower had suddenly lost hot water.

Passionate. Mark called her that. Could she be? She'd never been before. She liked missionary sex and knew it hadn't been Brian or Paul's favorite, at all. She lacked the ability to explain what about it turned her on. But Mark had known. Had known that she wanted men to stop asking so many damn questions and just take her already.

She got out of the car and slowly walked to the door. She was wearing heels, a skirt, and a blue silk blouse. She hadn't known what Mark would want. She went to knock, but couldn't bring herself to do it. She wasn't this woman. Mark had known things about her.

That much was true. But she wasn't what he was looking for, surely. She turned to go and took two steps when she heard the front door open. She stopped, but couldn't turn around.

Within seconds Mark was behind her, hands on her shoulders. "Just have dinner with me, Abby," he said. "We'll talk. That's all."

"That's all?" she asked.

"If that's all you want, yes."

Abby took a deep breath and decided she may as well put all her cards on the table. "I called a friend. A friend from college. She knows where I am. Your address. If I don't call her back by midnight…" She left the rest unspoken, not wanting to give voice to her fears.

She felt his hands squeeze her shoulders. "That was a good thing, Abby. The smart thing. Just dinner. Come inside."

She turned and looked up at him. He leaned down and brushed his lips lightly against hers. "It'll be okay," he whispered. "I promise." He led her back to the house.

She smiled when she saw the kitchen island crowded with takeout boxes. "I thought you cooked."

He grinned. "I do, but I figured you needed something familiar. Comfort food." He handed her a box of Shrimp Fried Rice and some chopsticks. "Let's sit on the couch."

Abby tucked her legs up under herself and plucked out a shrimp. "So, how does this work?"

Mark twirled some noodles. "Well, there are rules."

She nodded. "I figured. You have rules and I obey them. Like a prisoner or-"

He stopped her. "We both have rules."

She glanced at him. "I get to have rules?"

Yes. As many as you want. They're called limits. Sometimes limits are soft. Like things you may not be comfortable with right now, but you might try later. Sometimes limits are hard. Things you'll never, ever do."

"I don't want to be whipped," she said suddenly.

"Then I won't whip you."

"Can…I mean…do you do that? Like with a bullwhip?"

He shrugged. "I know how. I don't care for it. Like I said, I'm not into causing women that much pain."

"What *are* you into?" she asked.

"A lot of things."

She smirked. "That's cryptic."

He grinned. "This is about you. Not about me. For right now we're going focus on you and you alone. We'll get to me later."

"What if what you want freaks me out?"

"Then we don't do it," he replied matter-of-factly.

"Well, then what do you get out of it?" she asked.

"You. Any way you'll let me have you."

Abby was startled. "But you could have any woman-"

"But I want *you*. Plus, I'd rather play here, at my house, instead of at the club."

Abby's eyes widened. "You go to a club? Here in town? What if people recognize you?"

Mark shook his head. "It's in Sioux Falls. Usually once or twice a month."

Her eyes widened. "And people...watch you? Watch you do what we did?"

"Yes. That and more."

Her mouth dropped open. "I could never do that."

"I'm not asking you to go there with me."

She considered this. "What are you asking me to do?"

He considered *that*. "Tell me one of your fantasies."

She let out a harsh breath. "That's...kind of private, don't you think?"

He gave her a look. "Abby, we're negotiating kinky sex. It doesn't get more private than that."

"Yeah, but, I have to...tell you things?"

"Yes," he said firmly without hesitation. "You have to tell me everything."

"Why?"

The corner of his mouth twitched up. "Otherwise how do I know if I'm doing it right? That's one of my rules. You tell me everything. So, tell me something. Something easy. The tamest thing you can think of that you've never done."

She bit her bottom lip as something popped into her head. "We can't do it."

He grinned. "You have to let me know what it is first, honey."

"No. I mean, it's too late."

"Too late for what?"

She cleared her throat and squared her shoulders. "Meeting in a bar and... not telling each other our names."

He nodded. "Sex with a stranger. It's common. Especially for women."

"Why?" she asked. "Why is it common?"

"No judgment. You won't see him again, so who cares what you do?"

Abby blushed as she thought about the many, many times she'd thought about that scenario. She'd go to the bathroom, and come out and he'd be waiting. He'd push her back inside and rip off her panties. No one would know. It was safe because there were people outside the door. But it was also naughty because there were people outside the door.

But in her fantasy she was never in danger. She never got punched or choked or hurt. "I don't fantasize about men hitting me," she said firmly.

"Good because I would never hit you, Abby. And if you wanted that, we would be incompatible."

"I don't know much about this," she admitted. "I don't know where to start."

"Okay. We'll start with the basics. Oral? With a condom, of course."

Abby's eyebrows furrowed.

"What?" he asked.

"I've never done it with a condom. But then they were always my boyfriends, so..."

Christ. She was negotiating safe, kinky sex with a guy who was not her boyfriend. Could you have safe, kinky sex? Wasn't that a contradiction in terms? She glazed over the not-her- boyfriend part, choosing not to dwell.

"Anyway," he said, "it should be off the table, since I can't do it for you."

"You can't?" She had to admit that hearing him say it out loud was a little disappointing.

He glanced at her. "I don't know you that well, Abby, and we can't exchange fluids without a medical exam."

"Oh," she said, feeling stupid. "Right. Exactly. So, there's sex. But we already did that. So, I think we're in the clear. We should just eat the rest of this and I'll go home and-"

"No," he said firmly and she immediately quieted. "There's more to sex than just sex. Have you ever let a man tie you up?"

"No," she said a little too loudly. "I said no chains."

Mark smiled. "Abby you have a very narrow view of BDSM. Stop picturing crying women and torture. Did you cry when we had sex?"

"No," she admitted.

"Did I torture you?"

"No."

"Okay, so stop letting your imagination run away with you."

"But I don't know what to imagine!" she told him. "I've never done it."

"We'll start with bondage," he informed. "Something light and easy."

"What if I don't like it?"

"Then you have a safeword."

"A what?"

"A safeword. A word that you say to stop everything. If you get upset or too scared or something's bothering you, you say the safeword and we stop. For us, your safeword will be 'cantelope'."

She stared at him. "Cantelope," she repeated.

He nodded. "It's a strange word, out of context. Couldn't be mistaken for anything else. You say it, I stop."

Abby continued to look at Mark. She set the container of Shrimp Fried Rice down on the table. "Mark."

He looked at her, eyebrows raised.

"That's the dumbest fucking thing I've ever heard in my life!" she nearly shouted. "A word? *A safe word*? What the fuck about it is safe, Mark? It's a word! Is it a magic fucking word? Do the chains suddenly fall off and I get whisked away to my own bedroom on a magic, fucking carpet? What the fuck is safe about a *word*?!"

Mark stared at her for so long she sank back into the couch. "What?" she asked finally. "I'm just supposed to accept that?"

His face broke out into a smile. "No. You're not. You're the first woman to ever understand what a stupid concept that can be. I'm proud of you for calling me out about it."

He was so far from offended at Abby's outburst that she couldn't help but laugh.

"But you know me, Abby. We're friends. And you set up your safe call. I won't tiptoe around the elephant in the room and not admit that once you're tied up, I could hurt you for quite a while before your friend knows there's a problem. I know it's something you've at least considered, or you wouldn't have called her in the first place."

He put a hand on her knee. "This is the scary part, Abby. The part where you have to decide whether to trust me or not. But you do know me. You've been alone with me a few times. Your weirdo radar never went off and nothing bad happened to you."

She frowned. "I'm scared."

"I know. But the question is can you trust me enough to set it aside? I'll talk you through everything. I'll explain it all as we go. I'll show you what I'm going to do and you'll still have time to decide."

Abby looked away and chewed her lip. "You'll show me first?" she clarified.

"Yes."

Abby wondered what she was so upset about. He was an ex-army ranger and much stronger and larger than she was. If he wanted to hurt her tonight, he could easily have already done it. "Okay," she said finally. "Show me."

Mark squeezed her knee and led her into the bedroom. It wasn't particularly scary at all. The walls were blue and the bed was large with a wrought iron headboard. The comforter was dark gray. There were no whips, or chains that she could see. No rack, no iron maiden. This made her feel a lot better. It looked like a normal bedroom.

Mark led her to his dresser against the wall. He opened it and produced a leather cuff about two inches wide with two silver clips on either side, plus a buckle. She grimaced at it. "I thought it was supposed to be silk scarves?" she said.

He smiled. "Sounds romantic in theory. The reality? Not so much. They tighten up if you pull on them. They can cut off circulation and even cut the skin."

Abby's eyes widened. "Really?"

He nodded. "Silk scarves sound sexy, but they're not safe. The three things we need to worry about are being safe, being sane, and that everyone consents to what's happening. Okay?"

She took a deep breath. "Okay."

"I'm going to put this on you, just so you can feel it." He opened the buckle and encircled her wrist with the cuff. He fastened it and then took hold of the silver clip and shook it. "Hurt?" he asked.

"No," she told him. It was snug, but not tight and not uncomfortable at all.

"Feel too tight?"

She shook her head. "No, it's okay."

"Good." He let go of her wrist and walked over to the bed. Lifting up the corner of the mattress, he drew out a silver chain.

"Oh," Abby said.

He smiled at her reassuringly. "I know. No chains. But this isn't the kind you were thinking of, right?"

Abby examined it. It was smaller than she'd pictured. Gleaming and polished, not dirty and rusted. It wasn't any thicker than her thumb.

"They're strong and easy to clean," he told her. "But most importantly, they won't hurt you."

Between the chain, the cuff, and the wrought iron headboard, she could never get away. Mark must have read her expression because he lifted her chin to bring her gaze to him. "We're just going to cuff your wrists. Not your legs this time."

Abby eyed the chain and the bed. "And you promise not to hurt me?" She knew that was silly, a promise could be easily made and just as easily broken, but she looked into his eyes, searching for anything, any small hint of danger or a lie. Sarah had said she trusted him. Abby just wanted to be sure.

Mark brushed the back of his fingers down her cheek. "Never."

Try as she might, she could see nothing but gentleness and kindness in his eyes. "Okay," she said quietly. "Just the wrists." Not that it really mattered, but to Abby being bound completely seemed like a lot to take on for the first time.

Mark slid his hand around the back of her neck and pulled her close, kissing her forehead. "Good girl," he told her and her stomach fluttered a bit.

He brought over the other cuff and put it on her wrist. "Undress for me," he told her.

Abby hesitated. Having a guy rip your clothes, you ripping your own clothes off in a fit of passion, those were acceptable. But doing a strip tease in front of Mark when her heart was hammering in her chest? That did not seem possible. He sensed her reluctance. He turned, opened the closet door and took down the fluffy white bathrobe hanging on the back. "Would you prefer to get undressed in the bathroom, Abby?"

"Yes," she told him, taking the robe gratefully.

"Okay. It's the second door on the right. The second door."

Abby headed past the closed first door and entered the bathroom. It was enormous with a white tile floor and white walls broken with a strip of glossy black diagonally set tiles waist high, encircling the room. To her left was a small linen closet and a large black cabinet housing the white porcelain sink. In the corner was a tiled shower with a large glass door. Against the far wall, tucked under the window, was a large, white clawfoot tub.

It was beautiful. She wondered if Mark had bought it this way or had decorated it himself. She didn't know why a man would choose a tub like that, but it looked damn inviting.

She slowly unbuttoned her blouse, removed her bra, and unzipped her skirt. She laid her clothes on the chair to her right and examined the black cuffs against her pale skin. She was about to let a man chain her to his bed. It sounded crazy if she thought about it for too long. Then she pictured Mark as that man, and it still seemed crazy, but kind of exciting, too. She slipped on the oversized robe and stepped out of the bathroom.

Opposite the bathroom door was a room with an open door. It was a small home office with a desk, some bookshelves, and a computer.

So, she'd seen Mark's bedroom, his bathroom, and now his

study, all of which had the doors open. But the door next to the bathroom was closed. Mark had said the bathroom was the second on the right. Had said that twice. But had he said not to go in the closed room?

No. He'd just been making sure she knew where the bathroom was. Right? But this door was closed, which made her wonder. She hesitated, almost reaching for the knob.

"Abby."

She jumped and jerked her hand back. She grabbed the lapels of the robe and held them tight around her. Mark was smiling at her. "Snooping?"

"No!" she snapped, but she could feel her face turning red.

"It's alright. You want to know what's in there?"

"No. Yes. No." She sighed. "Do I?" she finally asked.

"Probably not. That's my torture chamber."

Abby gasped and Mark came toward her. He grasped her shoulder, turned her around and reached for the doorknob.

"No! I wasn't snooping! I-"

The door swung open and Abby's wave of hysteria abruptly turned into a fit of giggles. There was a treadmill, a weight bench, a balance ball, and a rack of free weights against the wall.

Torture chamber.

"I prefer to work out at home rather than the gym." He left the door open and took her hand, pulling her to the bedroom. "Come on. The look on your face was priceless."

CHAPTER NINE

"You're evil," she accused with a smirk. Still smarting over the workout room scare.

"Nope. I swear only to use my powers for good."

His lips came down on hers. It was a hot, demanding kiss that had her thighs quivering. He ran his hands through her hair and over her flushed cheeks. Fingertips grazed both sides of her neck causing her to shiver. He slipped a hand inside the robe and cupped her breast. His thumb rasped over her nipple and she clutched his biceps.

Mark had already taken off his shirt was wearing only his jeans. He tugged at the robe's tie and it fell open. He pulled her closer, pressing her bared chest to his. He slid the robe off over her shoulders and let it fall to the floor.

"Abby," he whispered against her mouth. "You don't know how long I've wanted to do this."

He pushed her back slowly to the bed and placed on hand on the back of her head and the other arm wrapped around her waist. He laid her down on the soft sheets. He kissed her senseless, nuzzling her neck and nipping at her shoulder. She was almost drowning in him when she felt him thread his fingers through hers, palm to palm. He drew her right hand up, above her head, toward the headboard. She tensed.

"Shhh," he told her. "It's okay, Abby. Everything's fine. Just relax."

He took her mouth with his again and she heard the soft click of the cuff being locked at the end of the chain. He quickly secured her other wrist. Abby's breath started coming faster. He put a hand under her chin and directed her gaze to his. "Abby, listen to me. Breathe. Just breathe, baby. Breathe in and count to three." Abby took a deep breath, counting in her head. "That's good. And let it out, counting to three. If you control your breathing, you control your heart rate. And if you control both of those, you can't panic. Look into my eyes. Nowhere else."

Abby breathed in and out, counting slowly and looking right at Mark.

"That's my good girl," he told her. He kissed her again, this time running a hand along the inside of her thigh. She instinctively spread her legs a little.

"There you go," he told her. "Spread for me, Abby. Let me touch your pussy."

Abby spread her legs wider and Mark rubbed her slit. Abby writhed underneath his fingers. Mark took his hand away and stood up. She watched in fascination as he unbuttoned his jeans and slid the zipper down. When he'd taken her at her condo, she hadn't seen him. She'd felt that he was large, but she was still surprised when he slid his jeans and boxer briefs down revealing a long, thick shaft that even now in its half-hard state was impressive.

When he caught her staring, she turned her gaze away. "You're allowed to look, Abby. I'm definitely looking at *you*."

She blushed furiously.

"Your nice, full lips, your beautiful breasts, your flat tummy, your curvy hips, those long legs. Hard to know where to start first." He pulled a condom out of the nightstand drawer and tossed it onto the bed beside her. "I guess I'll start from the bottom," he declared, "and work my way up." He got down on the bed, kneeling between her thighs and lifted her ankle. He kissed it. True to his word, he worked his way up her leg, licking and kissing.

He spread her legs, placed his thumbs on her labia and pulled them open. Abby gasped.

"You have a beautiful pussy," he told her. "All pink and red." He blew on it gently and she whimpered. "You need to get a checkup,

Abby, so I can taste it."

Her stomach muscles clenched, contracting her vagina. He chuckled. "So, you like your pussy eaten."

Abby frowned. Actually... "Not that much," she told him.

"Why not?"

"Um." Abby squirmed in the chains. The truth was neither of her exes really cared that much. If they bothered to do it, it didn't last long. She was brought out of her thoughts when he nipped the inside of her thigh. She yelped.

"Answer me."

"It's- it's just not that great. Guys don't care about that kind of stuff."

He looked up at her face and raised an eyebrow. "Am I like any guy you know?"

She thought for a moment. "No."

He opened her wide again, examining her. Abby felt her cheeks burn with embarrassment. Normally sex happened with the lights off.

"I love seeing you opened for me to use," he told her.

Abby wondered at that. Did she want to be used? Normally a declaration like that would make her think of cold, impersonal sex with no climax for herself. But he'd said he'd used her that first night. And while it may have been unlike anything she'd done before, it was far from cold or impersonal. And she had come twice. She decided that, for Mark, using her had a far, far different connotation. Oh, yes, she wanted to be used again.

Mark ran his fingers through the tuft of hair at the top and moved further down. "Do you shave or wax?" he asked, tracing his fingers along the bare lips. Abby never got a landing strip. She thought they looked weird. She just asked that they leave that part alone. He moved his fingers up again, felt for her hood and rubbed it.

Abby blew out a harsh breath. God, this was so weird. She was turned on, but being asked personal questions she didn't want to answer. It was an odd experience. "Wax. I get a wax every few weeks."

His fingers slipped down lower and parted her cheeks. Her hips shot up off the bed and she tried to twist away. "Don't do that!"

Mark laid one arm across her belly and flattened her to the mattress. "I'll look at any part of you I want to, Abby. There's nothing you can do. Have you been taken anally?"

"What?" Oh, God, she thought. Was he planning to-

"Has a man had your ass? Did it hurt? Was he not gentle or didn't prepare you properly?"

Prepare properly? How could you prepare for something like that? "No. No, I've never done that. That's- I don't do that. I won't do that." Well, that seemed like a stupid thing to say since she was chained to his bed and really had no ability to stop that from happening. God, what had she gotten herself into.

"We won't tonight," he assured her.

She sighed with relief.

"That kind of thing takes time for virgins. Especially for a man as large as me. But I am going to look at it, Abby. So you have three choices. You can pull your knees up and spread your legs for inspection. Or I can spank you. And then you can pull your knees up and spread your legs for inspection."

Abby licked her lips. "What- what's the third choice?"

"You say your safeword, get dressed, and go home."

Abby's stomach twisted. It was over? Just like that? "But- you said I could have limits."

"And you do. Hard and soft. Your hard limit is anal sex. You don't want it and we won't be doing it tonight. But there's no harm in looking, Abby. It won't hurt you. I won't even touch it. If everything is a hard limit, I'm afraid we won't be doing much. Give me this, and I'll reward you."

As if to illustrate what her reward would be, his thumb grazed her clit, making it throb in response. Abby gasped.

"Display yourself for me," he demanded quietly. "Let me see you."

Another stroke. She could feel heat pooling in her lower belly. She bit her lip and squeezed her eyes shut. He'd said he wouldn't touch her. If he broke that promise, she was out of here. Provided he'd let her go, of course, but she thought he would. He certainly wasn't going to kill her. And letting her go after hurting her meant she'd tear his life apart.

Slowly, she slid her feet up the sheets and planted them on the mattress.

"Good girl."

Abby flooded with warmth at his praise.

"Now spread," he coaxed.

She hesitated for the barest of moments then moved her feet further apart.

"More," he commanded. Her breathing quickened. "I know this is hard for you," he told her. "That's the point, Abby. Submission is not about doing what you want all the time. It's about pleasing me. And when you please me, I please you. Give and take. Does that sound alright?"

To Abby that actually sounded...normal. Wasn't that what a relationship was supposed to be? Give and take? If one person took everything and never gave back, well that would be unfulfilling to the other person, to say the least.

She parted her knees as far as they would comfortably go.

"Such a good girl," he said, stroking her inner thigh with a fingertip. "Now I'm going to have a look at what's mine for tonight."

He began a careful but erotic examination of her most intimate parts, starting this time with the thatch of curls at the apex of her vagina. He swirled a finger through them and then found her hood again. He gently pulled apart the folds of moist flesh until she felt the air on her exposed clit.

"Beautiful little pink pearl," he said, then blew on it. Abby jerked in response. "So sensitive," he observed. He gave it a light pinch. Abby gasped. "You're not afraid of a little pain," he told her.

"I- I don't like pain," she replied nervously. He pinched her clit just a tad bit harder and she squirmed.

"I said you're not afraid of it. Why would you be? Working on cars the way you do. And I've never had it done myself, but if I recall correctly, waxing involves ripping your hair out from the root." He chuckled. "No, Abby, you're not afraid of a little pain."

Suddenly, he smacked the inside of her thigh.

"Oh!" she yelped.

"That's a punishment. For lying to me," he informed her. "You don't mind pain, but you do like erotic pain."

Abby opened her mouth to protest again and he raised a finger at her. "Don't bother lying. Your pussy is wet as hell and getting wetter by the minute. Don't lie to me, Abby," he said more gently. "If you're embarrassed about the truth, we'll talk about it until you aren't. But don't lie. I will never lie to you. I expect the same courtesy."

He parted her labia and trailed a finger through her wetness. "There's no shame in liking this, Abby," he murmured. "Erotic pain is just additional stimulation, that's all."

Abby breathed deeply and her eyes fluttered shut. He called it erotic pain, which somehow did make it seem more acceptable. And her clit was buzzing now from all the...stimulation. She started to instinctively close her legs to increase the pressure on her clit.

"No," he said firmly and she opened her legs again. "Very good. That's all dominance and submission is, Abby. I tell you to do something and unless you absolutely can't for some reason, you do it."

Abby's mind reeled thinking of all things he might tell her to do. He spread her cheeks apart and she remembered pretty quickly what it was he was telling her to do right now. Let him look at her. She bit down on her lip and tried not to fight him, remembering the intense orgasms, plural, he'd given her the last time. She'd never come twice in a row and Mark seemed to know a lot about making women come and come hard.

"Very pretty," he commented. "Nice pink little rosebud. It's a shame you're so shy with it, but then again I'm glad no other man's ever been inside it."

Before Abby could really ponder his words, he let her go, opened the nightstand drawer and took out something small, holding it in the palm of his hand. "Now your reward for displaying yourself so well." He opened his hand and in it was a small purple toy. "Don't worry. It's brand new. I've never used it on anyone else. Do you have vibrator, Abby?"

She was still trying to get used to a man asking so many personal questions. She shook her head slightly. "No."

He turned it on and swept it over her tummy and down the inside of her thigh. She giggled. "It's small," he told her. "It's best for the clit, which you seem to enjoy having stimulated." He passed it over her mound and she jerked her hips a little. "Hold still," he commanded. "Do not move, Abby." He parted her legs wide with one hand, pressing on the inside of her knee. He touched the toy to her clit and she gasped. "Don't move or it's a spanking."

Abby tried to hold very, very still as he massaged her with the amazing little toy. But she got lost in the overwhelming sensation of it that she bucked her hips up into it.

"Bad girl," he told her, removing the vibe. He closed her legs, rolled her hips so her lower half was twisted and her left cheek was exposed. He smacked her hard.

Abby yelped. Smack, smack, smack. "Very bad girl," he admonished. Then he slipped the vibrator between her closed legs, holding it with one hand while continuing to spank her.

Abby cried out and yanked on the silver chains securing her to the bed. The warring stings of the slaps and the absolute eye rolling ecstasy of the toy were causing a slight sensory overload. She cried out again and tried to ride the hand holding the vibe, even with the spanking, it felt so good. She was breathing hard when Mark rolled her bottom back onto the mattress and spread her knees again. She hadn't come but she'd been so close. She whimpered in frustration.

"I'll be a good girl," she panted. "I promise. I'll be good. Please."

"Please what?"

"Please, let me come!"

Mark pretended to consider this. "If you want something from me, Abby, you have to ask the right way."

"I did!" she protested. "Please, please, please!" Mark shook his head and she was devastated. That little toy could send her to the moon and back in seconds. "W-what? What can I-"

" 'Please' is not the magic word," he informed her.

Abby racked her overstimulated brain to think of the right word. What the fuck? "I- I don't- I can't-"

"Sir," he said helpfully and Abby stilled.

"What?"

"Please, may I come, Sir."

"Oh, now wait a minute," she said. "I don't-"

He held up a finger to quiet her. "Only in the bedroom. And only when we're playing games like this. It's to help you, Abby. Help you to remember who is the dominant and who is the submissive.

Plus, it pleases me. And you want to please me, right?" He waved the toy a little to remind her of the stakes.

Abby glared at him. "You said I could have a reward!"

He smiled at her. "And I gave you a reward. Now, if you want to come, you call me 'Sir'. This is not a hard concept, Abby. The more you submit, the better the rewards."

Abby laid her head down on the pillow and stared at the ceiling. *Sir*. It wasn't such a hard word. God, she said it every day. 'I hope you enjoyed your stay, Sir. I'll be certain your room has more towels, Sir.' What would it mean to call Mark 'Sir'?

As if he could read her thoughts he said, "Hey." Abby drew her gaze down from the ceiling back to him. "It doesn't make you less of a person to show me respect."

Normally Abby would've responded with some smartass comment like he hadn't earned it. But then again, here was Mark Marsten who could have any woman in three counties, hell any woman in *Vegas*, but instead of being with any of them, he was with her. She should at least be grateful.

She licked her lips. "Please, may I come, Sir?"

He grinned. "Yes. But don't move, Abby. Hold, very, very still." He replaced the vibrator on her swollen, aching clitoris.

Abby fought hard to remain still. She clutched the chains and pulled hard, forcing her bottom down onto the mattress to keep from moving. She was afraid if she did, he'd take the toy away again.

She was gasping for air, which the room didn't seem to have enough of and squeezing her eyes shut. "Oh, God. Oh, God!"

"Don't move, Abby."

When she was almost there, he took the toy away. "No!" she howled. "I need to come! Please! Please, Sir!"

Mark chuckled. "Easy now, you saucy little minx." He quickly ripped off the top of the condom and rolled it on. "I want to feel that pussy tightening up on my cock when you do." He held her pussy open with two fingers. "Want my cock, pet?"

The wider he spread her, the more empty she felt. She needed to feel that stretch, that push/pull of being entered and filled up. "Yes! Yes, Sir. Oh, please fuck me, Sir!"

Mark shoved his cock inside her hard, causing her to cry out.

Then he quickly pulled out of her, causing an equally loud howl of frustration.

"Who controls your pleasure, pet?"

Abby didn't even stop to think. "You! You, Sir!"

"This pussy is mine to use, isn't it, pet?"

"Yes! Please, use it! Sir!"

Mark shoved in again, stretching her to her fullest. The sweet, sharp sting of being filled was heaven.

"Come on my cock, pet," he ordered, and began fucking her mercilessly.

Abby came hard on the third stroke. Undaunted, Mark still continued to fuck into her, taking his own pleasure from her sated body. He pressed the tiny vibrator to her clit as he pounded her.

"One more time, pet. Come one more time."

"I can't!"

"Yes, you can and you will. Come once more for me," he insisted.

He bottomed out against her cervix, balls slapping her ass with heavy thuds. The toy against her clit made her whole pelvis sing.

"Come," he ordered a third time and she threw her head back and screamed out her orgasm.

Mark had unchained her wrists and pulled her to his chest. "It's over," he told her. "You survived."

"Barely," she muttered against his skin, but she was smiling.

"*I* may not have," he said. "You are definitely a troublesome little pet."

She stiffened. "I don't like that."

"What?" he asked, rubbing her back.

"I'm not a pet. I'm a person."

He stroked her hair. "It's not meant to dehumanize you, Abby. It reminds me that I have a serious responsibility to you. To care for you and see to your needs, and never to forget that you haven't done anything like this before. Taking a sub through their first submission is a huge responsibility. I need to keep your feelings and your inexperience in mind."

Abby chewed her bottom lip and thought about that. "Okay," she said quietly. "That sounds okay."

"Tell me how you felt."

"Why?" she asked without thinking.

"Pet. I have thirty minutes. I *can* think up more ways to punish you. You belong to me until Midnight."

"It was scary," she replied.

"And?"

"And... exciting."

"Good. Scary is fine. I can work with scary. I like to keep subs off balance, anxious. It heightens the experience for both of us. But terrified is not the goal. You weren't terrified, were you?"

"No. But I was angry that you wouldn't let me come."

"I did let you come."

"Not without jumping through your hoops first!"

"The hoops are the point, Abby. If you could get yourself off as well as I do it, then you wouldn't need me or anyone else around, would you?"

"I don't come that way," she whispered.

"You mean hard?"

"Or more than once. I- it's never been like that. Sometimes I don't even come at all."

He squeezed her shoulder gently. "Well, now you know you can. I told you you're a passionate woman, Abby."

"But how did you know?"

He grinned. "I don't lack vision."

Abby wrinkled her nose. "I'm a project?"

"In a way. Don't misunderstand me, Abby. I like you. When I look at you I see a woman who loves her career, loves working on cars, loves old movies and expensive gin. A woman like you enjoys so many things and sex should be one of them. Even if it was vanilla sex, and you turned out not to be submissive, I wanted you to know that it could be good.

"I want you back here again next Friday," he told her. Before she could reply he said, "Take some time. Think it over."

"I thought I was a troublesome little pet."

"You are but you squeeze my cock so tight when you come it's Heaven. And I'm nowhere near ready to give that up yet."

Abby spent most of the week thinking about being chained to Mark's bed. It hadn't been anything like she'd thought it might be. Once the initial fear wore off, she was amazed to discover it had been...freeing. Was that right? She could barely wrap her head around the idea that bondage could be freeing, but it was. She was free to enjoy anything he did to her. No worrying about what to do with her hands. She also didn't have to worry about whether or not she was making him happy because he told her when she was and he...punished her..... when she wasn't.

She shivered a little at the memory of Mark's little punishments. A bite here, a smack there. Instant feedback on what she was doing wrong. And it had been a little daunting, showing herself to him like that, but he'd said she was beautiful. Abby watched a tall blonde stride across the lobby and toward the bank of elevators.

The blonde was pretty, with full lips and a decent sized chest. She was wearing a short linen dress with white heels. Abby looked down at her own black suit, blue button down shirt, and long pants. The only thing remotely sexy about herself were her shoes. But beneath all that, she felt...equal...to this woman who just weeks before would have seemed like some kind of untouchable goddess.

Mark could have this blonde, absolutely. No question. But it had been Abby chained to his bed and opening herself for his...inspection. Which she'd apparently passed, she added to herself, because he'd said he wanted her to return on Friday. It was only Thursday, but Abby already knew where she'd be on Friday night at 8 o'clock.

CHAPTER TEN

Friday had arrived and instead of slaving away at her desk working overtime, Abby left early and made a beeline for her car. She spent the rest of the afternoon prepping herself, washing her hair, making sure she was shaved in all the areas that mattered. She hadn't been sure what to wear and so opted for black slacks and a fitted t-shirt. She frowned down at the outfit now, outside Mark's front door. For the first time she found herself wishing she had sexier clothes.

Mark opened the door just two seconds after she knocked. Her heart hammered in her chest, but he seemed calm and composed. He took her purse from her again and kissed her on the lips.

"You ready?" he asked in a low, gravel tone that made her insides quiver.

She took a deep breath. "Yes," she replied.

Mark led her down the hallway toward the bedroom. "You'll need to get undressed," he told her. She balked at the bathroom door. He stopped to look at her.

"Um," Abby said, glancing from the bathroom door to Mark and back again. "Can I get undressed in the bathroom?" *Alone?* was the unspoken question. Between her poor choice of outfit and extreme nervousness she couldn't fathom dealing with undressing in front of him. Her mind was swirling with all the possible things he would do to her tonight and she needed time, also, to calm down.

Mark looked as though he would argue, but instead nodded and opened the bathroom door for her. "There's a bathrobe hanging on the door," he told her.

Abby undressed and laid her clothes on the chair. She put on Mark's robe and cinched it around her. She was still a bundle of nerves and her hand shook slightly as she reached for the doorknob. She found Mark already waiting for her in his bedroom.

Mark had been close to sending a rescue party into the bathroom because she was taking so long. He had to remind himself she was new and nervous. When she finally appeared in his bedroom doorway wearing only his own robe, he calmed himself again with a reminder that she was new to his world. He took a step toward her and drew her further into the room.

He slid the robe from her shoulders and saw Abby shiver. "Next time you'll undress in front of me." She held her breath. He leaned in closer. "Yes, Sir," he whispered in her ear.

"Yes, Sir," she repeated.

He kissed her temple. "Good girl." As he attached the wrist cuffs he said, "Tonight will be a little bit more challenging. You're going to remember everything I told you, about relaxing and breathing slowly. You don't need to think about anything or worry about anything. I just want you to feel."

He guided her slowly backward until she was up against the wall. He took her wrists and clipped them together then raised them above her head and attached them to a short chain on an eyebolt in the wall. Her arms were slightly bent to keep them comfortable. He put one hand behind her head and pulled her forward, sliding his tongue into her mouth. She opened to him instantly, teasing him with soft little licks of her own. To reward her, he slid his other hand down between her legs and rubbed her slit.

He pulled away as he felt the first drops of wetness between her thighs. "We haven't started yet, pet." He went to the dresser beside her and opened it. He glanced at her. "Eyes front, pet," he ordered. She turned her gaze to stare at the wall across from her. He pocketed a few essential items and returned to her.

He kissed her again, caressing her breasts and her stomach. She quivered deliciously at his touch. Then he plugged her nose. When she opened her mouth in surprise and for air, he pulled the gag out of his back pocket and slipped it inside her mouth. With a practiced hand he buckled it swiftly behind her head, faster than roping a calf.

Abby panicked, as he knew she would. She slammed back against the wall and tugged at the cuffs. He grabbed both sides of her head and forced her to look at him. Fear widened her eyes and he was damn sorry for it. "Abby," he said, speaking calmly and with authority. "Abby remember everything I told you. Breathe. Breathe deeply. One, two, three," he counted to encourage her.

The ball had holes in it to make breathing easier. He hadn't wanted to terrify her with visions of suffocating, plus he didn't want her to hyperventilate and pass out if she couldn't get enough oxygen just through her nose.

"Nothing bad is going to happen to you," he assured her. "Just breathe, honey. Deep breath now."

She started to calm down and control her air intake while her large, green eyes pleaded with him. He smoothed back her hair gently. "Everything's fine. It's alright. You can breathe. Is it comfortable?"

Abby shook her head vehemently. He narrowed his gaze at her. "Abby. I didn't ask if you liked it. I know you don't like it right now. I asked if it was comfortable. Is it pinching you anywhere? Hurting your jaw?"

Abby seemed to take a long time answering and he knew part of her was considering lying to get him to take it off. In the end she shook her head slowly.

"Good girl," he told her. "Just be honest. I will never let anything terrible happen to you. Now," he said, taking a small step back. "I know I told you about safewords and how you use them to stop the scene." Abby glared at him and he smiled, knowing she was now well past her initial shock. "But you can't safeword if you're gagged." He pulled out a small round plastic ball and held it up. He shook it and a tiny bell jingled inside.

"If you can't handle what's happening," he told her. "If you feel dizzy, or your wrists or arms start to hurt, if you have any problems with the scene, then you drop this and we stop." He reached up and opened her hand, placing the ball inside. She gripped it tightly. "Okay?" he asked and she nodded.

"I want you to stay calm, and focus on what you feel, pet. That's all you have to do. You don't have to jump through my hoops tonight. Just feel. Enjoy it. Everything will be well within your limits. I promise you that."

He reached into his other front pocket and took out a blindfold. She balked a little when she saw it but didn't drop the ball. "It's okay. This is just to help you focus on what you're feeling. You have the ball. That's your safe gesture. That's your control, Abby. If you need it, use it." He slid the ends of the black silk strip behind her head and tied them securely. She started to breathe erratically.

He ran his hands over her shoulders, breasts, and belly. "Easy now. Breathe. Just relax." He massaged her a little more until she calmed down. Then he went to the open drawer and took out an ostrich feather. He returned to her and swept the tip across her tummy. She jumped a little.

"Everything's fine, pet. Just a little sensation play. That's all." He brushed the feather over her nipples and they blushed a dark red. He ran the feather down one thigh and up the other. She whimpered slightly. "My pet likes that," he declared. He continue up her sensitive underarms and back down. He even wiggled it at the end of her nose and she growled at him from behind the gag. He grinned. Sassy pet.

He set the feather down and picked up a fur glove, slipping his right hand inside. He encircled her waist with his left arm and then ran the soft fur over one breast, then the other. Abby moaned.

"Not everything has to hurt or be scary, pet," he told her as he ran the glove over her stomach. He moved it over her hip to her ass and took a nipple in his mouth at the same time. She arched into him. He sucked the other nipple into a hard point as well and returned to the dresser. Abby was panting, but not terribly.

He poured oil onto his palms to warm it and rubbed it all over her breasts, pinching and rolling the now stiff peaks. Abby made the most cock-hardening noises and tried to push her chest into his hands.

"Easy, pet," he cautioned. "I can tell how much you love to be touched, but we've got one more lesson to learn."

He let her squirm a little in the cuffs as he watched her. God, she was fun when she stopped letting that head of hers rule her. He took out a thick black candle and lit the wick, setting the lighter down on the top of the dresser. It was a low temperature candle, made specifically for waxplay. She'd responded well to nipple stimulation as well as clitoral and he was interested in testing her threshold for erotic pain.

He brushed his free hand over her hip to let her know he'd returned to her and watched her immediately calm to his touch. She didn't like being left alone. He could only imagine the things her vivid imagination came up with when left to her own devices. "Not everything has to hurt, pet," he reminded her.

He brought the candle up and poured the pooling wax on his own arm, testing the height. Closer to the skin meant the drops were hotter when they landed. Farther away gave them a chance to cool off a little more before impact. He adjusted to just a little bit more than warm, but not particularly hot, and lifted it over her breast. He tilted it slowly.

Abby jerked back as the wax splattered over her left nipple. "Not everything has to hurt pet, but sometimes it does hurt, and we like it." He pressed his free hand to her stomach, holding her firmly against the wall and poured another few drops on the other nipple. He immediately checked her hand, but she hadn't dropped the ball. In fact, she was gripping it so tightly her knuckles were turning white.

He slid the hand that was bracing her against the wall down and ran his fingers between her thighs. She was slicked and warm. He ran his fingers through her dampened curls. Soon she'd forgotten the wax and was humping his hand. He slipped a finger into her cunt and poured more wax over her breast.

She twisted a little, but came back to his hand, desperate for more stimulation there. He inserted another finger. She groaned loudly and wiggled her hips. He pressed his thumb to her swollen clit and rubbed it while dropping more wax. She didn't move away this time.

"Good girl, pet. Just feel."

He continued to fingerfuck her and drop the wax, inching closer to her tits each time, increasing the heat. When she finally bowed her back trying to get away from the drops, he backed off. As long as he kept her aroused, she had a very nice threshold. The wax would leave her skin pink and tingly, but wouldn't burn or even hurt after a few hours.

When even he couldn't take anymore, he withdrew his hand, blew out the candle and knelt down in front of her. He set the candle down beside him and took hold of her leg, placing it over his shoulder. He sealed his mouth over her wet pussy and she shuddered. He lifted her other leg and when she was resting fully on his shoulders, he ate her delicious pussy with abandon.

She was drenched and tasted like fresh spring rain. He shoved his tongue as far inside her as it would go. She bucked her hips, grinding his face. He'd waited a long time for this and fuck it if she came right now, he wasn't going to stop.

He licked and sucked the cream out of her, stopping only to nibble her clit which made her shriek behind the ball gag. He spread his hands wide over her ass cheeks and held her against him. He attempted to slip a finger between her cheeks, but she clenched and made a noise of protest. He stopped and resumed feasting on her cunt. He would figure that out later, because god damn if he wasn't going to have every fucking part of her now that they'd started.

He let go of her ass, unbuttoned his jeans, and took out his cock. He gave her pussy a few more generous licks and then slowly stood up, holding her legs and wrapping them around his waist when he reached his full height. He lifted her up and sank her slowly down onto his erection. She pressed back against the wall and breathed hard through the gag.

"Open that pussy for me, pet," he told her. "Take me all in. Come on now." She relaxed and he felt her open slowly, sliding him in. "Good fucking girl. Such a good pet." He fucked her slowly, holding her ass and lifting her at the same time he was sliding out of her, then he pulled her back down, inching into her again.

Their first time had been hard and brutal and yes, she'd loved it, but he wanted to show her he could slow it down and take his time, too. He settled into a steady rhythm as he gazed at her wax covered tits. God damn he'd *hoped* she would be at least a tiny bit adventurous and she was already far exceeding his expectations for a vanilla woman.

He gave her a slow, sensual fuck as reward for being such a good girl. His own reward came soon enough when he felt her pussy walls shiver over his cock and she started to come. Her cunt was like a fist, tightening up around him. It'd been years since he'd fucked a woman without a rubber and he hadn't exaggerated, it felt like Heaven. She was so hot and wet and tight. He felt his balls draw up and he held tight to her hips as he pumped his load into her greedy, grasping pussy.

When they both finished, he carefully set her down on the floor. He stepped back and zipped his pants, watching her as she rested the back of her head against the wall. "You look so fucking good with my cum trickling down your thighs, pet." She blushed and he smiled. She wasn't quite ready to experience some of his other...proclivities, so he just watched and admired the view.

Finally, he reached up and squeezed her hands. "Pins and needles?" he asked. She jerked suddenly and he realized his mistake. "I meant do you have any numbness or tingling?" he asked, rubbing her hands. She sighed in relief and shook her head. He unclipped her cuffs and brought her hands down. He unbuckled the gag and removed it. She took in a deep breath. "Alright, pet?"

"Yes."

"Pet."

"Sir. Yes, Sir. I'm fine." She reached up to take of the blindfold, but he lightly slapped her hand.

"No." He picked her up and crossed the room, laying her down gently on the bed. He raised her hands and laid them above her head. "Keep your hands here. Don't move them," he ordered. "The blindfold stays on for just a little while longer."

He thought this was best as he reached into his back pocket and drew out a knife. He opened it quietly and began rubbing one of her breasts with his hand.

"What is that?" she asked, curiously. "What you did to me."

"It's candle wax," he replied, using the breast massage as a distraction from him scraping off the wax with the blade. She didn't even feel it and with the oil he'd applied before hand, it came off easily. "Not from a regular candle though. A special candle just for applying it to skin. Regular candles can burn way too hot and scented ones can cause irritation," he told her, lest she have any ideas about going home and experimenting by herself without his supervision.

"Did you like it?" he asked, already knowing the answer.

"Um."

He smiled even though she couldn't see him. "It's okay to say yes, pet. It was meant to feel just a tiny bit painful, but still really good."

"I liked it," she whispered. He leaned down and kissed her on the mouth.

"I knew you would."

He finished removing the wax and folded up the knife, pocketing it. He took of the blindfold and set it aside. "You did really, really well, pet."

She blushed and brought her hands down to cover her breasts. He pushed them away. "Don't do that. Don't cover up what I want to look at," he told her. He grasped her wrists and put them back over her head. Then took the towel he'd laid on the bed and began to wipe down her chest. He worked his way down to her belly. "Spread," he ordered and after a moment's hesitation, she spread her legs. He gently wiped her thighs and then her pussy. She was flushing crimson by the time he was done cleaning her.

"Do you need to call your friend?" he asked. She nodded. "I'll get your phone," he told her. "Call her now and tell her you'll call her again from your place in an hour. You aren't ready to drive yet."

He went to the bathroom and retrieved her purse, bringing it into the bedroom. He closed the door as he stepped out again to give her some privacy. When he returned, she was wearing his robe and picking up pieces of wax off the sheets.

"I'll just wash them," he told her and stripped the bed. She sat in the chair in the corner, as directed. She got up, though, when he brought a clean, fitted sheet from the closet and helped him re-make the bed. He climbed into it and gestured for her to join him.

She snuggled into his chest. "What other tricks can you do?" she teased.

"Everything."

"That's a lot."

"Yes, it is."

"Where did you learn it?" she asked.

"Overseas mostly. Clubs in Germany and Japan where it's more common."

"How did you know you would like it?"

He chuckled. "I spanked a girlfriend in high school."

She gasped and looked up at him. "No way!"

He nodded. "We were going at it one day and she was on top. Kept putting my hand on her ass. At first I couldn't figure out why she was doing it. She was obviously too shy to ask for what she wanted. So I took a chance and I smacked her. She loved it. First it was bare-assed hand spankings. Then she handed me a hairbrush one day."

"Oh, my God!"

He smiled at the memory. "She was a kinky little thing and I didn't want to ruin it by asking too many questions. I just knew we both loved it. I graduated, enlisted, heard about a spanking club in Berlin when we were on R&R. Turned out I liked a lot more than just spankings."

"Like whips?" she asked nervously.

"No. That's way too much for my comfort zone. I can do it. I've had lessons, but I don't like it, and I choose not to do it anymore, even if the sub wants it. I don't get off on hurting women. I do punish them, though. Usually with a spanking. If it's a serious offense, I'll use a cane."

"A cane?"

"It's made out of rattan. Long and thin. Hurts like a bitch. That's as severe as I'll go."

Abby looked shocked. "For what? Not calling you Sir?!"

He held her tightly. "No. I'm a harsh man, Abby, but I'm not abusive. I caught my submissive mouthing off to another sub in the club where I play. Embarrassing her, telling the girl she wasn't a real sub and not good enough to play at the club because she wouldn't do bondage. So I gave my sub a choice. She could go in the stocks and everyone there could take a whack at her ass with the paddle. Or five strokes with the cane from me. She chose the cane. But I dumped her anyway immediately after. Other people's limits are personal and are strictly between a submissive and their Dominant. It's nobody else's business or place to comment on them."

Abby was quiet for a long time. "Sarah can't do things like this," she whispered. "Because of what happened to her."

"Exactly," he replied. "Most people have no idea what a person's background is or why they refuse to do certain things and to insult them for their choices when you don't know the reasons behind them is not only rude, but it's also insensitive. And I don't tolerate that kind of behavior."

She cleared her throat nervously. "Am I- am I your submissive now?"

"No," he replied and he felt her tense in his arms. "We're just doing a few scenes together."

"Is it hard?" she asked. "Being your submissive? You said you were harsh. Is it difficult? I mean the things you do to them?"

He considered his answer. "Not really. Not for an experienced sub. But for you, yes, it would be a challenge. I have rules, Abby. Rules that I expect to be followed. And if they aren't followed, punishments are handed out. And they are not pleasant."

She shivered. "Like what? What rules?"

He debated how much to tell her. "I expect my submissives to be available for my use whenever I choose to use them."

She frowned. "But...I mean, what if they can't? I mean-" She lowered her voice. "What if they're...on their period?"

"They have two other holes, Abby."

She gaped at him. "Oh." Her cheeks flushed.

"Not only do I expect them to be open physically, they're expected to be open emotionally, as well. Meaning they tell me everything they think and feel about our sessions together. They're not allowed to hold anything back from me."

"They can't even have private thoughts?" she asked, incredulous.

"No. Not about the kink. Otherwise I have no idea if it's going well for them, or if things need to be tweaked or modified. I'm not a mind reader, Abby. I'm very clear and upfront about everything I expect from a sub and I won't tolerate anything less than the same honesty in return. If she does something I don't like, I'll let her know. I won't chew on it for days, bottling it up until it comes out at the wrong moment or disguised as something else. That's not fair. They have a right to know exactly what to expect and I have a right to know how well they're handling that.

"Their jobs, their friendships, their hobbies, that's all separate. I don't want to extend it outside the bedroom. I'm not interested in micromanaging a slave. But I need to know what's working and what's not in the kink department."

"Slave?" Abby asked. "You don't- I mean people don't-"

"Yes, they do. There are people, submissives, who give up all their power to another person 24/7. They're called slaves. Their Masters choose their food for them, their clothes, their friends, their leisure time activities, if they get any."

Abby gasped.

"But I have no interest in that," he assured her. "I just want to play in the bedroom, but I do demand a lot of my subs, sexually."

She nodded. "Right. Oral and...anal."

"That and other things," he decided to tell her. "I don't normally come in their pussies like I did tonight, but I know you and I trust you. I don't take chances with pregnancy. A baby is a lifetime commitment I'm not ready to make with just anyone. If they miss one pill...well, I won't risk it. But I don't waste seed, either. If I don't come in a condom, then they swallow it or take it anally. I mark my subs with my semen, Abby. It's probably a caveman thing to do, but it's still a rule."

She stared at him. "I...don't know if I could-"

"Like I said, it would be incredibly challenging for you to be my submissive, Abby. I wouldn't expect it all on day one, from anyone, but I would expect a solid commitment of training to work up to following the rules."

"What do they get out of it?" she asked.

"It's a fair question. Plenty of submissives just want to please their Doms. It's worth it to them to be challenged in order to make their Dominant happy." Abby scoffed and he held up a finger. "But usually that doesn't happen right out of the gate. With commitment and affection, comes the desire to please for its own sake, like any normal relationship. Plenty of vanilla people do nice things for their partners just because they care about them. But also, every sub has different needs themselves and it's the Dom's job to try and not only meet those needs, but to exceed them."

He grinned. "Personally, I start out with the basics. Giving them lots and lots of orgasms. And with you I'm going to be spending a fair amount of time eating pussy." Abby blushed. He didn't think he'd ever get tired of seeing that. "Getting your pussy eaten will pretty much be a standard reward for good behavior. Or possibly it's Wednesday and I feel like your eating pussy. Whichever."

She giggled.

"I demand a lot," he admitted. "But I try to give as much in return. I'm strict but fair."

Abby changed in the bathroom while Mark waited for her in the living room. When she emerged, he gave her a quick kiss on the lips. "Call me or text me when you get home so I know you made it," he requested. She nodded.

He wrapped his arms around her before allowing her to leave. "You did great tonight, Abby. Not letting your fear rule you and letting go." He gave her another, deeper kiss and swatted her ass as she headed toward the door. She laughed.

He closed the door after watching her get into her car and pull away from the curb. It was a tempting thought, Abby as his submissive. But it was a lot to wish for and he didn't want to set himself up for disappointment. He resolved to enjoy her for the time he had her and not think too much about anything else.

CHAPTER ELEVEN

On Monday morning Abby was again hunched over her desk squinting at printouts that were giving her a headache. She wished the memory of her weekend with Mark was enough to dull the pain of returning to work for Kessler. According to the budget he'd given her, they'd have to find even cheaper service vendors than they were already using. She shook her head at the ridiculous demands.

The Custer was losing money, that much was true, but skimping on amenities wasn't the way to counteract that decline. She might have thought that Kessler was skimming, claiming he was using higher quality linen and towel services, for example, but actually employing cheaper ones and pocketing the difference in cost. But so far all the vendors listed on the hotel's accounts were accurate.

She picked up a sheet for a Blue Orchid Floral Service and scanned the invoice. She frowned. She couldn't recall the Custer having that many flowers either in the lobby or the elevator vestibules. There were some large potted trees in the lobby, but not so many that it justified the enormous monthly fee the Custer paid to have the plants changed and maintained. She wondered how the Floral Service had escaped Kessler's spending cuts.

Even though she'd just arrived at work less than two hours ago, she glanced at the clock on the wall and groaned.

Mark slid out from underneath a 4X4 to find Hawk smirking at him. He wiped his greasy hands on a rag.

"You weren't at Maria's Friday night," Hawk announced.

Mark just looked him. "Why are you telling me shit I already know?"

Hawk grinned. "Vegas wasn't there either. In fact, neither one of you were there last Friday, either, if memory serves."

Mark sighed and stood up. "Well, aren't you Sherlock fucking Holmes?"

"You did her when you took her home that night, didn't you? Must've been damn good if you keep going back."

"No, that's *you*, Hawk, that doesn't sleep with them more than once."

Hawk's grin got impossibly wider. "So you did sleep with her. She freaky like you?"

Mark felt his cock swell a little behind his fly at the memory of how well Abby had taken to his dominance of her. He hadn't played with that many inexperienced subs over the years and unsurprisingly it intensified his attraction to her. Seeing her struggle with and ultimately give in to his demands was the ultimate aphrodisiac.

He turned away from Hawk to hide his burgeoning erection and sorted through some tools. He didn't know how far things would eventually go with Abby but one thing was for sure, next Friday wasn't going to come fast enough.

Abby froze as Mark ducked under her open garage door. Her first thought was that she was a bit of a mess. Her hair was pulled back, but not in any way that looked good. She had a ratty t-shirt on and jeans. She held a coupling in her dirty hand.

"It's not Friday," she told him, for lack of anything better to say.

He grinned at her. "Nope. I just wanted to see how you were doing with the car." He checked under the hood and examined the parts she had laid out on the tarp. "You really do spend all your time on this."

She nodded. "Yes, but the TV was delivered today. So, I was thinking of knocking off early and watching a movie. You could stay." Oh, God, she thought. Did she just invite him to watch a movie? It sounded dumb, even to her own ears. But then again, he was here without her having asked him over, so what did that say?

"I'll order pizza," he told her. "Unless you've learned to cook in the last week."

She shook her head. "No, but I shouldn't-"

"Abby, you can indulge once in a while," he told her in a tone that brooked no more arguments.

Abby washed her hands in the bathroom sink as Mark called in their order. He thumbed through the stack of unopened movies on the coffee table.

"I haven't seen any of these," he called to her. "Which one would I like?"

Abby thought about it. "Chinatown. He smacks her around. She likes him anyway. You'll love it." Mark laughed out loud.

Abby changed into a slightly less ratty t-shirt and came out of the bedroom as the doorbell rang. Mark paid for the pizza and they spread it out over the coffee table. He turned on the movie and she snuggled up next to him with a slice.

She managed to eat just one, but her thoughts were definitely not on the movie. Made bold, she supposed, by the beer she'd been nursing, she moved closer to him. Instead of being receptive to her advances, though, Mark shifted away from her a little on the couch. "Abby," he said sternly. "We're watching a movie."

She nuzzled his earlobe in response. "Do bad things to me," she whispered.

The corner of his mouth twitched a little but his eye remained cold steel. "No. It's not Friday. Now watch the movie."

Abby frowned. She didn't just want to be his Girl Friday. She sucked his earlobe. "It's Wednesday. You could eat my pussy."

He paused the movie with the remote. "If you don't stop, I *will* do bad things to you. And they won't involve eating your pussy."

Abby's heart beat an excited tattoo in her chest as she wondered what he would do. She bit his earlobe.

"Enough," he demanded. He tossed the remote onto the coffee table. He turned and grabbed hold of the hem of her shirt and yanked it up over her head. In one fluid motion it secured her arms behind her at the elbows with it. Abby grunted in surprise. He yanked her bra down in front, revealing her breasts and shoved her back onto the couch.

He threw one leg over hers and she heard him taking off his belt. For a brief moment she thought he was going to hit her with it then remembered when he'd told her to bite down on it. She pressed her lips together to avoid giggling excitedly. He was going to spank her. Except...he didn't.

He threaded the belt around her thighs and secured it, leaving her prone on the couch.

"Stay, pet," he told her, as if she could move anyway, and he went into the bedroom.

Abby tried to crane her neck to see what he was doing, but couldn't manage it. She heard her dresser drawer open and close and he stalked back out. He disappeared into the bathroom briefly and then returned. Abby was curious, afraid, and turned on all at once.

He unfastened the belt, unbuttoned her jeans and yanked them down to her knees along with her panties. She yelped. He brought his closed fist up to her face. "Open," he demanded.

Abby was startled by the order, but parted her lips. He stuffed a pair of her panties into her mouth. She tried to protest, but he didn't seem concerned. At least they were clean, she thought to herself, glaring at him.

He thrust his fingers into her pussy and pinched a nipple with his free hand. Abby tried to push her pelvis into his hand. She felt him part her with two of his fingers and his right hand released her breast. He reached around behind himself and produced her electric toothbrush. Abby's eyes widened in shock.

He stretched her even further and pushed it in, turning it on with his thumb. She twisted and bucked, but her t-shirt was holding her arms and her jeans were around her knees and she couldn't get any leverage. He picked up the belt again, wrapped it around her thighs, and tightened it, closing her legs around the vibrating invader. He buckled it snugly and sat back down on his end of the couch. He picked up the remote, turned the volume up slightly on the television, and resumed the movie.

Abby was bewildered. She attempted to apologize through the panties in her mouth, but it came out muffled and unintelligible even to her. It didn't take long for the reality of her situation to sink in. Her breasts were exposed, her pussy was stuffed, and the belt holding her thighs together was sending the vibrations of the toothbrush straight to her clit. In the back of Abby's mind she thought she might have made it to the five minute mark before the first orgasm hit.

She panted through the silk underwear and tried to regain her composure. Now that she'd finished, he'd let her go. She was sure of it. But when he didn't seem to notice her presence, she tapped his thigh with her foot. He slapped *her* thigh with his palm. "There's an hour and fifteen minutes left on this movie, pet," he told her. "You'll be still and quiet and let me watch it. Even when you come."

Come? she thought. She'd already come. For the briefest of moments she considered trying to relay this to him somehow, but he'd just told her to be quiet and still and she wasn't sure but she thought it was safe to assume if she tried to get his attention, there would be a punishment. Or at least, a harsher punishment than the one she was already enduring. Considering she'd never once looked at her toothbrush as a substitute vibrator, she wasn't sure what other things in her condo Mark could use to punish her with.

She laid back on the couch and looked at the ceiling, slowly reciting the alphabet in her head to distract her. She was on the fifth recitation when a prickly heat seeped through her pussy, though, and she clenched her fists. *G, H, I*, she thought, fighting it. Oh, God. Her clit seemed to swell. She felt the familiar clench of her vagina and bit down on the panties. She squeezed her eyes shut as a wave tiny little shocks and twitches surged up from her core and she clamped down on the toothbrush. A tiny little squeal erupted in her throat and she prayed he hadn't heard it.

By the fourth orgasm, she was no longer fighting. She felt her belly and her thighs tighten, but let it wash over her, keeping her eyes closed. She may have sighed softly behind the panties, but she wasn't sure. She didn't even notice when the movie was over. She did open her eyes when Mark lifted her off the couch and carried her into the bedroom.

He laid her down and unbuckled the belt, putting it aside. He parted her legs as much as he could with her jeans around her knees and slid out the toothbrush, setting it on the counter. He pulled the panties out of her mouth and rolled her over onto her stomach. She struggled just a bit as she heard his zipper come down and felt his cock slide into her. She couldn't come again. There was no way. She was too worn out.

"Shh, pet," Mark said, breathing into her ear as she rested her cheek against the pillow. "You've had your fun, now it's my turn. Just lie still. Nothing you can do about it anyway."

Abby felt her body go boneless when he said she didn't have to come anymore. She closed her eyes and sighed with pleasure as he fucked her. Keeping her bound by her jeans made her pussy tighter and it felt like heaven when he was thrusting in and out of her.

She lost track of time, but was aware when he pushed up into her one final time and she felt hot jets of cum spilling into her womb. She turned her face into the pillow a little and smiled a secret smile. No other pet got this. She was his special girl. Mark's special pet.

He gently pulled out of her and began undressing her slowly. He removed the t-shirt that was binding her arms and then unfastened her bra. He pulled her jeans and panties all the way off and covered her with the sheet. She felt him kiss her temple.

"Sleep now, pet. But you need to work on your endurance."

Abby drifted to sleep after he turned the light off, bathing the room in darkness.

She woke in the morning and wandered out of the bedroom. Mark had cleaned up while she'd slept. He'd put the pizza away and cleaned the coffee table. Their dishes and glasses had been washed. Abby washed her toothbrush with dish soap, knowing she'd never look at it the same way again. The man was an evil genius. He'd promised to use his powers only for good.

She wrinkled her nose knowing that when she brushed her teeth it would probably taste like detergent. She sighed. It was a small price to pay for four orgasms. Fucking evil genius.

She got dressed and headed in to work, walking quickly past her boss's office. She checked the reservation log on the computer and generated a few random keys for spot checking and then headed through the lobby. As the elevator doors were closing, a female voice asked her to hold it. She pressed the button and a tall, slim woman slid in between the doors.

Abby smiled at her then realized it was the same blonde she'd watched Susan check out last week. Abby watched her press the button for the third floor and the two women rode up in silence together. As the elevator dinged and the door slid open again, the blonde got out. Instinctively, Abby stepped out, too.

The blonde slowed and gave her a glance out of the corner of her eye. "Oh, sorry," Abby said politely and skirted around her quickly. She looked down the hallway at the housekeeper loading towels into the push cart. "Wendy!" she called out and made her way over. Abby positioned herself to the side, so she could see the blonde in her peripheral vision. She proceeded to talk to Wendy about housekeeping supplies and the weekly schedule while watching the blonde use a key card to enter room 312. She smiled at Wendy as the room door closed down the hall. "Well, don't let me keep you any longer. Just stop by my office if you need anything."

Abby headed back downstairs and logged into the reservation computer. Room 312 was currently occupied by a Mr. Don Barnes. She searched for a reservation history and apparently Mr. Barnes was a quite the regular guest. He stayed at the hotel at least twice a month.

Ten minutes later, Abby, armed with a clipboard knocked on the door to Room 312. Several minutes passed and the blonde answered. Abby smiled politely. "Hello. I'm so sorry to disturb you. I'm Abigail Raines, the Assistant Manager." Abby looked down at her clipboard. "It seems we had a sort of mini flood in the room above yours." She leaned in and said in a conspiratorial tone, "Never leave towels in the bathtub," she said. "Anyway, I'm just filling out the work log and I need to know if there's any damage to the ceiling in your bathroom as a result. If there is we need to get someone in here right away."

Beyond the blonde's shoulder, an aging, potbellied man in trousers and not much else glared at her. Then he stomped to the bathroom. He came back out in a huff. "No. There's nothing there."

Abby kept the smile. "Well, thank you so much. I'm so sorry to have disturbed you. Will you let me send up a complimentary bottle of champagne for the trouble?"

The man's scowl disappeared, but the blonde remained stoic. "Yeah," he told her. "That's- that'd be fine."

"Excellent. Consider it on its way. Thanks again."

Abby backed out of the door way and headed to the elevator. As the doors slid open on the lobby floor, her path was blocked by Kessler. "What are you doing?"

Abby looked startled for a moment then held up the clipboard, revealing the customer complaint that she'd faked. "I was overseeing a problem with the plumbing up on four."

"Then why were you on three?"

"In case of water damage," she said cooly. "I need to fill out the clean up order and I needed to know the full extent of the damage."

His face relaxed a little. "Is there any?"

Abby shook her head. "Thankfully not that we're seeing. We'll have to keep any eye out for mold, of course, but I think we caught it just in time."

Kessler rubbed his face. "Alright then. Good. Great."

"I also have this month's supply order ready. I'll need you to check and sign."

Kessler waved her off. "Just send it through. I have a meeting today."

Abby nodded and watched Kessler walk away. She headed back to her office, closed the door and slumped in the chair. After a few moments, she dug her cell phone out of her purse and hit a number on speed dial.

"Coral Canyon. This is Chase. How may I help you?"

"Chase."

"Abby!" came the effeminate male voice over the line. "How's the sticks?"

"Not terrible. Not good. But not terrible."

"Well, hurry up and come home with your tail between your legs, girl, because no one runs this town like you do and you are sorely missed."

Abby smiled. "I miss you guys, too. But I am firmly entrenched."

"Say it ain't so," Chase admonished.

"It is. But listen, I have...a question."

"Hmmm, sounds intriguing. Lay it on me, girl."

Abby looked up at her ceiling. "I have a stable behind my hotel."

"A stable? In Grizzly Adams country?"

"Men are men everywhere, Chase."

"Yes, they are," Chase agreed.

"How do I protect myself?"

Chase sighed. "Little Abby Raines. Never does anything easy."

"Nope. Not me."

CHAPTER TWELVE

Abby had a long list of vendors spread out over her desk when she looked up at the clock above the door. It was almost five and she was ready to get the hell out of there. She abandoned her paper tornado, pulled on her blazer, and retrieved her purse from her desk. She locked her office door and nodded to Susan as she headed out the front doors.

Halfway down the block to the parking structure, her phone rang. She smiled as she dug it out of her purse. "Are we going to watch another movie tonight?"

"Actually," Mark replied, "I was wondering, since you're from Vegas, how are you at poker?"

"What kind of poker?" she asked, her heels clipping on the hard concrete. "Hold 'em? Stud? Omaha? Pai Gow? Chicago? Crazy Pineapple?" She paused. "*Strip poker?*"

Mark laughed. "I'm going out on a limb and assuming you know how to play. Thursday night is poker night at Shooter and Slick's place. So, obviously clothes will be staying on. But you and I can play our own game sometime. I definitely wouldn't mind a beautiful, naked woman parading around my house."

Abby laughed. "Please. I'd take all your money. *And* your clothes. *You* could walk around naked for *me*."

"Intriguing," he replied. "I'm willing to risk it. But not tonight. How 'bout I come pick you up at your place?"

Abby liked Sarah and the rest of Mark's friends were definitely a fun bunch. "Yeah. I'm just getting off work so give me time to shower and change."

Mark showed up close to six thirty. Abby had thrown on some jeans and a short sleeve blouse. She was surprised when he took her into his arms and kissed her as though he hadn't seen her just last night. He rubbed his hands along her bare arms. "You look great, babe, but you need a jacket. I brought the bike."

She grinned. "Okay," she told him and took a short, black leather jacket out of the coat closet and slid it on. As she was zipping it up, Mark pushed her against the closet door and sealed his mouth over hers. "We may never make it out of here," he told her. "I've been picturing you naked for the last hour. Bound, gagged, and at my mercy." She shivered at his words. He grinned at her. "I think you like that idea," he whispered.

Abby rolled her eyes to hide her embarrassment. She liked that idea *a lot*. She grabbed the arm of his jacket. "Come on," she ordered.

She locked the front door and followed him to his Harley. He got on first and she threw her leg over, settling in behind him. Before he started the engine, she tapped him on the shoulder. He turned his head. "So, you're gonna fuck me on this bike soon, right?" she asked.

She watched, feeling triumphant, as his jaw twitched. She leaned forward, lips to his ear. "I think you like that idea," she teased.

"So much I might do it right now," he replied in a gravel tone.

Abby had the good sense to be quiet. Chuckling over his defeat of her attempt at sass, he turned the bike's engine over and pulled away from the curb. Abby slid her arms around his waist. She couldn't decide which was more dangerous, the bike or the biker.

The Sullivan house was a large log cabin that sat just outside of town. It was nestled at the end of a country road in the hills and the sun was just setting behind it. Mark led her in through the front door without knocking and Abby saw that everyone else had already arrived.

Shooter took her jacket and hung it up. He mentioned Sarah was in the kitchen and Abby announced she was going to see if the other woman needed any help. She located the kitchen, which she could have done without the aid of Chris' directions because of the mouth watering smell.

"Vegas!" Sarah cried as she saw her.

"Hey, Slick," Abby replied. "Need any help."

Sarah nodded. "I could use the head of lettuce in the fridge chopped while I finish these enchiladas.

"Um, yeah. I can probably do that," Abby told her. But before she could, she felt two large hands clamp down on her shoulders.

"Cover me," said a deep baritone voice. "I'm going in." Hawk attempted to skirt around Abby and further into the kitchen, but Slick brandished a rolling pin.

"Out!" she demanded.

"Damn it, Vegas!" Hawk bellowed, turning on her. "You were supposed to cover me!"

Abby stared at him. "With what?" she demanded.

"I don't know! Your feminine wiles!" he shot back.

"That doesn't work on other females!" Sarah snapped. "Now go wash your hands! I'll send Vegas out with chips and dip."

Abby was impressed by the tiny woman's ability to order around a man three times her size. "How do you get them to listen like that?" she asked.

Sarah laughed. "Easy. I'd just stop cooking. None of them is willing to risk it. Especially since Tex has been...busy." The brunette gave Abby a sly smile. "He's not cooking as much as he used to since he met you. They aren't going to risk pissing me off and going back to ordering pizza."

Abby blushed and washed her hands in the sink. "I'm not much of a cook. Which is about the same as saying I'm not much of an airline pilot. But I can follow orders." She froze as she realized what she'd just said. Sarah giggled, though, which made Abby laugh, too. Twenty minutes later, after the cabbage was reasonably chopped, Abby stepped out onto the deck, balancing the bowl of chips and the guacamole dip precariously.

"So, it's your weekend off," Hawk said to Mark. "You gonna head to that club of yours like you do? Or are things with Vegas-"

"Hawk," said Shooter flatly, looking past the large man at Abby.

Abby ducked her head and quickly walked forward. She pushed the bowls onto the table. "Here," she said brightly. "I didn't make the dip. So...it's edible." She spun and practically sprinted to the door.

"Abby," Mark said from behind her and she heard him pushing back his chair.

"I have some more tomatoes to chop," she told him. "You just hang out here." She stepped inside and nearly broke out into a run back to the kitchen, but Mark caught her arm.

"Abby, stop," he ordered.

She shook her head. "I wasn't listening. I was just delivering food. I- I don't-" She swallowed hard. "None of my business. You said I wasn't...your type, really. I get it. You were up front about it. I'm just a charity case."

He tilted her head up to meet his gaze, brushing his thumbs over her cheeks. "Hey. You are my type, Abby," he assured her. "I'm not going to the club. I have no plans to go there anytime soon. And you are going to earn yourself a red ass if you ever talk about yourself that way again. You're nobody's charity case."

"But I'm not your submissive," she reminded him.

He sighed. "Abby, I explained that to you. It would be-"

"Challenging," she finished for him. She'd understood that. Or at least the general idea of it since he hadn't been too specific as to what would be expected of her other than to be at his beck and call sexually, which she pretty much already was. That and she'd have to learn to swallow. And anal. She cringed inside a little. But he had said he wouldn't expect her to jump right in. She could put a toe in, maybe, and test the waters. "I want to try," she said firmly.

Mark didn't respond for a moment. "You'll have to follow all my rules. And obey. No matter what," he told her.

"But not everything right away, you said."

"Abby, it won't be easy, even in the beginning, not for you."

"Will it hurt?" she asked, chewing her bottom lip. "A lot?"

"I will hurt you, yes. A little. But I won't harm you," he replied. "I won't break the skin or cause physical damage, either permanent or temporary. But the things I do to you won't always be things you want or even like. They'll be for my pleasure alone."

"But I get pleasure, too, right? I mean you said lots of orgasms and... other stuff." She blushed furiously at the memory of him devouring her pussy.

He pretended to think about it. "Sixty-forty, I'd say. Maybe seventy-thirty." She glared at him and he laughed. "I mean in your favor, pet." He leaned in closer and whispered into her ear. "You'll like most of what I do you if you give yourself permission to."

She couldn't help but smile a little. "Do I still get a safeword?"

He nodded. "Absolutely. But I expect you to think about it before you use it."

"Do I get punished for using it?"

"Never. But expect to have a long and involved discussion about why you used it and how we can avoid you using it again in the future."

"I want to be your submissive," she whispered.

He closed his eyes and took a deep breath. "God damn it's going to be hard to wait until tomorrow night." He opened his eyes again and looked down at her. "8 o'clock, as usual. Bring an overnight bag, and come prepared to obey."

"Yes, Sir," Abby replied as a shiver of anticipation raced down her spine.

CHAPTER THIRTEEN

On Friday evening, Abby stood in her bedroom, completely unable to decide what to bring. She settled on wearing green silk blouse and black slacks she already had on and packing a pair of jeans and a red cotton t-shirt for Saturday. He hadn't told her to bring anything to go out to dinner. She packed her toothbrush, a black, short satin nightgown with lace edging and a pair of sandals. Her thoughts were racing as she drove to his house.

She'd browsed the internet a few times to learn more about BDSM over the last few weeks, but it appeared pointless to investigate. It seemed to run the gamut from just blindfolds to elaborate rope bondage to needles and something called fire play that she didn't click on but she knew whatever it was, she was totally saying 'cantelope' before the Bic got flicked. It was impossible to know what Mark would be into and she didn't care to see even the occasional photo of whipped, crying women in chains.

He'd said he wasn't into causing pain and that she could ask questions and that was good enough for her at the moment. She pulled up in front of his house and she'd just stepped onto his lawn when he came out to meet her. He gave her a quick kiss and took her bag from her, shouldering it as he led her into the house. They went straight to the bedroom and he set her bag down on the empty chair.

He kissed her again, this time on the forehead, and squeezed her arms gently. "Are you ready?"

She nodded. "Yes, Sir."

He turned to the dresser and opened it, turning back, Abby saw he held a black leather strap with silver rings and buckles. Her eyes widened a little.

"This is your play collar," he informed her. "You won't ever wear it in public. Only in private. It's lockable, but I won't do that. He opened it and showed her the inside. It was smooth and supple. "It'll be comfortable. If it isn't, you'll tell me."

"Okay."

"I'm a dominant man by nature, Abby. It isn't the kind of thing you just turn on and off on a whim. I will tone it down to the best of my ability day-to-day, but when you're wearing my collar, you are my pet. And you will obey. You don't need to ask permission to speak, but you will address me as 'Sir'. You forget sometimes and I let it go. That won't be happening from now on."

Abby swallowed hard. "Yes, Sir."

He slipped the collar around her neck and fastened it. He slipped a finger between the leather and her skin, checking the fit. "Does it feel comfortable?"

Abby had to take a moment to adjust. It wasn't tight, but it was definitely not like anything she'd ever felt before. She could swallow comfortably, she noticed. She nodded to him.

"Good." He moved to the bed and sat down on the edge. "Now undress for me."

Abby took a deep breath and unbuttoned the cuffs on her blouse. He had told her the last time that she would undress for him and she'd tried to mentally prepare herself for that.

"When you're wearing the collar, you'll be naked at all times, unless I provide you with something to wear." Abby's fingers faltered on the buttons and she looked at him. He smiled at her. "Rule number two, pet."

Just walk around naked? Abby couldn't really picture herself doing it. She pushed the mental images away and slid the blouse off her shoulders. She laid it across the arm of the chair. She slid off her mules and pushed them underneath the chair with her toe. She unfastened her bra and laid it over her blouse. Being naked while the other person wasn't was definitely...strange. She unzipped her black

TEX

pants and let them fall. The last thing to go were her panties and she closed her eyes as she slid them down.

Mark came over to her and stood in front of her. "Arms behind your back, pet. It's time for me to look at what's mine."

Abby felt her face flush as she clasped her hands together behind her back. It caused her chest to stick out, which was apparently the point, she thought. Mark put his hands on her shoulders and slid them down to her breasts. He cupped one in each hand and ran his thumbs over her nipples. "Much better," he declared when the dusky peaks were tight and hard.

His hands moved over her stomach and swept down over her red curls. Abby made a soft, feminine noise in her throat as he rubbed her clit. She made an even louder noise, this time of protest, when he took his hand away. "Turn around, pet." Abby turned, desire sitting languid in her lower belly, but she stiffened at his next words. "Bend over and spread your cheeks for me." She hesitated. "Pet," he warned. "If I have to do it myself, it's a punishment."

Abby didn't think being punished on her very first day, first hour, as Mark's submissive would be a good thing. She spread her legs, bent forward at the waist, and parted herself to his gaze.

"Hold yourself open to me," he ordered as she felt his finger dip down her channel. She gritted her teeth to keep from moving away or saying no. He ran a finger over the puckered hole. "Next week we'll start your anal training and I want you to stay properly groomed. Keep getting waxed," he told her.

"Yes, Sir," Abby whispered.

"Stand up now."

She breathed a tiny sigh of relief and stood up. She turned to face him. He pulled out the wrist cuffs. "Offer your wrist to me," he prompted and she held out her arm. He secured first one, then the other. "Now," he told her as he fastened the second cuff. "In order for you to *stay* properly groomed, you first need to *be* properly groomed. Come, pet."

Abby was a little flustered, but followed him out of the bedroom and into the bathroom down the hall. She watched as he took a large towel off the towel rack on the wall and laid it out on the floor. "Lie down, please," he instructed. "Head near the wall."

115

Abby knelt down on the towel and positioned herself across it. Mark got down on one knee beside her head. "Give me your wrist," he ordered and she brought it up over her head. She heard a metallic snap. "Now the other." Another snap and Abby realized she was latched to something.

"This," he told her, "is an exercise in trust. I want you to relax and spread your legs." She took a deep breath and opened her thighs. "Good girl. You need to hold completely still, pet. For the whole exercise. If you move, if you're uncooperative in any way, you could get hurt. Do you understand?"

"Um, no, Sir. I mean, I get it. Don't move. But why? What-"

"I'm going to shave your pussy."

Abby had no idea what to say to that.

"I love your hair," he told her. "It's beautiful. But it's not as beautiful as you. And it blocks my view of your clit. You're to be open to me at all times. That means when I look at you, I want to see all of you. So when you're wearing my collar, you will be naked and properly groomed so I can enjoy looking at what's mine."

Abby drew in a few quick breaths. No one had ever talked to her this way. Well, obviously no one had ever said, 'I'm going to shave your pussy.' But neither had anyone told her she was beautiful. Or how much they wanted to look at her. Naked. Mark wanted to look at her naked. *All the time.*

"Pet," Mark said, interrupting her thoughts. "What's going on in that head of yours?"

"You think I'm pretty," she whispered.

"No," he corrected. "I think you're beautiful. And you're going to stay that way by keeping still so I don't cut you, right?"

"Right. Yes. Yes, Sir," she stammered.

"Good girl." Mark stood up and she heard him running water at the sink but couldn't see from her position. He returned and knelt on the towel between her legs. She felt a warm cloth wet her down and heard the familiar hiss of a shaving cream container. He slowly applied it to her mound.

She felt his hand on her lower belly and then felt the gentle scrape of the blade. He worked methodically, rinsing the razor and reapplying it, periodically wiping her with the washcloth. Abby had never experienced anything more intimate in her life. She felt his thumb press down on her clit and she lifted her hips off the floor.

"Pet," he admonished. Abby panted. "Control yourself," he ordered. "I'm covering your clit so it doesn't get nicked." Abby groaned in frustration. "Do not come, pet. Apparently right now four is your limit before you collapse from exhaustion. Until we work on that, you're not to come unless I give you permission. And, pet, you do not have permission. *Do not come.*"

Abby pressed her lips together, squeezed her eyes shut, and willed herself not to move as Mark shaved around her clit, nudging it occasionally with his thumb. He rinsed it with the warm cloth and then tugged at her labia, stretching it and she felt the slow glide of the blade even though that part of her was already bare. More warm water trickled between her thighs and he pulled her other lip, tending to it. Thankful there wasn't that much to do since she had a standing wax appointment every two weeks.

Mark rinsed her off and unlocked the cuffs. When she sat up, he kissed her lightly on the lips. "That was very, very good, pet. Now, I want your pussy completely hairless from now on. Make sure it all gets done properly before we play."

"Yes, Sir."

He gathered the small bowl, the razor, and the can of shaving cream and stood up. "I want you to hurry up and take a bath," he told her after he'd put all the accoutrements on the counter and was now unbuckling her cuffs. He took hold of her chin and forced her gaze to him. "You still do not have permission to come. Make the bath quick and then come into the bedroom."

Abby nodded and started to run the bathwater after he left, shutting the door behind him. As she slid into the warm water she noticed an array of white bottles lined up on the small shelf. She picked one up and examined it. Orange Blossom shampoo. She opened it and caught the sweet, light scent. Her favorite. The second bottle was conditioner and the third was lotion. A large bar of handcrafted soap, also orange blossom, sat unused in a white tray.

She smiled to herself as she realized he'd seen her handsoap in the kitchen and some lotion, a cheaper version than the one he'd bought for her, in her bathroom at home. She bathed a dried quickly, lamenting that she couldn't spend more time in the large tub. She found Mark in the bedroom and her immediate instinct was to kiss him, but she stopped short just in front of him.

"What's wrong?" he asked.

"Am I allowed to kiss you?"

He grinned. "I can make an exception," he teased. She had to stand on her tiptoes without her heels and he lifted her up a bit to press his mouth to hers. When he set her back down, he asked, "What was that for?"

"Orange Blossom. You noticed."

"It's impossible *not* to notice you, Abby."

Abby smiled to herself as Mark opened the dresser drawer and took out a pair of leather cuffs. "Lie down," he told her and she moved to the bed. He crossed the room to her and she was prepared to offer him her wrist again, but instead he took hold of her ankle. He buckled the cuff and withdrew a silver chain from underneath the corner of the mattress. He clipped it and rounded the foot of the bed.

"Are you okay, pet?" he asked, as he buckled the other cuff.

Abby remembered to keep her breathing even and nodded. "Yes, Sir." Bondage wasn't all that hard, she'd discovered, once you got past the initial burst of fear. So, this time Mark was going to cuff her completely. It was a little nerve wracking, but she trusted him. When he finished, the cuffs were snug and the chains were short, spreading her legs. Her newly shaved pussy felt overexposed and she fought hard not to cover it with her hands.

Mark slid a finger into the second cuff, as he'd done with the first, checking the fit and then turned back to the dresser. Except, she realized, he didn't go to the dresser. Instead he picked up the chair beside it, which had contained her discarded clothes and overnight bag, but was now empty. He set it in the middle of the room a few feet back from the foot of the bed.

"What are you doing?" she asked.

Mark looked up at her. "Pet. Rule number three is: You don't ask questions. If you're confused about an order I've given you, you're allowed to ask for clarification. But it's not your place to ask me what I'm doing or why I'm doing it. Not everything will even have a reason behind it other than 'Because I feel like it.'

Understand?"

"Yes, Sir." Abby watched as he left the chair, and rounded the bed again. He opened the nightstand drawer to her left and took something out. He pressed it into her hand. When she opened it, she recognized the small clit vibrator. She closed her eyes and suppressed a groan.

"I told you it would be challenging," said Mark. "Even from the beginning."

He took a seat on the chair, which faced her straight on. Her shaved, exposed pussy displayed for him. Abby tried to tell herself that he'd obviously already seen it all, having just shaved her, but it was still difficult.

"I think you know what I want, pet," Mark told her in that dark, low tone of his that always made her stomach do flip flops. "But if you need me to, I'll give you a direct order. Masturbate for me." Mark leaned back in the chair. "You're not getting uncuffed until you come. And don't take your eyes off me once you start. Am I clear on that? If you close your eyes or look away, that's a punishment."

Abby nodded. "Yes, Sir." She took a deep breath, twisted the bottom of the toy to its on position and slid it down between her legs.

Her face flushed crimson as Mark, rather than looking at her pussy, looked right into her eyes. His gaze was hard steel, but darkened somewhat by desire. She wanted to look away from that gaze that never missed anything, but she remained in control of herself and maintained eye contact. The second the vibe hit her clit she groaned. His message was clear. She couldn't hide from him as his submissive. He'd told her every part of her would be open to him, but Abby had never really considered the deeper meaning of his words beyond the basic sexual connotation.

She'd never touched herself in front of anyone. It was such a private, personal act reserved only for the shower or the safety of her bed, hidden underneath the covers. It felt terrifying and wanton all at the same time. She felt herself start to get wet and circled her clit with the toy.

"Finger your hole. I want it covered in juice."

Abby slid her hand between her swollen pussy lips and felt her own slickness on her fingertips. She pushed her middle finger inside herself. She thrust it in and out while pressing the vibrator against her clit. Mark was still looking in her eyes and not at her pussy. "Taste yourself," he ordered and she froze. She felt split down the center. She wanted to please Mark. She really did. Because pleasing him meant he'd please her. But this was too difficult a task.

Masturbating in front of someone was new, to be sure, but the act itself was as familiar as anything else in her life. One she'd done thousands of times. But taste herself? No. She'd never done that. Before she'd meant to, she shook her head no. Mark stood up and she stiffened. Punishment. She'd get a punishment now for disobeying.

"I'm sorry," she whimpered. "I just-"

"It's alright. I'll help you," he told her. He leaned down, putting his hands on the bed and buried his face in her snatch. She gasped and raised her hips off the bed. His flattened tongue drove her insane, pushing past her labia and lapping up her juices. For good measure, he shoved his tongue into her hole a few times. Abby was on the brink of orgasm when he pulled away. He climbed up over her and before she could react, he sealed his mouth over hers, driving his tongue inside with the same force.

Abby closed her eyes and dropped the toy onto the sheets. She wrapped her arms around him and pulled him close. She was surprised that she didn't find the taste unpleasant at all. Or maybe it was just Mark's taste that she didn't wholly object to. As he took her mouth, his hand found her pussy and rubbed her expertly. His tongue slid in and out of her mouth with the same rhythm as his finger down below and Abby was drowning in pleasure.

He withdrew from her pussy and brought his hand up. "Suck, pet," he commanded, and held his index finger to her lips. She took it in her mouth, hoping that he would make her come soon if she was good. He pulled his finger out and kissed her deeply. His hand found hers and brought it down. He entwined his fingers with hers and together they played in the growing wetness between her legs. He brought their hands up to her mouth, breaking their kiss. She dutifully parted her lips and licked their fingers.

"I'm going to fuck you a lot, pet," he told her quietly. "And never with a condom. I may not always finish in your pussy. I may choose to use your mouth to come. You need to get used to the taste."

He got back off the bed and settled back down into the chair. "You still need to come," he reminded her and Abby picked up the toy and pressed it against her engorged clit once more.

He had a power over her, that much was certain. But she didn't think it was just the domination stuff. He made her *feel* things, incredible things. The sweet torture of near-orgasms that crept slowly to the edge, but then receded, which left her partially frustrated but mostly desperate for more. A hunger for pleasure that hadn't been there before she'd met him. The heady excitement when she knew she'd see him again and couldn't stop herself from wondering what he'd show her next.

She met his eyes across the bed and began to fuck herself slowly, despite her raging desire for an orgasm. She did it the way she thought he would if this were a different night, a different exercise. She slowly, thoroughly, lubed up her finger and brought it to her lips without hesitation. Mark's eyes went darker still as he watched her suck, pushing it in and out of her mouth like it was his cock. She hadn't given him head yet, but she knew he was thinking about it now.

She had a strange power, too, she realized, even though she was the one chained to the bed. Mark wanted her. And every task she completed, every order she followed, made him desire her even more. Abby never felt powerful during sex, despite her long list of do's and don't's. She'd only felt meek and unsure and unfulfilled.

One thing was certain, Mark would never leave her feeling unfulfilled. She'd already had more orgasms with him than in either of her long-term relationships. She definitely didn't feel meek, lying here on display like some wicked seductress. And she no longer had to feel unsure about anything. Because nothing was hers to control. All she had to do was whatever Mark told her to do.

She swirled her wet fingertip over one nipple, then the other and trailed it back down to her pussy. She stuck two fingers into her tight hole and nearly laughed as she shocked herself by hoping in that instant that Mark would stretch her pussy to better accommodate that beautiful cock of his. She humped her hand slowly, increasing the rhythm until she was fucking herself furiously. She came with a keening cry, watching Mark intently, and knowing he could have anyone he wanted but in that moment, he only wanted her.

CHAPTER FOURTEEN

Tex tried not to grin as he watched the wicked little witch chained to his bed try and chip away at his control. The show she was putting on for him was far and away better than anything he'd expected tonight. His cautious little pet was turning into a fucking minx. And he loved it. Thank God she had no idea how close she was coming to achieving her apparent goal of having him drop his pants and fuck the hell out of her right now.

The little sex kitten was sucking her finger like a cock and he decided it was time to work on her oral skills. She had a long way to go in her training and the sooner they started, the sooner he could have her in the way he wanted. She came loudly and he got up and took the vibrator from her. He set it on the nightstand and began to unbuckle her cuffs.

He laid down on the bed next to her and pulled her against him. "That was very good, pet. I loved watching you. Did you enjoy doing it?"

She snuggled closer to him. "Yes, Sir."

He leaned down and kissed her, tracing his tongue along her bottom lip and teasing her mouth. "I love the way you taste," he told her. He brushed her hair back from her face. "It's time for you to return the favor, pet." He looked down at her, gauging her response. She didn't look all that surprised. She nodded, albeit not terribly enthusiastically.

"You don't like it?" he asked her, gently.

"I'm not very good at it. Plus..."

"Swallowing is an issue for you."

She nodded.

He held her a little tighter against him. "Well, it's one of the things you're going to learn to do this weekend. You might like it eventually. Or you might just learn to tolerate it. Either way, it's going to happen. You don't need to worry about it, though. I'm not going to make you try and figure it out by yourself. I'm going to tell you exactly how I like it."

He stood up and unbuttoned his jeans. He stripped all his clothes off and laid them at the foot of the bed. He laid back down and pulled Abby over him so she straddled his legs. He lifted his semi-hard cock. "See this spot?" he asked her, fingering the underside of the head. "That's the sweet spot, pet. When it's time to suck me, and I'm not fully hard yet, you take your tongue and you lick it. Do it now." Abby leaned forward, extended the tip of her tongue and took a swipe. "Good girl. Now keep licking it. Slowly. Just a few times."

Abby did as instructed and he ran his fingers through her hair. "Now put just the head in your mouth and suck it. Not too hard and just the head." She sealed her lips around the mushroom head and sucked gently. When he was at full mast, he took hold of his shaft and tugged it up. "Start at the base," he told her, "and lick up toward the head."

Her wet, smooth tongue bathed his cock in short little swipes, working its way up to the sensitive tip. "Now. go back down, all the way to the base," he told her, and then he laid the rock-hard cock against his stomach. "Now, I want you to get lower," he told her, pressing down on her shoulders with his free hand. "And very slowly, very gently, lick my balls."

Abby must not have ever been asked to do that or thought of it herself because she looked up at him in surprise. "Go on, pet," he encouraged. "Watch your teeth and be careful. Get each one nice and wet."

Tex closed his eyes for a moment, enjoying the feel of her hot breath and warm tongue loving his sac. "Take one into your mouth," he ordered. "Suck on it for a little bit." He threaded his fingers through her hair and pulled her closer. Without having to be told, she released it with a wet pop and immediately started on the other. Tex groaned. "Such a good pet."

He waited a few minutes, enjoying the hell out of it, then pushed her back a little. "Now it's time to suck, pet." He pushed the shaft back down and angled it toward her mouth. "Just take in a little at first, then more."

She wrapped her lips around the head again and then slid him further into her mouth. He let go of it and she instinctively attempted to reach up replace his hand with her own. "No," he commanded, pushing her hand down and putting it on his thigh. No sense in letting her learn bad habits he'd have to break her of later. "When you suck cock, pet, you use your mouth only. We're in this position because I want you to be comfortable for your first time. But normally you'll be on your knees, hands tied behind your back. Just work it with your mouth. Move up and down on the shaft."

For her part she did what he asked, fucking his dick with her mouth. She was hesitant to take much in, but Tex didn't comment on it. It was enough to learn the basics first. Between shaving her, watching her finger herself, and now this, he was more than ready to finish. He took her head in his hands, not forcefully though. "I'm going to come, pet." She faltered. "Just relax and take as much in as you can."

A few more caresses of her lips and he felt his balls draw up. He thrust up a little bit into her open mouth and began to pump thick jets of cum. Abby only managed to deal with the first one before she gagged a little and backed up. He let go of her head, not wanting to force her. The rest of his load spilled across his stomach.

"I'm sorry," she told him.

He took hold of her upper arms and pulled her closer. "It's fine. You did a great job, pet. Really." He took hold of his still-hard cock and moved it to the side. "I want you to take one lick," he said firmly.

Abby didn't argue outright, but she pleaded a little with her eyes. He cupped the side of her face with his other hand. "One lick will not kill you. Now, do as I say."

Abby held her own hair so as not to let it fall into the sticky mess and hesitantly took one lick of the sperm. "Swallow it," he commanded. She grimaced, but complied.

He continued to stroke her hair. "You were a very good girl, pet. But if you want to be an excellent pet, you'll finish up the rest. And excellent pets get rewarded for their good behavior." She considered this at length. "It'll go down easier if it's still warm, pet," he informed her. "And like I said, I have something special for you if you do."

Abby took a deep breath, closed her eyes, and reluctantly cleaned off his belly with her tongue. "Very good," he crooned. "Now, open your mouth and show me."

Abby opened her mouth and stuck out her tongue. He nodded then pulled her up against him and held her. "You're doing great, Abby," he whispered into her ear. "So much better than I hoped."

She relaxed a little and then he patted her shoulder. He got up, pulled on his jeans and went to the closet. He pulled out the fluffy white bathrobe and handed it to her. She put it on and he removed the collar from her neck. He sat her on the bed and removed the ankle cuffs, placing them all into the dresser against the wall.

He led her out of the bedroom. They made their way down the hall and into the living room. He led her around the corner and turned on the lights in the formal dining room. At the head of the table was a silver cake stand with the lid on top. He pulled out the chair and gently directed her to sit in it. When she was settled, he lifted the lid, revealing a small chocolate cake with fresh raspberries on top.

She smiled. "But I can't eat it," she told him.

He rested his hands on her shoulders. "Actually, you can. It's dark chocolate and a whole lot of vanilla substituted for sugar. I told you that you don't have to eat crap from cardboard boxes. If you can put together an engine, you can put together a recipe." He leaned down and kissed the top of her head. "I like cooking for you, pet. If you don't have time to learn, I can at least feed you properly while you're here."

He handed her the fork and poured her a glass of red wine from the sideboard and set it down in front of her. "Here," he told her. "We're done playing for tonight." Abby picked up the fork and took a tiny bite of the cake. She closed her eyes and moaned. Tex thought it was a damn good thing he'd already gotten off or she'd be bent over the table right about now.

He was in the kitchen doing the dishes when she appeared several minutes later, carrying the stand and the empty wine glass. "I can't eat anymore," she announced.

"Did you like it?"

She leaned against the counter and rolled her eyes heavenward. "I loved it."

He grinned. "Turns out vanilla goes really well with dark chocolate," he teased. She swatted his arm.

He pulled her overnight bag out of the closet and let her have the bathroom. As he pulled up the waistband of the shorts he usually slept in, she appeared in a black silk nightgown that hung mid-thigh. He pulled her into his arms and kissed her. "Hmm," he said, eyeing her body. "Maybe we're not done playing."

He was only teasing, though, instead he picked up a DVD off the top of the dresser. "I rented this," he told her.

She laughed when she saw it. "It's not as good as Chinatown, but as far as sequels go, it's still pretty good."

"Well, I'm glad I actually got to watch the first one," he said as he put it into the player. "After having to subdue a ravenous little sex kitten."

"I have no recollection of those events, Senator," Abby declared, climbing into his bed.

He grinned at her and slipped in beside her. "Really?" he asked. "Want me to get your toothbrush and refresh your memory?"

"No!" she squeaked then cleared her throat. "Um. Nope. Let's just watch the movie."

She didn't make it through the whole movie, though. A little more than halfway through she'd fallen asleep curled up against him, her head resting on his chest. Tex fingered the tiny strap of her nightgown. He'd brought vanilla women home from Maria's a fair amount and though he didn't mind having a woman sleeping in his bed, he had to admit he'd never watched a movie with one. As he watched her sleep, he had all kinds of thoughts he really shouldn't be having. "You are a dangerous little pet," he whispered. He settled back against the pillow to finish the movie.

In the morning, he woke before she did and slipped into the bathroom. When he was finished showering, he threw on a pair of jeans and decided to wake her. He leaned down and pressed his lips to hers. She made a soft noise in her throat as she roused and slid her arms around his neck.

"Time to get up," he told her.

She stretched and made a face. "It's Saturday. How can you be up this early?"

"It's not that early," he told her. "Take a shower and come to breakfast, pet."

Abby paused as she was getting out of bed. He watched her as she came to the realization that they would resume playing. In fact, they would be playing the entire day, but he didn't want to tell her that now. She nodded and headed off to the bathroom with her overnight bag.

Tex was in the kitchen stacking pancakes when she appeared. Her hair was a little damp and swept up off her neck. She was naked and he smiled his approval. He picked up the collar on the island and secured it around her neck. "Have a seat," he told her. "Breakfast is almost ready."

He set down a glass of orange juice in front of her and then went back to the island, balancing two plates in each hand. In front of the empty chair next to her, he set down a stack of pancakes. In front of Abby, he set a small bowl with half a grapefruit and some sugar substitute sprinkled on it. He suppressed a grin as she scowled.

"I saw the bowl of grapefruit in your kitchen," he told her casually. "I assume that's what you normally eat for breakfast." Abby looked longingly at his own plate. "Of course," he declared, "you'd probably rather have my breakfast. Whole wheat pancakes. Fresh blueberries." Abby gave him a withering glare. He ignored it. "I think you know what you have to do to get it."

Abby put her palms flat on the table and took a moment to decide. He let her think it over without comment. Finally, she pushed back her chair and stood up. She turned to face him, knelt down on the tile floor and... amazingly... put her hands behind her back. Tex felt a surge of desire that started in his stomach and shot all the way to his cock. A dangerous little pet.

He undid his fly and pushed his jeans all the way down. He wanted to see exactly how much of last night's lesson she retained. She moved a little closer and rubbed the underside of his cockhead with her tongue. A quick riot of sensation shivered through him but it settled into a very pleasant, growing warmth as he gazed down at her. She licked and swirled the head then took it into her mouth and began to gently nurse on it. She even remembered his balls, nuzzling them and sucking on each one in turn.

She rose up fully on her knees and took him into her mouth, moving up and down on the shaft rhythmically. Her technique was decent he mused, but it was still the big finish that was going to be the problem. "Just relax," he told her. "It's time, baby." She tensed just a little and, as before, managed to take in the first spurt but started to draw back. He put one hand on the back of her head and wrapped the other one around his cock. "Hold still and keep your mouth open," he commanded in a firm voice.

He pulled his cock out of her mouth so she wouldn't panic and directed the rest of the semen across her face, specifically her open mouth. Abby made a small noise of either protest or surprise, but she couldn't really move with his hand on the back of her head. He put his fingers underneath her chin and forced her mouth closed.

"Swallow," he ordered. Abby's throat convulsed as she did. "Open," he told her and she opened her mouth again. "You look good covered in my cum, pet, but it goes in your mouth, doesn't it?" He took the first two fingers of his right hand and slowly scooped up all the drops on her lips and cheeks and fed them to her. "There now," he said, pushing his slicked fingers onto her tongue. "It doesn't taste bad. It's just that you tense up at the end."

With the hand on the back of her head, he pulled her forward. "Clean my cock, pet," he demanded. She bathed the head with her tongue. "Next time," he told her as she worked on him, "it'll be the same. You either swallow it when it comes out, or I feed it to you. Either way you'll get used to the taste. But I'd prefer it if you tried hard to swallow for me. I eat your pussy for you, don't I, pet?"

"Yes, Sir."

"So, it's only fair that you take this for me. I lick up all your cream, pet. You will lick up mine."

"Yes, Sir."

He pulled up his jeans and fastened them and then pulled Abby to her feet. He kissed her deeply and then directed her to the chair. He pushed away the grapefruit and pulled his own plate over so it sat in front of her. "Good girl," he said squeezed her shoulder gently.

When she was finished, he washed the dishes as she sat at the table. He dried his hands off on the towel and glanced at her. "I think the pancakes were a nice reward, but I want to give you a better one," he announced. Abby turned in the chair to look at him, her expression full of anticipation.

"There's a catch though," he informed her.

"What?" He raised an eyebrow at her. "What, Sir?" she corrected.

He crossed the room and stood in front of her. "Open." Her eyebrows knitted together but she opened her mouth. He brought up his hand and stuck his pinky into her mouth. "Suck on it." Still confused, she did as she was told.

"All this talk of eating your sweet pussy has made me hungry, pet. I want that hot, wet hole riding my tongue." Abby shivered in response. He wiggled the pinky in her mouth. "You've had my cock in your mouth. This seems small by comparison, doesn't it?"

She nodded, looking up at him. She kept her lips wrapped around the small digit. "If you want me to eat that pussy, then this," he wiggled the pinky again for emphasis, "is going in your ass while I do it." Abby's eyes widened and she stopped sucking. "It's small. It won't hurt. And would it influence your decision at all if I told you that I wouldn't put it in until you were begging me for it?"

He pulled out his finger so she could answer. "I would never beg for that," she told him.

He grinned down at her. "I can guarantee you would. And I've already promised no penetration until you do."

She thought about this for a long time. "Are you going to pull my fingernails out one by one until I ask?" She was partly joking, based on her tone, but the look in her eyes told him she was in fact slightly concerned that his methods of persuasion would involve pain.

"No," he told her. "In fact, I will amend the rules of the game to say that the only thing that will touch you, until you beg for my finger in your ass, is my tongue. So, obviously, there will be no pain of any kind."

"Your tongue?"

"My tongue," he repeated.

"And that's all?"

"That's all I need to reduce you to a horny, desperate, needy little pet."

She smirked at him. "Your tongue is talented, but not that talented."

"So, it's a deal, then?"

"Deal," she said with confidence.

CHAPTER FIFTEEN

Abby was drenched in sweat, yanking on the chains that were firmly attached to the posts of the bed. She was spread eagled, legs wide, and she was pissed. "Fuck!" she shouted. "Fucking fuck!"

Mark shook his head at her. "Such language, pet."

Why? Why had she ever thought she could beat him at his own game? She'd actually been pretty turned on from blowing him earlier. Who wouldn't be at the sight of a beautiful, rock-hard cock just inches from their face? She'd assumed that it would only take a few licks, maybe a few penetrations with that magic tongue of his and she'd be over the moon before the subject of her ass and his little finger ever came into play.

Abby could totally handle Mark touching her with only his tongue. But that was not her problem. Right now her problem was that Mark was no longer touching her with his tongue. And she was just shivering on the edge of orgasm when he stopped. She must've telegraphed her impending release in some way although she wasn't dumb enough to have yelled out anything so obvious as 'I'm about to come!'. He still knew somehow that she'd been dangerously close.

God! It was impossible to hide anything from this man. He was such a complete and total...

"You're such a-!" she shouted.

"*Watch it,*" he snapped forcefully, causing her insides to twist. "I'll only touch you with my tongue to play. But I'll still spank the hell out of you for punishment if I have to. And it won't be the kind of spanking you'll enjoy."

Abby licked her lips. "Please, let me come. Sir."

He smiled. "I'm glad you asked nicely, pet. Now...ask me for something else. Nicely."

Abby panted and shook her head. Mark drew himself up over and traced his tongue along one of her distended nipples. "You taste so good, pet," he murmured. "I could do this all day long."

All day? There was no way Abby could take this for five more minutes let alone all day. She could use her safeword, but she was fairly certain Mark wouldn't let her come if she did. After all, an orgasm hadn't been promised.

She closed her eyes and groaned. "Okay," she relented.

"Okay, what?" he asked, lazily licking the other nipple.

"Okay, put...put your finger in."

Mark paused. "That wasn't asking nicely, pet."

Abby squeezed her eyes shut tighter and then opened them. Why did he make everything so difficult? "Please," she begged. "Please, put your finger in. And lick me," she added just in case he forgot.

"Put my finger in where?"

"My ass! Please, put your finger in my ass! Sir!"

He grinned. "Of course, pet. If that's what you really need."

She felt him insert the digit into her drenched pussy, lubing it up gently. His tongue made a few light flicks against her clit. She felt the finger slide down and instinctively clenched her cheeks together to prevent the impending invasion, even though she'd asked for it.

"Oh, please don't hurt me," she whispered.

"Shhh," he replied and kissed her pussy. "I would never hurt you like that. Now, open up for me."

She took a few deep, calming breaths and slowly relaxed.

"Such a good girl." He took a long, slow lick of her pussy and she sighed, tilting her hips toward his face. She felt the tip of his finger press against her tight hole and tried to remain open to him. He parted her pussy lips with his tongue and delved into her wetness. She opened even further, welcoming the soft, warm invader. As she pushed into his mouth, she was also slowly working his finger into her ass by herself.

He moved his tongue further away from her by degrees, forcing her to push her pelvis up more and more if she wanted that contact on her pussy. The consequence being the finger was inserted more and more. When she finally shoved her aching clit against his mouth, the finger seated itself deep inside her. It didn't hurt and since her reward for being a good girl was Mark's coma-inducing tongue on her needy bud, she didn't complain. In fact, rather than complain she said...

"Oh, God, yes!" She yanked at the chains again, but this time not in frustration.

Mark pulled away a bit. "Fuck my finger, pet. Just a little harder. I don't want you to come just yet. Fuck it, baby."

Abby threw her head back against the pillow and ground her ass into his hand.

"That's it, baby," he encouraged. "Fuck yourself." He leaned down again, teeth barely grazing her clit and she bucked and thrashed.

"Oh, please more!" she begged.

"You want more?"

"God, yes!"

Abby gasped loudly as she felt his ring finger press against her and stretch her sphincter.

"Oh, God!" she shrieked. It wasn't painful, precisely, but the sudden stretching was shocking, nonetheless. Mark buried his face in her pussy and she was soon too overwhelmed with sensation to care.

She came loudly, in much the same way Mark had earlier, which was to say all over his face. He licked her clean as tiny shockwaves still pulsed through her. He slowly slid his fingers out of her ass and lowered himself over her, kissing her deeply so she could taste her own juices on his lips and tongue.

"That was beautiful, pet." Abby wantonly licked his lips, cleaning him thoroughly of her juices. "You loved it, didn't you?" he asked when she finished.

She smiled dreamily. "Yes, Sir."

Mark released the chains and cuddled with her on the bed for a few moments. "It's almost time for lunch," he informed her. "On your knees, baby."

Abby got off the bed and knelt between his legs. He pulled down his jeans and she began her ritual of tongue bathing his shaft and balls. This time she was slow and methodical, all the way through, pep talking herself right up to the end. His fingers threaded through her hair and she knew it was almost time. *Calm, relaxed, swallow it as it comes out*, she told herself.

This time she managed to swallow two jets before she gagged a little and then had to just use her mouth as a receptacle, catching all the semen and holding it until she could force herself to swallow it down. She was disappointed, but Mark didn't seem to be.

"Very good, pet. Show me." She opened her mouth for him so he could inspect her. "You're almost there. It'll be a lot easier for you if you can swallow it as it comes out rather than holding in your mouth until the end. But you'll get it."

After lunch, Abby took a nap on the couch with her feet in Mark's lap as he watched television. She woke up alone, tv off, and sat up. Mark was in the kitchen working on dinner. "Come here and help," he called out to her.

She made a face and walked over. "If you want to eat it, you probably shouldn't let me help."

He laughed. "I have faith in you. This," he told her "is what we call a knife." He said it slowly and sarcastically. She glared at him. "This is an onion." He set the onion down on a cutting board. "Now, the secret to cutting onions is you leave the hairy end on."

"I thought you liked the hairy end off."

He shook his head. "Sassy little bitch," he muttered, but he was grinning.

She took the knife from him and cut according to his instructions. "Do I get to shave your balls?" she asked him.

He laughed. "No. Sorry, pet."

She scowled. "So, we're definitely not equals."

"We are," he argued. "Equal, but opposite." He pulled a coin out of his pocket and set it on the counter in front of her. "Has two sides," he told her. "One can't exist without the other. No matter which side is facing up, it's still worth twenty five cents."

Abby chopped the onion silently and decided she liked that explanation. Equal but opposite. She could accept that.

After lunch, Mark rinsed the dishes and she placed them into the dishwasher. He dried his hands and turned to her.

"I have a gift for you," he announced.

Abby's heart skipped as she remembered the Orange Blossom shampoo. She tried not to look too excited but her mind was racing, wondering what it was.

He turned away from her. "Come, pet."

He led her not to the living room, or even the bedroom, but instead to the bathroom. She suppressed a giggle imagining bath salts, fragrance pearls, and hours upon hours of relaxing in Mark's amazing bathtub.

He opened the cabinet and took out a small, red paper gift bag and handed it to her. She pushed aside the white tissue paper and reached inside. Her fingers connected with something hard and smooth as glass. She grasped it and pulled it out. She stared at it. Well, the glass part made sense, because it was, in fact, made of glass. She frowned at it for a moment, trying to figure it out.

It looked a little like a dildo. Except that it was short. Very short. Only three, maybe four inches long. It had a flared base and a rounded tip. She looked up at Mark and back down to the toy. Suddenly her cheeks flared as she realized what it was.

"It won't hurt," he declared. Obviously he understood that her sudden embarrassment meant she knew exactly what it was.

He took the bag from her and reached into it again, this time pulling out a small bottle of lube that she'd apparently missed. "If you use this," he told her, "then you'll have no problem at all. It's a very small size," he assured her. "You'll be able to wear it comfortably for long periods of time."

Abby swallowed hard and looked up at him. "Long..." she cleared her throat nervously. "Long periods of time?"

"At work."

Her heart plummeted to her stomach and her eyes grew wide in shock. "*At work?!*"

"We need to work on stretching you, Abby," he informed her. "There's no way you take me comfortably right now. The sphincter is a muscle, like any other muscle. It needs to be worked on to achieve the best results."

He took the empty bag and set it on the counter. Then he took the plug from her, popped the cap on the lube, and began applying copious amounts to the rounded tip of the anal plug.

"One of my rules, pet, is that you be available to me in all ways. Every part of you will belong to me. Including your ass."

Abby started breathing heavily as she watched him prepare the mini-torture device. Her heart pounded rapidly in her chest.

"Calm down," he ordered without even looking at her. "I will never lie to you and I will never push you beyond what you can handle. This will not be terribly painful. There will be a slight burn as the larger part of the base slides past the sphincter, but it won't be unbearable."

He moved past her, lowered the lid of the toilet and set the plug, with it's flat, glass, circular base directly onto the seat. He stepped out of the way and gestured to it.

Abby couldn't move.

"The insertion will probably be easiest if you sit on it and ease it in slowly. You can do it yourself in the morning and then wear it as long as you can throughout the day. As your body grows accustomed to it, you'll be able to keep it for longer periods of time. This one is small, the smallest available, so I'd recommend some thong panties to help hold it in."

Abby tried to breathe slowly as she attempted to absorb everything he said. He grinned at her and ran a finger down her cheek. Leaning in he said softly, "Surely you have thong panties."

She blushed again and bit her lip. She merely nodded.

He cupped her face in both hands and kissed her. Her mouth opened instinctively to him and his gently seductive tongue. "Put it in you, Abby," he murmured against her lips. "Show me what a good pet you can be."

Abby swallowed again and gathered her courage. She reminded herself that she signed up for this. She'd practically begged for this. And she wasn't going to give it, or Mark, up so easily. She stepped around him. Positioning herself over the toy, she reached down and put one hand on the seat to steady herself and parted her cheeks with her free hand.

The tip was cold, but not shockingly so. She gasped anyway,

despite her determination. She angled a bit until she felt she had it right and began to sit. Slowly. So very slowly. In truth she might have hovered over the thing indefinitely if her knees and thighs could have held out that long. But they couldn't, and she slowly sank down.

The tip wasn't painful. It was about the same diameter as Mark's two fingers, which she reminded herself had gone in relatively easily.

"Go slow," Mark reminded her. "Don't jam it or force it hard. Just go slow and steady but do not stop."

She nodded, concentrating hard. The toy slid further in, expanding her as it went. It was a little uncomfortable the further it went and she wasn't sure how she would manage to deal with that for even just a few minutes, let alone all day. She took a deep breath and pushed down. She squeezed her eyes shut as the largest part stretched her. She gasped.

Just as she thought she couldn't finish it, the toy slid in quickly. More quickly than she anticipated, and the smaller stem-like portion gave her instant relief. She felt herself closing up around the base as her cheeks hit the cool plastic of the toilet seat. She sat, perched delicately, her stomach fluttering crazily and her hands gripping the edge of the seat.

Mark nodded and reached out to take her hand. He pulled her up, which gave her a momentary spike of panic as she worried the plug would pop out.

As if he suspected what she was worried about, he said, "Hold it in."

He turned her around and parted her cheeks with both hands, inspecting her. His fingers brushed over the smooth base and he tapped it. She moaned as it jiggled inside her. It was foreign, and wicked, and forbidden, and she had no idea what to think about any of it so she closed her eyes.

Mark's fingers found her pussy and stroked gently. "So beautiful, pet."

Later, as he helped her dress, she gingerly fingered the plug before she pulled on her panties. Mark kissed her on the temple. "I expect a text tonight when you've taken it out," he told her. She paused and looked at him. "Also one every morning after you've put it in and then a follow-up text when you remove it."

She gaped at him, but he looked unruffled.

"I need to keep track of how long you're keeping it in," he informed her. "So I know where we are in your training."

Abby felt slightly disconnected from everything as she gathered up her things and prepared to go home. As she left the house, she wondered about it all. She had a toy in her butt, and a Dom in her life, and she wasn't sure how either of those things was going to work out long-term, but it was definitely like nothing she'd ever experienced before. *Mark* was like nothing she'd ever experienced before. There was something simultaneously chilling and thrilling that he could get see into her so clearly and bring out things she'd never known were there.

On Monday, Abby entered the lobby and made a beeline straight past the receptionist with barely a nod such was her certainty that anyone who looked at her could tell that she was a horrible pervert with a glass plug in her butt. She clenched instinctively as she made her way down the hall to the office, fighting off they very palpable fear that the thong's tiny strap would not be capable of holding the damnable thing in.

Earlier that morning, she'd texted Mark to say she'd completed her task. He'd responded by saying he was proud of her and he wouldn't be opposed to her sending a photo. She'd refused and he'd pretended to be disappointed but it had made her smile.

She gingerly lowered herself into her office chair and willed her heart to stop hammering away. She shifted a little in the seat and was surprised to find that, like sitting in the car, it was not altogether unpleasant. It didn't hurt at all and though it wasn't exactly what she would call comfortable, she thought she could live with it. Though she dreaded the moment when she would have to actually leave her office. Which happened all too soon, to her liking.

She gathered her daily reports and practically goose-stepped down the hall to the office's copy room. Normally she didn't shut the door, but today she felt that it couldn't hurt to put as much as she could between herself and other people. Having a secret was exhausting, worrying about whether it was obviously just by looking that something was out of the ordinary.

In the relative silence and safety of the copy room, Abby brushed one hand over her rump for about the hundredth time that morning, checking that the outline of the toy wasn't visible underneath her slacks. But she was assured it was not. She closed her eyes and remembered Mark's hand caressing her bottom just after she'd put it in for the first time. First her bottom, then...

Her own hand stopped at her hip and she fanned herself with a sheaf of papers. Masturbating in the copy room definitely was not an option. There wasn't even a lock on the door. And though Abby had discovered that she was far more sexually adventurous than even she would have guessed about herself, she wasn't quite that naughty.

But the copy room was hot with the door shut and the copier's fan blowing hot air into the tiny room. And her ass was filled like it had been with Mark's own fingers....

"Gah!"

She threw open the lid, grabbed her originals, and crammed the rest underneath her arms. She stopped by her office just long enough to toss the entire lot onto her desk and headed off toward the relative safety of the bathroom.

It was a small, private room with, above all, a deadbolt on the door. Her heels clacked on the tile floor as she turned and leaned back against the heavy wooden door. She didn't know how she could survive days of this torture. She unfastened her blazer and shook the lapels, fanning herself. The chilled air of the bathroom made her nipples tighten underneath her sheer bra. It seemed like everything was working against her today.

Finally giving in, she unbuttoned her slacks and slid one hand down over her silk panties and closed her eyes as her fingertips found her aching bud, straining against the dampening fabric. She rubbed it rhythmically, simultaneously clenching her cheeks to feel the plug invading her. She slipped her hand into her panties and pushed a finger into her pussy.

"Sir," she whispered to herself in the deserted bathroom.

She pictured herself chained to Mark's bed anticipating whatever wicked thing he was about to do to her that she'd never before imagined. He knew everything about her. Everything she was afraid to admit as much to herself as anyone else.

Her pussy spasmed, preparing for the throes of an orgasm. When it hit, her muscles clenched, and she rode the wave of ecstasy while biting her bottom lip to keep herself from crying out. She only let out a small whimper as she reeled from the aftershocks. She took in a deep breath and her body went boneless as she leaned slack against the door.

It was because she had been so quiet that the sharp crack of the plug hitting the floor after it slipped out of her ass was so impossibly loud.

CHAPTER SIXTEEN

It was going on 4 pm and Tex was washing his hands with lava soap in the garage's utility sink. He glanced at his watch and scowled. Abby hadn't texted him. And while he was pleasantly surprised with her efforts as his submissive thus far, she wasn't anywhere near adept enough to have kept the plug in all day. So she had failed to text him when she took it out.

After drying his hands he tapped out a text of his own and sent it to her. He grated as he waited for her reply.

'It's out," she admitted.

He sighed. 'How long did you make it?' he answered back.

'A little while,' was her vague reply.

"Reinsert it,' he commanded. When she failed to text back he paced the break room until he finally looked down at the screen of his phone. 'Be at my house for dinner tonight. 7 pm. Be on time.'

She didn't respond to that one, either, but he knew she'd seen it. He sighed again and grasped the doorknob to head back out into the garage bay. She was new to all this, he reminded himself and he wouldn't punish her too harshly this time. After all, she couldn't be perfect at everything.

At a little before 7, he heard her car pull up outside his house and he set down his chopping knife to answer the door for her. She looked sheepish and uneasy as she stepped inside and he took her jacket from her, hanging it up. To allay her fears somewhat, he took her in his arms and kissed her deeply. For a moment, she did melt into his arms the way she always did when he kissed her. One hand gripped her hip and the other ran a slow circle over the other, then back to caress her cheek, and slipped down.

She gasped and his jaw tightened.

"It's not in," she blurted out, even though that was obvious.

Tex stepped back and regarded her.

"I- it's- I..." she struggled.

He held out his hand. "Give it to me."

She hesitated, which only made his irritation grow.

"Abby," he prompted.

Reluctantly, she reached into her purse and pulled out the toy. She handed it over. Tex looked down at it and frowned. Obviously this was going to require more than just dinner to work out.

Tex watched Abby for a moment, gagged, hands bound behind her back, and kneeling beside him on the kitchen floor. He nodded at the chipped glass butt plug sitting on the counter. "Are you trying to tell me you don't like my gifts, pet?" Abby shook her head, but Tex continued. "Because it seems like you don't. I bought it for you. Chose it specially. Never been inside anyone else but my little pet. And not only did you not keep it in, fail to text me when you took it out, but you destroyed it. Is this you telling me you don't want anal? Pet, are you ready to tell me why this happened?" He looked over his shoulder at her.

She lowered her eyes and shook her head slightly. He sighed. "And you're choosing punishment over telling me the truth?"

She nodded. Tex turned away. She might think she was getting away with not telling him what happened today, and he might go on letting her think that for a while. But, oh, she would tell him. Punishment was not a choice she made, just like keeping things from him was not a choice he would allow her to make.

He set the garlic cloves aside and picked up the ginger root and began peeling it.

"I think I told you in the beginning I would be harsh with you. I want to be sure you understand that. I will punish you, pet. Are you prepared for that?"

She nodded. *We'll see*, he thought. He carefully washed the ginger in the sink. He set it aside and washed his hands. As he dried them on a towel he turned to her. "Up," he ordered. He kept his face impassive as he watched Abby struggle to her feet with her hands behind her back. God, she was beautiful. Graceful in every way, even while bound. He was so fucking lucky.

"Come," he demanded as she finally made it to her feet. She walked toward him. He nodded to the island. "Bend over it. Put your cheek against the countertop."

Abby positioned herself in front of the island and leaned forward, resting against the surface. Tex was pleased at the sight of her curvy ass bared to him. With a feather light touch, he skimmed his fingertips over it. She jumped. He smiled. She was always so supremely aware of him.

He brought his hand down hard onto her right cheek. She made a slight squeak and jumped again. He slapped her other cheek, harder this time. She started to breathe heavily. He continued raining down blows, alternating cheeks and even reaching down and slapping the tops of her thighs. She was panting hard when he finished.

He turned to pluck a wooden cooking spoon from the holder. When he turned back, Abby was lifting herself up. He placed one hand on her back and pushed her back down. "That was just the warm up, pet. Now you're ready for your punishment."

She shivered involuntarily and he brought the wooden spoon down on her ass. It made a pleasing crack as it landed. She bucked and he gave her time to process the strike. "You will receive ten, pet. Do not clench your bottom. Every time you do, I will be forced to start over. Understand?" Abby nodded vigorously. "Good girl. That was one."

He brought the spoon down again and she jerked. He brought it up for a third blow and he saw her muscles clench in anticipation of the blow. He slapped her cheek with his bare hand and squeezed it. "Do not clench, pet." He gently began massaging her. "Relax. Do not clench." Abby took some deep breaths and slowly relaxed her cheek in his hand. "Good girl. Now we begin again." She tensed up again at his words. "Abby," he said, his voice full of warning. She forced herself to relax again.

He struck her across her left cheek. "One," he counted. He got to five allowing her time to recover between each blow, but she tightened up again. He gathered a fist full of her hair and pulled her up. In her ear he said, "You will be grateful for this instruction, pet, when we get further into the punishment. It is in your best interest to listen to me and obey. *Do. Not. Clench.*"

He thrust her back down and stuck another blow. He couldn't go back on his word. As her Dom she had to trust that he meant what he said in all things and she had a right to expect he would follow through with whatever promises he made. Allowing her to continue without starting over would not only show her he wasn't a man of his word, but would also allow her to think that if she kept defying him, she would eventually get her way and he would end the punishments earlier. He could allow neither of these things to happen.

Tex had not, however, made her any promises as to the severity of the spanking and so he could adjust within that framework. He did so by lessening the force of each blow. "One," he repeated. This time they made it all the way to ten. He set the spoon down and took a minute to watch her.

He was so fucking proud of her. She had only ever been spanked before by him and this was the first implement he'd ever used. She'd taken it well, breathing slowly when she needed to, calming herself when she had to. She'd corrected and mastered herself beautifully.

He rubbed his hand over her bottom, soothing it. "My good, good girl," he murmured and she shivered in response. He tapped her nicely pinked bottom lightly, causing her to jolt. "Stay, pet."

That was the punishment for failure to comply with his orders. The bigger problem, though, was Abby's inability or unwillingness to communicate. He couldn't add anything more or take anything away from their relationship unless he understood exactly what the problem was. So, to combat that, he'd temporarily taken away her ability to do just that. She could safeword if she needed to. Or in this case safegesture by dropping the cat toy in her hand, but he wasn't going to listen to her constant apologies for misbehavior and empty promises that it wouldn't happen again.

Promises were sacred, to Tex's way of thinking. From both the Dom and the sub. If you promised to submit unless you couldn't for physical, mental, or emotional reasons and agreed to explain what those reasons were, then you should honor your promise. Abby's problem was that picked and chose which parts of that promise she would keep. She could tell him what she couldn't or wouldn't do for physical reasons. But anything that skirted the border of the emotional or mental she shut down on him.

"I've been where you are, pet," he told her gently. "I've submitted. In exactly this way." She turned to look at him, eyes wide. "Surprised?" he asked. "I would never ask someone to do something unless I knew exactly what it was I was asking them for. For training purposes, I have been a sub to a female Dominant. It was difficult, uncomfortable at times, but ultimately I learned a lot. I'm only trying to help you, Abby. To explore with you what you're capable of, what you're interested in, what you don't like simply because it's strange and new to you rather than something that actually turns you off."

He picked up the finger of ginger root. Now the real punishment would begin. He came around behind her, and used his free hand to reach down and rub her pussy. She was a little wet. Probably had been through most of the hand spanking. He worked her pussy, rubbing her clit and thumbing her hole. She wiggled into his hand. "Oh, yes," he said quietly. "My pet likes that. I know you liked the hand spanking, pet. We'll discuss the spoon at a later time." She was probably too shocked and confused at the wooden spoon to analyze it clearly this time. Maybe she liked it, maybe she hated it. Too soon to tell.

He let her use his fingers until she tightened up, body ripe for orgasm, then he withdrew his hand. Abby moaned in disappointment.

"Sorry, pet. This is punishment." He allowed her a moment to calm down. "Abby," he said firmly. "You need to listen to me. Are you listening?" She nodded. "There are a few things you're going to need to know. One. This will hurt." She tensed and he saw it. "A lot," he added. "It will not harm you in any way. We've talked about this, right? The difference between hurt and harm?" He waited for her nod. "This will hurt, but it will not harm. Understand?"

He got a nod that he deemed satisfactory and reached down, stroking her pussy again. He wet his fingers and brought them up to her ass. "Easy now," he told her. With his other hand he guided the ginger root, which was about four inches total in length and twice the size of his thumb to her entrance. "Relax, pet, and accept this. This is my body to use and control, right? This ass is mine. To fuck, to lick, to punish. Now, your ass will be punished." He slid the ginger root in. "Stay calm. And do not clench."

Abby wasn't sure what Mark was doing to her. But then, she was never quite sure what he was doing. Hadn't he said that was the point? The spanking had been amazing. It hurt, but then the tingly sensation afterward had been exquisite. Then he'd hit her with something harder. She had been trying to figure out what it was. She hadn't seen him take anything from the bedroom. So it must have been something in the kitchen. One of the wooden spoons she suspected. The first blow had completely caught her off guard. Then she found herself trying to ward them off any way she could, which had proved difficult to do with her hands behind her back.

She had considered dropping the ball, but couldn't bring herself to do it. Mark had been in the army. Had been through much worse physical punishment than she could ever imagine. How much would she disappoint him if she couldn't even take a punishment spanking? She'd gripped the ball tighter and bit down on the gag and did her best to endure, but she was relieved it was over.

Then Mark had made a surprising revelation. A sub? She couldn't imagine it. Not by a long shot. Mark tied up at the whim of some woman's mercy. For a second she felt a pinch of jealousy. Not that she wanted to be some kind of Dominatrix. Lord knew she didn't have that in her. But this, what she had with Mark, this connection, these feelings. He'd had that with someone else? It bothered her to think about. Fortunately or unfortunately she didn't have to for long, because he called her 'Abby'.

Oh, the dreaded 'Abby'. 'Pet' was fun. 'Pet' she'd gotten used to now that she knew its meaning. But 'Abby'? 'Abby' meant scary BDSM time. 'Abby' meant something new and strange and possibly not wonderful was about to happen. 'Abby' meant "Brace yourself, darlin'." So she did.

And he stuck something in her. Hurt. He'd said it would hurt. But not harm. She would come through it, whatever it was. At first she'd thought he was going to fuck her. And yes that would hurt. Considerably, since she'd failed at her anal training on the first god damn week. But whatever it was it was not a penis. Probably not even a dildo. It didn't feel right. It was cold and wet, but smooth and not that big. It didn't hurt at all. Which had Abby more than a little confused.

Suddenly, he swept her up in his arms and carried her to the living room. He laid her on the floor and left the room for a moment. She heard the sound of running water in the kitchen and was lost in the confusion of the night when slowly, steadily, downright motherfucking *menacingly* whatever it was that was stuck inside Abby...began to hurt.

She immediately clamped down on it. *Oh, my god!* she thought. It hurt. No, it didn't hurt. It was starting to fucking burn! She squealed and clamped down harder. The burn intensified.

"Now, pet," came Mark's voice from just out of view. "Don't clench. Clenching makes it worse."

Abby bucked her hips. She could barely concentrate through the pain. Fuck. She felt like she was being set on fire from the inside. The ball. The ball. She still had the ball. She was about to drop it to signal the session needed to stop immediately when he said, "I'm considering ending our relationship." She stilled. She'd failed. The one thing he'd asked her to do, keep a damn plug in, and she'd failed miserably, or so he thought. But it had just come out. She hadn't planned on it. It was an accident.

As if he read her thoughts, he said, "Not because of the plug. Although that's a separate issue on its own, why you won't accept anal play. No. My biggest concern is trust. I don't trust you. You don't trust me. Even though you promised, swore to me, that you would. Part of trusting me is telling me what's happening. Why things aren't working; what things need to be changed. You're not giving me that, Abby. And relationships like these cannot work without it."

Several things happened to Abby at once. The first thing was she realized she did not want to lose Mark. The second thing, that only reinforced the first thing, was she realized that while he'd been talking, she'd stopped clenching her ass. And the pain that was there before was now just a mild burning sensation. He'd told her not to clench. The spanking with the spoon had been to exercise her ability to control her reactions. He had given her all the tools she needed to endure this punishment and if she would just listen to him, it would have gone much more smoothly.

Would she have even been punished at all if she'd just been honest? As she thought about, she realized, yes, Mark would still have punished her. But maybe not with this last part. She started to cry. Mark took pity on her, knelt down beside her and removed whatever it was that was inside her. She looked up at him, tears streaming.

"Will you talk to me, Abby?"

She nodded and he reached behind her head to unbuckle the gag. She gasped as it came out. "Please," she begged. "Please, don't leave me."

Mark sat down on the floor beside her, picked her up and settled her into his lap. "Honey, I'm not trying to manipulate you. I'm really not. I do think maybe you're not ready for this. Or maybe it's not for you. I have no idea. Because you won't tell me. And so whether you're a submissive or not, you're not ready to be *my* submissive."

"I- I just need more time," she insisted. "It's moving so fast and it's all new and things are happening-"

"What things?" he prompted. When she didn't answer, he said, "Abby, what things? And if you think it's moving too fast, just say so. Don't break the things I give you in some passive aggressive attempt at controlling our relationship."

"I didn't!"

"Then how did the plug get broken?"

Abby swallowed hard. "It- I- it came out."

"That still doesn't explain how it broke."

She blushed and looked away. He immediately grabbed her chin and forced her to look at him. He didn't repeat himself. He only stared at her, eyes boring into her until she cracked. "I came," she admitted.

For once she'd actually surprised him because his eyebrows shot up. "You came?"

She nodded. "In the bathroom. I- it just- it was there, in me, and it freaked me out that people were around and they might figure it out somehow. And then, then it didn't freak me out and..."

"You liked it."

"Yes. And I couldn't take it anymore. So I went into the bathroom and I...masturbated. I was up against the door and I had my panties down and when I came, the plug popped out and hit the floor. It chipped the side. It was an accident."

He grinned. "You know, I thought my biggest problem with you would be the things you don't like. Not the things you do. What's going on with the anal play?"

She hesitated, but only for a second. "It feels...dirty. I mean, it *is* dirty."

"You get it waxed regularly. Before you even met me."

"Yeah, but that's different. It's not inside. It's just-" She sighed. "I don't know. Dirty."

"But when you're alone, it gets you excited enough to masturbate in the bathroom," he pointed out.

"Well, no one's there to know."

Mark was quiet for a long time. Then he unlocked the cuffs and removed them. He swept her hair to the side and unbuckled the collar. She drew in a sharp breath. "Calm down," he told her in his silky smooth voice. "It doesn't mean anything. I just want a serious conversation with you, no collar. No Dom, no sub. Just me and you." When she was free of the restraints, he set them on the coffee table. "Go to the bedroom, put on a bathrobe."

Abby looked at him, confused.

"If you're naked," he explained, "and I'm not, you're still the sub. Go put something on so we can be equals." She nodded and headed off to the bedroom. She couldn't resist spreading her cheeks and looking at herself in the mirror. It didn't look like anything back there. Oh, her cheeks were rosy red from the spanking, but there was no evidence of whatever he'd done to her later and it didn't feel like anything at all now. She shrugged on the bathrobe and went back out to the living room.

Mark had gotten up off the floor, thrown away whatever was on the table, and was washing his hands. "What was that?" she asked him.

"Ginger root. It burns, more if you clench down on it, but it won't do any damage and if you leave it in, the effect only lasts about 15 or 20 minutes." He dried his hands on the towel. "But you've got to be careful of your hands because you don't want it to get in the eyes."

"It really hurt," she told him.

"Because you panicked and forgot everything I told you."

She hung her head. "I know."

"It's alright," he said, drawing her into his arms. "You did amazingly well through the spanking. I was very, very proud of you."

"Really?"

"Very. Did you like it?"

"I don't know," she admitted. "The first part with your hand. But I don't know about the spoon."

He nodded as if he'd known this already. The microwave, which she hadn't noticed had been on, beeped. Mark took a mug out of it and dropped in one of her teabags. "Come sit with me," he told her and headed toward the couch.

She sat on the end, pulling her knees up underneath her and clasping her mug in both hands.

"When I told you I was thinking about breaking it off, you started crying," he said.

"I- I don't want it to be over. I just...I don't know if I can do all the stuff you want. Some of it's just really out there for me. It's hard."

He nodded. "The hardest part isn't fear. Everybody has that and they get over it eventually. The hard part is what you're wired to think is acceptable versus what's not acceptable. For you, anal is dirty. Plus, nice women don't do it, am I right?"

Abby nodded.

"Abby, I'm going to explain something that's pretty tricky. Very advanced. I've done it, on both sides, and I've been doing this a long time. The idea will seem very strange to you and the reality will be extremely terrifying."

She scoffed. "Oh, good. 'Cause I needed this to be *harder*."

He smiled. "How much do you want me?" She looked up at him. "I'm not fishing for compliments," he assured her. "I'm asking how far you would go." Before she could answer he said, "Knowing that my first priority, always, is you and what you need. I said 'need', Abby. Not 'want'. What you want is very different in this case from what you need."

Abby took a sip of her tea. "What do I need?" she finally asked.

"You need to get over your inhibitions about your body. Of which there are many, but the one we're concerning ourselves with right now is anal."

"I don't have inhibitions about my body," she protested. Mark merely raised an eyebrow at her. "Moving on," she said. "How do we do that, give me what I need?"

"You give me you."

She frowned. "I did."

He shook his head. "I mean completely. It's called consensual non-consent. You give me your one-time consent to do anything to you. Anything I want. Total control. Anything you say after that initial 'yes', whether it's 'no' or 'stop' or 'cantaloupe' doesn't matter and will be ignored at my discretion."

Abby drew in a breath. "Mark."

"I will not harm you, Abby. There won't even be much pain. Not physical anyway. What you went through tonight was far and away worse than what I will do to you if you agree. Trust that. The issues will be mostly mental. And you will say 'no', Abby. You will ask me to stop. You will beg me to stop. But I will not. And in the end, you'll be better for it. If you can trust me."

"What- what will you do?"

He gave her a look. "You know better than to ask, don't you?"

"You said you don't want that. Total control. You said that's not-"

"I don't want it. Not forever. This will be for one weekend and one weekend only. We both have jobs, Abby. Lives. I'm not going to lock you in a cage in my basement for the next twenty years. It's one weekend. Starting Friday night and I will release you Sunday afternoon. If you never want to come back to me, I will understand. But I'm telling you, you will, Abby. You will be better for this. I can teach you to give yourself to me, to pleasure, and pain, and you will come to love it."

"You said no pain," she countered quickly.

"I said *some* pain. There will be some pain in the training. A small amount. Not the end of the world. Nothing you can't very easily handle. Like I said, your problem is psychological. And I can break you of that. But you have to trust me that I can."

"Break me," she whispered as a shiver ran down her spine.

"Yes, Abby. I will break you down. Totally. And then I will build you back up, better than you were before."

"And you can do whatever you want."

"Anything. You and your body belong totally to me. You will obey every command I give you or there will be punishment. That includes, especially, answering every question I ask you honestly and to the best of your ability. Punishments are not part of the training, Abby. I hope not to have to use them, but if I do, they will be unpleasant. Immensely. The training will feel like a walk in the park by comparison. The only promise I will make to you is that your needs always come first."

"I- I need to think about it."

He nodded. "It means a lot to me that you'll consider it. I'll give you this week to think it over. Like I said, we'll need all weekend." He leaned forward and took the play collar off the table and handed it to her. "If you decide to do this, come to me Friday night, 8 o'clock. Shaved the way I like you. Wearing this. The door won't open again until Sunday at 5. If you don't want to do this, or you can't, we'll just have to slow things way down until you can trust me."

CHAPTER SEVENTEEN

Friday afternoon Abby tried to concentrate at work and it worked for long stretches, but everything reminded her of Mark and if this week was any indication of 'slowing down' she didn't want any part of it. It was strictly radio silence for Mark while she was mulling over his request.

Life with Mark could be scary, could be exhilarating, always exciting. Life without Mark was....fucking boring. He'd promised no pain. No, scratch that. Little pain. If she submitted. Possibly big time pain if she disobeyed. But she needed it. So he said. Was he right? She tapped her pen against her desk.

What had he been right about so far? She wasn't afraid of pain. Didn't even mind a little bit of it during sex. She wasn't against BDSM because it objectified women. She was afraid of what would happen if she liked it. She wanted to give up control, to be allowed to feel and enjoy without being constantly worried about her performance. She loved the ball gag, despite all her initial fears and opinions of it. She liked the bondage. So far he'd been right about everything.

How far off base was it to think he'd be right about what kind of 'training' she needed? It's not like she didn't know him. She'd spent plenty of time alone with the man. If he wanted to hurt her, he could have done it already.

What she wanted. What she needed. She looked around her

office. This...was not what she wanted. At all. She wanted that knife edge of pain and pleasure, that heady anticipation when he was preparing to do something to her but she didn't know what. That thrill of confusion, shock, and excitement when he finally did it.

But Mark wanted more. He wanted anal. He'd been clear about that from the first night. If she was his, she was completely his. Why was she so worried about what other people thought anyway? She learned to ride a motorcycle despite what anyone thought. She learned to work on cars. The only opinions that mattered were hers and her Dom's.

She froze for a second. Her Dom. That was the first time she'd ever thought of Mark that way out of the blue like that. He was always just Mark. But he was more than that, wasn't he? He was her Dom, her teacher, her instructor. She closed her eyes and tried to hear his voice, dark with desire, that rumbling wave of timbre.

Good girl.

God, she loved it when he said that. She craved it. It thrilled her insides every time she heard it.

He was her Dom and she was his sub. She had to get over this hurdle. She headed home and went straight to the bathroom. She washed and dried her hair and then set about shaving herself. When she was done, she rinsed off, dried off, and opened the lotion he'd gotten for. She closed her eyes and breathed in the scent. She put some in her hand and rubbed herself all over with it.

Then she got dressed, putting on a button-down silk blouse and a black skirt with sandals that had a low heel. As she picked up the collar, she realized her hand was shaking a little. Well, of course she was nervous, afraid even. Who in their right mind wouldn't be? She put the collar in her purse and locked her front door.

Pulling up to Mark's house, she put her car in park and killed the engine. Her hands still shook a little as she pulled the collar out of her purse. She took a deep breath and fastened it around her neck snugly and then checked the fit with her finger as Mark always did.

She took her purse by the straps and opened the car door. She felt almost dizzy as she headed up the walkway to the porch. Before she could even ring the bell, the door opened. Mark appeared in jeans, barefoot, no t shirt. She wasn't sure what she'd been expecting.

Leather? One of those masks with a zipper for a mouth? She nearly laughed at the thought.

He stood back from the entrance to let her in. Behind her, he put his hands on her shoulders. "You came," he murmured into her ear.

"Yes, Sir."

He ran his hands down her arms and back up to her shoulders. "I'm so pleased with you, pet." She smiled and closed her eyes, leaning against him for support. "Are you ready to begin?"

"Yes, Sir."

Mark closed the door. She heard the snick of the deadbolt and fought off a shiver. It was just a lock, not the sound of a cell door closing. He ran one finger up the strap of her purse and lifted it.

"Heavy," he noted. "Did you bring your gun?"

"Yes. Oh! But not because of you or anything! I just carry it everywhere. I didn't think to take it out."

He chuckled. "It's fine," he assured her.

He set the purse on the entryway table. "Let's go," he told her, taking her hand and leading her into the living room. They didn't pause as they turned down the hall and toward the bathroom. She balked a little as she realized something was wrong. She didn't quite get it until they stepped inside the room. The door.

There was no door on the bathroom!

"Mark-"

He turned instantly and set that gaze on her that could stop a freight train. "I mean, Sir. Sir. There's no door."

"No. Your body belongs to me, pet. All of it. All your bodily functions are mine to control." Abby felt the blood drain from her cheeks. "You will inform me if you need to use the facilities and I will decide when and if I'll let you."

When? If? this was sounding a little insane. "Mark- Sir!" she corrected instantly. "I can't- I mean holding it all weekend? I don't-"

"Your body has needs. I understand this. Consumption, evacuation, sleep. But privacy? No. You don't *need* privacy, pet. You *want* privacy. But you can't have it. Not unless you're a good girl. You want privacy? Earn it, pet."

Abby looked around the bathroom helplessly. "Y-yes, Sir." God, she was going to have to be good girl. And fast.

"Strip," he ordered.

"I took a shower before-"

His hand snaked out and he grabbed the O-ring on the front of her collar. "Are you arguing with me? Already?"

Abby was caught off guard, but Mark wasn't hurting her. "N-no. No, Sir. I was- I was just...letting you know."

He nodded. "Now I know. Strip." He let go of her collar.

Abby unbuttoned her shirt, slid it off and draped it over Mark's outstretched arm. She unfastened her bra and did the same. It was, in a word, uncomfortable. She wasn't horny. She wasn't even remotely turned on and somehow disrobing in the harsh light of day in a room with no door seemed clinical and strange.

She slipped off her sandals and unzipped her skirt. She stepped out of it, handed it to Mark, and then removed her panties. She bent, picked up her shoes, and he took those as well. "Stay, pet," he told her and left the room.

She shivered even though it wasn't cold and wrapped her arms around herself. She looked around the room, but didn't see anything odd or unusual. Mark returned and immediately slapped her arm lightly. "Never hide yourself from me," he demanded.

"I didn't! I wasn't! I was just-"

"Never cover yourself in my house unless you've been given permission. Not with your hands, not with clothes, nothing. You will hide nothing from me, pet. No matter if I'm in the room or not. Understood?"

She nodded.

He brought up the wrist cuffs. "Offer yourself to me."

She extended one arm and he slid the cuff on, buckling it tightly. She held out the other one and he did the same. He checked their tightness and led her further into the room. He turned her to face the right hand wall. "Kneel."

Abby wasn't sure what was going on, but she knelt on the tile floor. Mark squatted down beside her, holding a double ended snap hook. He clipped one end to the metal rings on both cuffs and the other into a metal ring in the floor that she hadn't noticed before. She couldn't move or even turn around, only look over her shoulder.

Mark stood up and moved behind her. She heard the sound of the small linen closet opening behind her but couldn't see it. Her heart started to pound as she wondered what he was doing. She knew better than to ask.

"Have you evacuated your bowels today, pet?"

What? "What?"

"I'm being polite, pet. If you want, I can be more crude."

Holy Shit. Er, no, not Holy Shit. Most definitely not Holy Shit. "Um. Yes. Sir."

"How often do you have the need?"

Oh, my God.

"No, pet. I'm not God. I'm your Dom and I am asking you how often you move your bowels."

She'd said that out loud? Oh, man she was losing control of the situation. Then she almost laughed. Like she ever had control. But she had, hadn't she? Before this. Oh, yes, she had. She'd had 'cantaloupe'. And her long and silly list of limits. She'd had control and now she'd given it away.

"Pet?"

Her face burned. She was glad she wasn't facing him so he could see it. "Once. Once a day. In the morning."

"Good girl."

She breathed a sigh of relief. She was a good girl. Maybe she could get up off the floor at least, if she couldn't have a door.

"Lie down. On your side."

Well, damn. She wasn't getting up off the floor. She slid her knees down and lowered herself. Mark sank down behind her. He reached down and parted her butt cheeks with one hand. As she felt something push against her, she bucked. He let go of her bottom and slapped it.

"No," he growled.

She gritted her teeth and forced herself to relax as he parted her again. It took her a moment to realize the probe was his finger. It was covered in something. The lube she figured. She took deep breaths. Then she felt something else. Not his finger. But it wasn't cool and smooth like the plug. It felt strange and alien. Ha, like an alien probe. *Oh, God now is not the time for jokes,* she told herself.

"Hold still," he chastised and she realized she'd been wiggling. "Take your enema like a good girl."

She froze. "What? No! Mark, no! No!"

He slapped her again, this time on the thigh. "You will address me as 'Sir'. And you will take this enema one way or another. We can either do this now, or I can fig your asshole with ginger again. Over and over until you're begging me to let you have an enema. What do you want, pet? The enema? Or the ginger root and then the enema?"

Abby was panting now. Mark was holding her down at the hip. She couldn't get away. Even if he let go, she was still cuffed to the floor.

"I-" Fresh, hot tears stung her eyes. "I don't- I can't-"

"Decide. Right now. Or I will decide for you. You have very few decisions this weekend, pet. I suggest you take advantage of my generosity."

She closed her eyes and remembered the ginger, the burning. Why endure it and have to deal with the enema anyway?

"I-" she licked her lips. "I want the enema."

"I want the enema, please, Sir."

"I want the enema, please, Sir," she sobbed.

Mark leaned down and kissed her temple. "Very good, pet. Very good."

He parted her again and inserted what she now knew was a plastic tube into her. She heard a slight click and felt a warm sensation in her bowels. Odd, but not horrifically unpleasant.

"You're dirty," he told her. "Or so you think. So we will clean you. Inside and out. My fresh, clean little pet. Ready for her assfucking." She tensed. "We'll work up to it. Don't worry. We have a long weekend of training ahead of us.

Abby was quietly crying on the floor, unable to stop the tears, but not sobbing hysterically. She sniffled a little. "Please, stop."

"No, pet. Shh now. It's alright." He rubbed her back gently. "All nice and clean."

Abby felt a gurgling in her stomach and she clamped her thighs together. "No. No, no, stop." Mark ignored her. "It hurts!" she cried.

"What hurts? Cramps?"

"Yes!"

"Okay, okay," he said, sounding unruffled. She heard a click and the pain slowly subsided.

"Better, pet?"

She hated that she was forced to admit it was. "Yes," she gasped.

"Good. You'll tell me again if it hurts."

Abby felt her bowels getting heavier and heavier. "Oh, God. Oh please. Sir." *Yes, call him Sir. He likes that.* "Sir, it's...too much. I feel-"

"Like you have to go? It's normal. It's a small enema though. Just saline. You can hold it."

"I can't!" she sobbed.

"You can and you will," he assured her.

"No I-"

"You want some privacy when you go?" he cut her off sternly.

He wasn't seriously going to *watch* her go? It was unthinkable. "Yes!" she shrieked.

"Then earn it by being still and quiet and accepting your enema like a good little pet."

Abby swallowed and tried to focus on nothing but her breathing. Occasional spasms would hit causing her to groan. She felt his hand on her rounding tummy. "Hurting?"

"No, Sir," she whispered. He squeezed her, she moaned. "Good girl. Such a good girl. Are you dirty?"

"Yes," she groaned.

"Are we going to clean you?"

"Yes."

"Okay, then. Relax." She heard another click and felt a rush of warm liquid. She squealed and pressed her legs together. She heard a final click. "All done, pet. Hold it, please."

She groaned. "Please."

"Just for a minute. This is the only one for today."

"For today?" she whined.

"If I'd used soap, you'd need another one immediately after to rinse it out. Thank me for my thoughtfulness, pet."

"Th-thank you, Sir."

"Good girl."

He parted her cheeks and she reflexively tried to hold them

closed. "I'm just taking out the tube."

"No, don't."

"Pet, pet, pet. You don't want it in you, you want it in you. Which is it?"

"If- if you take the tube out I might-"

"Evacuate? I'll go slow. Hold it in. It'll be just fine. It's a small enema pet, it's not putting too much pressure on you."

He slowly worked the tube out and Abby started panicking, trying furiously to hold everything in.

"Oh, God," she gasped. "Oh, God I have to go."

"You did a very good job, pet. I'll give you some privacy." He unhooked her wrists and helped her up. He tossed the tube and the enema bag into the sink and propelled her toward the toilet. "I'll be back in ten minutes."

She sighed with relief as he walked out. She slammed the toilet lid open and waited as long as she possibly could hoping Mark was out of ear shot as she let go. The relief was instantaneous. Oh, God don't let there be another one, she prayed silently. I'll be a good girl. The best girl. The best pet ever. No more enemas.

She was washing her hands as Mark came back in. "Everything come out okay?" he asked, smiling.

She glared at him.

"Watch yourself," he snarled, his friendly demeanor instantly gone.

Abby's heart lurched. "Yes, Sir."

He set a bottle of liquid dishwashing soap on the counter. "Clean that," he said pointing to the tube. She set about that task as she heard him turn on the faucets for the bath.

"Into the tub, pet."

Abby nodded and stepped in. Strangely enough he hadn't filled it much. It covered her thighs and her lower belly but nothing else and there were no bubbles. He knelt down beside her and took the bar of soap off the shelf. He dipped it in the water and lathered it in his hands. She watched in surprise as he began to run his hands along her breasts, bathing her.

His hands skimmed her belly and she closed her eyes. Despite everything, his touch could still turn her on. She groaned.

"Feeling more relaxed, pet?"

"Yes."

"Good. Spread." Her eyes popped open and she stared at him. "Open your legs, pet. Now."

She slid them apart. "Good girl." His fingers, slick from the soap, curled into her and rubbed gently. Just as she was feeling happy again he said, "Turn over."

"What?"

"Hands and knees, pet."

Her eyes grew wide but his look said not to question. She bit her lower lip to keep from hyperventilating. He washed her pussy thoroughly and rinsed it with a cloth. Then she felt something hard and smooth nudging into her. She gasped and instinctively shot forward. He gave her ass a stinging slap. She yelped.

"Take it inside you, pet. Fuck it into you," he demanded.

She spread her fingers on the floor of the tub and gathered her courage. She pushed back, onto the object. It filled her easily, painlessly. With a click it hummed to life. "Oh," she cried in both ecstasy and relief. It was a vibrator.

"You may come if you want to, pet," he informed her. Then he set about to washing her asshole. She flinched and received another slap. "You will accept my touch, pet. Haven't I been kind? I gave you a nice, warm enema. I let you relieve yourself in private. I let you shove a vibrator in your cunt."

Whoa. Her cunt? He'd never used that word before. But strangely, it didn't offend her. The husky way in which he'd said it made her nipples tighten.

"Thank me for my kindness, pet."

"Thank you for your kindness, Sir."

" 'Please, wash my dirty asshole, Sir'."

Abby closed her eyes. "Please... wash my dirty asshole, Sir."

"Of course, pet. We want a nice, clean pet for fucking don't we?"

"Yes, Sir."

The vibrator ratcheted up a notch. "Good girl," he told her. "Hold still unless it's to come."

Mark rubbed a finger around her hole and she could tell by the slippery feel it had soap on it. He worked the tip in and she fought hard to hold still like a good girl. She must have done well because the vibrator went to a higher setting.

Abby cried out.

"Are you going to come, pet?"

"Yes!"

"That's a good girl. You like this, pet? Feels good, doesn't it?" He rubbed his soapy fingers all over her. Rubbing her asshole, skimming her clit, nudging the vibrator in deeper. God, it all felt so good.

"Yes, Sir!"

"You like having your asshole washed, don't you?" He tapped her clit and a jolt went right through her.

"Oh, God!"

"You like having your asshole washed don't you?" he repeated.

"Yes, Sir!"

"Such a good girl," he said. "Look at that cunt, holding that vibrator in. That's a greedy fucking cunt, isn't it?"

"Yes, Sir."

"Is your asshole greedy too?"

"I- I-"

The vibrator ratcheted up another notch.

"Yes, Sir!" she squealed, loving the feel of the toy.

"Tell me you want me to fill your asshole."

"I want- I want you to fill my asshole, Sir."

She heard the sound of the faucet turning and warm water cascaded down her ass and dripped onto her pussy, rinsing her. He turned it off after a few moments and then parted her cheeks as wide as they would go.

"Nice and clean, little pet. Such a pretty asshole too. Wet, and washed, and waxed. Does it feel clean?"

"Yes."

She felt something slippery against her exposed hole and she wiggled. "No," he warned and she stilled immediately. The familiar feeling of a heavy glass plug nudged her. "I got you a new present, pet."

"Th-thank you, Sir," she replied as he pushed on it. She groaned as it stretched her wide then settled into place.

"Not much pain, pet. As promised. Are you grateful?"

"Yes, Sir. Thank you."

"Then why don't you come for me and show me how much?" He tapped the plug and it sent a wave of sensation over her whole lower body. She came hard, clenching on the vibrator and crying out loudly as Mark pressed on the plug, keeping it in place.

When she recovered, Mark turned the vibrator off. "We'll work on your ability to hold things inside your ass while you orgasm," he told her. He drained the tub and helped her out. She stood on the tile floor as he dried her off, head to toe with a towel. "Spread," he ordered and slid the vibrator out of her. He left the plug in, however.

He set the toy on the counter and produced a thin chain from his back pocket. He clipped one end onto her collar and held the leather loop at the other end. "On your knees, pet."

Abby knelt and Mark turned. "I have more gifts for you," he told her. "Come."

CHAPTER EIGHTEEN

Abby crawled forward on her hands and knees. Mark, thankfully was not walking quickly and it was easy to keep up. Abby noticed two things right away, one, if she thought this was over or she was going to get some kind of break, her being on her hands and knees crawling behind her Dom pretty much killed any idea along those lines. And second, she was supremely aware of her ass. More than she'd ever been before. Sticking it up in the air with a plug filling it felt strange and exposed, but she dutifully followed Mark down the hall and into the bedroom.

The bedroom did have a door on it. She wasn't sure why she noticed that, but she did. Mark tugged on the leash, snapping her out of her distraction. "Up," he told her.

She got to her feet. Mark disconnected the leash. "Hands behind your head." She put her hands behind her head and laced her fingers together. He picked up a box off the dresser and opened it.

"These are not clamps," he told her. "These are purely for decoration because you're going to be wearing them for a long time tonight." He came toward her with a gold chain made up of three strands and had two small circles on each end. He thumbed her right nipple, making it hard and placed one circle over it. He tightened the tiny screw. It didn't hurt at all, but held the circle firmly in place. He did the same with her other nipple and let the slim chains hang between them.

He went back to the dresser drawer and returned with a pair of cuffs, just like the ones on her ankles. "Sit on the edge of the bed, pet." She complied. "Give me your foot." Abby raised her foot and he took it, buckling one cuff around her ankle. "The other." When he'd fastened them both he stepped up. "Now, we're ready for dinner."

She sat up and he snapped the leash on her. "On your knees, pet. Let's go."

Abby sank to the floor and crawled obediently after Mark. When they arrived at the dining room table, he tugged the leash. "Up."

She got to her feet. But instead of indicating she should sit in the chair, he instead bent, bringing one arm under her knees and scooping her up in his arms. He placed her gently on the table, in the center. "Lie down." Abby didn't hesitate and leaned back against the cool wood. Mark took one leg, bent it so her bare foot was flat on the table, and pulled a snap hook out of his pocket. He attached her left wrist to her left ankle. He rounded the table and did the same on the other side, rendering her immobile. She could lift her head and move it from side to side but nothing else.

"Delicious," he remarked and left the room.

Abby stared at the ceiling and tried not to think about the fact that her pussy was completely exposed, as were her breasts. She took deep breaths and tried to listen for any sounds that might indicate what Mark was doing, or going to do, but heard nothing. A few minutes later, he returned and she craned her neck to see him carrying a plate and a glass of water. He placed them, unbelievably, at the head of the table. He sat down and Abby understood he could see her exposed pussy and ass just a few feet from his face.

"I never turn down a good view," he told her and proceeded to cut a piece of steak off. Abby was slightly offended. After all this, she should at least get a steak dinner. She glowered, directing her gaze above her while Mark ate his dinner.

Just when she thought he was ignoring her completely, she was shocked out of her inspection of the ceiling when a drop of something freezing cold landed directly on her shaved mound.

"Oh!" she gasped and tried to close her legs, with no success.

She raised her head to see Mark dangling an ice cube from his water glass above her. It dripped down slowly. She tried to catch her breath. Then he pressed the entire cube to her clit. She screamed.

"Stop!" she shouted. "Oh, please stop!"

"What?" Mark asked mildly.

"Sir! Please, don't do that!"

"Do what?"

"Rub ice on me!"

"Rub ice on what?"

"My- my pussy. Stop!"

"Your what?"

"My....cunt. Please stop rubbing ice on my cunt, Sir."

"Whose cunt?"

She tugged at the restraints, then gave up. "Yours, Sir. Your cunt."

"Okay," he said, and shoved the cube inside her. Abby screamed again.

"This hot little cunt," he said as she lay there struggling, "that belongs to me, is melting that ice pretty damn fast. I have to tell you, I fucking love it. I love seeing things drip out this cunt, pet. Ice, cunt juice, my seed. I think maybe I'll put my seed in you and have you push it back out with your tummy muscles. While holding the plug in. Does that sound like a fun exercise?"

"Um." Abby had no idea how to respond.

"Well, it will be. But here's something you'll be a little surprised about when you feel it. A plug this big makes your cunt tighter."

"It- it does?" Tighter? She was snug enough as it was for Mark's large dick.

"It surely does. Fucking my pet with her plug in is going to be a whole lot of fun for the both of us." Mark continued with his dinner, occasionally watching her. When he finished, he stood up, gathered his plate and his glass and left.

Abby closed her eyes, trying to prepare herself for what was coming next. She heard Mark return and when she opened her eyes again, he took hold of both her legs behind the knees and pulled her forward until she was closer to the edge of the table.

She heard the distinct sound of him unzipping his fly. She whimpered.

"Excited or scared, pet?"

"Both."

"Honest answer. Good girl."

Tucked inside his hand was something small. Something almost flesh colored. It was a flat disc and Abby scrutinized it a moment before she realized what it was.

"NO!" She shouted, trying to move away from him.

"Easy, pet," he told her.

"No! No, no, no! Please. Please! I'm a good girl. I was a good girl! Please, no!"

"It's alright, pet." He placed the small piece of ginger root against her clit. She bucked and tried to fight him off, screaming.

But this time, the intense burning sensation did not come. It only tingled first, then steadily built to an almost buzzing sensation. "Oh, God!" she exclaimed and bucked her hips again, but this time not out of fear. She ached with need. She gasped and tried closing her legs to get the friction she needed.

"Pet?"

"Fuck me!" she shouted. "Oh, God fuck me!"

"Pardon?" Mark asked, grinning.

"Fuck me! Fuck me hard!" The ache got steadily sharper and she sobbed.

"You need my cock in you?"

"YES! YES SIR!"

Mark grabbed her legs, pulled her all the way to the edge of the table, and drove into her in one quick motion. She let out a shattering scream. He seemed huge! As he pounded in and out of her, he reached down and pressed on the plug. The added sensation of the ginger and the toy made her come instantly.

"Keep going, pet. Got another one in you, I suspect," he demanded, slamming into her. He pressed the ginger to her clit with his thumb and she howled with desire.

She felt all her muscles clenching as she came a second time, clamping down on his cock so hard she hissed. She couldn't tell if she was feeling pain or pleasure.

Mark came inside her then. She felt every pulse of his cock filling her tight pussy with his semen. After the last throb, he slowly pushed her back farther onto the table so her feet were resting on the flat surface.

Abby thrashed a little as she tried to catch her breath. When she did, Mark spread her legs wide with his hands. "Oh, yeah. Look at that," he murmured to himself. "Got a little tiny drop leaking out there. A dripping pet is a well used pet, isn't she?"

"Yes," Abby breathed. "Yes, Sir."

He pushed his thumb onto the plug making her groan. "We can get it out, though, can't we? Push it out of you. Push out the cum, not the plug."

Abby struggled to work her stomach muscles. She felt the plug slipping and he shoved it back in. "More," he ordered. She squeezed harder. "There it comes," he crooned. "What a pretty picture. You feel it dripping?" She nodded. "Push some more." When she did, he rubbed her inner thigh. "Good girl." He unlocked her wrists from her ankles and scooped her up off the table, setting her on her feet.

"Are you alright? Can you stand?" he asked.

"Yes. Yes, Sir."

"Pet."

"Yes, Sir?"

"There's seed on the table."

Abby looked down at the puddle. She felt Mark gathering her hair in his hands. "I'll hold this. Don't want a messy, pet. Go on. You know the rules."

Abby placed her hands on the table and bent down. She slowly licked up the still warm mix of their juices. "Every drop, pet." She swallowed it down obediently.

Mark pulled back on her hair, standing her up. He twisted her so his face was inches from her. "Such a fucking good pet. Licks her cream all up like a good girl. Hungry now, pet? Ready for dinner?"

She nodded, dazed. "Kneel here and wait for me," he told her.

When he returned he had another steak and a glass of water. He placed them at the head of the table. He sat in the chair and cut a piece of steak. He picked it up with his fingers and put it next to her lips. "Eat your dinner pet."

Abby took the meat in her mouth and chewed it. "Is it good?" he asked.

"Yes. Thank you, Sir."

As he cut another piece of steak he said, "All your needs will be met by me. If you're hungry, you eat from my hand. Understood?"

"Yes, Sir."

"Good girl. Take another bite." Mark fed her the whole steak, some potatoes, and held the water glass for her to sip from. She was too exhausted to be offended.

"Need to sleep, pet?"

"Yes," she said wearily. "Yes, Sir."

He gathered the plate and the glass and stood up. "Let's get ready for bed."

Mark allowed her ten minutes of bathroom time to pee and brush her teeth then made her crawl to the bedroom on the leash and even though she knew it wasn't there, she looked for a dog cage anyway when she entered the bedroom. He opened the dresser drawer and pulled out a pair of thong panties. "These are your size. Put them on please." She took them and looked at them. "They'll help keep the plug in overnight."

"Overnight?"

"Yes, pet. Your ass needs training if you're going to take my cock on Sunday."

She shivered and knotted the panties in her hand.

"Relax," he told her. "It's a process. It'll be a challenge, but we'll make it happen."

She pulled the panties on. Mark pulled her up to the bed, took off the leash, and attached another chain to her collar. This was was attached to the headboard. "If you need anything in the night, you wake me, and I will take care of it," he told her. He locked the chain to the bed with a silver padlock and then produced another, smaller one from his pocket. "Lift your hair." She felt him lock the buckle on the back of her neck. He put the keys in the nightstand drawer on his side. She could reach them if she wanted to, but it meant going over Mark to do it.

He shucked his jeans and slid into bed alongside her. "Pet?"

"Yes, Sir."

"Come here."

She moved closer and Mark leaned over her. He cupped her face with both hands and kissed her. There was no tongue, just a slow, gentle kiss. "You're doing so well, pet. I am so proud of you."

"I-" she stopped. Was she allowed to ask for anything? She didn't know.

"What pet?"

"Will you hold me?"

"Of course." He turned off the light and pulled her in close to him, arms wrapped around her. Abby drifted off into sleep quickly.

CHAPTER NINETEEN

In the morning, Abby forgot what was happening for a brief moment when she woke up. All she knew was Mark was next to her. And she smiled.

"Mornin', pet," he said. Right. Chains. Collar. Training.

"Good morning, Sir."

Mark unlocked the leash from the collar and the headboard and had her crawl down the hall to the bathroom.

He removed her panties and her plug. He tossed the panties in the hamper and set the plug on the counter. "I'm giving you ten minutes to use the toilet," he told her. "Then it's bathtime." She frowned. "No enema this morning," he told her. "Only tonight."

She sighed in relief and nodded. "Yes, Sir."

"Good girl."

Abby did her business quickly and washed her hands and the plug for good measure. Maybe she could escape that enema if she was extra good. Mark came in and saw her drying it. He kissed her on the forehead. "Like your present?" he asked.

"It's not so bad."

He laughed. "Bathtime, pet." He ran the water to the same level as before and bade her get in. He washed her with his bare hands and she didn't hesitate at all when he instructed her to get on her hands and knees. She bit her lip and said nothing as he washed her asshole inside and out.

"You dirty, pet?"

"No, Sir."

"Nice and clean inside?"

"Yes, Sir."

He rinsed her with the spray and brought the plug over. He lubed it up and inserted it with minimal effort. He rewarded her compliance with a finger fuck in her pussy until she came.

He brought her out of the bath and towel dried her. He attached the collar and she immediately knelt beside her. "Good girl," he said, obviously pleased. "Let's get breakfast." He led her to the smaller kitchen table and made her kneel beside it. He made an omelet with mushrooms, plated it, and brought it to the table.

He sat in the chair and Abby prepared herself to be fed again. But instead he said. "Pet. I'm really pleased with your obedience this morning. And I know this isn't quite as much of a treat for you as it is for me, but I want you to suck me off. Right now."

"Yes, Sir."

Abby maneuvered herself under the table as he unzipped his fly and his erect cock sprang out. She would probably never get over how beautiful it was. She happily enclosed her lips over his dick.

He groaned with pleasure and took her face in his hands. "It's really important to me that I be able to use all my pet's holes. And not only that, but all of them in an equal fashion. Do you understand what I mean when I say that, pet?"

Abby paused and looked up at him. She shook her head slowly so as not to dislodge the cockhead in her mouth.

He stroked a finger down the side of her face. "That means that the same intensity I use to fuck your cunt also needs to be done to your ass as well as your face."

She pieced together his words and started to draw back. He held her firmly. "Not today. Not even tomorrow. Not for either your mouth or your ass. But after we finish your anal training, I'd like to start training your throat. I want to facefuck you." She whimpered. "No," he told her. "You won't like it. But you'll learn to tolerate it as part of your service to me. Because you want to please me, don't you?" She hesitated then nodded.

"Good girl," he told her and came in her mouth.

She rested her head on his thigh as he finished his omelet. He stroked her hair with his free hand. When he finished, he carried his plate to the sink. "Do you want an omelet?" he asked her. "Or something else."

"That's fine. Sir."

He nodded and began making one for her as well. She watched him put the same amount of care and precision as he had into his own and he laid it on a clean plate and brought it to the table. He fed her, using the fork this time, thankfully, as she knelt beside him.

"Will it always be like this?" she asked suddenly, then winced. She wasn't supposed to ask questions. Oops. But Mark only gave her a puzzled look. "Will I cook for you? Obviously. Unless we want to live on PB and J, pet. You can't cook your way out of a paper bag."

She rolled her eyes at him. "I mean, will I always...eat on the floor?"

"No," he said. "This is a Total Power Exchange. To keep you in the right head space while you're here. I won't make you crawl, either." His eyes twinkled. "Well, not much. I do love the way your pretty little ass sticks in the air when you do. I use ginger root only for punishment. Unless you want me to put it on your clit again." She blushed and looked away. "Thought you might enjoy that," he told her. "I didn't think I'd enjoy bathing you as much as I do, it turns out. Might do that once in a while." She looked at him thoughtfully. "What pet?"

"Nothing. Sir. It's just that, you don't usually answer questions."

"Well, some questions are okay, and others aren't. I get that it's hard to know which ones are which. You know I don't like telling you what we'll be doing. That's what the checklist is for. So I know ahead of time what you are and aren't interested in. What's the best part of our sessions together, pet?" She grinned up at him. He rolled his eyes. "Aside from your cunt's insatiable need for orgasms."

She considered this. "The not knowing," she finally told him.

"Exactly, pet. It's normal to want to know. But it heightens everything when you don't. You just have to master yourself and refrain from asking. You'll find out when I let you find out. This is a demanding type of relationship, pet. It requires understanding, communication, and creativity on a level that other relationships never even sort of approach. It's relatively easy to keep a Dom happy. Not so easy keeping a sub feeling fulfilled.

"On some level they do really want to please their Doms, they wouldn't be a sub otherwise. But they have thoughts and feelings and desires and needs like any other person. They sometimes won't tell their Doms about them, maybe they don't think it's their place to ask for anything. Or they're afraid they won't get it. Very few subs are happy just serving. If they are they're usually slaves. I don't want a slave," he announced. "I want a pet who obeys only when she's wearing my collar."

She'd finished her omelet and he stood up, carrying the dishes to the sink. "Stay, pet." He left. Abby had no idea what was coming next, but she was relieved to think she wouldn't always be eating on the floor. She understood, in a general way, that this weekend was extreme, even for Mark, but she had no real idea of how a relationship like this worked long-term. What if she came home one night and just didn't want to have 'a session' as he'd called them? How pissed would he get? How many times could she say no before he dumped her for someone who would do what he asked?

Up until now it had all been just kinky play. *What will he ask me to do? Will I do it? How much will I like it?* Now her head swirled with questions. How many pets had he had? How long would he keep her if she chose to stay? How could she ever look someone else in the eye and ask, 'Would you put ginger root on my clit and fuck me?' Could she even do that? What if the guy freaked out? What if he told a bunch of people she was crazy? *Was* she crazy?

She didn't think so, but in the last 24 hours she'd been given an enema, been bathed by a man, fucked on a table while under the clearly aphrodisiac properties of a fucking vegetable, licked up cum, and was chained to a bed to sleep. Obviously she was crazy.

Why did all of this seem okay when she was horny and not so much when she wasn't? This seemed like a lot of trouble to go through just to get some anal sex. She sighed. It wasn't really about anal sex was it? It was about why she didn't want it in the first place, or said she didn't when she was secretly jilling off in the bathroom while toys were shoved up her ass. Fuck. She didn't want to look at that too hard. It had been so much easier to blame every guy she'd ever dated as being boring. Except she was the boring one, wasn't she?

Occasional blowjobs, no swallowing. No anal ever. No pussy eating. To be fair she didn't really have a no-pussy-eating rule, but now in light of everything, she probably didn't get it a lot because she wasn't all that jazzed about swallowing jizz. It was a give and take, just like Mark said, even if she was the sub and he was the Dom. They were both giving a lot. Well, he was. She was holding back.

She was startled out of her thoughts by Mark's return. "If you think about whatever it is you're thinking about any harder," he told her, "you'll have an aneurysm."

She smiled ruefully and was secretly thankful that he hadn't asked what she was thinking.

He had an armful of objects and he put them on the table. From her knelt position she saw some chains, her ball gag, and a velvet bag. "Stand up and come here," he told her. She did and he positioned her so her upper thighs were against the edge of the table. He attached a snap hook to both the rings on her wrists and the other end to the two chains. they snaked out in a V across the table and draped over the side. Mark bent down under the table and tugged the chain, she sprawled out forward on her belly. He attached one chain to each ankle cuff. She was stretched taut and couldn't move. Her breasts pressed against the table, but not painfully. Nothing was hurting, just a little unfamiliar.

She tested the chain, pulling on it. It tightened and pulled at her feet, almost causing her to lose her balance. *Better not fight the chain*, she thought. "Open," Mark demanded and when she opened her mouth he slipped the ball gag in. He fastened it behind her neck deftly.

"Pet, this next part will be challenging," he told her. "It will hurt. Nothing unbearable. But we're gonna stretch that little hole out today for your assfucking tomorrow." She sucked in a deep breath. "I don't want you to worry about that part. I promise you, you will love your assfucking. I know you don't believe me now. I know you think I'm gonna ream you, but I'm not. I told you I want to use your ass the same as your pussy, but that's not right now. After some training, we'll be able to do that. That's not something that happens in a weekend. Just relax and concentrate on following my instructions."

He tugged a little on the small glass plug she was wearing. "Push this out," he commanded.

She took a deep breath and pushed. She felt it plop out. Unlike the last time that happened, Mark caught it in his hand.

She heard the faucet running behind her for several minutes then Mark came back to the table, set a bowl of water down, and opened the velvet bag. She couldn't see what was in it. He moved in front of her and showed her a shiny metal plug with a hole in the end. He threaded two fingers through the hole and held it up. Abby thought it looked like a stainless steel Ace of Spades. She shivered.

"I know this looks pretty scary, pet. But it is not. It is the most comfortable plug available. Once it gets past your sphincter, it won't hurt. It'll just make you feel full. Ready, pet?"

She nodded and he stroked her cheek. "Good girl." He placed the metal plug in the bowl and walked back around to the other side of the table. Something else came out of the bag that she could not see and she felt Mark's hands rubbing her ass then sliding down to her pussy. She moaned at his touch and spread her legs further for him.

"Greedy fucking cunt," he teased, slapping her slit. She jumped and squealed, but the sensation had been oddly pleasant. "Oh, you like that?" he asked. He slapped her again. She made another high pitched noise in her throat. "Interesting. We'll have to explore that sometime."

He inserted two fingers in her and spread her wide. Then she felt a nudging and relaxed to accept whatever it was into her. She pushed back against it. "Good girl," Mark praised her. "Want that cunt full, don't you pet?" She found herself nodding enthusiastically. He pushed and something large slid inside her. It took a second to adjust. He patted her ass and came around in front of her. "Now. If at any time you panic, or something hurts beyond normal, or can't handle what's happening, you knock on the table twice. Got it?"

She nodded.

"You don't have your ball because this," he handed her a small object that looked like a car alarm, "is your reward for being such a good little pet this morning. Push the button." She did and the thing inside her vagina jumped to life. "It has ten different settings. You can experiment with all of them if you like." He moved out of her view and she heard the water sloshing in the bowl.

She braced herself for what was to come. Mark rubbed lube on her rear hole and she took a slow, steadying breath.

"Pet, I want you to push back on this, like you're pushing it out of you. It'll open up your sphincter and it'll slide in. It will hurt a little while the largest part stretches you. I won't lie about that. But you can take it. It's not a lot bigger than your glass one."

He slid his finger inside her and moved it around. She punched the button on the car alarm. The stimulation up front helped with the stimulation in the rear. She felt a heat at her puckered entrance. Not a strong heat. Not burning, just warm. The plug was warmed up and Mark slowly started to slide it in.

She pushed. She tried. But she fought the plug, straining against the chains and squeezing the car alarm so hard she might crack it at any moment. Mark was slow, but relentless in his invasion. "There is nothing you can do about this, pet. This is my choice and it will happen. Just relax and accept it. That's all you can do. If you fight it, it will only hurt more."

Tears sprang to her eyes as the widest part of the plug stretched her wide. She bit down on the gag. Just when she thought she might actually be ripped apart, the plug was seated and her entrance closed up around the narrower base. Mark gave the ring on the end a few tugs.

He rubbed her back and ass. "That's a good girl. Just accept it. It's not your choice."

She finally relaxed and he stepped away. When he came back he set a kitchen timer down in front of her. "Now, we're going to play a game," he told her. She glared at him. He gave her a raised eyebrow and she had the good sense to look contrite.

"I'm going to set this timer for one hour. If you can come five times or more with that egg inside your cunt and that plug inside your ass, I will give you a very special present. And I promise you it is a present you will like. Understand?"

She nodded. A present? So far his presents had been things that she eventually liked, but not always right away. What would it be?

She didn't care. Mostly. If she had to be stuffed this full of toys, she might as well enjoy every moment of it. She pressed the button and Mark set the timer.

"Don't test me," he warned, "Or try to fake an orgasm to get my gift. I'll be able to tell when it's not real, especially with you, pet. This anal plug is considerably bigger than the others, it won't pop out when you come." He walked out of her line of sight.

Abby concentrated on the setting of the thing he'd called an egg. She started randomly pressing the buttons. Some were too high and were actually uncomfortable and a few were so low she could barely feel them. The vibration of the toy also vibrated the plug and together her entire pelvis was humming.

She closed her eyes and let herself go to the sensations. Forty minutes later she was only up to three. Mark came up behind her and leaned down. "Are you humping the table edge, pet?" She blushed and leaned her head away from him. "You are, aren't you? Horny little bitch. Must not be just your cunt that's greedy. That fucking clit of yours is a demanding little thing, isn't it?" He slid his hand between Abby and the table. "Where is she?" Mark whispered in her ear. "Where's that pink princess? Come out and play, itty bitty clitty." He spread her hood with his first and third finger, pressing his middle finger directly onto her nub. She squealed. "There she is." He pinched it lightly. Abby shuddered into her fourth orgasm.

She was drenched in sweat, hair plastered to her face. She'd long ago lost track of the timer or anything else. Mark pulled the egg out of her and she only groaned when he slid his cock in its place. He took hold of the anal plug, twisting it and nudging it back and forth in time with his thrusts. "Come on, pet. Just one more. Can you come on my cock? Come for me, pet. You're so fucking tight with that plug in your ass. I know you're feeling how big my cock is right now."

Abby tried, but she couldn't go over the edge one final time. She felt every pulse of Mark's orgasm though. And she clamped down, despite the massive intrusion, trying to hold him in.

As she rested her cheek on the cool kitchen table, the timer dinged.

"Poor pet. Didn't make it to five." He unbuckled the ball gag and took it off. He smoothed her matted hair out of her face. "It was a nice try, though," he told her. He took the car alarm out of her hand. She'd been unaware she was even still holding it. Then he unsnapped the chains at her wrists. They slid off the table and landed on the floor with a thump. He bent down and unchained her ankles. He lifted her up and carried her into the bathroom.

He laid her down in the empty tub and removed all the cuffs and the collar. He ran a hot bath for her. He ordered her to lean back, wet her hair, and he washed it for her. She closed her eyes and leaned into his touch. He bathed her by hand, rinsed her, and toweled her dry. He fastened the ankle cuffs, the wrist cuffs and finally the collar and carried her to the bedroom.

CHAPTER TWENTY

He laid her down gently and she settled into the mattress. It wasn't until she felt his weight next to her and his hands rolling her to her side that her eyes fluttered open. She felt the tug of the plug. "Push out," he told her. She did and squealed as the widest part of the plug moved past her muscle ring. He quickly pushed something else against her and she tried to move away. "No!" she cried. "No more! I can't! Stop!"

"Hush," he told her, holding her down on her stomach, placing his large hand on her back, and pushing the next plug inside her. This was one bigger impossibly bigger and Abby cried out.

"I hate this! I hate you!" she yelled once it was fully inside her.

"No, you don't," Mark told her, pulling her into his arms. "You're exhausted and you're angry with me. You don't hate me."

"Why do you need this?" she demanded.

"We both need it," he told her.

"Why?!"

"I need it because I need to own every part of a woman. I love the feeling I get when a woman trusts me enough to let me control her. It's sacred to me when she knows she's putting herself, her safety, her life in my hands and she knows I will do nothing but cherish and pamper her for it."

Abby choked back a sob. "How many?"

"What?"

"How many have there been? Before me? Or are there some you still see?"

As upset as she was, Mark's voice remained calm and soothing. "Like this? None. I've only ever played in clubs. Most women you meet at clubs won't go home with you, for safety issues. That and they're scared to be outed. Club play is only half-real though. There's always a bouncer or dungeon master or some mentor looking out for everyone. They know it's safe, that's why they only play there. I've never dominated a woman in my home. Ever."

"But you have...equipment. Hardware. Metal rings in floors."

"Because one day I wanted to meet a woman that would see the risks and accept them anyway, because she trusted me."

"But I didn't trust you! I texted my friend. I set up safety nets."

"I know. And that made me like you even more. No smart woman is going to automatically give up control to a total stranger when she first meets him. And I'm only interested in smart women. You set up safety nets; you felt me out; you tested the waters. And then you came to me of your own free will and did something I never thought I'd ever ask any woman to do, give me total control over her body, even if only temporarily.

"I love that you did this. I can't tell you how much it means to me. I don't want to live this 24/7, but the fact that you would do this for me, even on a limited basis, means more to me than I could probably ever tell you."

"Why are you like this?"

He shrugged. "Why are some people born with green eyes and others blue? I have no idea. My parents had a great marriage. My mother submitted to my father." He chuckled. "Although I'm fairly certain it never even remotely resembled this. But he loved her for it."

"You're looking for a woman like your mother?"

He laughed. "No. You are nothing like my mother. Trust me. I don't think she's ever said a foul word in her life and she sure as hell never let a man tell her to masturbate for him. I mean I guess you're both independent and intelligent, but beyond that you don't have much in common. And you don't look anything alike."

Abby snorted. "Well, that's good to know."

"I'm a regular perv. Not a perv perv," Mark told her.

She considered this. "I'm not any kind of perv. Or I wasn't before I met you. Now I don't know what I am."

"Tell me what your last lover was like," he asked.

"I don't know if that's such a good idea."

"Why not?"

"Because earlier I had some thoughts along those lines and I didn't very much like where those thoughts were headed. I don't want to think about those thoughts."

Mark considered this. "This would be earlier in the kitchen where if I'd returned five minutes later you'd have run outside naked just to get away from me?"

"I wasn't going to run. I was just..."

"Having second thoughts?" he asked.

"Yeah, but not about you."

"What then?"

She sighed. "My last lover was boring. With a capital B. Which I never thought about much before, because I don't think about sex much. Or, really I do think about sex, a lot, but I don't think about having it." She frowned. "That made no sense."

"It did to me. So he was boring."

She shrugged. "I thought so, but now I think maybe I was the boring one. Because the ones before that were kind of demanding. But not in the way that you're demanding. Demanding in ways I didn't like. I don't know. Fuck. I'm tired. I don't know what I'm saying."

"Say it anyway."

"They wanted things from me. Wanted me to do stuff to them. With them. Like Jeff's girlfriend jumped out of a cake and gave him a striptease for his birthday, why can't I be cool like that? *Because I am not Jeff's girlfriend!*"

Mark laughed. A rolling belly laugh that shook the whole bed. "Pet, it would be next to impossible for you to jump out of a cake and take your clothes off. You don't like people looking at you sexually and you sure as hell aren't comfortable being the center of attention in that way."

"They wanted me to do everything. Like take charge. I thought they were boring. Or lazy, but-" She paused. "Shit! They wanted me to be like you! Am I so screwed up that people can't tell if I'm a Domme or a sub?!"

"No," he said reassuringly. "Not anyone who knew what they were doing. It was pretty obvious, though, that you were one or the other, at least to some degree. You're way too in control of everything. Very confident, very calculating. But a lot of type A people are Dominant in public and submissive in the bedroom. It didn't take more than a few minutes alone with you to figure out which side of the fence you were on."

She thought about this. "It was the hair thing, wasn't it?" she asked, remembering when he'd grabbed her hair on their first night together and asked her if she was ready to get fucked.

He chuckled. "Yep. Pretty tried and true method. Dominant partners will give it right back when their partners get aggressive. Subs will either submit or be confused by their reaction to it. Submissive people, though, don't always actually submit. Some are afraid of it and push it down where they never have to admit what they want. And a lot of Dominant people never raise a hand to spank anyone in their lifetime. Just because someone's a D-type or an s-type doesn't automatically mean they'll be open to exploring that.

"You have a lot of hangups," he told her. " 'Anal is dirty'. 'Don't look at me naked'. And some weird feminism thing that even you don't understand."

She scoffed. "It's not weird!"

"Pet, your philosophy, as I'm able to understand it, seems to be that a woman shouldn't submit to man, even if it's what she really wants. So according to you, there's something women shouldn't be allowed to do because they're female. Which would be just about the polar opposite of feminism. You hide behind labels so you don't have to deal with your sexuality. 'Slut', 'Good Girl,' these are important to you, I'm trying to figure out why." He nuzzled her ear. "I'm also trying to teach you that my version of a good girl likes to get fucked."

Heat pooled in her belly at his words and the liquid dark timbre in which he'd spoken them. She squeezed her thighs together. He kissed her, tongue sliding in and out of her mouth. One hand trailed down her back, drifting down, down, down until it found the plug and jiggled it a little.

She moaned.

"Only one or two more sizes to go, pet, until you're ready for me."

His other hand slid down her belly and his fingers played in her growing wetness. "Mmm. So fucking wet." He took her mouth again with his own. When her lips were swollen with kisses he pulled away and grazed his mouth over her bare shoulder. "Do I hurt you, pet? Beyond what you can bear?"

"No," she admitted. "I always think I can't take it, but I do. And-" she stopped.

"And?" he prompted.

"Sometimes I like it," she admitted.

"I know. That's why we do it. If you preferred being in the tub covered in cotton candy and whipped cream while I ate it all off of you, we'd do that instead. I like it when you discover something new about yourself. I love it when you accept it and let go enough to enjoy whatever that might be without being worried if you're a 'slut' or a 'good girl'. In exchange for giving you pleasure, I ask that you be available for my use whenever and however hard I might want to use you.

“I'll also display you for my viewing pleasure whenever and however I choose. My goal is that you choose to serve me in that way without being self-conscious about it, no matter where we are. Men are visual creatures and I love looking at beautiful women. Speaking of that, I think it's time for your present."

She turned to look at him. "But...I didn't...."

He smiled. "You almost made it. Four out of five wasn't bad and, pet, the sight of you humping that table, desperate to get off, was so fucking hot that deserves a reward all on its own." She blushed. "I love it when you accept what's happening to you and let loose." He threaded his hands through her hair and drew her gaze up to his. "You have no choice in this pet. I will stick things in you. Whatever pleases me at the time. You might as well just enjoy it. And because you did enjoy it, I will give you part of your present. But not all of it. Not yet. Come on. Up, now."

She got out of bed and he clipped the leash on the collar. She got on all fours and they headed to the bathroom. Mark took the chair from the corner, sat her in it and proceeded to brush her hair out until it was almost dry. Then he opened the linen closet and took out a bag, setting it on the counter. "Put your hair up and get pretty for me, pet. It's almost lunchtime. I'll be back in a few minutes."

He left and Abby got up out of the chair and walked over to the sink. The bag was a Nordstrom's bag and when she opened it she discovered a nearly fully stocked Chanel makeup set. Her mouth dropped open. There were foundation powders in three different shades, all appropriate for her skin tone, several eyeshadow compacts in varying hues, pencil liners. She was shocked. There were also several gently curved large hair clips in different color and patterns so she could comply with his request.

She picked up the brush, swept her hair off her neck, and secured it with one of them. Then she sparingly applied some foundation powder and light eyeshadow because it was only afternoon. She lined her eyes with a light brown pencil and stepped back to examine herself in Mark's large bathroom mirror.

She was completely nude. No collar, no cuffs and she was fascinated by her own appearance. She realized she'd never actually spent that much time just looking at herself. Quick checks in bathroom mirrors and department store changing rooms just to make sure her mascara wasn't smudged or the skirt she was buying fit properly were about the sum total of the time Abby spent examining herself.

Her breasts were on the larger side, but her areolas weren't that big. Her nipples were taut little nubs, not too big, not too small. She wasn't the pixie of magazines and ads, but Mark seemed to love her breasts. She ran a hand across her flat tummy. Spending hours underneath cars was definitely better than any crunches she might do at a gym. Her hips were rounded, but she thought about the way Mark liked to hang onto them when he was fucking her.

Abby talked a good game about stick figures and Marilyn Monroe being a size 14, but the truth was she was a little self-conscious, wasn't she? She knew her hourglass figure narrowed the pool of men who would be interested in her, but she couldn't do anything about the breasts without surgery and the hips just seemed to come right along with them. She was a size 12 and probably always would be.

Mark liked the way she looked, though. He was constantly touching her. Running a hand along her hip, cupping a breast, patting her ass, or spanking it. Displayed for his viewing pleasure. Like the dining room table last night. He'd opened up her most intimate parts and looked at them while he ate dinner! And it had felt at first strange and uncomfortable, but the way he kept running his hands on her calves and thighs and tummy had been nice.

Her hand went to her throat and she lightly rubbed the skin there. It felt different without the collar. She'd had it on non-stop since she'd first arrived and she could now feel its absence if she closed her eyes. Mark entered the bathroom and came up behind her. She started to turn but he slipped an arm around her grasping a breast in his hand. He pinched her nipple.

"You look beautiful, pet." his hand slid up to her throat and he wrapped his hand around it, but he didn't squeeze. "Missing your collar?"

She swallowed, increasing the pressure of his hand on her. "Yes, Sir."

He took her earlobe in his mouth and nipped it. "Such a good girl." With his other hand he produced the collar and fastened it snugly around her neck. He attached the leash. "Come, pet. Time for your present."

Confused, she knelt down on the floor. The makeup had been an extravagant gift. It must have cost a small fortune. She followed him down the hall into the bedroom. He unsnapped the leash and took a seat on the chair in the corner.

"Dress for me, pet."

She stood up and looked around the room, her eyes landing on the bed. Laid out on the comforter were a pair of black stockings with lace holdups, a matching lace garter belt, and a beautiful matching bra. She knew they were good quality and very expensive, judging by the metal hooks on the garter belt. The only thing missing were panties.

"Oh, Mark," she said turning to him.

He raised an eyebrow. "Excuse me?"

She licked her lips. "Sir. Sir, this is- this is too much. I can't-"

"Don't disrespect me in my own home, pet." He stood up. "Bend over and put your hands on the bed." She gaped at him. "Now," he ordered.

She was momentarily stunned and placed her hands on the mattress. "Bend over more," he said. "Show me that plug of yours."

She leaned down to her elbows, sticking her ass in the air. He came up behind her and delivered a resounding smack. She jumped. "Do you tell me what to do, pet?" he asked.

"N-no. No, Sir." Another smack on her other cheek.

"Do you make the decisions in this part of our relationship?"

She shook her head. "No, Sir. But-"

He smacked her again. This time harder. "The only butt is yours, pet, and it's going to be nicely pink and displaying my handprints now that you insist on arguing with me."

True to his word, Mark spanked her ass mercilessly as she tightened her fists in the comforter and struggled not to cry out in protest. Occasionally he paused to tug at the plug, twisting it and nudging it deeper into her as his other hand rubbed her pussy. When he was finished, she was panting hard.

"You're a mess," he told her. "Pussy juice running everywhere. Spread your legs, pet. You need to be cleaned up before you get dressed."

She moved her feet apart. "Wider," Mark demanded. When she complied, he knelt down behind her and slowly started licking her juices off her inner thigh. She gasped and surged forward. "Don't you move during your cleaning, pet. Understand me? The only time you move is to fuck my face to orgasm. Understand?" She tried to process his demand. Fuck his face? He pinched her clit and she cried out. "Pay attention, pet. I asked you a question."

"Yes! Yes, Sir."

"Good girl." He set about licking her thighs thoroughly. By the time he reached her pussy, she spread her legs even wider, giving him complete access to her. "Good girl," she heard him murmur against her skin. He spread her labia with his thumbs and licked inside her. She swiveled her hips, trying to take him deeper. He laid one arm across the front of her thighs and pulled her against his lips. With the other hand, he tugged and twisted the plug.

He was teasing her with short little licks, pulling back after each one causing her to move back, trying to prolong the sensation. The warring sensations of being filled by the plug in the rear but being left empty in front left her frustrated. She finally growled in irritation and shoved herself backward, grinding into his mouth.

He released her thighs and pinched her clit. He shoved on the plug, and pushed his tongue as deep into her cunt as it would go. She shuddered in orgasm. He was kind enough to wait until she finished coming before licking her pussy clean.

Mark got to his feet and gave her ass a final light slap. "My pet sure does love to be clean."

"Yes, Sir," Abby replied, feeling light headed.

"Well, get dressed. We don't have much time."

She got to her feet and sat down on the edge of the bed. Her ass tingled against the fabric from her spanking. Mark watched with interest as she rolled on first one stocking then the other. She stood up, fastened the garter belt in the back and fixed the clasps to the lace edging of the thigh high stockings. She put on the matching bra, perfect and in her size.

"You can get the panties if you can show me some respect for the rest of the day," he told her.

She met his gaze. "I'm sorry, Sir. It's just such a nice gift. No one's ever given me something so expensive before."

He scowled. "I assume someone's given you a gift before, pet. And you know it's only polite to be grateful. It's not your concern where the gift comes from or how much it costs. Only that I took the time and effort to pick it out for you."

"You picked it out?" she asked, surprised. "Like you went to a store and bought this for me?" She couldn't believe it.

He grinned at her. "Yes, pet. Slick and I went to that little dress and panty store she and likes so much and I had them made for you. Slick was sworn to secrecy so it would be a surprise. She helped with the makeup, too."

She smiled and bit her lip. "I can't picture you in that store. Surrounded by panties."

He squeezed her shoulder. "There is nothing I won't do to make you happy, pet."

"Sir?"

He raised an eyebrow and she looked up at him. She licked her lips nervously. "Can- may I suck you?"

He grinned. "So you really are grateful for your gifts."

"Yes, Sir."

Mark unzipped his fly and took out his hard cock. "Come here, good girl," he crooned, taking hold of the back of her neck and pulling her down. "Get your pretty mouth on my cock."

Abby knelt and took him in her mouth. She swirled the tip like he'd showed her and suckled greedily on the head. When pre-cum weeped out of the tiny slit, she devoured it. It tasted better than the actual cum, even though at this point, the cum wasn't all that bad as long as it was still warm.

"You forgot something at breakfast, pet, but I didn't punish you for it. Show me how much you want to avoid punishment this time."

She paused, released his shaft, and lifted it up, taking one of his balls into her mouth. "Such a good girl. I know you didn't forget on purpose. Love every part of me the way I love every part of you."

She licked and laved and sucked and rubbed her face in his crotch enthusiastically. "That's my good girl. Now, wrap your lips around my cock. Suck all my seed out. Take it in your tummy."

She took a deep breath and slid the cock into her mouth. She worked his shaft with her lips and tongue until he took hold of her head with his hands. "Here it comes, pet. Don't waste a drop."

Abby remained calm like he'd showed her and swallowed in time with the pumping jets of semen filling her mouth.

He pulled out and she struggled to catch her breath. "Let me see," he told her, lifting her chin. He inspected her lips and face. "Got it all. What a good little pet you are." She smiled.

CHAPTER TWENTY-ONE

Mark led her to the kitchen and directed her to stand. He unclipped the leash and handed her a knife. "Slice the tomatoes, please, pet. Surely you can't mess that up." His eyes twinkled as he teased her.

She scowled at him, took the knife, and began slicing. He handed her a red onion, black olives, a few hard boiled eggs. By the end she considered herself to be an excellent slicer. Mark mixed salad greens in a large bowl and tossed in the veggies. He pulled some potato salad out of a bowl in the fridge and set it on the counter. He made two plates, piled high with the nicoise salad and the potatoes.

Tidying up the area, he lifted his chin at her. "Come pet," he said, not bothering to put on her leash. But he didn't take their food. He led her out into the living area, picked up a large square pillow from the couch and set it on the floor next to the coffee table. "Kneel on that, pet." She made her way over to it and knelt. He retrieved a bag by the couch and set it down on the table. She glanced at it, but tried not to look like she was curious.

"I need to talk to you about respect, pet." Her heart sunk. She'd apologized for the gift debacle. "No, no," he said, catching her gaze. "I'm talking about in general. When you're wearing that collar you're representing me and all the things I've taught you. Your attitude needs to reflect your respect for me. No matter what. Understood?

"Now, you're in training and I know so much of this is new to you and a little daunting, so I'm going to help you out as best I can." He produced her ball gag. "There are rules, little pet, to this thing that we do. Rules I don't make you play by because I don't really care about them myself and some of them are contrary to what I personally want and believe.

"One of these rules is eye contact. Most Doms don't allow their subs to look them in the eye. It reinforces their dominance over the sub. But I prefer it. I need it. Especially since you spend so much of our time together on speech restriction. I can see everything about you in those expressive little eyes of yours and, for better or worse, so can everyone else. Open."

He fastened the gag. "So rule number one is this: If you are unfamiliar with a person or in an unfamiliar environment and you are wearing my collar, you will only make eye contact with me and me alone."

Abby felt the blood drain out of her face and suddenly her heart beat a rapid tattoo inside her chest. She looked down at herself. She was nearly naked, not wearing panties. Also, she and Mark had just made lunch, so whatever he meant about an unfamiliar environment, it was clear to her he had no intention of taking her out of the house today. So that meant only one thing.

Her eyes widened and she shook her head violently, straining to speak even though she was gagged.

Mark grabbed the o-ring on the collar and shook it a little to break her panic snap. He raised a finger and put it in her face. "Respect. You will show it. You've given yourself to me and that's the last word on the subject. I know what you want. I know what you need. And I am well aware of your hard limits, pet. Trust me to respect them even though I don't have to this weekend."

He released her collar, stood up, and pulled a riding crop out of the bag. He swung it. It landed hard on his own thigh with a crack that made her nearly jump out of her skin. "This is what's waiting for you if you do not do exactly as you're told. You will respond to all commands quickly and to the best of your ability, with no sass. None. I've gagged you for your benefit because that little mouth of yours sometimes shoots first and asks questions later, but sass won't be tolerated. Give me a nod if you understand."

Tears stung her eyes. She was struggling to keep it together. Why? Why would he do this? He *knew* she would hate it. The thought of another man's hands on her made her shudder. She couldn't do it. She wouldn't. *Oh, god,* she thought as fear gripped her. Would they hurt her? Would a stranger cum in her?

The tears she'd been fighting flowed freely and she begged him with her eyes. His face softened and he laid the crop on the table. He knelt in front of her and took her hands in his. "I know. I know everything that you're thinking, pet. I know everything you're afraid of. You have got to learn to trust me."

He released one of her hands and put his palm over her heart, spreading his fingers wide. "Some Doms think the only way to truly own a sub is to share them with others, that you can't own something unless it's yours to give away." She sucked in a sharp breath. "I don't believe that, pet. As long as you're with me, no other man will ever touch you in any way. You're a treasure, pet, *my* treasure, and only mine."

He wiped her tears and stood up. "Now. Remember what I said. Rules and respect. Make me proud, and I will give you another, better, present."

It was only a few minutes later that the doorbell rang. Abby felt dread in the pit of her stomach. Mark answered the door and if Abby's imagination hadn't sufficiently upset her enough, it kicked into overdrive as a tall, svelte, blonde woman walked into the house. She was wearing a short sleeved pink silk blouse, a long black skirt, and high heels.

Mark kissed her. Kissed her! On the cheek but still. Abby's fear turned to loathing. As Mark gestured for the woman to enter the living room, the blonde's steps faltered a bit as she spotted Abby kneeling on the pillow next to the couch.

"Well, now," she said, smiling. "Isn't this a surprise?"

"Sabrina, this is my pet."

Sabrina assessed Abby with shrewd eyes. Abby met the woman's calculated gaze. "Pet!" Mark admonished. "Eyes down." Abby lowered her head, but not before taking in the full measure of the woman's beauty.

Sabrina declared, "She's breathtaking. Even with her obvious lack of training."

"I agree. Have a seat."

Sabrina thanked him and took a seat on the couch nearest Abby. Mark offered her a glass of wine.

"Pet," he said when Sabrina accepted. "I left a bottle and two glasses on the kitchen counter. Fill them both and bring them here." Abby flinched at the request. Mark's hard gaze bored into her and she got up off the floor, rather ungracefully she thought to her own chagrin as she was certain Sabrina the middle-aged bitch never did anything that lacked the grace and poise of an Old Hollywood Starlet.

As Abby passed in front of them, Sabrina said, "Now I know who the plugs were for. Very nice. And I can see she's already been punished today. I can just make out a handprint."

"She's got two more to plugs to go before she's ready, but she's doing well," Mark replied.

Abby's face burned. They were looking at her ass and talking about it. She stomped into the kitchen and spied the wine that she had thought was for her. If the kitchen hadn't been in full view of the living room, she'd have taken that ball gag off and spit in the glasses.

She half considered just taking the damn thing off and heading out the door. But Mark would never let her leave. He'd catch her and whip her with that crop of his. As she poured the wine, she glared out at the two of them talking in hushed tones.

Was Sabrina a sub? She hadn't called Mark 'Sir,' so she obviously wasn't his sub right now, but had she been? No, she couldn't be a sub, Abby realized, because she wasn't allowed to make eye contact with the bitch. The bitch was a Domme. She felt a little better about that. She wasn't any sort of competition, not that such a thing was possible anyway with Sabrina's classic good looks and slender figure. There was no way Abby could compete with her.

She brought the drinks out to the living room and handed them each a glass, careful to keep her eyes from meeting Sabrina's. Abby looked, instead, at the floor. The bitch had killer shoes. The kind Abby saved for six months to buy when she was still in school. Mark thanked Abby while Sabrina pretty much ignored her presence. Abby went back and knelt on the pillow. She kept her knees closed tightly together, not wanting to expose any more to Sabrina that she already had.

In the middle of his conversation, Mark said, "Pet, why are you hiding your cunt from me?"

Abby's head snapped up and she stared at Mark. Her eyes involuntarily slid to Sabrina, who only raised a perfectly arched brow at her.

"Pet, that's two rules broken," he informed her. "You hid your cunt from me and you made eye contact with someone who hasn't given you that permission. Stand up."

Abby's heart thudded and her eyes darted to the crop.

"If you take longer, it'll be harder on you," he warned.

She got up.

"Come here," he demanded. He got up, gripped her wrist, and turned her around. "Bend over. Hands on the table."

Abby hesitated, then realized that hesitation would cost her even more so she bent down quickly. She watched Mark slide the crop out from beneath her. She tensed as she waited.

"Unclench, pet," Mark told her. She took a deep breath and relaxed. The crop hit her right ass cheek hard. She yelped. "That's one for eye contact." The crop whistled through the air again, striking the other cheek. She bit down hard on the gag. "That's another for hiding yourself. Now you can stay in this position so we might better admire you."

From behind her Abby heard Sabrina exclaim, "Oh, Mark. Her skin!"

"It pinks up nicely, doesn't it?" he replied.

"Have you caned her? That pale skin would show off the stripes exquisitely."

Abby tensed. Caning? Mark said that was the worst of the punishments he doled out. Would they do that now?

"Not yet, but believe me there've been times I've wanted to."

They both laughed.

"Is she a slut?" Sabrina asked.

Abby bit down on her ball gag and suppressed a growl.

"No," Mark responded. "She likes the usual. Nipples, clit, and spankings, but she's not heavily into pain."

"Pity," said Sabrina. "Victor would have loved to borrow her. A painslut with pale skin that marks like that? After her training, of course. She'd never spend a minute out of his cage the way she is now. She's perfectly suited to you though."

"Perfectly," Mark agreed.

"Are you planning-?" Sabrina started.

"We're a long way off," Mark said curtly, cutting her off.

Abby turned her head to try and look at them. A long way off from what? Caning? Being a painslut? She shuddered. She'd never be that. Mark said he knew that. So what then? A...slave? Mark said he didn't want that either. But what if he did? What if he just didn't want to scare her by telling her that in the beginning?

"Eyes front, pet," Mark ordered.

"I understand completely," said Sabrina. "All things in time."

Mark invited Sabrina to join him for lunch. *My lunch*, Abby thought angrily. And she was ordered to serve them both. The nerve! Abby tossed the plates unceremoniously onto the table in front of each of them, getting more and more angry by the second.

Sabrina gave Mark a look. He grinned at his lunch companion. "All things in time," Mark repeated.

Sabrina smiled back beatifically. "Indeed."

"She's a sexual submissive," Mark declared, as he pulled Abby down to the floor by her collar. "Domestic service will never be her strong suit."

Abby looked in Mark's eyes. Despite his outward calm, even jovial tone, his eyes told her he was furious with her. She looked away. It was his fault for bringing this woman here and parading Abby in front of her like a show dog.

Mark and Sabrina ate their lunches and discussed people and things Abby neither knew, nor cared too much about. She got that they knew each other from a club in Sioux Falls and that Sabrina had several subs. At the mention of a favored female of Sabrina's, Abby looked up for a moment, curious. Female? So she had a relationship like Abby and Mark had... but with other women?

Sabrina caught her looking and Abby flushed scarlet and looked away.

"Mark?" said Sabrina abruptly. Abby's stomach twisted. Sabrina was going to bust her for eye contact again. "May I have a glass of water?"

"Absolutely. Pet, ice water for our guest."

Abby careened out of the dining room and made a beeline for the kitchen, desperate to get away from Madam X and her canes. She returned with the glass of ice water, not spit in, even though from the separate dining room no one had been able to see her. She set it down as politely, respectfully, as possible in front of the Domme, trying to buy some goodwill over the eye contact blunder. She returned to Mark and knelt down beside him, keeping her eyes to the floor.

When they finished, Abby cleared the plates, respectfully, and set them in the sink, respectfully, and joined them in the living room. She knelt down on her pillow, respectfully. She'd pretty much do anything to avoid a caning.

"Shall we start?" Sabrina asked Mark.

Mark nodded and Abby froze. Sabrina had told. And she was going to be punished. She pleaded with Mark, trying to make him understand that she hadn't meant to offend that time, she'd just been so surprised. He barely spared Abby a glance as he got up. "I'll get your things," he told Sabrina.

"Thank you," the genteel woman replied.

When Mark was gone, Abby gritted her teeth against the gag telling herself that appealing to the mercy of the woman beside her would do more harm than good.

The woman's quiet voice shattered the silence. "Maybe if you play nicely, you'll avoid the bite of my cane, little pet."

Abby flinched and almost looked up. Almost. Mark reentered the room carrying a large purse that obviously belonged to Sabrina. He handed it to her. Sabrina stood up and rummaged through it. Abby began to breathe heavily. She couldn't a fit a cane in that bag, could she? What else had she brought? Some medieval torture device, Abby knew. She was going to suffer for that breach of the rules. She nearly collapsed in relief when the woman brought a small notebook and a pencil.

She handed them to Mark. "Would you be a dear?"

"Absolutely," he said taking them from her. Sabrina rummaged through the bag again and came up with something small that fit in her hand.

"Stand up, little pet," Sabrina said. "Let's have a look at you."

Abby got to her feet and took a few steps toward Sabrina. Mark settled himself onto the couch.

"Offer her your wrist, pet," Mark ordered. Abby glanced at him, but he was opening the small notebook.

Abby held her arm out and envisioned a nun with a ruler slapping it. Instead, Sabrina took the cloth tape measure in her hand and encircled Abby's wrist with it. Not knowing what was happening or what to do, Abby stood perfectly still, keeping her gaze locked on the measure. Sabrina gave the measurement to Mark, who wrote it down. She gestured for the other wrist, which Abby gave freely, and measured it as well.

"Put your foot on the chair," Sabrina told Abby. Abby looked at the chair confused. Sabrina put her hands on her hips. "I know you don't expect me to bend over for you, little pet. Doms never place themselves lower than the subs."

Getting it, Abby quickly moved to the chair and put one foot on the cushion. Sabrina measured her ankle. Abby would have thought the woman was measuring her for cuffs except she then ran the tape around Abby's thigh. Weird. When her other ankle and thigh were measured, Sabrina ordered Abby to turn around and she took off the play collar. She measured Abby's neck. Then replaced the collar.

"Turn around," she told Abby. Abby complied. "Take your bra off." At this Abby hesitated for a second, but then remembered that lingerie makers preferred to measure that way. She reached behind herself and unfastened the garment. Sabrina took it and laid it gently over the arm of the chair. Instead of measuring Abby though, she reached out with both hands and cupped Abby's breasts.

Abby gasped and tried to step back. "Don't be childish," Sabrina said in a clipped, harsh tone that made Abby freeze. At odds with her frosty tone, Sabrina's hands were gentle and warm, slowly massaging Abby's breasts and then pinching her nipples until they hardened.

"She responds well," Sabrina told Mark.

"Very well. I'm very pleased with her."

"Decorative jewelry is nice for long sessions, but these could take piercing well," Sabrina said, rolling Abby's nipples between her fingers. "I'd go horizontal, not vertical. For weights."

Abby's eyebrows knitted together in confusion. Horizontal? Vertical? Weights? What?

Seeing her puzzlement, Sabrina released her and slowly unbuttoned her own blouse. She laid it over the arm chair. She had a beautiful white lace bra on underneath which she started to unclasp. Abby didn't know what to do. When Sabrina slid the bra down her arms she revealed that her own nipples were pierced.

"Touch the piercings," she ordered.

Abby looked at Mark. For one thing, she was relieved that Mark was not looking at Sabrina. In fact his casualness about the whole thing was at odds with the fact that a topless woman was in the fucking living room! Instead Mark was looking at Abby. Expectantly.

She turned back to Sabrina. "Go on," Sabrina demanded. "They don't hurt me. They certainly won't hurt *you*. Touch them." Abby tentatively reached out with one hand and touched the silver ball on top of the small bar.

"These are vertical," the woman informed her. "I prefer my subs to be pierced horizontally."

Abby's hand jerked back and her heart thudded as she stole a glance at Mark. "He may pierce you," Sabrina told her. "He may not. We're just discussing what's possible." She reached out and took hold of Abby's breasts again. "These are lovely," she told Mark, squeezing gently. "She'd need a decent size gauge to show them off, if you were so inclined." She released Abby and said, "On your knees, little pet."

Abby knelt, feeling a little dizzy from the turn of events. The Domme lifted the front of her long skirt, slowly revealing her shapely legs. She revealed her bare pussy to Abby, who, on her knees, was looking directly at it. There was a silver ring the size of Abby's thumb at the top.

"This is a horizontal," Sabrina explained. "Some women can't get their hoods pierced because they don't have enough skin. Touch it."

Abby looked helplessly at Mark, who again had nothing to say on the subject. She slowly reached out and fingered the little circle. Sabrina moaned approvingly. "If done right," she continued, "it enhances sensitivity. Nipples, too."

Abby had to admit she was a little fascinated. She'd never, ever seen anyone with body piercings. It looked like it hurt, but when she touched it, Sabrina seemed to enjoy it.

"Lie down on the table, pet," Mark told her.

She could only look at him. He stood up, gently took her arm and positioned her with her ass on the edge of the table. He laid her back until she was resting on the surface. "Spread your legs," he told her.

Abby hesitated, but slowly spread her feet and thighs apart.

Sabrina took a pillow from the couch and deposited it on the floor between Abby's legs. She knelt this time, in front of Abby and Abby sucked in a breath as she felt the woman's hands on her mound.

Sabrina spread Abby open. She whimpered and Mark said, "Shh, it's alright, pet."

Sabrina inspected Abby's cleft. "Well, she's got a beautiful full hood," the older woman declared. Abby gasped as she felt a finger prodding her nub. She wiggled her hips in response as Sabrina pushed her finger. "A piercing would look absolutely gorgeous on a girl like this."

Sabrina took hold of one of Abby's labia, pinching and pulling it. Abby made a noise low in her throat. "If she were mine, I'd pierce these, too," Sabrina said. "Use them to open her up." As if demonstrating, Sabrina spread Abby's labia wide and dipped a finger into her. Abby groaned behind the gag.

"So responsive," said Sabrina admiringly as she spread Abby's juice onto her clit. "A piercing would have her coming constantly just by walking around."

Sabrina shoved a finger inside Abby and curled it. Abby bucked her hips off the table. Sabrina got up, still fingering Abby and moved to the side of the table. She knelt down again and took Abby's nipple between her teeth and bit gently. Abby shrieked, but her pussy tightened up on Sabrina's finger.

"I see what you mean about just a little pain. She certainly doesn't need much."

"No." Mark replied and knelt between Abby's knees and gripped the plug, half pulling it out and shoving it back in while Sabrina licked Abby's nipple and teased her clit between two fingers.

Abby felt the incredible fullness of the plug which steadily built as Mark pulled it a little further out then then slammed it back in. She arched her back up off the table. The third time, the plug came all the way out, stretching Abby wide until she was crying behind the gag. She was tortured between Sabrina's sweet frigging and Mark's painful extraction. Her body was at war with itself.

Mark immediately replaced the plug with the head of another. She tried to cry out in protest behind the gag. She knew this one would be bigger, more painful. She tried to move her legs, but Mark slapped her thigh with his free hand, stinging her. He seated the plug despite her tears and Sabrina fingerfucked her mercilessly to orgasm through the pain.

As she lay panting, nostrils flaring, Sabrina stood up. "Entertaining," she declared. "You should thank your Dom, when you can, for allowing you to come during your training. Speaking of coming, I was rather...intrigued...by your little display, pet. Mark?"

"Yes, Sabrina?"

"Can your little pet service me?"

"As you wish."

Abby watched in equal parts shock and fascination as Sabrina hiked up her skirt again and straddled Abby's chest. She watched, like a small animal hypnotized by a large snake, as the topless woman licked her own fingers. "Mmmmm. You taste every bit as good as you look, little pet. Would you like to know how I taste?"

Abby could scarcely breathe. Taste? No, she couldn't do that. She didn't even know this woman. Mark knew her, sure, but still....she shook her head no. Sabrina sighed. "Disappointing. I thought you'd appreciate something in your mouth other than that ball gag." She pressed her skirt to her belly. "Touch me."

Abby couldn't move. Couldn't do anything. The woman's bare pussy was just a mere foot away from her face. "I touched you, little pet. You could at least do the same."

Abby brought her hand up, but was unsure what to do. Everything was weird. In reverse. She'd only ever touched herself. Personally she liked to stick two fingers in her pussy and pinch her clit with her thumb and forefinger. But that wasn't an option here because her hand was upside down. It was a puzzle she couldn't solve.

Her eyebrows knitted in confusion.

"Pet?" Mark asked.

"It's alright, Mark," Sabrina assured him. "Listen to me, little pet. Rub your finger along my slit."

Abby extended her index finger and gently traced the woman's seam. Sabrina rocked her hips in encouragement. "Now, part my lips and feel around to see if I'm wet enough."

Abby's finger slid in between the labia. It was hot. Like temperature hot. Sabrina was very warm. Abby supposed she knew that on a superficial level having felt herself, but touching someone else made her more aware of it. Sabrina was wet, too. It was a slippery slickness that she gathered on her fingers and rubbed them together. It felt exactly like her own. She rubbed two fingers into Sabrina's inner labia.

"One finger first," Sabrina instructed. "Like I did for you."

Abby inserted her index finger. Sabrina made a noise of contentment. Abby curled her finger. She couldn't do that to herself and so it had never occurred to her to do so. But Sabrina had done to her and it had felt amazing, so that must be the right thing to do. Sabrina moaned.

"Your little pet's a fast learner."

Abby looked at Mark but his expression was unreadable. She couldn't tell if he was happy with what she was doing or pissed. Was she cheating? She didn't think so. Mark had invited this woman and then she asked him if she could use Abby. He'd said okay.

"Put your thumb on my clit," Sabrina commanded, knocking Abby out of her reverie. She pushed her thumb into Sabrina's clit, tucking it under the silver ring. Sabrina rocked harder. "Stick another finger in my cunt."

Abby pushed her middle finger in and felt Sabrina tighten in response then relax. Christ, but the woman had good muscle control. Abby watched intently, then for some reason slid in her ring finger as well.

"Cheeky bitch," Sabrina said, but she was grinning down at Abby.

It was then that Abby let go. She reached up with her other hand and flicked the silver ring with her finger. Sabrina thrust her hips forward. Abby was amazed. Seeing this no-nonsense ballbuster lose control was interesting to say the least. She began rhythmically tapping the piercing in time with her fingerfucking. She felt Sabrina's insides tense up as she came.

When the Domme recovered, Mark helped her off the table and she set her skirt to rights, then putting on her bra and blouse. She smoothed back her shoulder length hair and suddenly no one looking at her would know she had two nipple piercings, a pierced clit hood, and had just ordered a gagged sub to bring her to orgasm. She could have been any other business woman out for a lunch break.

Mark walked her to the door, leaving Abby on the table. Abby closed her eyes and spent a minute trying to process everything that had happened this afternoon.

CHAPTER TWENTY-TWO

What the hell had that been? Especially that part at the end where she really, really wanted to get Sabrina off in a huge way? That was...unexpected. She heard the door shut and knew Mark had returned. She opened her eyes and he sat her up. Her bottom stung a little from the insertion of the bigger plug. He unfastened her gag and she worked her jaw up and down, stretching the muscles.

"Are you alright?" Mark asked.

She looked up at him. "I don't know," she answered honestly. "Are you?"

He frowned at her. "What do you mean?"

She rubbed her hands on her thighs. "Um. I don't know. Are you mad?"

"About what?"

"I- I don't- I mean...was that...cheating? Because you said she could do it. And I didn't know, and I didn't want to make anyone mad, and I didn't know if I was allowed to say no, and-"

"Stop," he ordered and sat down on the couch. "Pet, come here."

She got up and stepped toward him. He pulled her into his lap. "Did you like it or not?" he asked.

Abby hesitated. She had no idea how to answer that. Would she have done it if she was out to lunch and a blonde sexbomb cornered her in the bathroom and said, "Kneel before me and fingerfuck me?" Probably not.

"Pet, stop thinking so much and tell me exactly what's in your head right now."

"I can't tell if I liked it," she said quickly. "I didn't feel ....that thing that I feel when you make me do stuff."

"What thing?"

"Like, I don't know. Like there's this thing in my stomach that flip flops every time you tell me to do something."

"You get excited."

"Yeah, but that's such a....mundane word for it. It feels like more than just that. Because I've been excited before. I mean I've had orgasms. It's not just being horny."

He considered this, then nodded. "Okay. I don't get a thrill from submitting because I'm not a sub, but I do get one when my submissive does what I ask her to do, so I think I understand. You didn't feel any particular way about being dominated by Sabrina."

"No. But I liked...what we did. I mean she's pretty. Beautiful even. I haven't seen that many gorgeous women close up like that." She paused. "Poor choice of words." Mark chuckled. "It was, I don't know, new and different and interesting and exciting, just not in any of the ways that being with you is new and different and interesting and exciting. But I was kind of worried that you were mad. Because I couldn't tell what you were thinking. You didn't order me to do what she asked. You just...stepped aside almost and I didn't know if you were pissed at me and just didn't want to make a thing out of it in front of her."

Mark shook his head. "She saw you looking at her when she mentioned her subs are female," he told her. Abby stiffened. "Relax, pet. No punishment. I promise. She said you didn't seem rude. You seemed...curious. And then embarrassed because she caught you being curious. She asked me if you'd been with other women."

Abby blushed and looked away. "I- no. Not really."

"But you've done something with another woman," he surmised. "Or fantasized about them."

"Just- just one really. In college, I had this friend. We got drunk and kissed at a party. I'd always thought she was pretty. It was nice. But she had a boyfriend and I don't even really know if it could have been anything anyway. I mean women are okay. Sometimes some women click for me while most of them don't. But I prefer men, so it wasn't worth pursuing. Are you mad? It's not like I've dated women or anything. It just happens sometimes that I'm attracted to one. You were so distant..."

"I'm not mad, pet. She asked me if she could explore your curiosity and I told her she could. She's a lesbian and an experienced Domme. She knows homosexuality can be a hot-button issue for some people. That's why I didn't do or say anything to stop it or encourage it. I didn't want you to feel like you had to do anything you weren't comfortable doing just to please me and I didn't want to stop you if you were interested in seeing where it led. I'm not mad as long as you don't want to switch teams on me."

She laughed. "No, I don't."

"And as for the cheating, I was there and I was watching, so no, it's not cheating. But, pet, if you think you want to see if it leads anywhere, then you come to me and we'll discuss it. Anything you do away from me that I don't know about, whether it's with a man or a woman, is cheating and I won't tolerate it. And I don't mean that as in I'll get the cane. I mean it's over. Period. BDSM is so far down the rabbit hole, trust-wise, that one serious fuckup is usually all it takes to break a relationship permanently. Lies can't be tolerated. I would never cheat on you and expect the same amount of respect."

She nodded. She could see exactly what he meant. This required so much more trust than anything she'd ever done before. It was exhilarating, but terrifying as hell And if someone lied and abused that trust, it would have serious consequences. She frowned as she remembered something. "Mark?" He looked at her. "What- what are we a long way off from?"

"What?"

"You told Sabrina we were a long way off from something. But you didn't say what."

He furrowed his brow. "That's not your concern, pet. And not your place to ask."

"How could it not be my place to ask? What is it? Are you going spring something on me that I can't handle? Well, what happens then? Is it over because you kept this thing from me that you want, but wouldn't tell me about and it turns out I can't do it?"

"This is not a discussion we're going to have." He picked her up, set her on her feet and got up himself. "Come on. You still need your lunch."

"No," she balked. He turned to stare at her. "What do you want?"

"Pet, you are dangerously close to a punishment. You do not question me. I will tell you what you need to know when I feel you should know it. And not before. Now let's go."

"You want a slave, don't you?" Abby blurted out.

Mark narrowed his eyes at her. "I've already told you I don't."

"But how do I know that's true? How do I know you're not just- just- brainwashing me so I'll accept it when you finally tell me that's how it's going to be?"

"Brainwashing you? Do you hear yourself?"

"But you already have! I sit on the floor, I eat from your hand, I walk on a fucking leash! I'm your dog!"

"For the weekend! For *this* weekend so you can work out whatever issues you've got."

"Well, I don't think it's working!"

"Really? Because you've got a four inch stainless steel butt plug in your asshole that says I know exactly what I'm doing. You are tired and hungry and it's affecting your judgment. You need to eat and then rest for a while. Now, stop arguing with me and let me take care of you. And trust me, pet, you are not my dog. I've treated you very, very well so far, but if you keep pushing me, I swear to God I will start treating you like a dog and I promise you that you will understand how easy you've had it these last two days."

She rolled her eyes at him. "You do treat me like a dog. And that's what you've wanted all along! The only thing missing is a cage and a shock collar."

"Fine. You're a dog."

He surged forward. She froze in fear and then tried to back up, but he caught her by the ring on the collar. He took out the leash from his jeans pocket and clipped it on. "Move, bitch." He jerked the chain and she was forced to follow him. He led her to the bedroom.

She was too terrified to say anything. He flung open the dresser drawer, grabbed a pair of stainless steel handcuffs and had one on her wrist before she even knew what was happening. He brought her other arm around behind her back and secured it.

"Come, bitch. It's time to eat." Mark led her down the hallway with her hands cuffed behind her back. He led her into the kitchen and wrapped the leash around one wrist as he opened the refrigerator door, pulled out a pyrex dish of what appeared to be a marinating chicken breast and dumped it unceremoniously into the garbage. He tossed the dish into the sink.

Abby supposed that was going to be her lunch. He opened a cabinet door, brought out a bowl, and slammed it on the counter. He opened the pantry, took down a box of cereal and dumped some into the bowl. He led her over to the sink. "Kneel, bitch."

"Mark. *Sir*," she corrected.

"Bitches don't speak. Ever. Speak again and I will gag you and then no lunch for you. Kneel."

She knelt down as carefully as she could. Not that she cared about eating lunch, but she was seriously wary of pissing him off further. He set the bowl down in front of her. "Eat."

He dropped the leash, stepped on it with his foot, and then turned away from her, running the water in the sink. He started washing the dishes and she looked down at her bowl. She bent down precariously and took a bite. As far as punishments went, she wasn't sure if she preferred a spanking or this. At least if she was being spanked, Mark was looking at her, paying attention to her. He was focused solely on washing the dishes and the only thought he had for her was standing on her leash so she couldn't run away. Like a stray dog.

She continued to take small bites of the cereal to please him. She'd eaten almost the whole bowl when he picked it up off the floor, dumped the rest in the trash and washed the bowl and set it aside to dry.

He slid the leash out from under his boot and tugged it. She got to her feet and stumbled after him. He stopped in the bedroom and grabbed the two padlocks from the nightstand drawer along with a set of keys. He led her into the bathroom. He turned her around, padlocked the collar to her neck and tugged the leash down. She immediately knelt down. He locked the end of the chain to the bolt in the floor. He used the keys to unlock the handcuffs from her wrists. Then he left. All without saying a word.

And if she sometimes thought Mark's orders were scary, Mark not giving orders was much, much scarier. He was gone a while and she'd thought maybe they needed a cooling off period. She didn't know how long it was before he returned and when he did, the first thing she heard was a loud thump in the hallway. Mark appeared in the doorway with, of all things, a large cordless drill. She watched in silence as he set it down, brought the bathroom door into view, and aligned it with the holes in the frame.

He set about re-hanging the door and for some reason Abby knew, instinctively knew, that while she'd been so desperate for a door when she'd first arrived, having him hang it up now was bad. Really, really bad. She didn't want that door. For no reason that she could name, she started to cry quietly.

Mark finished with the door and closed it, leaving her alone again. She was trying not to get upset when he returned just minutes later with another bowl. She heard the faucet running behind her and he set the bowl down in front of her against the wall. It had water in it. It was not a dog bowl, just a cereal bowl, but the message was very, very clear. Mark left the bathroom.

Okay, Abby told herself. Okay. She wasn't hurt physically, everything was fine. They just needed some time out and Mark needed to make a point. So she would sit here, like a good girl, and wait until he was in a better mood.

This time, Mark was gone a while. So long that she actually picked up the bowl and drank from it. Then she picked at the tiles on the floor. Then she counted the links in the leash. Then...she was regretting drinking the water.

She had to pee. Bad. She'd had to pee for a few minutes now and set about finding a way to do that. The toilet was too far. Out of desperation, she had considered the tub, but it was also out of reach. That left the towel hanging on the wall in front of her. And that was just...no. She had to call Mark. Maybe bitches didn't speak, but they had to pee, and that surely trumped the restriction.

She was about to call out 'Mark' when she checked herself. Sir. Always 'Sir' when she had the collar on. "Sir?" Her stomach fluttered as she called out. What if he was still mad? What if he punished her for speaking? What if he punished her for speaking before he let her pee? No answer. "Sir?" she called again, louder.

She heard boots coming down the hall and steeled herself for whatever was to come. He was a reasonable man. He would understand. The door opened and he stood there, arms crossed over his chest. "Thought I made myself clear about speaking. Speak one more time and it's the cane."

She scowled. Not at him. But at her dilemma. Can't speak. Gotta pee. She pressed her lips firmly together and directed her gaze meaningfully at the toilet. "You've got to piss?"

She nodded.

Mark took out the keys and unlocked the leash from the floor. "Let's go for a walk, bitch." He turned to leave and she crawled frantically after him. Walk? Where were they going? Was he really going to lead her around while she had to pee to make her hold it longer? Pee punishment. That was one she hadn't thought of. She started counting to distract her. One Mississippi. No, no, no. No water. One alligator, two alligator, you do not have to pee. Three alligator, these are not the droids you're looking for. Hold it.

Mark led her to the back door and opened it. She froze. He tugged the leash. She couldn't go outside. She was topless and although she had on a garter belt, she no panties and a giant plug sticking out of her ass. Outside was not an option.

"Bitch," Mark said menacingly. "You piss on my carpet and I will rub your nose in it."

Abby's heart hammered. Trying to maintain her composure, she peeked out the door. Mark's yard was large, bordered by trees, and she didn't immediately see any neighboring houses. She tentatively stepped outside. She prayed that he would only make her crawl around for a few minutes before he had mercy on her. Holding it was not something she'd ever been that good at.

She crawled carefully down the deck stairs and onto the grass. At least the grass was soft on her knees, she thought. Alright. Crawl, don't think about it, Crawl, don't think about it.

"Well?" Mark asked her. She looked up at him confused. She was on a leash. If he didn't walk, she couldn't walk. Was she just supposed to crawl around him in a circle? "Thought you had to piss."

Her eyes widened and her jaw dropped. He was not-

"So piss. I don't have all day, bitch."

He was. He honest to God was telling her to pee in the grass. Once she got over her initial shock she realized she had two options. She could beg. Begging would absolutely result in a caning. But it might also result in her being allowed to use a toilet. Or she could suck it up and pee in the grass. Pain, humiliation, pain, humiliation. These were not choices she wanted to have to make. She started to cry.

Would Mark let her go inside if she asked? She had no way of knowing. In the end, the prospect of asking, being told no, and then having to endure a caning was too scary and she slowly, carefully spread her knees apart in the grass. She sobbed uncontrollably as she released her bladder on the lawn.

When she was done, Mark turned and led her back up to the house. Abby couldn't crawl and wipe her nose at the same time so her face was a mess of snot and tears when they reached the bathroom again. He locked her to the floor and abandoned her. She pulled the towel off the bar and wiped her face with it. Then she curled up with it on the cold, hard tile floor.

Mark returned some time later. He silently undressed her, put on her wrist and ankle cuffs, and led her to the kitchen. He attached the leash to the table leg with one snap hook and cuffed her hands behind her back with another. He set down a bowl of oatmeal. At least it was hot, she thought. She balanced precariously again, leaning forward just enough to eat the porridge, but not fall face first into it. Mark sat at the table and ate silently.

At this point Abby was pretty hungry. She'd not had the whole bowl of cereal and so as humiliating as it was, she licked the bowl clean. Mark took it away and washed the dishes then released her hands from behind her back and led her back to the bathroom.

He snapped them together in front of her this time and attached her to the bolt in the floor, forcing her to her hands and knees. He left and returned with something she'd never seen before. A large bar, like a police baton, but not quite as thick. Before she could wonder if he was going to beat her with it, he quickly attached it first to one ankle cuff then the other, keeping her feet apart, and as such her knees. She was immobile.

He came up behind her and the ball gag appeared in front of her mouth. Reluctantly she accepted it. He fastened it and reached down to pull out the plug. Abby grunted in pain as he removed it. She felt a squirt of cold lube on her ass and knew what was coming though she dreaded it. Then a thing larger than the damn hose slid into her. It was a little smaller than the last plug and didn't hurt at badly. It also didn't feel cold or warm like the plugs could be made to feel, so she didn't know what it was.

She heard a hiss of air, rhythmic and slow and felt the thing in her ass getting bigger, stretching her. She bit down on the gag as it expanded inside her. When it finally stopped, she dropped her head, wearily. She heard the tell tale click and felt the first warm rush of water. She was determined not to cry. It filled her bowels slowly, twisting and churning, and her belly felt heavy.

Mark occasionally squeezed her tummy, checking for cramping she guessed, and she supposed she was grateful for that.

Another click. Then another. When she became too agitated from cramping, he slowed down the flow and let her adjust. He detached the bar holding her feet apart then she felt his hand on her ass and knew he was going to pull out the hose or nozzle or basketball or whatever it was inside her ass. There was a soft click and a release of air as it slowly deflated. He carefully pulled it out. She clenched tightly trying not to make a mess on the floor. She sure as fuck didn't want him rubbing her nose in that.

He unclipped her cuffs and she had a momentary panic as she wondered if he would make her go on the lawn again, but she heard the toilet seat lift. "Go," he told her.

The pressure in her belly didn't give her time to think about whether or not she wanted to do this in front of him. She sat on the seat and breathed a sigh of relief through her nose as she let go. Thankfully, it was all just water. Probably not the kind of water she wanted to think about or even see, but water just the same. She turned and flushed it immediately. She wiped her tears and then herself as she waited for the tank to fill up again and flushed a second time.

Mark took off the ball gag and the collar and set them on the counter. He took her by the arm and directed her not to the tub, but to the shower stall next to it. He turned on the water, tested it, then pulled down the spray nozzle and hosed her down, starting with her breasts. He rinsed her thoroughly then took a bar of soap from the caddy and scrubbed her with it.

It was some kind of harsh soap, the kind that he used himself. Not what he had bought for her. Not her Orange Blossom.

He scrubbed her pussy and her ass, inside and out, but didn't tease or even be really gentle. He wasn't hurting her, but knowing what she could be having compared to what she was getting hurt in its own special way. There were a lot of ways to be a dog, Abby decided. And they all fucking hurt in their own special ways.

She was numb even though the water had been warm by the time he pulled her out and toweled her off. He reattached everything but the ball gag and secured her to the floor again. She felt him part her legs and winced at the cold stream of lube on her ass. She grit her teeth and vowed not to beg. She would not say no. She would not say stop. She would endure. She'd fucked up and this was the penalty.

She didn't know it if was better or worse that Mark sure as fuck didn't seem to be getting any kind of twisted thrill out of all this either. Why would he? He'd loved giving her her gifts. Her soaps and shampoos and makeup and gorgeous lingerie. He'd cuddled her in his lap and held her when she asked and even fed her from his hand when he knew he had to be the Dom, but he didn't want to force her to eat out of a dog bowl.

I promise you that you will understand how easy you've had it these last two days.

But he'd been wrong. She hadn't had it easy. She'd had it *good*. Damn good. Near fucking perfect. And there might have been a little whipping and a little anal play that she didn't care for, but she'd had it good. She knew the rules. She didn't choose to obey them and now she was being punished.

She bore down, pushed hard when he started the insertion. Just like he'd told her. But it was harder. So much fucking harder. Not only was the plug bigger, but she wasn't aroused, which always seemed to have the magical effect of lessening the pain.

You should thank your Dom, when you can, for allowing you to come during your training.

Well, now wasn't that the truth? He'd been rubbing her and fingering her and fucking her to get those plugs in and that had helped. A lot. Because insertion was hard work. But once they were in, and he was tugging on them while eating her pussy or fucking her hard, it was heaven. Sheer heaven.

She cried out from the pain, but didn't beg. She took it like a good girl and wished she was 'pet' instead of 'bitch'.

Mark finished the insertion and gathered up his tools. On his way out, he turned out the light and shut the door. That soft click shattered her insides as much as a cane or a punch to the gut. She was in her cage. It was bigger than a dog cage, but it had a door and a cold floor and a water bowl and, most importantly, no Mark.

She pulled the damp towel of the wall and cried into it.

CHAPTER TWENTY-THREE

In the morning, Abby woke up, face still swollen from crying. It was Mark who had woken her, coming in the door. He pulled out the plug, unlocked her, and said. "Go. You have ten minutes." Then he left. Well, at least she didn't have to shit on the lawn. She did her business and he stuck her in the shower for another hosing off.

She was back on her hands and knees for this morning's plug insertion. She held it together as best she could and crawled down the hallway to the kitchen where she was chained to the table leg and ate cereal out of a bowl with no hands. But she was undeterred. Today was Sunday. The last day. And today she would win him back.

She nudged the cereal bowl away with her nose. Mark looked up from his scrambled eggs. "Not hungry, bitch?" he asked.

Abby nodded yes and fixed her gaze to Mark's crotch. He was silent a moment. "Hungry for my cock?" he asked.

She nodded again.

He took a bite of eggs. "It won't change anything. Besides, we don't have time. Your training is ending early. I'm taking your ass and then you're going home."

Abby didn't mind not being able to speak because she didn't know what she would say to that. She waited patiently for Mark to finish his breakfast.

In the bathroom, Mark attached her to the floor and used the bar again to spread her feet. She took the warm salt water enema without complaint and did not cry when she had to evacuate in front of him. He washed her in the shower, dried her, and replaced all her restraints. He put a plug in her, but it was one of the medium sized ones and in truth she barely even noticed it.

He led her down the hall to the bedroom. Abby discovered that at this point, she wasn't even all that nervous, so many things had been shoved in and out of her ass this weekend that Mark's cock would probably feel good by comparison.

He bid her to stand by the bed and fished two large straps out of the dresser drawer. He buckled first one, then the other, around her thighs. Her first thought was that Sabrina had been measuring her for restraints, though what anyone needed their thighs restrained for was a mystery to Abby.

He took the pillows off the bed and stacked them neatly in the corner. He laid her down, face up, which was also odd to her, and drew out two chains attached to each end of the head board. He secured her wrists to them.

Then he took two snap hooks and latched her ankle cuffs to her thigh cuffs, drawing her knees up almost to her chest, but still allowing her legs to part. It was an odd position, but not uncomfortable. She wondered if he was going to fuck her pussy first then turn her over.

She watched him undress, pulling off his gray t-shirt and jeans and boxer briefs and laying them on the chair. From the nightstand drawer he retrieved a bottle of lube and got up on the bed, kneeling between her spread thighs. He poured some into his hand and with the other, pulled out the plug. He set it aside and rubbed the lube all over and inside her ass. Then he reached down, grabbed hold of his cock, and slowly leaned into her, pushing the head against her entrance.

Abby couldn't believe that they were doing anal facing each other. She'd never imagined that to be possible. But after he inserted the head, he took hold of her legs and pushed them back, rotating her hips and giving him full access to her. He slowly pushed inside.

She gasped as he stretched her, holding back a groan. He worked his way in an inch at a time. She was breathing through clenched teeth.

When he was fully seated inside her, he held himself still, allowing her body to adjust to him. He slipped one hand down between them and began to gently massage her clit. She closed her eyes and concentrated on the sensations. She felt full, but not hurting. Her clit was coming to life. He slipped a finger in her pussy and worked it around. Soon she was panting with excitement. Then the fucking began.

He braced himself on the bed with one hand, still playing with her with the other and began slowly moving in and out of her. His tongue touched her nipple and an electric current shot straight to her clit. She grabbed the chains and started trying some way, any way, to fuck him back.

God, it felt so good. He licked the other nipple and then bit it gently. She cried out, pulling on the chains, back arching. He pinched her clit and she came. Hard. There was nothing inside her pussy so her juices leaked out, covering the base of his cock. He thrust harder taking only a few measured strokes before releasing inside her. She could feel each throb as his cock swelled, stretching her. He waited until the pumping subsided then carefully pulled out, replacing himself with the metal plug. Abby was so dazed she barely noticed.

He got dressed and unshackled her. The last thing to go was the collar and she felt a momentary pang at its loss. He'd laid her clothes out for her on the chair back and left the room.

Abby's mind was a flood of thoughts as she dressed. First off, in retrospect it seemed silly that she'd been so afraid of it. It had been good. More than good. Pleasurable even. She'd had a better time doing anal than she'd ever had with straight sex with previous boyfriends. But it was oddly hollow and she knew why.

There was no connection. It had been lost. Or buried. Or severed. He hadn't looked at her eyes so she'd closed them to avoid thinking about it. He hadn't called her his good girl. He hadn't driven her wild with desire and she knew from experience he was more than capable of that. She wondered if it was over between them. She was too afraid to ask.

She slipped on her sandals and left the bedroom. Mark was in the living room, sitting in a chair. She spied a large Nordstrom's bag by the door. A glance inside showed her purse on top. She didn't know what to do or what to say. "Goodbye" sounded permanent. "See you soon" left him the opportunity to say, "I think not."

So, Abby flipped the lock on the front door, picked up the bag and said the only thing that came to mind. "I'm sorry I couldn't be what you wanted." Then she left, closing the door behind her with a soft click.

When she got home, she went straight to her own bathroom, which was nowhere near as nice as Mark's she thought for the umpteenth time. She set the bag down on the toilet lid and got undressed. She removed the plug and ran a bath for herself. Inside the bag her lingerie had been laid on top so she took it out and set it on the counter. He'd included the panties which she'd never gotten to wear.

Next came her makeup. She set it down on the counter as well. Marveling at his generosity. She pulled out the shampoo bottles and the extra bars of soap he'd apparently stocked up on. She froze.

At the bottom of the bag was a dove gray box. She didn't even need to see the side to know what it said.

Make me proud, and I will give you another, better, present.

Holding her breath, she pulled the box out of the bag and took the lid off. Tears stung her eyes as she looked inside. A pair of size 8 black leather five inch heels gleamed in the light of the bathroom.

Motherfucking Jimmy Choos. He'd remembered. She sat down on the floor and sobbed.

CHAPTER TWENTY-FOUR

Tex swore and threw the wrench that had just slipped, again, and smashed his thumb. It hit the tool chest and left a small dent in the metal.

Hawk looked up. "Try not to destroy the place, cowboy."

Tex scowled, but said nothing.

"Not for nothing," Hawk said, standing up and wiping his hands on a rag. "But how long are you planning on moping around like a kid who lost his favorite toy?"

Tex shook his head. "I'm not moping."

Hawk smirked. "Cowboy, that's some Grade A moping you're doing. The only people who mope better than you are twelve year old girls."

"Shut up."

"Can you just say you're sorry?" Hawk replied.

Tex sighed. "Fuck off."

"Not to me, dummy. To her!"

Tex sighed again and shook his head. "No."

"You are one stubborn asshole," Hawk declared.

"It's more than that," Tex admitted. "We're not right for each other. I knew it wasn't gonna last. It's no surprise."

"Nothing ever lasts with you," Hawk pointed out. "But this is the first time I've seen you give a shit that it didn't." Tex didn't resond. "So fucking apologize already and get your woman back. Maybe you should get on *your* knees. I bet that'd work."

Tex picked up a second wrench. "I wouldn't be opposed. I'm not too good to grovel. But everything's moving way too fast. If I didn't slow the train down, it was going to derail and take both of us out."

"Sure about that?" Hawk asked. "Could've just been in for a wild ride."

Tex shook his head. "Can't say it would be worth the risk."

Hawk laughed. Tex glared at him. "Never thought *you'd* be worried about taking a risk."

Tex turned his back on his friend and re-focused on the engine in front of him.

Abby took a rare day off and fired up her laptop. After a few days of crying and cleaning out the local grocery store of Haagen-Daas she'd decided it would be more productive to simply get Mark back. Which, unfortunately was easier said than done. She knew he'd withdrawn from her for asking too many questions. He'd already told her that he wouldn't entertain her curiousity. She'd panicked when she thought he was looking for slave and broke that rule pretty thoroughly.

Now that she was calmer, she thought maybe she'd better find out exactly what it was she was so afraid of. Because it occured to her that she had a lot of opinions for someone who knew nothing about BDSM before meeting Mark. So far, everything Mark had showed her had been initially frightening, but ultimately acceptable. Granted peeing on the lawn was a low point in their relationship, but she'd brought that on herself and had no one else to blame for it.

And how could she be angry with Mark for holding back when that was all she. herself, ever did?

Love was about sacrifice. That much she'd always understood and believed. And so far, Abby had done none of the sacrificing. It was Mark who was putting off the things he truly wanted in an effort to make Abby comfortable and happy. She felt like a petulant child in the wake of her outburst. Like a little girl throwing a fit because she didn't get everything she wanted. Even if Mark wanted a slave, he hadn't asked Abby to try that. He'd never even brought it up. It was entirely possible that "We're a long way off," was a polite way of saying, "She'll never be able to do that."

Abby looked at photos of cages, some of which actually went *under* the bed, but shook her head. There were no cages in Mark's house. And she woke up every morning in his arms, even if she was chained to bed. He'd never make her sleep away from him, she decided. As a Master he could trade her or give her away, but he'd said he'd never share her. And Mark was a lot of things, but he was not a liar. Or a manipulator. Not in the negative sense. He'd promised to always see to her needs, and he always did.

As she researched, she discovered some Masters treated their slaves as true property. Things to play with and pass around, but never give any attention to beyond that. Other Masters professed that their slaves were their ultimate possessions that were to be cherished above all other things and cared for as though they were priceless. Abby decided that if Mark was a Master, he'd be the latter.

What would it be like to be owned by Mark? His house was immaculate, despite the fact that he was a mechanic and that was a dirty, messy job. His Harley was beautiful, always polished and perfectly tuned. She closed her eyes and pictured the soaps, and makeup, and shoes. And the orgasms, and the chocolate cake, and the bone melting kisses that he never seemed to get tired of bestowing upon her. Being Mark's pampered and most prized possession sounded like a dream. But it wouldn't always be like that. It would be hard. Like pissing-on-the-lawn hard sometimes. But she was beginning to see what he meant about sacrificing for the one you love.

Because even if she didn't quite love Mark, yet, she could *see* herself loving Mark. And see him loving her. Mark was honest, and kind, and reliable, and above all a good man who, despite his sexual leanings, never treated her as less than a person or less than capable of doing anything she wanted to do.

Abby dug in with both heels, at that moment. She wasn't losing Mark. He was the only good thing she had here. Had *anywhere*. And as long as he kept being Mark, Abby was going to be everything he wanted her to be.

Tex unlocked the front door and stepped inside his darkened house. He stopped short when he saw Abby. He had no idea how she'd gotten in.

She was naked, kneeling, wearing her collar, wrist and ankle cuffs, even the thigh cuffs which were attached just above her thigh high black stockings. She'd left off the garter belt.

For a moment his cock surged with desire.

She had her gaze directed at the floor. She was also kneeling with her knees spread apart and the the back of her hands resting on her thighs, palms up.

Classic Slave Presentation, he thought.

At first he was surprised. Then he was angry. How had she learned that? He sure as fuck didn't teach her that.

"What are you doing?" he snapped.

Abby didn't lift her head. "Pet is here to serve her Master."

Jesus Christ. *Master.* And she was even referring to herself in the third person. He was about to tell her to stand the fuck up and put on some clothes when he stopped himself. A niggling thought entered his brain. In war you used any tool at your disposal, took advantage of every opportunity. And Abby may or may not have realized it, but she'd just given him an opening. He pocketed his keys and tossed his leather jacket onto the chair beside her.

"And who is your Master, pet?"

"You, Sir."

"Is that so?"

"Yes, Master. Pet wasn't ready to serve before. She's ready now."

He spotted a piece of paper on the coffee table that he knew he hadn't left there. He strode to it and picked it up. It was a standard TPE contract. She'd already signed it.

"What is this, pet?"

"Pet's contract. Pet signed. Pet serves."

"Pet, this is a no-limit, Total Power Exchange contract. For life or until I release you."

"Yes, Master."

"Where did you get it?"

"Pet downloaded it off the internet."

Ah. Well, at least she hadn't sought another Dom.

"And this is where you learned the slave position?" he asked her.

"Yes, Master. Pet knows 5 positions."

"Is that right?"

"Yes, Master."

"Present yourself to me for inspection," he commanded.

Abby placed her hands on the floor in front of her and laid her forehead between them, ass in the air. He walked around her, coming up behind her and stopped. His heart thudded in his chest. On Abby's left hip, right at the top of her ass cheek was a scrolling black tattoo.

TEX.

So many different emotions ran through him all at once he couldn't even identify them all. His cock only felt one thing, though. Raging lust. He took a silent, steadying breath.

"Pet, what is that on your ass?"

"Pet's mark of ownership."

"I didn't ask you to do that."

"Pet wanted to please her Master."

"You chose a permanent mark instead of a piercing?" he asked in wonderment.

"Pet thought perhaps Master wanted to pierce her himself."

Holy fuck, Tex thought, reeling.

"And you would let me do that?"

"Pet's body belongs to her Master."

Tex couldn't pierce her if he wanted to. He lacked the technical knowledge, but he was stunned she'd taken it this far. He drew his gaze away from the tattoo and a glint of silver caught his eye. "That's not one of plugs I gave you." He knew they were all present an accounted for in his drawer these last few weeks and though she'd broken in and retrieved the collar and cuffs tonight, that still wasn't his plug. The shape was different.

"Pet bought it," she replied.

Tex bent down and felt the smooth round base. "What size is it?" he asked.

"Three and a half inches in circumference, Sir."

Roughly the same as the largest one he'd ever used on her. He knew from experience that his own plug that size was painful for her during insertion.

"Pet did it the way Master likes," she added.

"The way I like," he repeated.

"Pet gives herself an enema at night. Then bathtime. Then the plug."

Tex rubbed his hand over his face. "Pet, you hate enemas."

Abby wiggled a little on the floor. "Pet doesn't mind them so much now. Except...she prefers that you do it."

Tex clenched his fists and fought the urge to yank out the plug and fuck her asshole right there on the living room floor. "Why do you prefer I do it?"

"Because Master touches pet all over and makes her feel safe. Pet doesn't like the enema, but Pet likes that. And Master is careful with lube and with the cramping. He... doesn't want to hurt pet. He just wants a clean pet."

The corner of his mouth twitched a little. He could hear the question that wasn't really a question. "Pet, where did you learn to give yourself an enema?"

"Pet's enemas aren't like yours. She sits on a bag. It doesn't go in as far. But pet learned by watching videos on the internet."

"And you came across punishment enemas," he finished for her.

She hesitated. "Yes, Master," she said quietly.

"I would never do that to you, pet." A tiny little sigh of relief passed her lips. "I do use the enemas to clean you. But I also love giving them to you. With other subs it was merely for hygienic purposes. But with you, I love seeing you filled up, by me. I know it scared you and hurt you the times we did them, but I didn't think you'd accept the erotic aspects of receiving one during your training, so I didn't try to confuse you."

"Erotic?" she asked.

"Yes, pet. Very. If you can relax enough. In fact, we're going to do it right now." He picked up the pen she'd apparently left on the table, signed the contract, and set the pen back down with a loud clatter. "Crawl to the bathroom, pet."

"Yes, Master."

Tex walked behind her, enjoying the view of her beautiful ass, now displaying his name proudly. Once inside, she positioned herself to kneel in front of the floor bolt, putting her hands down in front of it.

"No restraints, pet. You're doing this for pleasure, remember?"

"Yes, Master."

Tex turned on the tap to its hottest setting, letting it run a bit. He washed his hands and when the water was as hot as it would get, he pulled the stopper on the sink, filling it up. He opened the cabinet and took out his supplies. When the sink was full, he shut off the tap and put the unopened bottle of water in it to warm up while he set out the bag, the hose, and the smaller nozzle rather than the inflatable one. He took down the small container of sea salt and the spoon and set them aside. He attached the hose to the bottom of the bag. He opened the medicine cabinet and took out the small tube of lube and slid it into his pocket.

Once the bottle had heated up nicely, he broke the seal on the top, carefully poured in a teaspoon of the sea salt, and shook it to dissolve. He poured the entire quart of water into the 4 quart black bag and ran the hook through the top. He hung it up on the small, discreet hook near the top of the mirror to free up his hands and then held the nozzle down over the sink, releasing the clamp to expel the excess air from the tube. When only warm salt water was flowing, he clamped off the hose again.

He picked up the bottle of lotion on the counter and crossed the room to hang the bag on the towel bar above Abby's head. Then he ran the length of tube down the wall and along the floor beside her. He knelt down beside her, placed the lotion bottle on the floor, and massaged her ass with both hands. He couldn't resist the urge to pass his thumb over the tattoo.

"I love this," he admitted to her in a low voice. In truth he more than loved it. It sent hot licks of desire coursing through him just to look at it. To own a woman this beautiful? It was almost too much to hope for.

Abby sighed in pleasure at his touch. He parted her cheeks, took hold of her plug, and gently tugged. "Push out, pet." She squeezed at the same time he pulled and it slowly worked itself out. Abby moaned, but he noticed that she wasn't quite as tense as she had been with him before. She must be getting used to the plug.

He finally had it out and set it aside, pulling out the tube of lubricant from his pocket and squirted some into his fingers. He parted her cheeks with his hand and rubbed one lubed finger over her hole. It went in easily and she wiggled her hips in response.

"Like that, pet?"

"Yes, Master."

"Good girl. Spread your legs a little more. Open up for me."

She moved her knees apart on the floor giving him a view of her most intimate parts. He slid his other hand down and rubbed her freshly shaved pussy.

"Getting wet down there?"

"Yes, Master."

"Reach down and hold your pussy open with one hand so I can see," he demanded.

She balanced a little to the right and spread her labia with her left hand, opening it for him. It glistened for him and he smiled appreciatively.

"Mmmm. Beautiful. Prettiest cunt I've ever seen. Do you feel pretty, pet, displaying yourself for me?"

"Yes, Master," she breathed.

He worked another finger into her asshole and watched her pussy contract pleasingly. God damn. She was going to look so fucking gorgeous when he finally fisted that tight twat of hers. He had a feeling that once he did, she was going to come so hard she might snap his wrist. He almost chuckled thinking it would be well worth it.

All things in time, though.

"Okay, pet, you can put your hand back on the floor now."

He picked up the hose and squeezed more lube on it, rubbing it all over the hard plastic with his finger. Then he pressed one finger to Abby's asshole again, giving a small push until it gave way. He inserted a second finger and fed the well-lubed nozzle between them, slowly inserting it.

Abby didn't have much to say about it, but then again she wouldn't after having a three and a half inch plug inside her just minutes ago. The nozzle was considerably smaller than that. He wanted her to have as little discomfort as possible and since the end goal wasn't anal sex, he didn't need to keep her hole stretched open enough for him to use later.

She contracted down on the nozzle nicely and he rubbed her cheeks, soothing her. Then he release the clamp just enough to get a small flow. Abby made a small noise as the water started flowing. He let go of the nozzle and slowly began rubbing her all over. Her ass, her thighs, her pussy.

"It's just a small one tonight, pet. It won't be too hard," he assured her. "You'll tell me if there's cramping."

"Yes, Master," she whispered

Tex didn't much care for being called Master. And for damn sure didn't like her referring to herself in the third person as if she'd obliterated her own identity in order to serve him. In fact, he was very surprised that such a confident, independent woman would agree to go that far. Abby had maintained their relationship out of the idea that what they were doing was, usually, pleasurable for both of them, or pleasurable enough for her most of the time. Enough so that the unpleasant things like punishments and anal sex were worth the trade off in her opinion. She must have realized, through her research, that a Master/slave relationship meant that her pleasure was no longer important and subject only to the whim and generosity of the one she served.

He knew some Masters from the club who believed in service so much that they never let their slaves orgasm and punished them harshly if they did. Things like cunnilingus and kissing were abhorrent to them as they believed it was the slave's duty to serve the

Master and never, ever the other way around.

Had Abby read about that? About the fact that at any time he could stop seeing to her desires as he saw fit? It humbled him to think she'd be willing to sacrifice her own happiness please him. Not that he would *ever* let that happen. But she had to have known it was a risk and she'd accepted it anyway.

Slavery wasn't legal, of course, and he couldn't force her to remain with him. The contract didn't mean anything other than an understanding on the part of both parties what their relationship would entail. Some contracts went on for pages and pages filled with detailed rules and expected behavior for the slave. Abby's hadn't had any. She hadn't known what his rules would be but she'd signed anyway. He couldn't legally force her to stay, but she was choosing to be here and try anyway.

She whimpered a bit. "Master? It hurts a little."

He nodded to himself and stopped the flow with a click of the clamp. He slid his hand from her back to her belly and rubbed gently. When he felt her relax he asked, "All better pet?"

"Yes, Master. Thank you."

"Ready for more?"

"Yes, Master."

He released the clamp, a little bit more this time and then rubbed her breasts, squeezing and tugging a little on her nipples. She panted a little.

Tex picked up the hand lotion and, moved to her side, kneeling down again, he poured some into his hand. It wasn't the lotion he'd bought for her. It was just basic non-scented stuff he used to keep his hands from becoming too calloused. He began massaging it into her skin, starting with her shoulders.

"Filling up nicely, pet?" he asked.

"Yes, Master," she replied as she leaned into his touch.

He worked his way down her back, kneading and pressing gently. When the lotion had been rubbed into her skin, he went back for more and started on her breasts. He slowly brushed his hands down to her belly.

"Nice little round tummy. I love to see you filling up for me. Any pain, pet?"

"No, Master."

"Good. Good girl. You're doing so well."

The lotion had been rubbed into her underside and had left his own hands nice and smooth. He pressed his hand to her pussy, running his fingers through her slick folds. She sighed as he inserted a finger into her hungry hole. She instinctively started rocking back and forth on it then gasped, halting.

He smiled. "You can feel all that warm water moving around when you do that, can't you?"

"Yes, Master," she breathed, astonished.

"What did it feel like, pet?"

She pursed her lips. "I- pet was surprised."

"Did it feel nice?"

"Pet doesn't know."

"Try again."

Abby leaned back slowly, testing things out. She slowly moved her hips forward and back, taking his finger further and further into her. She stopped. "Pet feels full," she told him, and edge of concern to her voice. "Like she might...."

"Expel?" he finished. "You won't. The nozzle's in tight. You're completely safe from embarrassment, pet. I promise you. Just relax and see if you enjoy it."

Abby began rocking again. He pushed his thumb against her clit and with his other hand, squeezed a nipple. "Oh!" she cried out, and began to move faster. She kept it up for a few moments, but stopped, head down, panting hard.

Tex moved toward her head, cupped her face and kissed her deeply, thrusting his tongue in and out. "You're so fucking good, pet," he murmured into her mouth. "Tummy filling up, nipples hard, cunt soaked. Is my pet enjoying her enema?"

She nodded and swirled her tongue around his. He started very gently massaging her belly again while kissing her. She made the most cock-hardening noises into his mouth. He glanced at the bag and saw from the translucent indicator on the side she'd almost taken the full dose. He released her, and heard a groan of her displeasure as he left her. He smiled. He knelt behind her and clamped off the flow.

He lubed up her plug and firmly took hold of the nozzle. "I'm going to remove the hose, pet. And put the plug back in. Be very still and don't move. Be a good girl now. We don't want a mess."

She adjusted her position and he slowly tugged on the nozzle. She whimpered a little nervously. "It's all right," he told her. "You're doing beautifully. Just hold it. Hold," he commanded. "Hold it." He pressed the plug against her sphincter and pushed slowly but steadily. It breached her ring and plopped into place with little argument from Abby. *Such a good girl*, he thought.

He tossed the hose aside and unbuckled his belt. He knew she heard him because she looked back over her shoulder. But she didn't say anything. He slowly unzipped his fly, letting her hear that too. He pushed his jeans and boxer briefs down to just above his knees. He didn't need any prep time for himself. He was already rock hard. He nestled himself between her legs and sat back on his heels.

He took hold of her shoulders and pulled her up to kneeling. "Come here pet," he crooned. "Let *me* fill you up now."

He fingered her slit a little, making sure she was ready and then guided his cockhead toward her cunt. With his free hand he tapped the plug. She gasped. "Plug's in nice and tight. There won't be any accidents. I promise you. Now sit on my cock, pet. Take it in your cunt."

Abby reached down and pressed two fingers to his shaft, positioning them both then slid down onto his erection. God it was incredible. She was soaking wet and the plug pressed against him as he took her pussy.

"So tight," he murmured in her ear. "My pet's so nice and tight. So wet," he added. "Loved your enema, didn't you baby?"

"Yes, Master," she cried out as he cupped her breasts.

"Now just relax and let me fuck you, pet. Close your eyes, and just concentrate on what you feel." He began thrusting, sliding his shaft in and out and tweaking her nipples simultaneously. When he had a steady rhythm, he ran his hands over her belly, careful not to press down. Just a gentle caress. "So full. Such a good girl. Look at that round tummy. It's so beautiful. Pet, do you want to please your Master?"

"Yes!"

"Then come pet. Come with Master's enema filling you up and

his cock in your cunt, ready to fill you up with seed. Come for me now."

He hadn't taught her to come on command. They weren't anywhere near that level of training. So he moved his hand down, one pinching a nipple and one pinching her clit, giving her that little pain/pleasure spike she needed to go over. She tightened up on him exquisitely and howled out an orgasm. It sent him spiraling into his own, his cock pulsating, jetting cum into her hot snatch.

When they both finished, he held her back against him, cuddling her in his arms. "That was amazing," he told her. "I've never done that before, fucked a sub while she was holding her water." It was true. In the past, enemas had been strictly prep for anal sex and so he always refrained from taking their pussies first so it didn't lessen the orgasm of that final goal. He'd given erotic enemas, though, to help subs who were embarrassed by them. The massage had not been new.

The sharpness of his desire to fill Abby surprised him. He'd always admired a full tummy, or a cunt full of fist, but he'd never been this lustful for it. Something about her soft, curvy body taking in whatever he wanted to give her filled *him* with a desire that he'd never felt this strongly before. And the fact that she'd enjoyed it, too, made it so much better. It raised their intimacy level, he thought, these shared, naughty passions.

He smiled to himself and kissed her temple. "Did you like it?" he asked her, already knowing the answer, but wanting to hear it just the same.

"Yes, Master," she replied dreamily while resting her head on his shoulder.

"Such a good girl." He lifted her up, sliding out of her. He raised himself to his knees and set his jeans to right, not bothering with the buckle. "Stand up, pet. Time to release."

She stood and looked at him, eyes pleading, but saying nothing. He stood up, too, and kissed her forehead. "I'll take the plug out and give you some privacy. I'm not into that and neither are you," he assured him. He could see her visibly relax. "When you're done, take your cuffs off, but leave the collar and get in the bath. Call me when it's time to wash you, pet."

"Yes, Master."

He shut the door firmly behind him. He took a seat on the chair in the living room and rubbed his face with one hand. *Master*. He glanced at the signed contract on the table. He didn't want it, not permanently, but it was like leading a starving man to a buffet and setting him loose. The possibilities were endless. But some of his ideas were just acts, sexual acts that would be pleasing in the moment, but without her understanding, her acceptance, her *enthusiasm*, they would seem hollow.

But God he wanted her. Every part of her. *Now*. He took a deep breath, sat back in the chair, and laid his arms over the arms of chair. One indulgence. He might allow himself *one* while he had the full blanket authority to command it. And it might make him a bastard, he decided, but in the end his desire for her won out. One indulgence. If she passed his test.

Minutes later she called to him and a fresh wave of interest and excitement shot through him as he slowly rose and went to pamper his brave little pet.

CHAPTER TWENTY-FIVE

After bathing her gently in the tub, he dried her off methodically and led her out to the living room. He set a pillow on the floor for her and bade her to sit on it. He was not a Dom given to forbidding his pets to use the furniture, as others were. But he needed to continue to reinforce that, for the time being, he was Master, and she a mere slave. He took a seat in the chair again and drummed his fingers on the arm for a few moments, watching her.

She kept her gaze lowered respectfully, hands open, even her lips were slightly parted. Like a good slave. He appreciated the effort even though he didn't care for it. She was distant from him like that. The connection he sought in her eyes wasn't there anymore and though he'd known all along that he liked it and needed it to be a good Dominant to such an inexperienced woman, he hadn't known just how much he would crave it when it was missing from their relationship.

He realized now that in the bathroom, he'd taken her from behind because he couldn't stand being denied looking into her eyes. He could have ordered that, he was the Master after all, but he was going to play this little scenario she'd set out for them both to its fullest.

"Tell me about the first time you had sex, pet."

He knew she was surprised because her mouth widened a little, but she didn't look up at him.

"How old were you?" he prompted.

"Pet was fifteen."

"Who was he?"

She hesitated. "The brother of a friend."

"Older than you?"

She nodded. "He was twenty, Master."

Tex frowned. That was one hell of an age difference. Tex might be considerably older than Abby now, but she was at least a woman, not a girl.

"Have all your boyfriends been older?"

A flash of something crossed her face. It was...pain? he wondered. She might have been embarrassed if that were the case and he'd guessed it. Or surprised that he would ask. But pained?

"No, Master," she answered. "The other two were my age."

So it was this boy, this *man,* who'd been the problem. "What was his name?"

"Finn Donovan."

"How long were you together?"

There it was again. That fleeting look. "A few days, Master," she said quietly.

He leaned back in the chair. Days. *Days.* That did not jive with the Abby that he knew. She might have jumped into bed with Tex on a sexy, alcohol induced whim, but her other two boyfriends had been long-term.

"Tell me the whole story," he commanded.

She looked a little lost at the request, but she opened her mouth to speak, anyway. "Finn was her friend's brother. And he picked up Natalie a lot from school. He- he started talking to pet. Made her feel special. Said he understood things."

"What things?"

"That pet wasn't allowed to date boys. That pet had to go to a Catholic High School for girls to keep boys away. One day Natalie wasn't there outside the school in the afternoon, but Finn was. He offered pet a ride home. She said 'yes'."

Tex didn't like where this was going. *At all.* But he didn't want to take the risk of expressing it and possibly have her shut down on him.

Abby continued. "Finn didn't take pet home, though. He drove behind the school. He kissed pet. She'd never been kissed before." Abby hung her head in shame. "Pet liked it," she whispered. "But then Finn drove her home. Well, two blocks from home so Dad didn't see, and the next day, Finn was waiting for her again.

"They went behind the school and he kissed her. And kissed her and kissed her and touched her under her shirt and she liked that too. He said she was pretty. He said he knew how much she'd been wanting it and that was true. Pet couldn't talk to boys and so boys were all she thought about."

Tex understood that. The minute you made something forbidden it could backfire and grow like an obsession in the mind.

"Did you ever tell him no?"

She nodded. "The third day. He wanted pet-" she shifted uncomfortably on the pillow. "He wanted pet to give him a blow job. But pet didn't know about things like that. So, she said no. Finn said that was okay. He understood. So, he wanted to put a finger in. Just one. It wouldn't hurt, he said. And it didn't. Pet liked that, too."

She was crying. Not loudly or even very noticeably. If you weren't looking directly at her, you'd never know it from her voice. But tears ran down her face. Tex fought the urge to go to her. She needed to get this out. They couldn't go anywhere until he figured out what it was that had her so god damn tied up in knots about sex. He prayed to God she hadn't been raped. Not forcefully at least. It was pretty god damn clear, though, that a twenty year old man had no business messing around with a sixteen year old virgin and that was definitely rape of another kind. But Tex hoped the man hadn't hurt her badly.

"The fourth day, the last day, Finn wanted pet to suck him, but she couldn't. It seemed so...alien to her. She couldn't see how anyone did that. Mary Elizabeth Cartwright sucked dick. That's what everybody said. That and she was a slut, even though she didn't go all the way. Still a slut, they said. But Rita Granger only had sex with her boyfriend, and everyone said that was okay. Boyfriends were okay as long as you didn't have a lot of them.

"Pet asked Finn to be her boyfriend. So sex would be okay. And then she wouldn't have to put his dick her mouth. The finger felt good and Rita said it hadn't really hurt when her boyfriend had sex with her, so pet thought it would be okay. She had a boyfriend who thought she was pretty and so everything would be okay.

"Finn said he already was her boyfriend. And he put on a condom and tried to get pet ready, but she was nervous. He did it anyway. He said it would be okay. But it hurt and it wasn't like pet thought it would be. He didn't even kiss her. Then he drove her two blocks away from home. And pet didn't see him again for two weeks, but when she did, he acted like he didn't even know her. Just picked up Natalie and drove away. Pet never told Natalie. Pet didn't want anyone to know she was a slut just like her mother."

Tex sat up a little straighter. Whoa. "Who called your mother a slut?"

"Dad. Pet woke up one night when she was twelve and heard them fighting. Pet peeked through the crack in her door and heard Dad call Mom a slut, over and over. Then he slapped her twice. But Mom didn't cry or even apologize. She just went to their bedroom, packed a suitcase and left. She didn't even come to pet's room to say goodbye."

Holy Shit. Tex's heart thudded in his chest.

"Dad never paid much attention to pet before, but after Mom left he did."

Fear uncoiled in Tex's belly. Oh, Jesus Christ, no. He braced himself for the worst. But he was intensely relieved when it didn't come.

"Dad started making pet come to the garage with him after school. He wouldn't leave her alone in the apartment anymore. He said pet wasn't going to be like Mommy, not if he could help it. He never said the word 'slut' to pet, but she'd heard him say it that night and she knew what he meant. He said no boys, ever. And pet had to change schools, to a girl's school.

"Pet was bored in the garage, so she learned about cars. It was okay, fun sometimes even. Walter showed her everything. He was so nice. Dad never minded that pet spent time with him. But one day another man working in the garage touched pet's hair. Pet didn't even feel it, didn't even know he'd done it. But Dad saw it and hit him with a tire iron. The man never came back to work and the next day Dad made pet cut her hair short."

Tex rubbed a hand over his face. It could have been far worse, but it was still horrible enough. The man was so intensely angry at being cuckolded by his wife that he'd turned his daughter into a virtual boy so he'd never have to face her eventual sexuality. Tex could only imagine Abby having to go through puberty in that house, getting her period and needing to buy bras. It would have sent her father into a tailspin. No wonder she wore fuck-me lingerie under her boring clothes. She'd been denied having a sexual identity for her whole teenage years and even though as an adult she hadn't been able to act on most of her desires, she still wanted to break away from her conditioning in some small way.

Tex picked up the contract, tore it in half and tossed the pieces in the fireplace. Abby gasped. "No!" she shrieked and tried to move past him to get to it. There wasn't a fire going so she couldn't hurt herself, but he still wouldn't let her get it.

As she struggled, he reached behind her and unbuckled her collar smoothly with one hand. It was then she really lost it, sobbing hysterically. "No! Don't! Don't leave! Don't send pet away!"

He tossed the collar, too, into the fireplace and cupped her face in his large hands. "Abby stop."

"Please!" she begged. "*Please!*"

Her panic was distressing to see. His heart was breaking for her. "Shhh," he said and kissed her on the mouth. "Trust me, good girl. Trust me."

Abby stilled a little at his words and he bent her back until he was supporting her in his arms and laid her on the floor, her head on the pillow she'd been sitting on.

"Shhh," he soothed her and kissed her while running his hands all over her body. "You're not a slut, Abby. You're not bad. You're a woman who likes to make love and you're perfect. Sweet and clean and beautiful. My Abby."

He liked pet. Pet was fun and exciting and sensual and gave him what he needed. And maybe Abby liked being pet because as pet she could do things that Abby wouldn't normally do and tell herself it was all okay. But Abby needed to know she was accepted for who she really was.

Tex made love to her slowly, kissing her now exposed throat and shoulders and collarbone. He sucked her nipples, first one, then the other, and dipped his tongue into her belly button on his way down to her pussy. He slid his hands underneath her ass and lifted her up, feasting on the delicious crevice between her thighs.

He even parted her ass cheeks and slipped his tongue along her sensitive hole. He hadn't replaced the plug after the bath and was now allowing himself his indulgence. He took a long, slow lick from her asshole all the way up to her clit, over and over, until she was drenched and swollen with passion. He pushed the back of her thighs to tilt her hips and swirled his tongue around her rear entrance and pushed it inside. She gasped and contracted, but didn't protest.

He tonguefucked her ass slowly. She'd started out smelling and even vaguely tasting like the soap he'd used to clean her during her bath, but her pussy got more and more wet until all that luscious juice ran down the crack and onto his tongue. It was heaven. Pure heaven.

He knew the anus had thousands of hyper sensitive nerve endings. He also knew a lot of women were hesitant about receiving pleasure in the way he was giving it. He loved making women completely and totally vulnerable to him both physically and emotionally. Then, instead of punishing them for it, giving them intensely pleasurable experiences as a reward for opening themselves to him. Abby was no different. In fact with her Tex's need to pleasure was increased ten fold. She was by far the least experienced woman he'd been with since his own high school days and he wanted to show her, teach her, that nothing that felt good to everyone involved was off limits.

"Say my name when you come, Abby. Say it for me, please," he asked.

Abby, in a move that made him simultaneously incredibly happy and the hardest he'd been all night, wrapped her arms around her own legs, holding them up so he could get to that delicious little rosebud. "Oh, baby," he said, approvingly. And pushed his thumb inside her pussy as he ate out her bottom.

She came explosively, screaming his name. He unleashed his massive erection and nudged the head into her pussy. She convulsed around him then opened up and he slid right in. He went balls deep and then back out again, slamming into her, hard. The wet sounds of their fucking were mind blowing because it meant she'd been creaming for him the whole time. She'd loved it and her reward was a head spinning orgasm while his reward was a sloppy-wet cunt that grasped and squeezed and contracted, doing everything it could to get him in deep and hold him there.

He shuddered through an orgasm, emptying his load into her. He rolled onto his back, taking her with him, still inside her. They were quiet for a long time. He ran his fingertips up and down her back.

CHAPTER TWENTY-SIX

"You're keeping me," she sighed into his chest.

"I am. For now."

She tensed.

"Abby, we need to talk."

She lifted her head. "What? What do I keep doing wrong? Just tell me what it is. Whatever it is, I'll- I'll try. I'll-"

"Abby, I don't want a slave," he assured her.

"What then? I don't understand. Why just for now? Why is it already half over? What-"

"I want a wife, Abby." She stilled on top of him. "I'm not asking you," he clarified. "I am not proposing. Believe me. If I ever do, it won't be on my living room floor. But, yeah, I'm tired of bringing home vanilla girls and being left unsatisfied. And I'm tired of the club scene with women who won't take a chance on me.

"I'm not saying we have the potential to go the long haul. I'm not saying we don't. I have no idea, Abby. It's like getting to know two separate people. Abby and pet. I need to know if I'm compatible with both. And you haven't been doing any of this long enough to know if it's what you really want long-term or if you're just experimenting because you've never really felt free to be sexual before. And even if you do like it, you might outgrow me or decide you don't want a life like this."

He sighed heavily. "I'm sorry as hell Sabrina ever said anything.

She didn't mean to. She's just a good friend and she knows I've been keeping my eyes open for a committed relationship. And when you called me on it, I wasn't sure what to do because, honestly, if some woman I barely knew said she wanted to get married and have babies, I'd probably run for the hills thinking she was more than a little nuts.

"And Abby, what I did to you that final night was wrong. You're too young and too new to the life to handle punishments like that and I had no business degrading you like I did. Especially when you said it was a soft limit. Honestly I'm surprised you'd even forgive me for it. I fucked up. I didn't want to tell you the truth and chase you away, so I did the next dumbest thing and punished you so harshly that it still might have chased you away.

"I haven't known what to do these last few weeks. I wanted to see you and apologize, but I didn't know how upset you were and since you went out of your way to avoid me I thought maybe it was best to leave you be for a while. You're so damn young, honey. It's hard. I want to be the one who opens you up and finds out what's inside you, what makes you Abby. But at the same time, you haven't lived much and maybe you don't want to be tied to one person, even if it's just for a while, even if right now you think you do."

He took hold of her chin and met her gaze. "I'm not perfect, Abby. I don't have all the right answers. I don't even know if it's a good thing for you to be with me given your inexperience. All I know is, the more you show me of you, the more I want. It's like a spark inside me caught fire and I have to know more.

"Baby, I'm a hard man sometimes. I want things that are hard to give simply because it's hard to give them. And maybe once all the newness wears off you'll figure out that you just want a nice, safe vanilla boyfriend and every once in a while you crack open a bottle of wine and ask him to spank you. Fuck, Abby, I'm not even sure I know exactly what *I* want anymore. I used to know. I used to know myself precisely but you....do things to me."

"Like what?" she asked quietly.

"Like enemas. I've given them. I've enjoyed that my subs have enjoyed it. But I've never really cared that much about them one way or the other. But fucking hell. Seeing you on your knees, submitting to me, taking all that water inside you, it makes me rock fucking hard, Abby. That's never been one of my fetishes, but I think it is now. You're changing me. And it scares the shit out of me."

Lightening the mood, Abby suddenly giggled. "Poor choice of words," she told him.

He grinned and rolled his eyes. "God, Abby I see you and I just...I wonder what's fucking possible. What's off limits just because it seems like it ought to be and not because it really should be?" He sighed. "I'm not even making sense."

She shook her head. "It makes sense to me. You think I've ever let a man put his tongue where you did tonight? I wouldn't have even let a guy *talk* to me about that before I met you. It just always seemed so...taboo. Dirty and wrong. But you showed me I'm not dirty. And you made me all sparkling clean inside and out just so I could let go and give that part of myself to you. I've never come that hard before."

She put her hands down on the carpet and pushed herself up, careful to keep his penis still lodged in her. "Let's not stop, Mark. I don't want to stop. Not now. Not yet. I couldn't bear it if you showed me all these things and then took them away. There's no fucking way I could ever talk to someone else and ask for these things you do to me. I don't know even know what half of them *are*!"

He chuckled. "But Abby-"

"No!" she protested. "Let's just keep going. And if we hit a stumbling block, we get over it. Somehow. And we just keep going until we hit a wall and have to end it if we can't find a way over. I don't know if I want to get married, Mark. I agree we don't know each other well enough yet. But my first thought wasn't '*hell no*' and that's something, right?"

He looked at her a long time. "Are you sure?"

"Yes, Master," she replied, grinning.

"Abby," he said, warning her.

"Yes, Mark. I'm sure." She thought for a moment. "Except, new rule, no peeing on the lawn."

He pulled her back down to him and hugged her. "Jesus God, I'm so sorry about that. I was so fucking mad that you wouldn't obey and I was mad that you wanted to know all my secrets but wouldn't tell me yours and I fucked up. I used to think that not punishing a sub in anger meant just not hitting them. But now I know all kinds of punishments can hurt when they're applied wrong. I'm so, so sorry, Abby. Why did you even do it?"

"Because I was afraid of the cane."

He let out a long breath. "Oh motherfuck me. I know how to use the cane in a hundred different ways. Not all of them even hurt. I was just trying to scare you into obeying. Abby please forgive me. I know I have no right to ask for it. I didn't break your hard limits, but I knew that would be a lot for you to handle and I made you do it anyway just to prove a point."

"If I hadn't forgiven you, I wouldn't be here," she told him. "And I was never really mad at you, only myself. It was obvious you didn't like what you were making me do. But I kept making you do it to me."

"Abby that's insane. I had all the power. You had none. None of that was your choice."

"I think it was."

"Abby, it was a no-limit, nonconsent weekend, I was respons-"

But Abby was having none of it. "If I had stood up on that lawn and told you that my mother was a slut and I was terrified of being one too, would you still have made me go?"

He didn't even have to think about it. "No. I would have stopped everything, taken off the collar, and we would have talked about it."

Abby put her hands on his chest. "Okay. So it may have been no-limits for *me*, but *you* have limits, Mark. If you'd seen that I was about to open up, you would have made that a priority because our relationship isn't about punishing me, it's about actually having a *relationship*. And, okay, it may be a relationship that includes spanking and ginger root and enemas but it *is a relationship*, not just a- a- service that you buy from me with soap and lingerie and expensive shoes.

"We both had communication issues that weekend. And you may be a lot of things, Mark, but you're not a sadist and you're not some kind of creep who gets off on degrading women by making them piss outside like an animal."

Mark's mouth twitched. "Don't judge other people's kinks, Abby." She gave him a sharp look and he smiled. "Okay, yeah, there's some stuff that even I, *secretly*, think is a little fucked up. But the key word here is *secretly*. Don't say it out loud when you're with other people. Judge silently, little grasshopper."

She nodded. "I remember. Rules and respect."

Before he even thought about it he said, "There's my good girl."

She looked at him, eyes hopeful. "So, does that mean you'll try? With me?"

He smiled. "Yes, pet. We'll try."

Abby got off him suddenly and went for the collar in the pile of ashes of the fireplace.

"Leave it," he told her.

"But-"

"I said leave it," he commanded, zipping up his fly. He got up off the floor and held out his hand to her. "Come on." She took it and together they went down the hall to the bedroom. Mark led her to the center of the room. "Turn around and face the wall," he told her. She did and heard him pull open one of the dresser drawers. Then she felt a slight pressure as he slid another collar around her neck. He buckled it and guided her to the full length mirror off to the right, hanging on the back of the door.

Abby gasped in delight. It was beautiful. It was leather and similar to her black play collar in width, 2 inches, but the similarities ended there. It was fur-lined in a rich, dark green and the leather itself was a lighter jade. Instead of one ring in the middle, it had two hanging a few inches apart from each other. In between them was a silver plate and a filigreed 'pet' inscribed on it.

"I had it lined," he told her, "because you wear collars longer than any other woman I've ever had sessions with and I want you to be as comfortable as possible."

"Mark, it's beautiful!" she exclaimed. Then blushed. "Sorry. Sir."

He laughed. "I'm glad you like it." He kissed her forehead and returned to the drawer. "I had a full set made, wrists, ankles, and thighs. All the same." He brought the wrist cuffs over and attached them. They were the same two-tone lush green and had o-rings.

"So she *was* measuring me for cuffs," Abby declared.

"She makes them. And other items. She's very skilled. I told her I needed a set made and she asked if we could have lunch. So I invited her over. I think she assumed I just wanted a nicer play set. But I wanted you to have something no one else had worn for me. And I wanted it to be completely yours. Hence the 'pet' engraved on the front. I've never called anyone else that."

She turned to look at him. "Really?"

He shook his head. "No. It never occurred to me until I first saw you and I thought, "She's so fucking cute I just want to pet her and take her home."

She laughed and shoved him a little. "I knew you were up to no good! With your little grin and your wandering eye."

"Honey, when a woman as fine as you bends over under the hood of a car, I'm going to notice."

She sighed. "And here I was hoping you were admiring my fine skills as a mechanic."

"Well, to be honest I wasn't really watching that. I figured if you fucked it up, I'd just fix it and we'd get to hang out longer. Or if you fucked it up royally, we could have it towed and then I'd give you a ride into town on my Harley."

She shoved him again. "Sexist pig," she said, grinning.

He shrugged. "My mama fixed tractors. But like I said, you don't look like my mama and how lucky did I get to find a fine-ass woman who can also fix an engine? In my experience pretty girls are used to getting by on their looks and not much else. You were a very welcome surprise."

She reached up and fingered the plate on the collar. "Thank you for this. I really do feel special. Thank you for the gift. All my gifts. I love them."

He eyed her skeptically. "Then why aren't you wearing the shoes I bought you?"

"Because they're $800 a pair and I would kill myself if they got scuffed on your bathroom floor! If you want to see me wear them, then take me to dinner."

"Did you just wrangle me into a date?"

She crossed her arms in front of her chest. "Maybe I did."

He raised one eyebrow. "Pet. You're wearing my collar. You failed to address me properly and you're covering yourself in my presence."

She looked down and immediately dropped her hands.

Tex grinned at her. "I'll give you a three second head start before I take you over my knee and spank that ass."

Abby's eyes grew wide. She squealed and sprinted out the bedroom door and down the hall.

"One," Tex called out. "Two...Three!" He ran after her. She made it to the living room, but he grabbed her easily, cutting her off before she could round the couch and put it between them.

"Oh!" she shrieked as he tossed her on the couch and clipped her wrists together behind her back.

"Too easy," he declared. "I've had more trouble with calves."

He watched her struggle a bit, getting turned on in the process. He finally sat down next to her, pulled her over him and settled her ass on his lap.

"Yep," he declared. "I think I like my brand on your ass." He gave it a light slap and she yelped in surprise. "Now pet, it should be ten for not addressing me properly and ten for covering yourself in my presence. Count out loud for me. And do not clench."

She shivered and he figured she'd gotten the message. He massaged her ass, ran a finger down her slit and then just when she was starting to get interested, he slapped her hard. She gasped. "One," she said.

"Louder."

Slap. "Two!" she cried this time as the blow landed on the other cheek.

He brought his hand down on the back of her left thigh. She squealed. "Three!"

He rubbed each spot and then brought his hand down between her thighs. She was warming up nicely. Another slap to the other thigh. "Four!"

"Why don't we play a game, pet?"

She wiggled against him. "Sir?"

"I said it *should* be ten for each offense. But I think I'll make it easy on you. If you can come before I get to twenty, then we can stop."

Abby struggled a little. "But...but my hands are tied!"

Tex grinned. "Indeed they are, pet. Indeed they are."

"How am I going to come? Are you going to finger me?"

He scoffed. "No. Of course not, pet. I've only got two hands and one is holding you on my lap and the other is delivering your punishment. Silly, pet."

"But-"

"Alright," he said, exasperated. "I'll give you a head start. *Again.*"

Abby hesitated. She hesitated for so long Tex wasn't sure wasn't going to do anything but lie there and take the spanking. But then she began to move. She laid her cheek on the padded armrest of the couch and slowly started moving her hips. He was mesmerized by the sight of her.

He rubbed his hand on her ass. "There you go, pet. Got it all figured out. Such a smart girl."

Abby made a soft noise in her throat and ground her clit into his thigh. Watching her hump his leg was one of the most entertaining things Tex had ever had the pleasure to witness. Seeing Abby so turned on that she dropped her inhibitions was always the highlight of their times together. When she was good and into it, he came down with a resounding smack on that gorgeous ass. She jolted.

"Pet?"

"Five," she panted.

"Better hurry."

She grunted and groaned and swiveled her hips, trying desperately to get more friction on her clit. God, she was so cute. He brought his hand down twice in rapid succession. Abby could barely concentrate between the stings of the spanking and the loving her clit needed to come.

"Six," she cried out. "Seven."

"You're almost halfway there, pet," he told her and slapped her thigh.

"Oh! Eight!" Abby growled and started humping furiously.

He struck two more times and she howled in frustration.

"N-nine. Oh, god. Ten," she gasped.

"Hmm, we're done." He unclipped her cuffs. "Turn over, pet."

"W-what? We're not-" she was having trouble catching her breath. "You said twenty."

"Stop telling me what I already know and turn over," he

commanded.

Abby rolled over in his lap. There was a small sheen of sweat on her brow and he wiped her hair away from her eyes.

"I've had a flash of brilliance, pet," he told her. She eyed him warily. "I can spank you and help you get off. All at the same time. Would you like that? For me to help you?"

Her eyebrows furrowed at him. She was trying to see the angle. "I don't- um- yes, okay, Sir," she said cautiously.

He frowned at her. "Ask for my help, pet."

"Sir, will you please help me come? So my punishment can end early."

"Certainly, pet. Here." He unlocked the cuffs and quickly shoved her left leg off him so her foot hit the floor, spreading her legs. He slapped her soundly on her mound.

Abby shrieked and bucked her hips. "Oh! You can't- you can't-"

"I believe I said spanking. I didn't specify ass or cunt."

She gaped at him. "Oh, wait, I-"

He slapped her again. He wasn't hitting her nearly as hard as he would have done to her ass, but hard enough to get her attention. He saw her breath catch, and her pupils dilate. "Rub your tits, pet. Tug on those nipples. That'll help you come."

Abby didn't comply quickly enough and he slapped her again. She jerked frantically in his lap. "You're up to thirteen, pet. If you don't get working on those titties of yours, you're never gonna come in time."

Abby could see she'd lost the fight and laid her head back on the armrest. She cupped her bare breasts in her hands and began slowly massaging them, between her fingers she squeezed her nipples which were dark and flushed.

He slapped her clit lightly again. A little softer this time. "Just relax, pet, and take your pussy spanking like a good girl. I'll keep track for you. That's fourteen."

A little bewildered, she began tugging on her nipples and moving on his lap. He gave her another tiny tap. Her cheeks flushed as she watched him in wonderment. He slid two fingers of his right hand into her cunt and started patting her mound rhythmically with his left. Once she got over the shock, she closed her eyes and started trying to thrust her pussy toward his fingers.

Every time she did she was punished (rewarded?) with a smack on the pussy. At first she was apprehensive about it, but if she wanted to get the fingers, she had to take the slap. It wasn't long before she didn't care. Her mouth was open and she was panting hard and Tex felt the muscles of her pussy start to contract on his fingers. He gave her one final hard smack to the clit and she erupted in a shuddering climax.

She opened her eyes, dazed. He smiled at her. "See what a good girl you can be when you try?"

He picked her up and carried her to the bedroom. He removed her collar and cuffs and put them away. She curled up next to him in bed, snuggling, and he put his arm around her, holding her tightly. "Go to sleep, Abby," he ordered quietly.

"Thank you for keeping me," she murmured.

"Thanks for being such a good girl," he replied, but he didn't think she heard him as she seemed already asleep.

In the morning she wasn't quite as tired. "You slapped my pussy," she accused as they were brushing their teeth.

He glanced at her in the mirror. "I was there."

"You slapped my pussy!"

"Abby, if I'd asked you for permission to slap your pussy what would you have said?"

"No!"

"Uh huh," he said, rinsing his mouth out. "And what did we discover about slapping your pussy, dear?" he asked in an intentionally patronizing tone. Her face reddened and she was very busy arranging her toothbrush in the holder. "That you like it," he told her.

She opened her mouth in what he knew would be a protest and he raised a finger. "This part of our relationship is exactly the same as the other part of our relationship in that we do not lie to one another."

She scowled. "You slapped my pussy," she muttered.

"Keep irritating me and I will *whip* your pussy."

She gasped. "You wouldn't!"

He grinned at her. "Well, not without your gag in because, honey, you already come like a fucking banshee and if I whipped your pussy the neighbors would hear your orgasm all the way to the end of the block. Caleb would show up we'd have to explain what I was doing to get that sound out of you. And Caleb is a cool guy for a cop, but I'm pretty sure he only has one definition of pussy whipped, babe, and that ain't it."

She glared at him out of the corner of her eye. "I wouldn't come from that."

"Oh, yes you would. You're not heavy into pain, but you like a little. And if I warmed you up nicely, I could do a fair bit to every part of you and you'd beg me for more." Abby scoffed. Tex kissed her on the top of the head. "Are you gonna stay here while I go to work today or head home? How did you get in here by the way?"

"I borrowed the key from Sarah."

"Figures. Women working together."

After one final kiss goodbye, Tex straddled his Harley and headed off to work for the day. He strolled into the garage a little after eight.

"You're late," Shooter called from under a Ford.

Tex was unconcerned. "You and I have something in common now."

Shooter slid out on the rolling board and looked up at him. "I'm never late."

"No. I mean a woman showed up at my house last night with my name tattooed on her ass, and I've gotta tell you, Shooter, if you were half as surprised as I was then you were pretty god damned surprised."

Hawk laughed. "I thought that was a good thing in your world, cowboy."

Tex gave him a lopsided grin. "Depends on the woman."

"So, what'd you do?" Easy asked.

Tex's half grin morphed into a full one. "Tied her up and did nasty things to her most of the night."

"Can she still walk?" Shooter asked.

Tex shrugged. "Well, she's back to sassing me this morning, so I guess I didn't do any permanent damage."

Shooter smiled. "So, you and Vegas are finally back together. 'Bout time."

"We're seeing how it goes," Tex cautioned.

Shooter grinned. "Uh huh. *When's* the wedding? I need to pencil it on the calendar. Give the boys time off."

"We're just seeing how it goes!"

"Right," Shooter said. "Like it was just lunch for me and Slick?"

"She's young!" Tex argued. "Maybe she doesn't want to marry a dirty old man like me! She doesn't know yet and neither do I. We're. Seeing. How. It. Goes." Shooter was still grinning. Tex glowered. "I do terrible things to her, Chris. Terrible, dirty, *depraved* things. She may decide she doesn't like them."

"Ack!" Shooter said, getting shaken out of his shit-eating grin. "No details! No details! I don't want to know! As long as it's, what's that thing, safe, sane and consensual, I don't want to hear!"

"I totally want to hear!" said Emilio. "What do you do to her?" he asked, fascinated. "Like you make her take it up the ass and stuff?"

"*Oh, my God!*" Shooter yelled and glared daggers at Emilio. "First off, seventeen is way too young to know what that is. Second, if you're lucky enough to get it in the *front* door, you buy her dinner and flowers. Entiendo?"

"And wear a condom," Hawk supplied.

"That's right!" Shooter snapped. "Always wear a rubber. You know that. If some little girl shows up here carrying your baby, I will beat your ass."

Tex turned to Emilio. "Abby is a highly intelligent woman. I don't *make* her do anything, Emilio," he said in a gravelly tone to let the kid know how serious he was. "She's with me because she wants to be and everything is her choice. Always. No means no, kid."

Emilio held up his hands. "Okay, I got it, cowboy."

Tex nodded. "You just worry about graduating from High School, boy. Plenty of time for women later."

"She really got your name tattooed on her ass?" Hawk asked, amazed.

"Says 'Tex.' Big as Texas," he replied.

Hawk considered this. "You must be one hell of a Dominatrix."

Tex scowled at him. "Dominatrices are women."

Hawk looked confused. "Don't see your point."

Tex flipped him off.

"Well, now that the band's back together," Shooter said, "Are we all going to Maria's tonight?"

"Hell, yes," Tex replied.

CHAPTER TWENTY-SEVEN

Abby was on her second martini when she eyed Mark from across the table they were occupying. Doc and Easy were finishing up a game of pool while Hawk was flirting with some cowgirl in a dark corner. Shooter was at the bar, talking to Maria and keeping an eye on his wife, who was serving drinks in the busy establishment. Abby gulped down the gin and set the glass on the table. "I think we should play for it," she announced.

Mark looked from Doc's combo shot to Abby. "Play for what?" he asked, confused since they hadn't actually been discussing anything.

Abby leaned toward him and indicated the pool table. "If you win, you get to pussy whip me," she said in just above a whisper. "And if I win, I pussy whip *you*. This seems like the fairest way."

Mark suppressed the urge to laugh. "I agree that it does seem fair, but since I lack the appropriate equipment for being pussy whipped, what do you suggest we do about that? Because you're not whipping my cock or my balls."

Abby grinned. "If I win, we do whatever I want. All day tomorrow. Shopping, lunch, maybe a movie."

"Shopping," he repeated.

"I try things on. You hold my purse and tell me I look good in everything. Shopping."

He eyed the table and then looked at her. "You're two drinks in the bag and you want to play now?"

She nodded. "I could still beat you."

He grinned. "You're on. Do we need to shake on it?"

"What? You don't trust me?" she asked innocently.

Doc beat Easy and Mark stood up. "Gentlemen," he announced. "We'll take those."

Abby held out her hand to take the cue from Easy. "You two are going to play?" the youngest man asked. He scrutinized Abby. "Aren't you half drunk already?"

Abby glared at him. "Shut up," she said, reaching for the cue.

Easy swung it away and she nearly stumbled trying to reach it. "You're totally hammered," he declared. Then he handed her the cue. "My money's on Tex," he called out to Doc. "Vegas is sloshed."

Doc considered this. "I don't know. She's wily." He pulled out his wallet. "I got fifty bucks on Vegas. Tex is toast."

Mark racked the balls and Shooter wandered over. "What's up?" he asked the group.

"Vegas may or may not be drunk," Easy answered, "and thinks she can beat our boy."

"I say it's a hustle," Doc declared. "She's gonna kick his ass."

"Really?" Shooter asked. "You think she can take him?"

Doc shrugged. "Like I told the kid, she's wily. Breaking into people's houses and shit. She's probably a criminal mastermind."

Shooter thought about this. "Yeah, I can totally see your reasoning." He pulled out his own wallet. "I got fifty bucks on the redhead."

"Jesus," Tex said, annoyed. "Do none of you have faith in me?"

Shooter grinned. "Against Vegas? Nope. Hawk!"

The large man ambled over and spied the stack of bills on the edge of the table. "Are we settling our tab already?" He checked his watch. "Seems early."

"Nah," said the lieutenant. "Tex and Vegas are gonna play a game."

"Oh, shit! I'm in! My money's on Vegas. No doubt," he said, slapping down a bill.

"Fuck all of you," Tex announced loudly. "Except Easy. He's my only friend."

Easy frowned. "Actually if she weren't piss drunk I'd change my bet," he admitted.

Mark flipped him off. All the men laughed.

"You want to break?" asked Mark, with a shit-eating grin.

"Up to you," Abby told him, chalking her cue.

"Oh, then you go ahead," he told her, still grinning.

Abby knew he thought she couldn't do it. He'd probably played against a lot of girls who didn't have enough cue control or strength to break up the rack. She leaned over the table, hand on the felt, and lined up her shot. She hit hard and with confidence, splitting up the grouping nicely, sinking two balls to boot.

"Damn it," said Easy and everyone laughed.

"Stripes," she called brightly, rounding the corner for another shot.

"You're gonna be *wearing* my stripes if you lose," Mark growled.

"Oooh," said the men, gathering to the side to watch.

Abby missed her shot and glared at Mark.

"That was kind of hot even if I don't play that way," Hawk mused.

"What do you get if *you* win, Vegas?" Chris asked.

She grinned. "He has to come along on a girl's day out. Shopping, lunch. I'm thinking of throwing in a mani-pedi, too."

The men laughed hysterically. "I don't think he has enough money to pay someone a fair wage to touch his feet," said Hawk. "A whole year's salary wouldn't cover it. Oh, my God, paint his nails! Please!"

Mark sank his shot and stood up. "No nail painting. I didn't agree to that."

Abby rolled her eyes. "I meant for me. While you hold my purse."

Mark sank two more balls, but missed a third. Abby was on a run of two when he bent over and whispered, "You are going to come so hard at the end of my crop." She bounced her shot off the ten ball and swore loudly.

"Cheater," she hissed.

He grinned. "Hey. In the army we had to learn to shoot amid distractions. Why can't you?"

Abby scowled as she stalked around the table. They were down to the finish now. Mark only had the eight ball left and she still had two balls in play. They were desperate times. As he lined up his final shot, Abby walked into his line of view and turned to the men. "Oh, hey," she said, casually. "I don't think you guys ever got to see my tattoo!" She spun and bent over, lifting her skirt all the way over her hips and pulling down the waistband of her panties a little.

"Holy Shit!" Easy yelled.

"Damn!" said Hawk.

Mark sank the eight ball, but the cue ball went in after it. "God damn it!" he shouted.

Abby pulled up her panties and let her dress fall back down. "Wait!" said Easy. "Was there a tattoo? I missed it! I was too busy looking at her ass!"

"I gotta go," Hawk announced. "I gotta find some hot babe and try not picture your girlfriend's ass while I'm doing her." He looked at Abby. "Unless you're gonna take off more clothes. Then I'll stick around and wait for the whole visual."

Mark glared at Hawk. "Go. Away." He came up to stand beside Abby and laid a resounding smack on her bottom. She jumped. He leaned down to her ear. "Bad," he half-whispered, and tapped the base of the medium sized plug she was wearing that was hidden by her panties. She sucked in a sharp breath.

"So much for shooting amid distraction," Easy muttered.

Shooter and Doc laughed. "Well, in his defense, the army doesn't have women in black lace panties popping up on courses to test their focus on the mission," Shooter replied.

Mark took his beer off the table. "We should email them about their oversight. If the enemy gets wind of our weakness, we'll never win another war."

Abby had one more martini and Mark steered her out the door to his Hummer. She giggled as he reached for the door with one hand while pressing her up against the vehicle, kissing her and letting his free hand caress her bottom.

At the house she kicked off her shoes and pulled her dress off over her head. She threw it on to the floor. After Mark got his shirt and jeans off, she pushed him back on to the bed. "I want to be the Dom tonight," she slurred.

"Oh, is that so?" he asked, grinning up at her.

She crawled up over him, straddling his thighs. "Uh huh. I want to tie you up."

"Nope, sorry. No bondage while either of us is drunk. That's a rule."

Abby frowned. "Fine. But I'm still in charge."

Mark smiled. "Yes, Mistress Vegas. What do you command?"

Abby laid herself over his lap, panty-clad ass in the air. "Spank me," she demanded.

He laughed. "That's not being a Domme, honey. That's topping from the bottom."

She giggled. "That sounds like a cooking term. Spank my ass!" Mark's hand came down with a sharp thud. Abby squealed. "Yes!" she cried, grabbing the sheets. "Harder!"

"Yes, Ma'am," Mark replied, slapping her cheeks in quick succession, each blow getting progressively stronger. He tugged down her panties and she kicked them the rest of the way off. His slaps stung, sending a pleasant warmth all over her rear end. She wiggled furiously, pressing her pussy against his hard cock. He reached down, rubbing her ass with one hand and twisting and tugging the plug with the other.

Abby panted. "You're going to fuck me now!" she told him. She ripped off his underwear and straddled him, facing away. She lifted the thick shaft and guided it upright, positioning herself over it. She slammed down onto it. Mark groaned happily and she gasped in delight. She reached back and grabbed one of his hands that were resting on her hips. "Do that again," she ordered, guiding his hand to her ass.

Mark resumed toying with the plug as he raised his own hips, fucking her forcefully. "Like that?" he asked.

"Yes!" she cried, shoving herself down to meet each of his upward thrusts. Every time she came down, her ass filled with the toy as her pussy stretched to accommodate his erection. The sensation of being full nearly brought her to orgasm way too early. Mark slapped her bottom with his other hand. "Oh, Fuck yes!" Abby gasped. "Whose cock is this?" she demanded.

"Yours, Mistress," Mark answered playfully.

Abby reached down and rubbed his balls. He groaned appreciatively. "Whose balls are these?"

"Your, Mistress," he repeated but it came out a little more hoarse as she teased them.

Abby growled and put her hands on his thighs for balance as she rode him hard. "I want to come. Make me come."

"You need to come, Abby?"

"Yes! Please."

"You want to come?" he asked again.

"No!" she answered suddenly. "I need to. I need to come. Give me what I need!"

Mark slapped her ass over the tattoo. "Who does this ass belong to?"

"You, Sir!" she replied immediately.

Mark reached up and grabbed a large fistful of her hair and pulled her back. With his other hand he slapped her mound hard. "Whose cunt is this?"

"Yours, Sir!" Abby shrieked as the vibrations from the slap made her whole lower body tingle.

"Then come for me like a good girl," he ordered.

Abby clamped down on him hard. Her back arched and Mark cupped her breasts, pinching her nipples through her powerful orgasm. When she was done, he grabbed her hips and drove into her mercilessly until his balls drew up and he pumped her pussy full of cum. Abby collapsed on top of him with his dick still inside her.

"Is it really mine?" she asked dreamily.

He kissed the side of her head. "Of course it is. It's never been anyone else's. But don't get any ideas about thigh-high boots and bullwhips," he said with a chuckle. "There's only one Dom in this relationship." Then he stopped to consider it. "Okay, maybe you can dress up for Halloween. Because even I can admit that would be damn sexy. And you can still top from the bottom when you're drunk. It's cute."

Abby sighed. "I am no good at being a Domme."

He laughed. "Well, you're not a total loss."

She perked up. "I'm not?"

"You definitely have erotic pain figured out. I think your little kitten claws might have drawn blood on my thighs."

She smiled. "You liked it."

"I fucking loved it. And clearly I should let you be on top more because you go from a kitten to an unleashed tiger." He turned her head toward him and kissed her on the mouth. "I knew my fiery redhead was in there somewhere."

CHAPTER TWENTY-EIGHT

Tex dutifully held Abby's purse again while she took an armful of bra and panty sets into the fitting room. He smiled politely at Megan who grinned back but kept her distance. He appreciated that. He'd been in here before, with Slick. It was where he bought the garter belt set for Abby when she agreed to try the non-consent weekend.

During that visit, Megan had been extremely flirtatious, despite Tex having made repeated comments about needing something for his girlfriend, though he'd never mentioned Abby by name. But on this visit, the second Megan had caught sight of Abby coming through the door Mark had been holding open for her, Megan had become a consummate professional. She wasn't above flirting a little to make a sale, apparently, but drew the line at alienating the man's significant other right to her face. Tex was grateful that Megan was keeping a polite distance from him out of deference to Abby.

He spied a white corset on a metal wire torso on display to the side. "Megan," he said, gaining the attention of the seamstress. She hurried right over. "Do you have anything like this in Abby's size?" he asked.

Megan smiled. "Yes. Absolutely. I'll get them!" she said and weaved her way through racks and displays, disappearing behind the large screen. She returned several minutes later, arms full. She laid out the corsets on the sales counter. Tex looked each one over thoroughly. There was a nice blue one with black trim that he liked. The white one had too much lace on it for his taste. There was a red crushed velvet with see through black lace laid over the bodice that he liked as well, but his eyes were drawn to the black one. Megan followed his gaze. She picked it up.

"This one is classic," she told him. "The pinstriping makes it work with a skirt or trouser suit. It has a full bust that sits a little higher to look more professional, but I cut a bit of a sweetheart dip for it so it still looks feminine. It has steel hooks on the front for decoration, but it's fully laced in the back." She turned it over to show him. "So it can be worn over a silk blouse."

Mark nodded and picked up the red one next. "This one also laces in the back," she told him. "But the hooks in front are functional, too. So she can put it on herself."

At this point Abby emerged from the fitting room. Mark looked up at her. "Try this on for me, please." He added the 'please' because his mother raised a gentleman, but there was no mistaking the tone in his voice. He'd let her have her day, without complaint or interference by him, but he'd seen what he wanted and he was going to get it.

Abby nodded and set down the garments she had in her arms. She took the corset from him. "Yes, Mark," she replied.

He smiled. He knew the 'Mark' was for Megan and the true meaning behind it was "Yes, Sir."

Megan accompanied her to the fitting room to help her get it on and Abby stepped out in a pair of black panties and the red corset. His cock started to harden. The bustline was low, revealing the creamy swells of her perfect breasts. The laces were cinched to accentuate her hourglass figure. It sat slightly low on the hips.

He loved having her naked most of the time, but there wasn't anything wrong with having her on display in other ways. Especially looking so lush and feminine like she did right now. Part of him wished her hair was down, but other, more rational parts of him knew it wasn't a good idea to put that much temptation in front of him.

He nodded to himself and picked up the pinstriped corset. He set it down on top of the pile Abby had placed on the counter. "We'll take these," he said, indicating the pile. Then he pointed at the corset Abby was wearing. "And that one." He took out his wallet and set his debit card down on the counter.

Abby hesitated before heading back to the fitting room. "Mark."

He gave her a stern look. "You pay for lunch."

To her credit, she didn't argue with him in front of the shopkeeper. "Okay," she replied and returned to the fitting room to change.

Megan bagged up their purchases and Tex thanked her for her help. He gave Abby's purse back to her and carried the shopping bags out the door to the Hummer. When he closed the rear door and started up the passenger side to help Abby in, she stood in his way. He was prepared for an argument, but that wasn't what he got. She stepped up to him and kissed him lightly on the lips. Then she grinned at him in that sassy way she had.

"Thanks. I heard about you," she purred.

"Oh, yeah?" Tex asked, curious where this was going. "What'd you hear?'

She reached up and ran her fingers through his hair. "That you were a really good Daddy. Take your girls shopping. Watch out for them on their *dates*."

The corner of Tex's mouth twitched up. Generally speaking, he didn't do much roleplaying, not on the level of, say, Shooter and Slick, who Tex accidentally walked in on one time at the garage playing out one of their favorites: Boss and the Naughty Secretary. As far as Tex knew, Shooter hadn't had any real interest in role play before he met his wife. He smiled as he thought about the things men would do for their women.

"Well, you heard right," he told her. "Of course I take care of my girls. You see my ride," he said, gesturing to the Hummer. "Would I have it if I wasn't the best pimp in town?" He rubbed her hip, just above her ass. "Now, you've got your Daddy's mark on you. And we bought everything you're gonna need to look pretty for your *dates*. It's time for me to test the merchandise." He opened the back door and helped her inside, sliding in after her. He closed the door with a soft click and started unbuckling his belt. She moved closer to him and watched him pull out his semi-hard cock. All the rear windows had privacy glass, so no one could see in.

"Suck my cock, sugar." He took hold of the back of her neck and pulled her down to his crotch. "Show me what a good job you can do."

Abby slid her tongue over the sensitive underside of his cockhead, licking it like her favorite lollipop. Then she parted her lips and took him in. She suckled the head gently until he was fully erect. Not having access to his balls with her mouth, she slid her hand up the inside of his thigh and cupped his crotch.

She couldn't take in the full length of him because they hadn't worked on that yet, so she compensated by enthusiastically moving her mouth up and down over his shaft. She paused to lick the drops of pre-cum that had emerged from the slit. Satisfied that the head was once again clean, she went back to fucking his cock with her mouth.

Tex leaned back and closed his eyes. She gave great head now that he'd taught her how. He smiled remembering how her initial reluctance had turned to enthusiasm over the long weekend of training. It was great, but it wasn't fantastic. He nearly groaned trying to restrain himself. He needed her. Soon.

He rubbed the back of her neck, allowing her to set the pace, not trusting himself to put forth too much effort. He felt his balls tighten and his hand tightened on her neck in response. He felt her draw in a deep breath and began rhythmically swallowing his cum. When the last drops squeezed out, she licked her lips and his cock thoroughly and looked up at him, sensually opening her mouth so he could see.

He brushed his fingers lightly along her cheek. "Daddy's got a brand new girl," he told her, approvingly. He fastened his jeans and his belt then pulled her close and kissed her. She reached for the door handle, but he stopped her.

"Oh no, pet. One good fantasy deserves another, don't you think?"

She looked at him, eyebrows furrowed. "What do you mean?"

He pulled her hand away from the door. "I mean, I'm done. But you're not." He twisted his body so he was leaning up against the door and pulled her onto his lap, her back pressed against him. He took his right hand and pushed the inside of her right thigh, causing her foot to move to the floor. "What are you doing?" she hissed.

He chuckled. "Relax. No one can hear you. You don't need to whisper." He pulled up the hem of her dress, revealing her panties. "Of course, if you scream like you sometimes do, we might have some 'splaining to do. You're not wearing a collar. So this will have suffice." He slid his left hand around her throat, holding it gently. He could feel her pulse hammering away. "Now," he announced. "I want your hand inside your panties."

"Mark," she protested. He flexed his hand ever so gently across her throat. "Sir," she corrected, and he could tell by her breathing that she was getting excited, despite her misgivings.

"Hand inside your panties," he repeated. "Now, pet."

Abby slipped her left hand into her black lace panties and made a small, feminine noise that he heard as well as felt with his hand encircling her throat. As she fingered herself, he put his lips to her ear. "Look," he whispered. "Look outside. All those people," he said, his own gaze following the sidewalk shoppers, talking on cell phones or with each other, carrying their own bags.

It took a firm hand, absolute confidence, and a deep understanding of your submissive's desires, capabilities, and limits in order to command them to do something they otherwise wouldn't normally do. Tex knew that Abby *wanted* to be sexual, but often downplayed that part of herself because of her childhood. For her, submission was a release, a way to admit and allow herself to enjoy desires so secret that she even hid them from *herself.*

A woman who wore as much lingerie as Abby did, *wanted* to be looked at, admired, lusted after. But between her father's iron-fisted upbringing and her fear of being rejected because she had a body like a 1940's starlet instead of a 2000's waif, she kept it under wraps. Or, more accurately, under gender-neutral business suits that gave no hint to the tantalizing lace and silk hidden underneath.

Tex moved his mouth over her ear. "They can't see us, but we can see them, can't we, pet? Just a few feet away from where you swallowed my cum." Abby shivered and he grinned. "It's different when your head's not buried in my lap, isn't it? Being able to see them. Watch them. Do you think any of them had their fingers in their cunts this morning? Like you're doing now?"

"Yes," she breathed.

He licked her earlobe. "My greedy little pet, rubbing herself in public. Can't get enough, can you, pet?"

"N-no, Sir."

"That's how I like you. Greedy, and horny, and following my instructions. Is that pussy wet?"

"Yes, Sir."

"Good girl. I like it soaked. You're going to wear your sopping wet panties to lunch, pet. No changing just because you bought fresh ones. Fuck, I love smelling you when you're turned on."

As luck would have it, a sedan actually pulled into the lot and started backing in just two spaces down from them. Tex had pulled the Hummer straight into the spot facing the brick building, so he and Abby were now looking directly across the back seat at a guy in his mid-forties with salt and pepper hair parking his BMW. Abby gasped.

"Keep touching yourself, pet," he commanded, his voice full of warning. "If you don't get off, I will get you off. And then I'll make you *keep* getting off until you're crying, begging me to stop."

Abby threw her head back against his shoulder. With her free hand she actually pressed *his* hand a little harder against her throat. She moved her hips languidly, riding her own hand. "Fuck," Tex growled. "There's my good girl. Are you looking at him, pet? Keep looking at him. He's so close. So fucking close."

Abby held his hand harder against her delicate throat. Mark didn't tighten his grip though, choosing instead to let her control how much pressure to exert. They hadn't done anything like breath play and he suspected she wasn't actually trying it now. She just wanted to reinforce his dominance over her since they were in an unfamiliar environment and there were no other outward trappings of her role as his submissive, such as being naked while he remained clothed or wearing her play collar. She needed that reaffirmation of their respective roles as submissive and dominant.

He took his right hand, which had been resting on her hip, and slid it around her waist. He pulled her against him in a steel grip, a primitive sort of bondage that required only flesh and bone. Abby was trapped in his embrace. She couldn't fight or get away. She was also completely and totally *free*. And she recognized it, knew it for what it was, because she writhed against him passionately, the wet sounds of her fingerfucking competing with the soft moans in her throat.

"Come." he commanded. "Come for your Owner, pet."

She shuddered and arched her back, then slammed back into him again as she came, not loudly this time but still fiercely, panting and squirming and grinding in his lap. He held her until it was over then he trailed kissed down her cheek and along her jaw and on that spot behind her ear that made her putty in his hands.

"My precious little pet," he whispered in her ear.

CHAPTER TWENTY-NINE

They sat outside on a sidewalk cafe since it was a beautiful afternoon. True to his word, Mark had made her go to lunch in her wet panties. Abby shifted slightly uncomfortably in the seat as he grinned at her. She narrowed her eyes at him.

It sometimes astonished Abby how much Mark knew about her, without her having to say anything at all. She couldn't tell if it was because she was that easy to read or because Mark had super secret psychic abilities. She wouldn't be surprised if it was the latter. She glanced at the menu and ordered the house salad. As they waited for their lunch, she announced, "Maybe after this we'll head to the nail salon for a mani-pedi."

Mark narrowed his own eyes and she smiled. But also true to his word, he didn't object. It was pretty obvious to Abby at this point in their relationship that Mark was the most reliable man she'd ever met. If he said he was going to do something, he did it. If he said he wasn't going to do something, then he didn't. Abby's other boyfriends had been ridiculously unreliable, making plans and breaking them at the last minute or making plans with other people and not bothering to tell her about it.

Mark kept things from her, that was true. But that was part of the Dom/sub dynamic, she'd discovered. It reinforced his control and kept her constantly guessing. And while she may not always be comfortable with that, she also understood the she wasn't supposed to be. But in the other vanilla part of their relationship, Mark never did that. He always kept her in the loop about his plans. He was always honest, always reliable, and always showed up when he said he would. Mark was a man she could count on.

"On second thought," she said, "I'm tired. I think we should just finish up lunch and call it a day." She couldn't be sure, but she swore he visibly relaxed at her words. She smiled to herself.

At his house, Mark took most of the bags from her and helped her carry them into his bedroom where he laid them on the bed.

"I have something for you," he told her.

Abby's heart fluttered. "A present?"

He shook his head. "No."

She tried to reign herself in. Mark had just spent quite a bit of money on her this afternoon. Abby wasn't greedy. She didn't expect Mark to give her gifts every minute of every day. But it was hard to contain her excitement at the prospect. Because Mark's gifts weren't like other people's gifts. Whereas her other boyfriends could barely be counted on to toss her a birthday card or maybe some tickets to a show she'd been dying to see, Mark's gifts were truly amazing.

With Mark, it wasn't the money. He was truly the embodiment of 'It's the Thought that Counts.' Because Mark's gifts were incredibly thoughtful. Shampoo in her favorite scent, shoes from a designer that she'd only mentioned in passing during a casual conversation. Mark's gifts were the direct result of him being *genuinely* interested in everything about her. And that was a feeling that Abby had never had, from anyone.

He turned to the dresser and her heart skipped a beat. But instead of opening the top drawer, his hand passed over the second and down to the third. He gripped the handle and pulled. She held her breath. A whip? More chains? Some strange and terrifying thing she never knew existed? She resisted the urge to close her eyes as it slid open.

Except it was empty.

She blinked at it.

He turned to her and grinned. It took several long seconds before Abby actually understood. Her jaw dropped.

Ignoring her, he walked to the closet and opened the door as well. "There's space here for you, too."

Crossing the room back to her, he held up his hand. Abby tore her gaze away from the half empty closet to the small silver key glinting in Mark's hand. She plucked it from his fingers and turned it over to examine it.

"Now you don't have to borrow one from Slick when you to want to surprise me."

He gave her a quick peck on the lips and left the room.

Abby stared at the dresser and the closet for a long time after Mark left the room. She looked down at the key in the palm of her hand. She suppressed the urge to squeal with delight. She stuck the key in her purse, pulled out some of the things she'd bought earlier, including the red corset, which was gorgeous. She added a pair of jeans she'd bought at the mall and a blouse to the pile and began putting them away.

Out of curiosity, she opened the top drawer again and fingered the toys there. A few of them looked scary, like gigantic plugs, and a few of them were scary and also *odd looking*. And even though she examined every inch of a six inch stainless steel tool that looked like a tiny pizza cutter except with spikes on it, she still couldn't figure out what the hell that would be for, so she put it away. She wasn't sure she wanted to ask Mark about that just yet. He might mistake her curiosity for interest, and she didn't think she wanted her curiosity to kill her cat, especially not with a medieval torture device.

She thought better of putting the red corset away and instead began to undress, hanging her blouse up in the closet and folding her trousers and putting them in her new drawer. She chose a pair of elegant black stockings that Mark had bought for her and sat on the bed to put them on. They were luxurious and topped with a two inch wide band of lace. She slipped her high heels back on and put the corset on, pressing it against her back and fastening the hooks in front. She crossed to the mirror and took her hair down, shaking it out over her shoulders.

The black lace overlay of the corset went well with the black stockings and the overall look was that of a courtesan or an upscale, turn of the century cabaret girl. Abby ran her palms over the front of the bodice. She'd never felt sexier. She turned back to the dresser, searching for the best way to please Mark after he'd been so wonderful today. She made her decision and attached her collar and cuffs.

Halfway down the hall, Abby was grateful that Mark's bedroom, hallway, and living room were carpeted. Because otherwise her knees would be bruised to hell and back from all the time she spent crawling around. She rounded the corner of the long hallway and tightened her jaw. She had the ball gag secured, hanging loosely around her neck over the collar. In her hand was the small plastic ball with the bell inside. In between her clenched teeth was a black leather riding crop she'd located in the toy drawer. Mark was on the couch, channel surfing, but stopped when he saw her. The look in his eyes had been liquid dark and scorching.

She was slightly disappointed that the only reaction he had was a slight twitch in the corner of his mouth. But his eyes darkened, like they always did when he was aroused. She sighed inwardly and wondered what the hell it would take to actually *surprise* this man. Determinedly, she crawled up to him and stopped. He took the crop out of her mouth.

"Pet?" Mark asked casually.

She looked up at him and considered batting her eyelashes at him but didn't want to turn the whole thing cheesy. Especially since, truth be told, butterflies were crashing around in her stomach in anticipation and anxiousness. "Sir. Please, whip my pussy."

He reached down, took hold of one of the rings in her collar and pulled her up to her knees. He kissed her fiercely, tongue taking possession of her mouth. "Of course, pet. You know I love pleasing you."

He turned off the television and tossed the remote onto the couch. He affixed her gag properly and then directed her to lean over the coffee table so her ass was exposed. She hadn't put on panties in order to accommodate her request. *Her request.* She'd asked him to whip her most sensitive parts and she hoped to God he was telling the truth about her loving it because she was more than a little nervous.

The whip ended up on the couch alongside the remote, and Mark got to his own knees beside her. He tilted her head, so her cheek was resting on the cool, smooth wooden surface of the table and she was facing him. The ball was in her left hand. She clutched it tightly. He began by rubbing her ass with his hand, massaging it. She closed her eyes as some of her trepidation melted away.

He started with light slaps with his bare hand and as they increased in power, he rubbed her warming skin between each blow. Abby loved this part. Ever since that first spanking with the belt in her mouth, she'd come to love the sharp sting of his hand and then the spreading warmth that came right after. He paused and rubbed his hand between the dampening folds of her pussy.

"Don't come, pet," he ordered. "I know you like your spankings, but if you come, we can't have some real fun." Abby bit down on the ball gag and tried to keep from humping his hand. He tapped her inner thigh. "Time to turn over."

He helped her lie down on the table, ass as the edge, feet spread wide and resting on the floor. He massaged her lower belly and moved down to her thighs, purposely skipping her pussy. She whimpered in frustration. "I know, pet, I know," he said gently. "Just hang on. For me." He tapped her cunt lightly and she jerked. "Hold still," he said firmly. "I can strap you to the table if I have to, but I'd rather you do as you're told."

The slaps were lighter than they had been on her ass, but they send ringing vibrations straight to her clit. She closed her eyes and tried to breathe deeply. He inserted one finger into her pussy and she reflexively clamped down on it.

"Now, pet," he admonished. "You're going to have to open back up for me. We're going to get some more fingers in there. A lot more." Abby opened her eyes and looked at him inquisitively. "I won't hurt you," he promised. "But I want my fingers stretching you out. Just like your ass, I'm going to start training your cunt to take a little more. I'd like to fist you."

Abby panicked and started shaking her head vehemently. "Shhh," he calmed her. "Not today. But we're going to talk about it. I want this cunt filled with my hand."

He pushed another finger in and Abby let go of her fear. She wiggled and spread her legs, trying to get him deeper. Her ass stung as it pressed against the table but it's wasn't an overwhelming sort of pain. He slapped her mound lightly with his other hand. She barely noticed the third finger.

"Getting nice and wet now, pet. Your pussy's just opening right up for me. It knows who owns it, doesn't it?" She whimpered behind the gag and nodded. "Has your cunt ever gotten this wet or opened this wide for another man?" She shook her head. "No," he agreed. "That's because it belongs to me. It's my cunt. And I'm going to stretch my cunt just a tiny bit more. He folded his pinky finger in and pushed it inside her.

The burn of the stretch caused her to pull away from him, but he pressed a hand onto her stomach, pinning her down. "Now, now. If you really think you can't handle it, then drop the ball, but don't try to get away from me. You won't make it far. I'm not putting any more in. Just these four. Now relax for me and open yourself up or drop the ball."

Abby planted her feet a little wider and drew in a slow, deep breath. Mark slid his fingers in further. "Such a good little pet." He worked her gently, letting her juices soak them both. "Don't come, pet," he warned. "Let me know when you're too close. Do not come."

Abby rocked her hips in response to Mark's slow fucking and alternately squeezed and relaxed around the invasion. She felt him sliding in, inch by excruciating inch. She felt vulnerable to him, exposed, and it was such a turn on that she cried out suddenly behind the gag. Mark removed his hand. She protested the loss of his fingers and the empty feeling it left her with.

He chuckled. "See? When you let go you really love what I do. You're going to love having my fist in you, baby. Just wait and see. Someday. Someday you'll take it for me." He picked up the crop and instead of hitting her with it, slowly rubbed the triangular end against her bare lips. He pressed harder, moving the thin shaft along her slit. The first blow hit and was a surprise. It hit her inner thigh. He continued a firm tapping along the inside, getting closer and closer to her spread open sex but then stopped just before he reached it. Abby sighed, partly in frustration and part relief.

He repeated the same thing on the other leg, stopping just before the pussy. Another tap came down just above her pubic bone. He slapped her mound with the tip, not hard, though. She whined, caught between wanting more and wanting it to stop before it got worse. Mark spun the rod in his hand and traced the handle along her slit. With his free hand, he spread her wide and slid it in.

"Fuck it, pet. Fuck it like it's my cock. Show me how much you love my whip."

Abby wiggled and bucked her hips, trying to take the handle deeper. It seemed a little shocking to her to fuck something that wasn't even really a sex toy, but that also made it kind of hotter. Naughtier. She felt like Mark's wanton little pet, driven insane by desire, humping tables and legs and fingering herself in parking lots. And all of it was so deliciously bad. He yanked the crop out and slapped her pussy with it. She continued to hump the air like she was still being filled by toys, fingers, cocks...Mark's fist. He rained down blows from her clit to her slit to her inner thighs, and Abby, having been brought to the edge so many times during this session only to be denied relief, screamed behind the gag as she came in a rush, her pussy clenching and grasping frantically at nothing. She started to cry in frustration mixed with relief.

Mark threw down the crop, grabbed her off the table and laid her on the floor. He hurriedly unzipped his jeans and released his cock. He drove into her hard. Her orgasm had only just subsided and the sensation of the sudden invasion was right on the border between pleasure and pain. He covered her with his massive frame and fucked her hard, pulling out and slamming back in. She felt a second, stronger orgasm building in side her. She grabbed and clawed at him, trying to pull him deeper inside her.

"I know," he told her, slamming into her again. "I know, baby. You need my cock inside you to come hard." He grabbed her wrists and pinned her arms above her head with one hand. He kept ramming her, getting close, grinding his pelvis into her mound to stimulate her clit. Abby fought against his hold, not really wanting to be free, just enjoying the feeling of being helpless. "That's right," he growled, slamming her hands back into the padded carpet. "You just have to take it. *Take. my. fucking. cock.*"

Abby screamed again and bit down on the gag hard, another more powerful orgasm ripped through her. She sobbed and fought and screamed, never wanting any of it to stop. Ever. She was reduced, once again, to Mark's crying, needy, greedy fucking pet and she wanted nothing more than to crawl onto his lap, cock impaling her in whichever hole pleased him most, and stay there forever.

Mark had taken off the gag and moved them to the more comfortable couch. He was stretched out across the length of it and she was on top of him, snuggling against him. "How do you know everything?" she asked him, trailing her fingers along his arm.

He chuckled. "You *tell* me."

She frowned. "No, I don't. I said I did not want my pussy whipped. And you told me it would make me come."

"I've got a pretty good idea of where your pain threshold is at the moment. I know how hard to spank you to make you come, and how hard to make you cry for punishment, without actually seriously hurting you. Your brain tells you some things are wrong or scary but, like I said, your body trusts me. It knows who owns it. Your brain will catch up. You can't undo two decades of programming in just a few weeks. You're trying, Abby. You're really, honestly trying and that makes me incredibly happy."

"But don't you want anything?" she asked quietly, half interested and half anxious about the answer. "You made me tell you my stranger fantasy, but you have some, too, right? So far, everything has been for me. I...want to do something for you. But I don't think I could do fisting," she added. "It's- that's too much. I can't. And I don't think that's just my brain. My pussy can barely take your cock. But do you want anything else?"

He brushed her hair lightly. "Abby, I appreciate the offer. But I've been doing this for a long, long time, and the things I want, you're not ready for them. Not yet."

"Can we try? Can you- I mean- is there like a triage? Can you pick an easier one and we'll give it a shot? I really, really want to do something for you."

"Abby-" he protested.

She straddled him, getting up on her knees. "You said people do that. Subs. They do things just to make their Doms happy. I want to do that. I want to make you happy. I might fail, but at least I tried."

He considered her for a long moment. "Alright," he said finally. "There's a specific fantasy that I couldn't do with girls in clubs for various reasons. If you're really serious, we'll try tomorrow. But, Abby, parts of it will not be pleasant for you. It's my fantasy, strictly for me. What you want doesn't enter into it. You can safeword if it's too hard for you, but you won't get pleasure out of some of it."

"We're trying it," she declared firmly.

"Well, I'll try to take it easy on you, and-"

"No," she interrupted him. "It's your fantasy. You get it exactly the way you want it. No adjustments just for me."

"Okay," he agreed. "It won't be scary at all, but it'll be a challenge. I'll do it the way I want, and if you can't take it, you safeword."

She nodded. "Deal."

He grinned up at her. "I'm so glad I gave you a drawer."

"And a key," she reminded him.

"And a key."

Abby grinned. "Though, I have to say, I'm surprised you didn't just put in a doggie door."

He grabbed her and rolled her off the couch, coming down on top of her, but cushioning the back of her head with his hand. "Oh, you're going to get it!" He pinned her down with an arm over her chest and tickled her belly just below the line of the corset.

"Stop!" she shrieked.

"Oh, no. You bad, bad girl!"

"I can't breathe," she said, laughing.

"You sassed me, pet! And sassy little pets get punished!"

He tickled her until she was panting and her face was probably as red as the corset. He dragged her back up to the couch and sat her in his lap. "Tomorrow," he informed her. "We'll try it tomorrow."

Abby knew better than to ask what 'it' would entail. "Tomorrow," she agreed and hoped it was something she could do.

CHAPTER THIRTY

Abby stretched and felt the other side of the bed. She found it empty. Opening her eyes she found Mark, across the room, sitting in the chair. He was watching her intently. For a moment she was simply happy to see him and happy that he was apparently happily watching her. But then she remembered that today was the day.

She gave him a tentative smile. "Sir?" she asked, even though she was wearing her silk nightgown and not her leather collar.

Mark leaned forward in the chair and put his hands on his knees. He was wearing a pair of jeans and nothing else. His bare feet were planted on the floor. "Bath time, pet," he informed her. "Take as much time as you need and come back to the bedroom."

Abby nodded and climbed out of bed. As she washed herself she tried not to think too hard about what kind of fantasies a guy like Mark would have. He said it wouldn't be scary. Just challenging. And she'd survived challenging before. She dried off, and unsure of what to do with her hair, she left it down but brushed it out. She headed back to the bedroom and scanned the room for anything that looked out of the ordinary, but it was exactly as she had left it. Mark attached her collar and pulled out a pair of white stockings. He handed them to her. Silently, Abby sat on the edge of the bed and rolled them on.

He indicated she should stand up and she did. A shiver of anticipation shot through her. He walked her to the wall, where the eye bolt was anchored above her head. The spot where he'd cuffed her and dropped wax onto her nipples. But she wasn't wearing cuffs now, only the collar. Mark put his hands on her shoulders and positioned her with her back to the wall, facing him. He traced one finger over her lips. "What's your safeword?"

"Cantaloupe."

"What is it?"

"Cantaloupe," she repeated more firmly.

"If you can't do this, it doesn't mean you're a failure. It just means you're not ready. I already know you're not fully trained, but I'm a selfish bastard and I want this now. In fact I've been trying like hell to hold off, but since you offered..." He gave her a sly grin.

She swallowed hard, getting a little nervous now, but nodded.

Mark attached the wrist cuffs and clipped them together behind her back. "Kneel," he ordered. She very carefully got down on her knees as Mark watched silently. "Put the soles of your feet against the wall."

Thrown off a little by this direction, Abby hesitated then moved backward and set the soles of her stockinged feet against the wall. Mark unzipped his jeans and stepped out of them, tossing them on the bed. His semi-erect cock was just inches from her face.

"Suck me," he ordered.

Abby nodded. She tongued the head as she'd been taught and swirled her tongue around it. She licked her way from the tip to the root and back up again and then ducked down a bit to take one of his balls into her mouth. When she was sucking on the other one, Mark threaded his fingers through the hair on top of her head and gently but firmly pushed her back until her head made contact with the wall behind her.

"Open," he growled and Abby opened her mouth as much as she could. Mark shoved his fully hard cock in and pulled out immediately. She gasped in surprise. "Keep your mouth open for my use," he demanded and drilled into her again.

She was completely restrained, with her hands cuffed behind her back and the wall behind her cutting off any avenue of escape. Mark's hands were in her hair, not hurting her, but holding her head firmly at any rate. All Abby could do was withstand the assault. And it was no doubt a full-on assault on her mouth. After a few warm-up fucks, he moved closer and shoved his entire cock in, hitting the back of her throat. She gagged and he retreated. He allowed her to catch her breath and then plunged in again.

Abby started to panic a little when her throat sealed around the cockhead, cutting off her air supply, but almost immediately he would pull back out again. He removed himself fully from her mouth after each thrust, giving her ample opportunity to safe word if she needed, but she struggled to continue. Her eyes began to water and he thrust into her harder, holding himself in for longer periods of time. In reality, the thrusts were mere seconds, but to Abby, not being able to breathe, felt like minutes. She fought and squealed, but didn't use her safeword.

She couldn't stop the tears, which were a direct result of the gagging. Mark ignored them and continued to brutally fuck her throat in short increments. Abby couldn't suppress her gag reflex and fought for air every time. She sobbed as he pulled back, out of her throat, and used her mouth to jerk himself off to a climax. When he was ready to come, the hand in her hair tightened and he drove forward. He held her forcefully as he pumped his load directly down her throat. Abby gagged and choked and fisted her hands behind her back.

He withdrew his cock which was covered in her saliva. It ran from her mouth in long strings and through her tears she knew she looked like a mess. He unclipped her cuffs and cradled her in his arms. He stood up and carried her to the bed, sitting on the edge, with her in his lap.

"I'm okay," she told him, breath hitching. "I'm okay."

He hugged her tightly. "We haven't worked on that yet, the deep throating. It's something I'll require eventually, but I jumped the gun with it today."

Abby took a deep, shuddering breath. "So, was that it? Was that...what you wanted?"

"No, pet. That was just the first part. This session will take all day, though that was one of the hardest parts. And you made it through. I'm so happy with you, pet. You made me really proud, taking it like that."

"Really?"

"Mmm hmm. And your reward is relaxing on the couch while I make pancakes."

Abby sat, cuddled in the white fluffy bathrobe and devoured Mark's pancakes as he waited on her. He refilled her juice and made fresh, hot cakes, putting a new one down in front of her as she finished up the last. "Are all the rewards as good as these pancakes?"

He smiled. "Yep. I made the dark chocolate cake, too."

"Oh, you really want me to be your love slave."

He kissed her on the side of the head. "All day long, pet." He leaned down and put his lips next to her ear. "The next part will be easy for you."

She smiled and took another bite of pancake.

After breakfast she rested on the couch watching an old movie while Mark did the dishes. She dozed and he woke her gently by kissing her. "Time for round two, pet," he whispered.

He led her into the bedroom and attached her ankle cuffs. He restrained her to the bed and brought out her ball gag. "This is just for you," he told her while fastening it. "Because I know you like it."

Abby lay naked, spread eagled on the bed while Mark lapped generously at her pussy. When he deemed her wet enough, he took hold of her hips and slammed into her forcefully. Abby grabbed the chains and held on. Mark's cock, as before, was punishing, but true to his word, she liked it this time.

He pulled out all the way each time, the ridged head of his shaft grazing her clit and then pounded back in. She came long before he did. He collapsed on top of her, cock stuffing her, and reached over to open the nightstand drawer. He drew out two silver balls attached together by a black cord.

Abby made a noise behind the gag.

He smiled down at her. "These are to keep my cum inside you, pet." He pushed one in with his thumb, then the other. They weren't huge, about as big around as the glass butt plug he'd given her. He unbuckled the gag.

"Um, how long do they-"

"Until I take them out for you."

"Yes, Sir."

Abby got up and took a few steps. The balls bumped up against each other inside her as she walked. She froze and looked at Mark. He grinned at her. "That's another part that you'll really like," he told her.

Abby tried hard most of the afternoon to ignore the riot her body was staging at her expense. After she fetched Mark his shirt, then his socks, and a bag of pretzels, she slammed the beer he'd ordered down on the coffee table.

"Is this part of your fantasy?" she demanded, glaring at him. "Me as your waitress slash valet?"

"Honestly? No. But, pet, I see how you are when those balls move around inside you and I was inspired to improvise."

Abby walked over to the couch, tossed the bag of pretzels aside and straddled him. She pushed him back against the couch and gave him a death stare. "Make me come. Now."

He raised an eyebrow at her.

"Sir. Make me come, now, Sir."

He took hold of her hips and pulled her down onto his crotch. "Make yourself come, pet."

He let go and spread his arms out across the back of the couch, refusing to touch her.

Abby, undaunted, placed her hands on his shoulders and began rocking her hips over him, rubbing her slit along the fly of his jeans. The harder she rocked, the more the balls clacked together inside her.

"What if I made you put these inside you before you go to work?" he whispered.

Abby didn't pause. "Then I'd put them in, Sir. And I'd think of you every time I moved." She leaned down and bit his lower lip gently.

"Fuck," he murmured. "Send you to work, full of my cum, with those balls holding it in you. Fuck yourself on my lap, pet. Fuck yourself with your cunt full of my cum."

Abby rode him hard, maintaining eye contact the entire time.

She felt the slow, aching build up in her core and increased the tempo, now humping his burgeoning erection. For once she finished and he didn't, and that gave her some small measure of satisfactory revenge.

"Aw, Sir didn't come," she teased.

He narrowed his gaze at her. "If I didn't have plans for that ass later, I'd be spanking the hell out of it right now."

Abby pressed her lips together and suppressed a smile. She had pretty much figured out Mark's fantasy when she was chained to his bed. She leaned forward and kissed him. "My ass is yours to use, Sir."

He smacked her ass and then lifted her up, setting her down on the couch next to him. "I'm going to go make dinner before I fuck you and ruin the grand finale."

After dinner Mark skipped the dishes and asked Abby to follow him to the bathroom. She took a deep breath and steeled herself for what was coming. He folded the towel and laid it on the floor, bidding her to get on her hands and knees. The enema was warm and slightly more than she'd ever taken before. Mark was gentle and calming, but didn't tease her or make anything overtly sexual about it. She wasn't scared this time. They hadn't had anal sex since that first time, but she'd been wearing her plugs for at least a few hours everyday and she knew she could handle him.

He sat her on the toilet and gave her some privacy before returning to bathe her. In the bedroom, he put her on the bed on all fours and buckled her gag behind her head. He handed her the cat toy and took out a bottle of lube from the nightstand. He warmed it up with his hands before applying copious amounts to her sensitive hole.

"This has a numbing agent in it," he told her. "Not like the kind we used last time. The point of this is not to hurt you. It'll numb me a little too when I get inside you. So this is going to last longer than you're used to," he warned. He pushed his fingers, coated in lube into her hole and worked it around. After a while, Abby did feel a little less sensation. She could still feel that she was being penetrated, but the slight sting of the stretch was gone.

Mark positioned himself behind her and took hold of her hips. Unlike her pussy, he eased his cock in much more slowly until he fully seated himself inside her. She felt the pressure of being filled up, but no pain.

"Ready, pet?" he asked.

Abby took a deep breath and tightened her grip on the headboard with her free hand. She nodded.

Mark fucked her slowly at first, then faster. There wasn't much pain, just a stretching sensation. The balls in her pussy clacked mercilessly and because there was no numbing gel in her cunt, she felt it every time she moved. The vibrations went straight to her clit. He began slamming into her, reaming her hole, jiggling the balls, and setting her pussy on fire with need.

She'd understood Mark's intention for quite a while, but feeling it now, knowing that she had her Owner's cum in her belly, her pussy, and was about to get a hot load in her ass made her shiver with desire. He was claiming every part of her and the way he'd done it, was now doing it, so animalistic and brutal, it felt truly like being possessed.

She bore down on the invading shaft, trying to push him out of her, which she knew from experience would only facilitate his penetration to the deepest parts of her. She tried for a better grip on the headboard with one hand but couldn't get it. She felt desperate. Mark wanted her, and she wanted to be his. She dropped the cat toy.

He froze, mid-thrust. "Abby?"

She grabbed the head board with both hands and shoved hard, impaling herself on his cock. Then she pulled herself forward and shoved backwards again, fucking him as hard as she could manage. It only took a moment for Mark to regain his focus. He grabbed her shoulders and pulled her back on him.

"Oh, fuck!" he breathed. "Give it back to me, baby. Give it right back!" She pulled and shoved and met his thrusts with all the power she could muster. "Fuck! My pet wants my cum in her. She wants to get filled up, full of her Owner's seed."

Their flesh came together with slaps and smacks and guttural noises from both of them as Abby tried to match his desire with her her own, tried to give as good as she was getting. She came with a scream behind her gag, the silver balls pummeling her pussy as Mark drilled her ass. Though she was nearly spent, she readjusted her grip on the headboard and tried to keep pace with Mark, wanting to make it good for him.

His grip tightened on her shoulders and he thrust in and out a few more times before he came with a shout. Abby could barely feel it because of the numbing gel, but there was no mistaking the expanding and contracting of his cock as he shot his load deep into her ass. She let go of the headboard and put her hands on the mattress, barely holding herself up.

Mark took the stainless steel butt plug he'd left on the nightstand, coated it in lube, and slowly extracted his dick. When the head came out with an audible pop, he slid the plug in. Abby was ready, relaxed and accepting, having known he was going to do it. When the plug was seated, she finally collapsed onto the bed. He unbuckled her gag and threw it onto the floor. They were both still panting.

He grabbed her and pulled her close, nuzzling her hair. "You dropped your ball," he finally said.

"I wanted it to be good for you. I needed both hands to make it good."

He cupped her face in his hands and gazed at her. "Are you really mine?" he asked, as though he couldn't believe it.

"Yes, Sir. Always yours."

He kissed her deeply, tongue taking possession for a bit. She closed her eyes and pressed her body into him. When he released her, she was slightly out of breath again.

"I can't eat the cake," she whispered. "I'm too tired."

He sighed, contentedly. "Me, too."

"Lock me in so we can go to sleep, Sir."

He gazed at her a little longer, as though he was still unsure of it all. Then he nodded, bringing up the chain from the post and attaching it to her wrist cuffs, still giving her plenty of slack. He put the padlock on the back of her collar so it couldn't be removed and she turned on her side, away from him, but moved back a little so she was pressed up against him. He draped his arm around her. She brought his hand up, between her breasts and kissed his palm. She pressed it to her breast and he squeezed firmly, holding her in a gentle but iron grip. Abby drifted to sleep, feeling secure and satisfied.

CHAPTER THIRTY-ONE

On Poker Night, Abby headed directly to the kitchen when she and Mark arrived to see if Sarah needed any extra hands in the kitchen. The smells of her cooking were delicious as usual, but the normally bubbly older girl was looking a little down.

"What's wrong?" Abby asked, washing her hands at the Sullivan's kitchen sink.

Sarah sighed. "Nothing. It's nothing."

"No, really," Abby insisted. "Are you sure you don't want to talk about it?"

Sarah paused and turned to Abby. She chewed on her lower lip then peered around Abby at the doorway to the kitchen. "Okay," she finally said. "But not here."

Intrigued, Abby watched Sarah adjust the flame on the chili she was simmering and both women headed upstairs to Chris and Sarah's master bedroom, away from the men.

Abby gaped at the huge framed picture of the badlands in the moonlight that hung over the bed.

"That's where we got married," Sarah informed her, perching on the edge of the bed.

"It's beautiful," Abby replied.

Sarah nodded, but then was quiet again.

"You can talk to me, Sarah," Abby assured her. "Whatever it is, I won't tell anyone. Not even Mark."

This seemed to have an impact because Sarah nodded. She sighed heavily. "We're trying to have a baby," she announced.

Abby gasped and threw her arms around her newest friend. "Oh my God, that's awesome!"

Sarah returned the hug but not as enthusiastically. "Yeah, it is, but..."

"But what? He doesn't want a baby?"

"No, he does," Sarah said quickly. "A lot. And so do I. And that's the whole problem."

Abby frowned. "I don't follow you."

Sarah scowled. "It's not working," she confided. "It's been months now. Plural. And nothing. And now my bathroom is filled with ovulation test kits and a thermometer and other things you don't want to know about, but we're not getting anywhere. And I'm okay with that," Sarah assured Abby. "I was on the pill and the doctor says it can take a while sometimes for things to go back to normal. But the problem is..." She trailed off and looked away.

"The problem is..." Abby prompted.

"The sex," Sarah wailed. "It's awful!"

Abby gaped at her, shocked. "Oh. Um..." This was really awkward. Not because Abby was uncomfortable talking about sex. God knew in her time with Mark she'd loosened up a lot when it came to physical pleasures, but Chris? Bad in bed? Abby couldn't picture the buff, handsome ex-Special Forces lieutenant being bad at anything at all. Least of all that.

"It didn't used to be," Sarah confided. "But now it's all scheduled and timed and all I'm ever thinking about is 'Is it going to work this time?' And I know he's frustrated. It's not fun for him anymore, either. I mean, we...we do some stuff."

Sarah blushed and Abby could not picture what it was that Sarah Sullivan did that made her face so red but she couldn't help but grin.

"We roleplay," Sarah whispered fiercely, as though Abby had forced the confession out of her even though Abby had done no such thing. "Or we used to," Sarah corrected. "But now the babymaking thing has tainted everything! The sex is more mechanical now. Tab A, slot B. I know he's not having as much fun as he used to."

"Ah," Abby said sagely. "I see the problem. Maybe..." She

thought for a moment. "Maybe you could try to spice up your sex life in other ways."

Sarah looked like a deer in headlights. "I can't do what you do."

Abby laughed. "No, you don't have to. You could do some other things though."

Sarah chewed her lip, nervously. "Well....like what?" she asked cautiously.

Abby grinned. "I have some ideas."

Shooter stood at the bottom of the staircase, listening to Abby and Sarah giggle through the closed bedroom door. He turned to Tex. "What are they doing in there?" he demanded.

Tex, relaxing on the couch, shrugged.

"Hey!" Shooter bellowed up the stairs. "Eating is cheating! Especially if I don't get to watch! What are you doing up there?" Shooter turned to Tex and scowled at him. "What are they doing?"

Tex laughed. "No idea."

Shooter looked over at Tex, pouting. "Well, how to you get Vegas to obey and tell us what's going on?"

"I don't. She only obeys me during playtime."

Shooter seethed. "Well, what good is that?!" He threw up his hands. "I can't believe two hot-ass women are getting it on in my bedroom and I don't even have a keyhole I can look through. *This house needs keyholes!*"

Tex laughed again and shook his head. "I have no idea what they're doing, but like I said, they're not getting it on."

Some minutes later, the women emerged from the room, still giggling hysterically. At the poker table, they kept exchanging knowing looks with each other which caused them to burst out into hysterics.

"What is going on?" Shooter demanded.

"Nothing!" his wife insisted.

"What where you doing up there?"

"Just girl talk!" Abby replied.

Shooter pointed his finger at both of them. "I sense shenanigans.

Slick? What's up?"

Sarah merely shook her head. Shooter looked to Tex for help, but Tex merely shrugged. "We could torture it out of them," Tex suggested. "But it probably wouldn't work."

Shooter grumbled and returned to his hand.

The next day at the garage, Tex headed to the office to print out an estimate for a customer who was dropping off his chopper for some custom work. When he opened the door, the sounds of loud moaning filled the room.

Shooter's mouth dropped open at the intrusion.

"What are you doing?" Tex asked loudly.

Hawk came up behind him in the doorway and glanced in. "Is that porn?" he asked, looking at the computer monitor which was turned away from them. "Are you looking at porn?" Hawk nearly yelled.

Easy came over, having heard the commotion from the garage area.

"I was not looking at porn!" Shooter insisted, even though the sounds of a woman clearly enjoying herself could be heard.

Hawk swept past Tex and reached for the computer screen. "I expressly remember the no porn speech," he said.

But instead of the monitor, Shooter was fumbling frantically with his phone, which he was trying to shut off. He finally did and slammed it down on the desk.

"Pervert," Easy teased.

"You!" Shooter said, looking angry now instead of contrite at being caught out. He jabbed a finger at Tex. "This is all your fault!"

"I didn't send you porn," Tex replied casually.

"No!" Shooter nearly shouted. "But my sweet, innocent, loving wife just sent me a 10 minute video of her shaving herself and using a vibrator! Where the fuck did she get a vibrator?!"

Hawk grinned. "I think the real question is if the video is only 10 minutes long, how come you've been in here for almost half an hour?"

Easy guffawed. "Because he watched it twice!"

Shooter surged up out of his chair, gathered up his phone, and shoved it into his pocket. He stormed out of the office, across the garage, and toward the parking lot.

"Don't spank in anger, Lieutenant!" Tex called after him. "And before you do anything rash like smash the thing, try doing her while putting it on her clit!"

Hawk and Easy laughed hysterically as Shooter, not bothering to look back, flipped them the bird as he stalked to his truck.

Almost two hours later, Shooter Sullivan returned, and to Tex's eyes, seemed a lot less angry than he'd been when he left. Tex grinned at him, but didn't say anything.

"I smashed the thing," Shooter announced as he walked past the men.

"Poor Slick," Tex mused.

"She can have one in any color but motherfucking purple," Shooter declared. "And as long as it's not bigger than me."

Tex bit his tongue to keep from laughing. "You know it'll tighten back up afterwards."

Shooter glared at him over his shoulder as he headed toward the office. "You have rules. I have rules."

"Yes, Sir," Tex replied with a grin.

CHAPTER THIRTY-TWO

Abby felt trapped behind her desk and ran her hand through her hair. She glanced at the clock for the thousandth time. She loved the Custer, but paperwork was not high on her list of favorite things. She picked up a vendor sheet for Blue Orchid Floral Services and frowned at it. Earlier that morning, she had done a walkthrough of the hotel. There were a few arrangements in the lobby. A pair of potted fruit trees that flanked the large grand staircase that led to the ballroom and a small arrangement in the elevator lobby of every floor, but that was all. Certainly nothing to justify the exorbitant fees the company was charging for providing and maintaining the Custer's floral arrangements.

She'd already submitted a claim to her boss to look for a cheaper company, as per instructed. But he'd informed her that they would be keeping the Blue Orchid as a contractor, and then proceeding to tell her she wasn't finding enough cuts in the budget. She'd wanted to hit him. Instead she'd picked up the phone and dialed Blue Orchid to try and negotiate a smaller monthly fee. She'd gotten no answer then and she got no answer now as she held the receiver to her ear with one hand and drummed her fingers on the desk with the other.

Unwilling to leave another voice mail, she scooped up the vendor sheet and decided to kill two birds with one stone. She could get out of her office for a bit while, hopefully, slashing her budget at the same time.

She stood up and smoothed down her knee-length black skirt. Her blazer was new, and fitted, and her dark blue silk blouse showed not a hint of the matching bra and panties that Mark had gotten for her. But she knew they were there and she had to admit it had always made her feel sexy to wear pretty underthings. More so now with the memory of Mark choosing them for her.

She grabbed her purse and headed to the parking garage on the corner. Traffic was light for a Monday and she only had to circle the block once to find the building she was looking for. She'd expected a nursery or a garden center, but then with that the Blue Orchid was charging for replacing a few lilies every month, they could afford to have an office space as well as a nursery.

She parallel parked on the street and headed through the three story building's lobby doors. The glassed-in bulletin board put Blue Orchid on the top floor and she slipped into the elevator. The doors opened across the hall from a pair of glass doors that were propped open. Abby walked through them and spotted a receptionist to the left. Which was a little irritating since every time Abby had called, she'd gotten no answer.

She smiled anyway at the woman behind the desk. The woman smiled back.

"Do you have an appointment?" the woman asked.

Abby shook her head. "No, I was-"

"That's okay. Helen isn't booked this afternoon. Did you bring headshots?"

Abby hesitated. "Um. No."

The woman shrugged. "It doesn't really matter. Helen's got a photographer that she likes to use, so between you and me and the lamppost she would've made you get new ones, anyway." She looked Abby up and down. "You from around here?"

"No," Abby replied.

The woman nodded. "I can tell. You're prettier than a lot of the girls we get here." She pressed a button on the phone and it rang back to the desk. The receptionist answered it quickly. "I've got a walk-in." She listened for a moment and then looked up at Abby. "Did you see us on the website?"

Playing it safe, Abby nodded.

The woman hung up the phone and gestured to the door off to the side. "Good luck!" she called enthusiastically.

Abby adjusted her purse on her shoulder and walked through the closed door. To her relief, an older woman in a fitted business suit was on the other side of the door, sitting on a couch. Abby glanced around to make sure they were alone.

The woman gestured for Abby to take a seat and so Abby did, even though she would have rather made a beeline for the elevator.

"Well, I haven't seen you before," the woman noted.

"No, ma'am. I haven't been in town long." To Abby's relief, the woman did not ask for a resume. Did hookers even have them? Abby doubted it.

"Tell me about yourself," the woman prompted.

Abby smirked inwardly. A typical question she, herself, would have asked any interviewee. She straightened in her chair. "Well, I just graduated," she replied, sticking as close to the truth as possible. "And I have student loans."

The woman nodded.

"I'd like to pay them off as quickly as possible," Abby continued. "And save a little money at the same time. Not a lot jobs pay that well."

The woman smiled. "No. Not around here. And not in this economy. Have you done this kind of work before?"

"No. But I knew someone who did. In another city. She said it pays well and the agency takes care of almost everything."

"True. We book your appointments for you. And bill the client. We give you a paycheck, courtesy of Blue Orchid Floral Services, which you don't have to hide from the IRS. Of course, any tips you make are yours to keep."

Abby nodded enthusiastically.

"We'll need to set you up with our photographer, for head and body shots."

Abby made a small noise of protest. Helen raised her hand. Absolutely nothing is available online. We keep portfolios here, which the clients are able to look through at their leisure. They choose from the book and we make the appointment. There will be total anonymity for you. You'll even choose a stage name so that none of the clients know your real name."

Abby settled back into the chair, trying to appear appeased by this explanation.

"Now that we've gone through the basics. I'd like to get a better idea of what we'll be offering."

It took Abby a moment before she realized Helen wanted her to stand up. She put her purse on the chair and stood in front of Helen, squaring her shoulders.

"Can you take your hair down, please?"

Abby reached up and shook out her hair, letting it fall across her shoulders. Helen waved her hand slightly and Abby unbuttoned her blazer. She draped it across the chair behind her. Helen waited, expectantly, and Abby drew in a deep breath. She was reminded of Sabrina's visit and the jangle of nerves she'd felt when she'd been in this situation before. But she'd survived once, and she could do it again. Running out now might make Helen suspicious, and if Helen called Kessler to say a mysterious redhead had come through the doors for an 'interview' it could end badly.

Abby slowly unzipped her skirt and pushed it down over her hips. She stepped out of it and placed it on the chair as well. She unbuttoned her blouse and shrugged it off. She stood in front of Helen in her high heels, thigh high stockings, panties, and bra.

"Very nice," Helen commented.

Abby turned around without being asked.

"You do anal?" Helen asked, with no small hint of surprised. Abby tried to hide her blush as she realized Helen could see the base of her plug. She cleared her throat.

"Yes, ma'am."

"A pleasant surprise."

Abby finished her turn and Helen gestured for her to take her bra down. Abby took hold of the straps and revealed her breasts to the older woman, who merely nodded in approval.

"I'll set you up with the photographer on Friday," Helen declared. "We have a small room here. I'll also book you with a long-time client for Saturday night. He enjoys reviewing our new talent for us."

Abby suppressed the urge to gag. Everybody wants a hooker, but only on their first day.

She quickly got re-dressed and left the office. The receptionist handed her an appointment card, that Abby took only to keep up the charade, but she tossed it directly into the garbage can outside the building's front doors. She flopped into the driver's seat of her car and took a deep, steadying breath. That had definitely been more than she'd bargained for. She didn't want to return to the Custer right now and it was too early to go home. So she cranked the engine of her Toyota and headed across town.

She pulled into the gravel lot of Burnout and parked beside Mark's Hummer. She got out and headed to the garage. Easy spotted her first and waved at her. As she stepped from the crushed stone onto the concrete, Mark crossed to her and leaned in to give her a kiss, careful to keep his dirty hands off her.

"Hey, baby," he said. "What's up?"

"Nothing," she replied. "I was just...around...and thought I'd see you.

Shooter came into the bay from the office. "Need more parts for your car, Vegas?" he called out.

She smiled and shook her head. "Not today," she called back.

It seemed deceitful and wrong not to tell Mark what had happened. Plus, she was still kind of weirded out by the whole thing.

"You okay, Vegas?" Hawk asked. Mark continued to gaze at her.

She cleared her throat. "I had a job interview today," she declared.

Mark frowned. "I thought you loved the hotel."

"I do! I'm not taking the job. I just went to check the place out and I ended up having an interview, instead."

"For what?"

Abby cleared her throat again. "Escort."

Mark's eyes narrowed. Hawk, Shooter, and Easy stopped what they were doing and stepped a little closer.

"Better be careful, Vegas," Hawk warned. "That's his Hillbilly Hulk face. The man is not happy. You better do some fast talking."

"How do you interview to be a hooker?" Easy asked.

Abby looked at Mark, and indeed he looked angry. "It was only an interview. A lot like the *interview* to be your girlfriend." Mark's face got impossibly darker and he dropped the rag he'd been cleaning his hands with.

"Meaning what?" Easy asked.

"I think it means she got naked," Shooter replied.

"I just went to check the place out," Abby insisted. "I didn't even know it was an escort agency. It was just a weird company on the vendor list for the hotel and I was looking into it. I didn't want to run out and look suspicious. So I had an interview, to play along." She smiled weakly. "Apparently I passed because they want me back for pictures and an audition. Which I'm totally not going to!" she added.

"Office," Mark ordered. "*Now.*"

"Ooooh," Easy murmured. Abby ignored him, but she still hesitated.

"Don't make me repeat myself, pet."

That got Abby moving and she moved swiftly toward the office door on the other side of the garage. Once inside, Mark slammed the door. He managed to maneuver Abby up against it without getting grease on her suit. His large hands were spread out on either side of her, though, flat against the door, pinning her.

"Did another man put his hands on you?" he demanded softly.

Abby shook her head vehemently, looking him squarely in the eye. "No. There was no man. It was a woman. And she had me take my suit and bra off. That's all. She just wanted to look."

"You should have left."

"I didn't want to look suspicious. I didn't want my boss to find out."

"Your boss is selling pussy out of the hotel?"

Abby nodded. Mark's jaw twitched.

"That was dangerous, Abby."

"I didn't know what it was."

"Some people in this town take their criminal activities very seriously. Your boss might be one of those people. Do not go there again."

She shook her head. "I won't. I swear. I really didn't know."

Mark leaned further into her, his cock pressing into her belly. "Pet," he said darkly. "You show yourself off again outside of my presence, I'll strip you naked and parade you around on the end of my leash."

Abby gasped, partly in surprise, and partly from desire since he was so close.

"I want to cum," he announced.

Abby licked her lips in anticipation.

"I can take you," he informed her. "But you'd get all dirty and have to go back to work. Or you can get on your knees and suck me off. Choose, pet. And don't keep me waiting."

Abby didn't hesitate. She kicked off her heels and pushed them aside. She knelt down on the floor in front of Mark, placing the soles of her feet against the door. She reached up and unzipped his fly. She pulled his jeans and boxer briefs down enough for his long, thick shaft to spring out. She tugged a little more until his pants were around his thighs, giving her enough room to work.

She placed her hands behind her back and leaned forward, taking one of his balls into her mouth. He was already rock hard and so it wasn't necessary to warm him up. She licked and laved got his balls soaking wet with her mouth, pausing only to look up at him periodically to see that he was pleased.

His hands remained flat on the door as he watched her intently. She gave him a small smile as she licked her way up his shaft to the head and then took as much in as she could. Mark didn't want his dirty hands in her hair and so she understood it was up to her to do the work. She took the hard length of him as far into her throat as she could, only gagging a bit before pulling back out. She repeated the process, attempting to swallow him down, which worked well.

Mark thrust his hips forward enough to move her back and she soon found herself pinned against the wall. Having experienced this before, she closed her eyes and relaxed her jaw to give Mark unfettered access to her throat for fucking.

It was the work of a few dozen thrusts before he unloaded down her throat. She swallowed quickly to get it all down. When his cock stopped throbbing, she released him with a gentle pop from her mouth and licked him clean.

He fastened his jeans and she was barely back on her feet before he had her pressed against the door again. This time he took her mouth with his own while she gripped his biceps with both hands, trying to draw him in as close as he could get.

"I want to see you again tonight," he whispered against her lips.

"Yes, Sir," she panted.

CHAPTER THIRTY-THREE

On Thursday, Abby and Tex appeared to arrive before everyone else at the Sullivan house. At least that's what they thought when they turned into the large circular drive. But one look at Shooter's ashen face when he opened the front door told them otherwise. He half-hearted waved his cell phone at them. "Tried to call," he said.

"What's wrong?" Tex asked.

Shooter shook his head and sighed.

"Where's Sarah?" Abby asked, looking around.

"Upstairs," the older man replied. "Bathroom."

Abby headed for the stairs while the men hovered in the living room.

Shooter shook his head again and pocketed his phone. "Test was negative," he told Tex.

Tex felt his heart squeeze a little. "Fuck," he muttered. "I'm sorry."

Shooter flopped onto his own couch and stared at the ceiling as though it wasn't the only separating him from his wife. "I just want help her. I just want to make this okay. But I can't. I don't know how to fix this."

Tex took the nearby chair. "What does the doctor say?"

"Doctor says wait. Give it time. Give it a *year*, they say, before they start tests. But you know Sarah." The older man fisted his hands in frustration. "She lost so *much* time because of that fucker. She's waited so long to have something even approaching normal. She doesn't want to wait anymore, Mark."

Tex nodded. "Slick's used to taking what she wants. Making things happen for herself. It's her way."

On the bathroom floor, Abby sat beside Sarah who was wiping tears from her cheeks. "I just had this whole plan, you know?" Sarah told her. "I came back and we got married. Right away. I sort of demanded it. We didn't do it the normal way. No wedding shower, no bachelor party, no honeymoon even. Not really. Just a week here in this house by ourselves."

She smiled as she remembered better times.

"I thought I'd get pregnant right away. And I figured we'd just, I don't know, keep going, you know? Babies, and barbecues, and Poker Night. Forever. Because that's how it's supposed to be." Sarah sighed. "I'm a terrible person."

Abby gasped. "What?! No, you're not!"

Sarah nodded. "Yeah, I am. Chris should be enough. I had nothing before I met him. Nothing and no one. I should just be grateful that I have this much. I shouldn't feel this way."

Abby got to her knees and leaned forward. She took hold of Sarah's shoulders. "You have every right to feel this way," Abby insisted. "And you deserve more than you have. So much more. You deserve everything you want."

Abby wasn't exactly sure how best to help her friend, but she knew she had to do something. She couldn't make babies appear, or dig up serial killers, reanimate them, and then kill the fuck out of them all over again, but there had to be something she could do to help Sarah and Chris. They needed it. Badly.

That night, back in her condo after Mark had dropped her off, she knew exactly what to do for them. She tightened her robe around her and fired up her laptop.

The next night at Maria's, Abby made a beeline for the table that the guys had snagged in the back, near the pool tables.

She slung her heavy purse onto the flat surface of the table. "Where's your wife?" she asked Shooter, looking around for Sarah. She located the waitress at the booths by the jukebox and waved her over.

"Need a drink that bad?" Easy teased, but Abby smirked at him.

"Nope. Well, yeah, always. But nope. Not this time." She opened her purse and looked at Sarah as she approached the table with a smile on her face.

"I come bearing gifts," Abby announced. Sarah looked surprised and a little confused. "Consider it a belated wedding present." Abby pulled out a large Fed Ex envelope that had already been opened.

Shooter glanced at Mark to see if he knew anything about this, but Mark shrugged. He didn't know.

Abby fanned out a handful of airline tickets and placed them on the table. Shooter reached for one first.

"All expenses paid. I booked us a suite of rooms at the Canyon. Consider it a bachelor party slash honeymoon all rolled into one weekend."

Sarah stared at the tickets. "Abby...this is too much."

Abby waved her hand dismissively. "It's Vegas. It's not about how much money you have. It's all about who you know."

"Sweet!" Easy declared, plucking a ticket off the table. "So we're all going to Vegas?"

"You guys need a reboot," Abby told Shooter. "And *that* I can give you."

"Oh, please," Easy whined. "Please, please, please say we can go to Vegas, boss."

Shooter looked at Sarah across the table. "You want to go Vegas, baby?"

Sarah bit her lip. "I'm not supposed to go to Vegas," she admitted.

Abby laughed. "Have you been banned from the Canyon?" Sarah's eyes widened and Abby laughed even harder. "Forget it. I'll unban you. It's not a problem."

"You can do that?" Sarah asked, gaping at her.

Abby nodded. "Of course I can do that."

Sarah looked at her husband. "Let's..." she said, "Let's go to Vegas."

Abby had arranged for a shuttle to pick them up at the airport and take them to the Canyon. The sun was fierce, as it always was in mid afternoon, and she was wearing her sunglasses. But they did little to dull the sparkle of the Coral Canyon with its shimmering facade, bright white and tinted glass with lush palm trees lining the front. She still thought it was the best hotel on the Strip, though she admitted to herself that she might be biased. The lobby's marble floors gleamed and the off-white walls made it seem a cool oasis in contrast to the desert.

They didn't even have to check in. Chase had been standing by, ready to spring into action when they arrived. Before she finished hugging him, their suitcases were whisked away to the upper floors where Abby had reserved several rooms that were connected via a large sitting room.

Their sitting room had large floor to ceiling windows that over looked the Strip. It was fairly impressive now, during the day, but Abby knew when the sun went down and the lights came up, they'd have a glittering view of one the most amazing cities in the world.

Sarah flung herself at Abby and nearly started crying. Abby laughed.

"It's so beautiful!"

"I know," Abby agreed. "I've always loved it. It really is the best hotel on the Strip. It's got the best views, the best pools, the best casinos. And we'll hit the shops downstairs tomorrow. They're some of the best in town." She looked around at the men who were also admiring the view. "But tonight's a busy night," Abby announced. "So you've got two hours to shower and get dressed because this town moves fast, gentlemen, and you've got a long night ahead of you."

Easy glanced at her over his shoulder. "You mean we've got like an itinerary and stuff? We can't just hang?"

Abby smirked at him. "Jimmy, why would you settle for *just hanging* in the entertainment capital of the world?"

Easy frowned. "But there's bars, and a pool, and strippers, and-"

"Jimmy," Abby said again, shaking her head. "Jimmy, Jimmy, Jimmy." She put her hand on his back and steered him toward the bedroom he'd chosen for himself. "I'll let you in on a little secret. Something I don't tell a lot of people."

Easy narrowed his eyes. "Oh, yeah? What?"

"I run this town."

CHAPTER THIRTY-FOUR

Abby led the group out the hotel's front doors and onto the sidewalk of the circular drive. "I arranged transportation for you guys," she announced, nodding in the direction of the hotel's garage to the left. "They'll pick you up here."

"Are we all going together?" Easy asked, eyeing the size of the group.

Abby shook her head. "Slick and I are on the town tonight. Try not to get into too much trouble."

"What are-?" Easy started to ask, but Abby turned her head in the direction of the garage again.

"Here's your ride," she announced.

"Oh, shit!" said Hawk as a sleek black Hummer limo glided onto the asphalt and pulled up to the curb. The driver's side door opened and an older man in a dark blue trouser suit and a button down overcoat stepped out.

Abby beamed at him and as he approached the sidewalk, she threw her arms around him. "Guys," she announced. "This is Walter. He's going to be taking care of you tonight while Slick and I are on an adventure of our own."

The older man smiled and nodded to the group, then turned to Abby. "I'm afraid the car you ordered isn't coming, Abby."

Abby's face fell. "Walter, Chase swore to me he ordered these cars."

Walter's grin perfectly mirrored Abby's frown. He slid his arms around her shoulders and squeeze. Turning her around he said, "I know, honey. But the boys got wind that the cars were for you. And, well, they just couldn't let you out on the Strip in a Lincoln Town Car."

As the group watched, a gorgeous blue and white '53 caddy with the top down made the corner and pulled up behind the Hummer.

"Whoa," said Easy.

Abby gasped. "Oh, Walter!"

Walter squeezed her shoulders again. "When you go," he told you, "you go in style."

The driver got out and handed Abby the keys with a wink. Abby squealed and turned to Sarah. "Your chariot awaits, Thelma!"

Sarah made an excited squeak of her own and threw open the passenger door

Abby adjusted the rearview mirror. "Take care of our boys, Walter!"

The older man smiled and gave her a small wave. "Will do," he promised.

Abby gave the men her own wave. "Have a good night, boys!" she called before she peeled away from the curb and headed toward the main drag.

Tex and the boys watched as the girls headed for a night in Sin City.

"Think they'll be okay?" Shooter asked.

Tex nodded. "Apparently, my girl really does run Vegas. I'd be more worried about us, honestly."

Walter chuckled. "Oh, not to worry, Sir. Ms. Raines has taken care of all tonight's entertainment for you."

Easy looked unsure. "A chick planning a bachelor party? I don't know. Are we gonna end up at a synchronized swimming show?"

Walter's eyes twinkled. It was clear he had no doubts about Abby or her plans. He opened the back door and gestured for the men to climb on board.

After they piled in and took their seats, Easy leaned toward the lowered partition between the driver and the passengers. "So," he said, clapping his hands together. "Which club are we hitting first?

Which one has the hottest chicks?"

Walter smiled and pulled away from the curb. "First stop is off-Strip, gentlemen."

Easy groaned. "Awww. I knew it!"

But Tex shook his head. "My girl's anything but boring, Easy."

Walter wasn't kidding about going 'off-Strip'. The large vehicle swung into an alley three blocks from the main drag. Walter got out and opened the back door for them. Easy looked around, particularly uneasy. Even Hawk looked a little cautious.

"Did anyone think to bring weapons?" Easy asked.

Walter herded the group to a steel door and knocked succinctly. It opened, revealing a large bouncer in leather pants and a black t-shirt stretched across his huge pecs. Tex was tempted to tell him the pants were less badass and more Siegfried and Roy, but kept his mouth shut. Walter produced a business card and handed it to the man. He nodded and stepped aside.

The five army rangers cautiously entered the building, making their way down a nondescript hallway. At the end they were greeted again. But not by a juiced up bodybuilder with questionable attire. This time they were greeted by a woman with long, silky brunette hair and the shortest red dress that Tex thought could still be considered clothing.

"Gentleman," she said, greeting them warmly. "It's this way."

Easy apparently approved because he shouldered his way to the front of the group and followed the siren across a well-appointed sitting room with cherry furnishings and a large, thick carpet that stretched nearly wall to wall. The group headed toward two large oak double doors that were closed. Apparently, the siren liked what she saw, as well, because she kept peeking over her shoulder at the youngest of the group.

She opened the doors revealing a large felt table with five chairs.

"Oh, sweet!" Easy remarked, temporarily forgetting about the siren.

As they took up the chairs, a side door opened and two women appeared, each carrying stacks of chips in racks. It was hard to look at the racks because of their racks. Both women were topless and only had on black short shorts.

Hawk laughed.

"Your stakes, gentleman," said the blonde, leaning over the table seductively to divvy out the chips.

The hostess took a brand new deck of cards from the solid oak bar off to the side of the room and placed them in the center of the table. She nodded to the other brunette, who set down her chips and headed to bar, returning with a humidor. She opened the lid and offered them some of the finest Cubans Tex had seen since his army days. The other took their drink order, explaining that everything was covered. Except tips, she playfully pointed out and grinned cheekily.

Easy leaned back in his chair and arranged his cards. "You're right. Not boring," he declared.

Tex sipped his scotch and smiled. "Nope. Not my girl."

Abby and Sarah pulled up in front of La Celestine, which Sarah had seen on the Food Network Channel. The valet grinned at the classic car and Abby led her friend straight into the lobby. The hostess made a beeline for them and greeted them warmly.

As they made their way across the dining room, Sarah kept close to Abby. "I've never eaten at a place like this before."

Abby looked at Sarah over her shoulder. "Well, don't get your hopes up. You're not eating here tonight."

Sarah's face fell but Abby smiled. "Well, you might," she amended. "If you do a good job."

Sarah's eyebrows knitted together. "A good job?" she asked as the hostess led them past the other diners and through the swinging doors of the kitchen. The slightly older girl's eyes got impossibly wide as she took in the gleaming stainless steel appliances and counter tops, the bright white of the chef and sous chef's jackets, and the mouthwatering smell of French cuisine.

Alphonse Remoude himself made his way toward them.

"Abby!" he cried, smiling. His arms were held wide.

Abby stepped into them and returned the older man's hug with enthusiasm.

"What have you brought me, then, hmmm?" he asked, stepping back and eyeing Sarah.

"Alfie, this is Sarah."

The chef looked her up and down and then nodded. To Abby he said, "We have a bouillabaisse with a spicy rouille that is to die for. And a steak béarnaise with sweet potato straws."

"Sounds amazing," Abby replied.

The Michelin star chef nodded and Abby made her way to the empty chef's table. Sarah attempted to join her but was halted by the Frenchman.

"No, no, no!" he said loudly. "We cook! You come!"

Sarah's jaw dropped as a sous chef handed her a jacket with her own name embroidered in royal blue on the lapel. She glanced at Abby who grinned widely at her.

"Make it good!" Abby called out as she took a seat. "I'm starving!"

Alfie had decided that Sarah had worked hard enough to join Abby at the table in the corner. Sarah slid into the booth looking incredibly joyful as a waiter slid the plates onto the table.

"I can't believe I cooked with Alphonse Remoude!" she gasped, grabbing a chilled water glass off the table and taking a huge gulp. "Oh my God!"

Abby took a bite of the seafood soup and moaned gratefully. "Well, you did an excellent job. This is awesome!"

"Do you know how to flambe a wine sauce?" Sarah asked.

"Nope," Abby admitted.

"Well, I do now!"

Both women sipped the wine that the waiter had poured and giggled happily.

The men played three hands and were about to start a fourth, if they could get Easy to stop tucking chips into the brunette's short shorts long enough to focus on dealing. But they were cut short by the hostess who had returned through the double doors.

"Your time is up, gentleman," she announced with a hint of disappointment in her voice.

"What?" Easy protested. "I want to stay! Let's stay!"

The hostess shook her head. "I'm afraid it's not on your agenda," she informed them. "But come see us again!"

The men gathered up their winnings after the waitresses cashed their chips in for them. Hawk tucked a large stack of bills into his jeans. "I feel like a high roller," he declared.

Shooter laughed.

In the alley, Walter was waiting for them, and they climbed back into the Hummer. Before they pulled away he passed a manila envelope through the open partition. Shooter took it and opened it. Tex leaned across the seat for a better view. There was a flyer, another business card with Abby's name on it, and a note in her handwriting.

A little bird told me that Vasquez is looking good tonight. Good luck! -A.R.

"What is it?" Tex asked, angling for a better look.

Shooter glanced at the flyer, the note, and then to Tex. "I think- I think your girlfriend just gave me an inside tip."

"What?" Doc demanded and snatched the flyer away from Shooter. Then he took the accompanying note. "Holy shit," he declared.

Easy examined the note. "Think it's true?

Hawk grunted. "I'm putting everything I got in my pocket on this kid," he announced.

Easy made a face. "Well, I lost my shirt, but I'm so betting on this dude. Maybe I can get some of it back."

Everyone laughed.

Walter drove them straight to the front doors of the venue but didn't get out. Valets opened all the doors for the men and they emerged into the spotlights and raucous crowd gathering for a Friday Night Fight in Las Vegas. As Walter glided away in the Hummer limo, Shooter pulled out the business card and, as instructed on the back, showed it to the valet. The young man led him in through the front doors and waved over a woman in slacks and a fitted blazer with a security I.D. lanyard around her neck. Shooter again presented the card and the men were ushered past the teeming crowds of people trying to get to the arena.

The woman led them to the end of a hall, used a key to activate a private elevator, and they rode it three floors up. She directed them to a small, private viewing room overlooking the ring. Shooter grinned and took one of the middle seats, pushing it back so it reclined a little. The men placed bets with the besuited woman who returned with their billets as they raided the bar for ice cold beers.

After dinner at La Celestine, Abby swung the Caddy into a parking lot on the Strip and killed the engine. She waggled her eyebrows at Sarah. Sarah looked at the brightly lit building in front of them.

"Oh, come on," Abby challenged. "Look but don't touch, right?"

The two girls walked quickly across the parking lot and the bouncer held the door for them as Abby shuffled Sarah inside.

After her eyes adjusted, Sarah's mouth dropped open. "Is it Ladies' Night?" she asked quietly, taking it all in.

"It's always Ladies' Night here," said a velvety voice behind them. Sarah jumped nervously as a perfectly chiseled shirtless man grinned at them.

Abby laughed, took Sarah's hand and grabbed a table up front by the stage. Sarah gawked at the performers as Abby ordered them drinks.

When Sarah was halfway through her first Long Island, a lithe but well-built guy with a long blonde ponytail sidled up to their table. Sarah's face turned bright red but she dutifully took one of the bills Abby had given her and closed her eyes as she tucked it into the waistband of his shorts. He blew her a kiss and danced away. Sarah giggled and took another long gulp of tea.

"He was hot," Abby declared.

Sarah nodded. "But I only gave him a dollar."

"Why?"

Sarah leaned forward and whispered conspiratorially, "Because

Chris is bigger."

Abby howled with laughter. "You've got a fine man. I can't argue with that."

Sarah smiled and nodded. "Mark's nice, too."

"Oh, yeah," Abby concurred.

Sarah wrinkled her nose. Apparently bolstered by the cocktail she blurted out, "Does he really gag you?"

Abby guffawed as a group of out-of-towners at the next table eyed them with shocked expressions. Abby sipped her own martini and nodded.

"Is it awful?" Sarah asked, looking slightly appalled.

Abby shook her head. "I love it."

Sarah looked as though she could not comprehend this. "But....why?!"

Abby thought for a minute, swirling her olive into her drink. "You ever had really bad sex? Like, it was his idea, but he's got one eye on the tv the whole time and you could be anyone at all? Or a sock?"

Sarah shook her head.

"Well, consider yourself lucky," Abby advised. "Because I have. And when Mark first gagged me, I thought I would lose it. But when I calmed down, I realized I'd never experienced anything like it." She leaned forward in her chair. "When I'm gagged, and I can't speak, it's like here's this absolutely gorgeous man, who is the most amazing lover I've ever had *ever,* and all he cares about, all he's thinking about, is me. He's watching my every reaction. He's looking to see if I like what he's doing. I've never been with a man who cared *that much* about whether or not I was happy. I've never been someone's whole world like that."

Sarah sat back in her chair, amazed. "I never thought of it like that."

Abby shook her head. "I didn't know it would be like that, either. But it's the most amazing feeling. To know someone cares so much."

After the fight was over, they headed back out front and waited for Walter. Once inside the Hummer, the older man grinned at them. "Win big?" he asked.

Hawk grinned back and pulled out a wad of cash and fisted it.

"Where are we off to next, Walt?" Easy asked, happily fingering his own, smaller stack of cash.

"Ice cream social, Sir."

Easy looked crestfallen. "Huh?"

"Ice cream social. It's the last stop."

Easy grumbled and sat back in his seat. "What's an ice cream social?" he grumbled.

"No idea and I don't care," Shooter replied. "I'm up for anything!"

Walter weaved through city traffic and put them back on the Strip in short order. Easy perked up when he pulled into the lot of a huge building that couldn't be anything other than a strip club.

"Now, that's what I'm talking about!" he shouted, slapping Doc on the shoulder.

Shooter frowned, though. "I don't know," he said quietly.

Easy shook his head. "Oh, no! This is a bachelor party! There are always strippers at a bachelor party! Slick knows that. It's a universal rule!"

But Shooter just frowned. "Maybe I should call her."

"You're not calling anyone!" Easy yelled and launched himself out of the car. "No one's coming between me and naked women!"

He sprinted for the door. Walter handed Shooter another business card that said nothing on the back. He reluctantly took it and climbed out of the car. Once inside, he presented it to the girl behind the counter who beamed at the men. She gestured for a group of women, one for each man, and the girls swarmed them.

They led the men into the main area, past the tables and the stages, and into a large private room. Shooter looked more and more anxious as they went. The room had chairs, all placed strategically in a circle. But not around a stage. They were surrounding a large, heart shaped bed with fitted plastic over the velvet mattress.

Another girl, topless with perky tits and an impossibly perkier ass scurried up to them. "Is one of you Shooter?" she purred.

The rest of the men glanced at their lieutenant.

Shooter squared his shoulders and looked directly into the face of the enemy, showing no fear. "Yes, Ma'am," he said stoically "But I am not-"

The girl giggled and produced a card from behind her back. She handed it to the large man.

Surprised, Shooter seemed to forget what he was going to say and opened the card. He pulled out a small, handwritten note.

Looking is okay, the note said. Touching isn't. Enjoy! Love, Slick

"Free pass!" Easy shouted. And the girls all cheered.

They bade the men to sit in the chairs and Easy pulled his girl directly into his lap. "What, pray tell," he said into her ear, "is an Ice Cream Social?"

The girl giggled and wiggled on his lap. "You'll see!" she declared.

And oh, did they see.

Two girls with ponytails, g-strings, and high heels wheeled in a small cart and placed it next to the bed.

The men watched in with a mix of adoration and amazement as the two little minxes climbed onto the bed, the cart within easy reach, and began to decorate each other as though they were living, breathing, ice cream sundaes.

At least the plastic sheets made sense now.

"Oh, my God," Hawk moaned as the little blonde ate the dark-haired girl's cherry, and then ate her cherry. Well, probably not her cherry, considering she was a stripper, but it was good to pretend.

A pretty little Asian girl sidled up next to Tex. "Want some company?" she purred, indicating that aside from Shooter, Tex's lap was the only other that remained unoccupied.

Tex grinned, but shook his head. "No, ma'am," he replied. "I'm playing by the same rules as my friend here," he said, jerking his thumb at Shooter. He did, however, dig some bills out of his wallet. "But if you'd get me a shot of Jaeger and a beer, I'd be grateful."

The woman toddled off on her impossibly high heels to complete the bar order.

Hawk lifted his own beer that he'd ordered a moment ago and

held it out to Tex. "To Vegas," he announced. And the other men approved.

"To Vegas!" they all joined in.

Easy grinned. "You should leave," he told Tex. "Right now. You should go back to the hotel, grab that woman of yours, and take her straight to one of those little Elvis chapels."

The men laughed. Tex smiled. "I don't see myself getting married by the King," he protested.

Hawk smirked. "I'm not one for marriage," he declared. "But buy that little woman a leash or something, cowboy. Don't let her get away."

Tex sipped his beer and watched Candy and Mandy wrestle in a sea of whipped cream, but all he could really think about was a sassy little redhead who needed one hell of a reward.

CHAPTER THIRTY-FIVE

In the morning, the group headed downstairs to the buffet. Easy came to their large table with plate stacked as high as he could get it without spilling.

"You know you can go back up," Hawk told him, shaking his head.

Easy flipped him the bird and shoveled in a mouthful of Belgian waffles. "Last night," he declared, "was amazing, Vegas." Abby grinned at him. "Out of curiosity, do you own any other towns? Berlin? Helsinki? Tokyo?"

Abby laughed. "Nope. Just Sin City."

"I never met someone who owned a whole town before," Hawk declared. "You think-"

"Abby?"

Abby felt her stomach tighten at the sound of her own name. She didn't even need to turn her head to know who it belonged to. But she did anyway.

The woman standing at the table was tall, especially since she had on high heels. A decent pair, Abby thought to herself, as she looked the woman over. But then Nicolette had always done better for herself than anyone would have expected from Louisiana sharecroppers.

She had on a crisp linen dress. Her hair was flaming red, much more so than Abby's. Abby knew it was a dye job just by looking, but a pricey one at any rate.

"What are you doing here?" Abby blurted out, getting out of her chair.

"I heard you were in town and I thought I'd come say hello."

Abby skirted around the table, took Nicolette by the elbow, and started pushing her toward the door. "Be right back," she called to the table of her friends.

As both women walked through the lobby, Nicolette protested. "Abby, really, I-"

"*Not. here,*" Abby snapped, jamming the button for the elevator. When the doors opened, she ushered the other woman in and pressed the button for her own floor.

In the relative safety of the suite, Abby slammed the door. "What are you doing here?" she demanded again.

"I came to see you," Nicolette replied. "You practically ran out of Vegas when you graduated and I never had a chance-"

"You had years, Nicolette," Abby snapped. "It's not as though you didn't know where to find me."

Nicolette scowled. "Well, things were complicated."

"I bet," Abby replied, crossing her arms in front of her chest.

Ignoring Abby's seething anger, Nicolette instead glanced around the suite. "You know," she said conversationally, "when Mick built this place, he promised me an apartment on one of the upper floors." She ran her hand over the back of the sofa. "When he died that bitch-"

"Enough!"

Nicolette at least had the good sense to look chagrined.

"It doesn't matter," Abby informed her.

"It's always mattered," Nicolette argued. "But now you're back and-"

Abby shook her head. "I'm not back. I'm just spending the weekend with some friends."

Ignoring that as well, Nicolette took an envelope out of her purse and tried to hand it to Abby.

"I don't want that," Abby declared.

"Abby. Be reasonable."

"I am being reasonable. This is your thing. Not mine. It has nothing do with me."

"It has everything to do with you!" Nicolette snapped.

"Why can't you just be happy?" Abby demanded. "I mean, you look like you're doing well for yourself, Nicolette. You look like you've got a good thing going."

Always temporarily sidetracked by a compliment, the older woman smoothed her dress and smiled. "I am. He's a doctor. But this has nothing to do with him," she said, getting back on track.

Abby sighed inwardly, having forgotten how focused Nicolette could be when money was at stake, or when she was feeling panicked. Nicolette looked good for her age, no one could deny it. But she was an aging ex-showgirl in a town full of younger talent and she obviously felt like she lacked the type of stability that comes from having a lot zeroes in your bank account.

Maybe the doctor was getting tired of her. God knew Abby certainly was.

"Nicolette," Abby said sternly. "This is a game you don't know how to play."

And it was true. Nicolette Boudreaux Raines always wanted more than she had and she always played high stakes. The trouble was, she never understood that the House always wins.

"Abby, we could try again," Nicolette pleaded. "I know...I know I wasn't always the best mother."

"Or ever."

Undeterred, Nicolette put on her best matronly face. "You could stay," she said. "We could spend some time together. We could....reconnect."

"I have a life. And it's not here."

Nicolette scoffed. "Nebraska is hardly-"

"South Dakota."

Nicolette laughed, sharp and brittle. "Is there a difference? Abby, this is Las Vegas. This is home. This is-"

"I have someone," Abby confided.

Nicolette actually looked surprised.

"I have someone and he's all I want."

Nicolette was silent for a moment. Doubtless trying to figure out why anyone would choose love over money. "Abby," she said in a voice verging on condescension. "You haven't even known him that long."

"I've known him long enough."

Nicolette sighed, irritated. "Abby, you can't possibly care that much for him. And if he cared about you at all, really cared, he would want you to have-"

Abby snatched the envelope from Nicolette and started to crumple it. Nicolette grabbed her wrist. "Do not throw away your future," she hissed.

"My relationship isn't for sale, Nicolette."

Behind them, someone cleared their throat and both women turned to notice that the rest of the group had finished breakfast and had come back to the suite.

Nicolette rearranged her features into a beatific smile and patted Abby's hand that was holding the envelope. "We'll talk more before you leave," she told Abby and breezed out the room.

Mark crossed the sitting room toward Abby. "Everything okay?" he asked.

Abby nodded. "Fine. Honestly."

"Who was that?" Hawk asked.

"No one," Abby insisted. To Sarah she said, "Ready to go shopping?"

Abby sipped her Bahama Mama and giggled at Shooter trying valiantly to hide his wife's ass from the general public. Abby had convinced Sarah that she could still look sexy in a bathing suit, despite her scars. They just had to find the right one. Claudia, the boutique owner, had come through with a hot little Brazilian suit that had side cutouts and a nearly thong back, but covered Sarah's chest and stomach.

Beyond Shooter's shoulder Abby saw two large men wearing suits and ties, at odds with the pools casual dress code, coming toward the table. Mark, ever attuned to her moods, swiveled his gaze to the approaching men. He tensed, but Abby leaned back in her chair.

"Ms. Raines," the older one said.

"Jack," she drawled. Jack Tallant was completely loyal to the Dugan family, but Abby wasn't about to let him get away with acting as though they barely knew each other.

Jack's only visible reaction to the familiarity was a slight twitch in his jaw.

"The Dugans would like to see you," Jack announced.

Abby smiled. "I'm assuming I have time to change."

Jack grunted something that might have been a yes and Abby stood up. Mark began to get up, as well, but Abby put her hand on his shoulder. "Stay," she told him. "They'll just make you sit in a waiting room. You won't see anything exciting." She gave Mark a kiss on the cheek and picked up her towel that she'd draped over the chair. Tightening it around her, she was escorted back into the hotel and toward the elevators.

At the suite, she quickly changed into a pair of linen trousers, black high heels, and a cream colored silk button down blouse. She grabbed her purse, double checked to make sure Nicolette's half-crumpled envelope was still tucked safely inside, and made her way back to the sitting room where Jack and Jack's Shadow were patiently waiting for her. She didn't bother to remind them that she knew perfectly well where the hotel's administration offices were located.

They took her to the ground floor, past the check-in desk, and down the long hall to an area of the hotel that guests never saw. She was ushered into the conference room where it seemed the entire Dugan clan was assembled to greet her. Or do battle. Which for them was the same thing.

Abby spotted Lucian Hilliard, who was head of legal for the Canyon as well as the Dugan family's private attorney. He smiled warmly at her, in direct opposition to the chilly reception the others were giving her. But then Lucian Hilliard had been overseeing legal operations for the Coral Canyon before any of these people had been associated with the resort. Before Mick Dugan's widow had gotten her claws into him and certainly before the Dugan heirs, Kyle and Gillian, had been born.

She took a vacant seat next to Hilliard and set her purse down on the floor.

"Abby," Kyle said by way of greeting, and also as a cue to start the meeting.

"Is this a short trip, Abby?" Claire Dugan interrupted, her sharp gaze boring into Abby from across the table.

Abby smiled, unruffled. "Just a weekend getaway. For my friends."

Claire's face remained passive. "Yes, we'd heard you'd taken a job up north."

Abby didn't bother to reply. The Dugan family surely knew everything about her from where she lived to what toothpaste she bought and where she bought it.

"Well," Claire announced, usurping the central role from her son. "I, for one, would like to congratulate you on your new job. Mick was always very supportive of his employees and their families. Since you're here for a visit, we'd like to offer you-"

"Ten million dollars," Abby finished for her.

There was no sense in dragging this out any longer than was necessary, was Abby's way of thinking. Plus, while the Dugans might appear to be a comical mix of a trophy wife past her prime, a grasping, laughably inept son, and an air-headed daughter, Abby knew looks were deceiving. Claire Dugan had as much to do with the operation of the Coral Canyon as her son and her daughter, while not the brightest of progeny, certainly could hire an army of lawyers who were.

Claire gaped.

"Abby-" Kyle scoffed as though she were being childish.

Abby picked up her purse. "We're in Vegas," she declared. "Let's gamble."

She pulled Nicolette's envelope out of her purse and set it face up on the table, close enough that Hilliard could see the letterhead. She tapped it casually.

"For 10 million dollars, I will sell you this envelope. But if you're feeling lucky, let's open it and let the chips fall where they may, so to speak."

Claire snorted, which was highly unladylike, but Abby was wise enough not to comment. "It's surely not the only copy."

Abby shook her head. "No. I'm certain Nicolette has her own

copy. But she can do nothing with it. Not without me. And I'm also certain Mr. Hilliard here has brought along a waiver that I'm supposed to sign relinquishing any claim I might make for a sum of...." Here she looked at Hilliard, who cleared his throat. He was clearly embarrassed by the Dugan's paltry offer.

"One hundred thousand dollars," he told her.

Now it was Abby's turn to scoff. "We all know I'm worth much more than that."

"Bitch," Gillian seethed.

Claire held up a hand to silence her daughter.

"Ten million," Abby repeated. "Or we open this envelope. And I book myself for an extended stay."

Gillian stormed out and Kyle looked like he might kill Abby rather than agree to that amount. Claire finally sighed and nodded to the lawyer. None of the Dugans stayed in the room, as though they couldn't be bothered to be associated with Abby for longer than absolutely necessary.

Hilliard smiled at her and produced a different sheaf of papers from his briefcase. Apparently he had anticipated that Abby wouldn't be going down without a fight. He filled in the appropriate numbers and called the casino floor to issue a cashier's check.

As they waited he loosened his tie. "You should stay, Abby."

Abby returned the smile, but shook her head. "I can't. This is not my town, Mr. Hilliard."

Undeterred the old man said, "It could be."

"Vegas killed my father," Abby said, somewhat wearily. "It killed Mick, too."

Hilliard sighed and nodded, his Old Vegas eyes showing that he understood that while the death certificates might say "Pancreatic Cancer" and "Heart Disease" it was years of trying to keep your soul relatively clean in this dirty little town that eventually did both men in. Abby silently wondered how long the old man in front her had left, and whether he thought it had all been worth it.

Twenty minutes later Hilliard handed her the check and offered her a heartfelt handshake.

Abby returned the friendly sentiment and headed back upstairs.

CHAPTER THIRTY-SIX

As Abby entered the suite, Tex stood up from the chair he was lounging in. She tossed her purse on the couch and kissed him.

"Sorry I took so long," she said.

"You alright?" he asked, stepping back to look at her.

She nodded. "Yep. Better than alright."

He smiled at her. "Good. Because if you'd taken any longer, I was coming to find you."

She laughed. "It was fine. Honestly."

"Well, you're late, but not that late. Come on," he told her. "It's time for dinner."

At the elevators, Tex pushed the button for the top floor rather than the ground floor where the Canyon's restaurant was located.

"Um," Abby started to say, but he shook his head.

The car traveled up to the top floor and they both got out. Tex led her to the end of the hall where he produced an electronic key card from his pocket. With a swipe, he unlocked the door to the stairway.

Abby giggled. "And here I thought I was the one who had this place wired."

Tex grinned at her as he held the door open. "Apparently it's all about who you know."

"Oh, is it now?" she teased as he led her to the roof.

Outside it was a beautiful evening, not too hot with only a slight breeze. A room service cart had been brought up and a small table, lined with a table cloth overlooked Sin City as the sun was beginning to set.

"Your friends had some ideas about the best place to eat in the city."

Abby looked out at the glittering oasis that lit up the desert surrounding it. "I've been up here," she admitted. "But I've never had dinner here."

Tex held out her chair for her and as she moved to sit in it he leaned close to her ear. "Always nice to be your first," he half-whispered.

She blushed in spite of herself.

They finished the meal just as the sun was about to sink into the horizon. Abby was about to head to the edge of the roof to watch, but Tex lifted up the tablecloth that was draped over the food service cart and fished something out of the lower shelf.

"Dessert?" she asked, hopefully.

"No," he replied and made his way over to her. "Like I said," he declared, producing a flat, blue velvet box. "Your friends have been very helpful."

She took it and opened it. Inside was a gold snake chain necklace with a large flower made of rubies and diamonds. It was the most beautiful thing she'd ever seen. She couldn't even begin to guess at the cost.

"Oh, Mark-"

"I love you. It's not just the kink, Abby. That's part of it, but it's not the only reason. I wanted to give you something you could wear all the time. No one at work will know what it means. And it's not a play collar, Abby. By wearing it, you're not required to obey me any more than you already do. That's still for the bedroom only. This is just...a symbol of our relationship.

"I know I just said I love you for more than kink, and then I gave you a collar. But it's also vintage. From 1950. Like the movies you love. I saw it and I knew it was perfect for you. It's you, Abby. All of you. The sassy, beautiful, kinky, adorable woman who knows all the lines to every classic movie. I want everyone to see how much I love you. Even if most of them won't know all the reasons why."

Tears rimmed Abby's eyes. "Mark-"

"Shhh. All that matters is you keep giving me you. That's the most precious thing you could ever give me. Your love, your trust, your obedience in the bedroom. I can't put a price on that. It's worth everything to me."

He took the necklace out and handed it to her while pocketing the box. Then he took it back, stepped around behind her, and slid it around her neck. The jeweled flower nestled perfectly in the hollow of her throat.

"I couldn't have wished for anything more perfect," she told him.

He took her in his arms and nuzzled her ear. "I feel the same way."

Back downstairs, the rest of the group showed up at the suite, ready to head downstairs and hit the casino. Sarah headed off to find Abby, who was still getting ready in the bedroom and was only there a few short moments before she let out a piercing shriek.

"Oh my God! Oh my GOD! OH MY GOD!"

Shooter glanced over his shoulder at the closed bedroom door, then to Tex who was positively beaming. "I got Abby a permanent collar," he announced proudly. The men were stunned.

Shooter rubbed his face with his hand. "Please. Please tell me it's not a spiked dog collar. You'll scare Slick."

Loud squealing ensued from the bedroom, but none of the men knew if this was a good thing or not.

Tex scowled at Shooter. "I wouldn't put a spiked dog collar on a *dog*, let alone a woman."

The bedroom door flew open and Sarah darted out. She threw herself at Tex and hugged him. "Oh, it's so beautiful!" she cried.

The men rounded the women to get a better look at Abby who emerged from the bedroom wearing a red dress that matched the jeweled flower at her throat.

"It's so beautiful!" Sarah proclaimed again. "It's a collar? It doesn't look like it. It's gorgeous!"

Abby laughed. "Well, it's a necklace. Vintage Tiffany's. Unless they know us, no one will know what it means."

Sarah squealed. "It's so perfect for you!" She turned to look at Tex. "Mark, it's...amazing!"

When Slick had calmed down, Tex looked at their friends. "Thanks, you guys. For being cool about it. It means a lot that we don't have to hide."

Hawk chuckled. "Are we gonna have a group hug now? Might lead to an orgy."

"Fuck you," Tex replied, but he was grinning.

Doc put his arm around Abby's shoulders. "Well, aside from Slick, I've never seen a man make a woman so happy. So whatever it is you're doing," he told Tex, "and I probably don't want to know what it is, but you must be doing it right."

At the craps table, Hawk laughed. "Now, you're going to be shopping for jewelry," he told Shooter. "You know this, right?"

Shooter rolled his eyes and shook his head. "Nah. Not me. Slick likes panties. Lots and lots of panties. We have weekday panties and week*end* panties."

The men laughed. "You mean they have Monday, Tuesday, Wednesday written on them?" asked Hawk.

"No. I mean the weekday panties are just Victoria's Secret. Thirty bucks a pair. Very cute, but no big whoop. The weekend panties she orders online. From *Paris*. I got excited and tore a pair. That did not go over well. Weekend panties are purely visual aids. Hundred bucks a pair."

Hawk coughed on his beer. "*A hundred bucks a pair?*"

"I know," Shooter said. "I know. But I figure, I have my bike, she has her panties. And it is sooooo worth it."

"A hundred bucks a pair worth it?" Hawk repeated.

Shooter grinned. "Well, each one comes with it's own little backstory. She's got this French maid thing. A naughty nurse thing.

She's even got some frilly little knickers for Princess and the Pirate. Every weekend is like Sexy Halloween. What am I gonna say? No more Sexy Halloween? Yeah, that's not happening. I love Slick's little panties. Plus they make her feel pretty, and that's worth every dime I make."

The men frowned. "You guys talked about maybe plastic surgery?" Doc asked

Shooter nodded. "Yeah, but she doesn't want to spend the money right now or have to be out of work with Maria needing so much help. Later, when things are calmer, we'll discuss it some more. I'm okay with whatever she does. I just want her to feel good about herself."

"Maybe you guys could get a his and her discount," Easy replied, lightening the mood.

Shooter chuckled. "No, my scars are rugged, manly scars that make me more attractive. Or so says Slick."

The girls found them, Slick apparently having lost at the roulette wheel. "What are you talking about?" she asked as everyone got quiet.

Her husband put one arm around her. "Nothing baby. Just...you know...weekend panties," Shooter told her.

Sarah rolled her eyes at him. "Weekend panties?" Abby asked.

Sarah turned to look at her. "He ripped my La Perla's."

Abby gasped. "Part of a set?"

Sarah's eyes narrowed. "Sheer lace balconette bra."

"Brute!" she cried at Shooter. He grimaced contritely.

"I lost," Sarah announced.

"I told you not to play," Abby admonished.

"I need more money," Sarah told Chris. He dutifully fished some bills out of his wallet.

"Don't cheat," he warned her.

Sarah stuck her tongue out at her husband, took the cash, and pulled Abby toward the Blackjack tables.

As they sat side by side at a table with two openings, Sarah looked at Abby and a smile crossed her lips.

"What?" Abby asked.

"I was worried, when you two met."

"Worried?" Abby shook her head. "No. You were right. Tex would never, ever hurt me."

"No, it was him I was worried about."

Abby was shocked. "Why?"

Sarah leaned in a lowered her voice. "Well, I've known him a while now. And he was always pretty open about the fact that he was...dominant. I tried to be upbeat and positive about it, but he had a laundry list of things he was looking for. I'm not even talking about the kinky stuff. I don't even know about that part. But he was holding out for an intelligent, independent, sexy woman who could hold her own against him outside of the bedroom, but still be strong enough to wear this," Sarah said, running a finger along the necklace. "And like I said, I tried to stay positive for his sake, but honestly it seemed like the tiniest sliver of a Venn Diagram, finding a woman who could be both."

Abby toyed with the felt at the edge of the table. "He's everything I want, too," she admitted.

Two hours later the group had splintered. Doc had found a woman at the bar and was about to close the deal with her. Easy and Hawk were trying to outshoot each other at the craps table. Slick and Shooter had wandered to off to no one knew where and Mark was busy nuzzling Abby's ear from behind.

"Ready to go upstairs and be naughty?" he asked quietly.

She smiled and ran her hands along his arms. "More than ready."

They practically sprinted toward the elevator and when they were inside, Mark jammed the button to close the doors before anyone else could get on with them. He pushed her up against the side of the car and ground his cock into her. She paused in their kissing long enough to hiss, "Cameras!"

"Let them watch," Mark declared, sliding a hand up Abby's leg, but stopping just short of truly indecent.

When the car stopped and the doors slid open, he tugged her out and hurried toward their door. After fumbling with the electronic key card for a moment, he finally got it and the door swung inward. They made it as far as the couch where he sat down, pulling her on top of him, and his hand found the spot he'd refrained from caressing in the elevator.

Abby moaned appreciatively.

And then the phone rang.

She tore her lips from his and glared at it.

"Ignore it," Mark ordered, reaching for the hem of her dress and pulling it up over her hips to reveal her panties.

It rang again and Abby groaned. "It might be important," she protested.

"Nothing could be that important," he decided, nipping her bottom lip.

The phone rang a third time and Abby sprawled across his lap to reach the extension on the end table.

Mark slapped her ass. She yelped.

"Bad girl!" he admonished, but he was grinning.

Abby picked up the receiver with one hand, balanced herself on her elbow, and rubbed her stinging cheek with her free hand.

"Hello?"

She listened for a bit, then glanced back at Mark over her shoulder.

"What now?" she asked. "You what?"

She rolled slightly off Mark's erection, making him groan, but only in disappointment.

"I'll be right there," Abby promised to the person on the phone and hung up. She slid off him and off the couch entirely and straightened her dress. "I have to run downstairs. I'll be back in ten minutes," she swore, fleeing for the door.

"You are so getting an ass whooping when you get back!" Mark called after her.

Riding the elevator down to the lobby, Abby smoothed her hair and attempted to fix the wrinkles in her dress. Glancing at herself in the hallway mirror, she thought she looked halfway presentable as she reached the Hotel's Security office. Not bothering to knock, she twisted the handle and let herself in.

Chris was sitting in one chair, elbows on his knees, hands covering his face. He looked more irritated than anything else. Sarah was sitting next to him, crying. When she saw Abby she gave a huge sigh of relief, but she didn't stop sniffling.

"Paul," Abby said, acknowledging the Hotel's lead detective.

"Abby," he said, doing a very fine job of hiding his grin. He jerked a thumb toward Chris and Sarah. "These two say they're guests of yours."

Abby nodded. "They are. What, exactly, did you say you picked them up for again?"

Chris merely shook his head.

"Prostitution!" Sarah wailed.

Abby struggled mightily not to laugh.

"I caught her soliciting him in the Hotel bar just off the casino," Paul intoned.

Abby shook her head. "I'll take them from here. Thanks, Paul."

Paul nodded.

Chris and Sarah may have been mortified, but they were far from the first married couple to attempt to spice up their sex life with a little role play in a Las Vegas hotel. Chris stood up and stalked toward the door. Sarah flung herself at Abby and weeped. Abby herded her friend out of the Security office and back toward the elevators.

"I'm so embarrassed!" Sarah cried.

Chris jabbed the button and the three of them stepped into the empty car. As the doors slid shut Sarah cried out, "I am not a hooker! *Why does this keep happening to me?*"

The next morning, Abby packed her bags and they were carried down to the lobby by the bellhops. She didn't miss Kyle Dugan standing near the entrance to the administration offices, making sure she was actually leaving town. She took one last look around the Canyon. She'd spent her entire life here, had always thought that she would live here. But times had changed. And, if she was being honest, there were memories here that she didn't necessarily want to keep.

Las Vegas was a town like no other. A jewel in the desert that shone like a beacon, an oasis. The trouble was, it could easily turn out to be a mirage. And by the time you realized the truth, it was usually already too late.

Mark took her carry on from her shoulder and slung it over his own. "We ready?" he asked her.

Abby looked at him and nodded. "Yep. Let's go home."

CHAPTER THIRTY-SEVEN

The next weekend, Mark had cancelled their Friday night session to work late at the garage. He'd told her he was swamped today, too, and that they were working to catch up from the weekend they'd lost in Vegas.

Abby changed into a pair of old jeans, boots, and a faded blue shirt and revved up the engine of the Camaro. She swung into the lot of Burnout and parked. After she killed the engine, which she noticed with no small amount of satisfaction no longer wheezed, she got out of the car and headed toward the open bay doors.

Shooter greeted her first, being closest to the doors.

"Hey, Vegas," he called.

"Shooter," she acknowledged. "I hear you're holding my man hostage for the weekend."

He nodded. "Got a bit behind." He grinned. "Was worth it, though."

"Hell yeah it was!" Easy shouted from underneath a truck.

Shooter laughed. "Tex can take a break, but I can't spare him for too long," he told Abby.

Abby shook her head. "Actually, I came to work."

"Really?" Hawk asked, sidling up to the two of them.

"Not entirely selfless, though," she admitted. "I want my man back tonight. And not so tired he can't work his other job."

Hawk glanced at Mark and laughed.

Abby jerked her chin toward the Camaro. "Brought my resume."

Shooter looked at the Camaro, which, granted, still needed a new paint job, but he couldn't have missed the purr of the engine as she'd pulled in or the lack of grinding brakes when she'd parked.

"Could use the help," the former lieutenant admitted.

"Just tell me where you want me."

"That's my job," Mark said, approaching the group. "What's up, baby?" he asked, pulling Abby in for a kiss.

"I came to help out," she told him.

"Hmm," Shooter said, pretending to reconsider. "So long as Tex can keep his mind on his own work and not staring at your ass all day."

"Does that go for us, too?" Easy asked from a few feet away. "Cause it's a fine ass. And I'm tired of working in a sausage fest."

Shooter ushered her into the garage. "When she's here, she's one of us," he declared.

Easy grumbled, but went back to the truck.

"Thanks, Abby," Chris said. "For everything."

Abby smiled at him. "That's what friends are for. Plus, and I said up front that I wasn't being completely selfless, do you think you guys could spare about an hour on Monday and come to the hotel?"

Shooter looked at Mark, who shrugged, not knowing what was up. "All of us?" he asked.

Abby nodded. "Yeah, I just need a favor. Nothing big."

Shooter grinned. "We can swing by."

"Great!"

Abby tied her hair up and got to work on a chopper that needed a new fuel line. Around noon, Slick brought lunch for the group, which Abby was supremely grateful for. She and Mark were the last ones in the breakroom and when Abby attempted to leave, he snagged her arm and pulled her back.

"He's right," Mark said, nipping her earlobe. "It's totally distracting having you here."

She giggled. "Well, I'm sorry to hear that," she told him. "Because I'm enjoying myself. In fact, working on that chopper has inspired me to get another bike."

Mark turned her around and pushed her up against the table.

"Not happening," he said.

His answer surprised her and she stared at him. "Why not?" she demanded.

He leaned in and kissed the side of her neck. "Because I don't care if it's on a bike, or in between the sheets, or right here on this table, if you think I'm giving up being between your legs, you'd better think again."

Abby let out a surprised laugh and he tickled her with his nose behind her ear.

"Work!" Shooter called from the garage.

She laughed again. "Come on. We've got to go."

She pushed Mark in the opposite direction and headed toward the parking lot where a man was pulling up with in a Ford Fairlane. He got out and she smiled at him. "Hi!" she said enthusiastically. "Help you?"

He eyed her warily. "Are you the receptionist?"

"Um, nope."

"Well...I'd better talk to someone else."

Shooter walked over at that moment. "Help you?" he said, repeating Abby's words.

The guy nodded. "Yeah, I need an oil change, tire rotation, and a tune up. But I don't have an appointment. And I need it back by the end of the day."

Shooter glanced at the Fairlane. "Can do," he replied.

The guy handed over the keys. Shooter turned to Abby. "Oil, tires, tune. Got it?" he asked, passing her the keys.

"Yes, Sir," Abby replied with a mock salute.

The guy spluttered. "Hey now!"

Shooter turned and gave the man a look that could stop a freight train. "You don't have an appointment. You've got a vintage car. You want a full day's work done in three hours. Have I got all that straight?"

The man looked helplessly from Shooter to Abby and back again. "Yes," he finally said weakly.

"Good," Shooter replied. "Glad we're on the same page." He nodded to both the man and Abby and walked away. Abby gave the guy a reassuring smile even though she'd much rather kick him in the nuts and headed toward the car.

"Oh, please be careful," the man pleaded.

Abby refrained from rolling her eyes at him. "Why'd you come to Burnout, Sir?"

His back stiffened. "Because it's supposed to be the best in the city!"

Abby winked at him as though that was all there was to say on the matter.

On Monday morning, Abby tore through her closet, trying on outfit after outfit. She had no idea what was appropriate attire for stealing a hotel. In the end she chose a pair of black slacks and a matching black fitted blazer. She figured it would hide bloodstains. She lifted a cardboard box from her kitchen counter and lugged it to her Camaro, stuffing it onto the passenger seat. Her arms ached by the time she managed to heft it onto the check-in counter in the lobby of the Custer.

Susan, bewildered, looked from Abby to the box and back again. "What's this?" she asked. Abby grinned at her.

"Susan," Abby half-whispered. "I'm going to make you an offer you can't refuse."

An hour later the private car Abby had hired arrived out front and Mr. Hilliard, looking sharp in a gray pinstripe suit, emerged. He took in the facade of the historic hotel and Abby saw him nod to himself before he came through the double doors of the lobby. He positively beamed when he saw Abby.

She took his coat and led him into the conference room. Checking her watch, she bid Mr. Hilliard to wait a few moments as she marched down the hall to Kessler's office where she could hear her boss and her boss's boss chumming it up behind the closed door. Without bothering to knock, she opened the door and breezed in.

"Alice!" Burton said, his jovial tone was clearly fake and there was a menacing edge to his voice as he spoke. "So, what's the big emergency?" the Custer's soon-to-be former owner demanded.

"Conference room," Abby snapped and without waiting for an answer, she turned and swept out of the room.

Kessler came out, hot on her heels. "Wait just a damn minute," he demanded. "Why the hell would you call Burton and why-?"

Abby whirled on him, her glare so penetrating that Kessler actually backed up a step. "Conference room," she seethed and threw open the oak door as though to punctuate her demand.

Kessler spied Hilliard and had no idea what he was in for but came into the room, Burton followed, looking vaguely amused at the whole thing.

Abby let Burton take a seat at the head of the table, with Kessler on his right.

"I'm on a tight schedule here, gentleman," Abby declared. "So let's get started." She shut the door behind her and turned to face the two men who had been making her life miserable since she arrived in Rapid City.

"This hotel is in trouble," she announced.

"Alice-" Burton said, clearly annoyed now.

"Abby!"

Burton looked taken aback at her sharp tone.

"My name is Abby. You should know it. Because I'm buying your hotel. For the bargain basement price of 3 million dollars. Plus a cash incentive."

Burton looked at Kessler and then at Abby. "What?" he asked and Abby could not stop herself from actually rolling her eyes at her boss who could not be less qualified to own a plastic Monopoly hotel let alone a gem like the Custer.

"I'm. buying. your. hotel," she said slowly, emphasizing that she though Burton was basically a moron.

Burton's jaw set. "It's not for sale."

Abby sighed and flipped open the briefcase she'd brought along with her. She grabbed a sheaf full of 8 X 10 glossies and tossed them across the table. They were surveillance shots of the working girls coming to and from the Custer.

Burton stared at them, but then regained his haughty air and sneered at her. "This is nothing," he told her. "This is bullshit."

Abby picked up the second stack of photos and flung them. They were license plates of the cars whose drivers availed themselves of the Blue Orchid's services. "This is just the polite version. For Mr. Hilliard," Abby said, nodding at the older man. "I've got your whores on video, too."

That part was actually a bluff. But Abby was a Vegas girl through and through.

"Now," she said authoritatively. "Like I said, I'm buying the Custer for 3 million dollars." She turned the briefcase around, revealing the rest of its contents to Burton and slid it across the table toward him. "The 3 mil is for the IRS, all nice and legal-like. This," she said, indicating the 2 million in cash, "this is yours to do whatever you want."

Mr. Hilliard opened his own briefcase and set out a bill of sale in front of Burton. "I think you'll find," the lawyer said, "that all our paperwork is in order."

Burton hesitated, staring at Abby and the pinstriped man. The phone's intercom light blinked and the tell-tale chime rang out. Abby pressed the button. "Ms. Raines," came Susan's voice over the speaker. "Your associates have arrived."

"Thank you, Susan. Send them in, please."

"Yes, Ma'am."

The door swung open and Mark entered first, followed by Hawk, Shooter, and Abby saw that even Easy had come.

"Gentlemen," Abby said. "These are my associates."

None of them said anything, but they were clearly curious, looking back and forth between Kessler, Burton, and Hilliard. Abby slid the pen across the table to Burton. "I think we're all pretty clear at this point on the particulars." She reached behind her into the waistband of her tailored trousers and pulled out her .38, pointing it at Burton.

"Holy fuck!" shouted Kessler. Burton's eyes widened, but he was too scared to speak. Mr. Hilliard said nothing. Neither did the four enormous ex-army rangers lined up against the wall. "Sign the papers," Abby demanded. "Take the check, and the cash incentive...*and get the fuck out of my hotel.*"

Kessler looked at Burton, who did nothing helpful, and then

turned to Hilliard. "Do something!"

Abby smiled and shook her head. "He's not going to help you. Mr. Hilliard was Slick Mick Dugan's lawyer for more years than I've been alive. He's Old Vegas."

"Very Old Vegas," Mr. Hilliard added, leaning back in his chair. "I suggest, Mr. Burton, that you accept the sum Ms. Raines is so generously offering you. You're lucky to even get that. In the event the police discover your... sidebusiness... all your assets will be seized, accounts frozen indefinitely."

Burton, finding no aid with Hilliard, looked at the men along the wall.

"They won't help you, either," Abby told him. "They're here to carry your bodies out the back door if you don't sign."

Kessler stood up suddenly. "Susan! Susan!"

Abby rolled her eyes. "Susan's not going to help you. I offered her a management job with a shit-ton of vacation time."

"What the fuck?" Kessler shouted.

"Bitches," Abby scoffed. "I know, right?" She pulled the hammer back on the .38.

Kessler looked at his boss. "You've gotta do something!"

Burton glared at him. "Like what? Go to prison? No, thanks." Burton picked up the pen.

"At least give me half!" Kessler cried. "I arranged everything. I set up the front!"

"And did a great job, too," Burton said sarcastically. "Since apparently any fucking bitch with a college degree could figure it out." The pen scratched loudly as he initialed the highlighted lines and then signed his name on the last page.

Burton stood up, picked up the briefcase, and stormed out the door with Kessler on his heels, begging for a cut.

The chime on the phone rang out again. Abby lowered the gun and hit the button. "Ms. Raines," said Susan. "The Asshole and The Complete and Total Bastard are heading outside. "Everyone's assembled in the ball room."

"Fabulous," Abby replied and disconnected.

She tucked the gun into the back of her waistband again, hiding it under her blazer.

"Thank you, Mr. Hilliard, for coming all his way."

The old man grinned at her and stood up. "It was worth it. Felt like old times." He shook her hand and headed out the door.

Abby picked up the sale paperwork and followed Hilliard out of the meeting room door. "Almost done," she told the men. The rangers followed her.

Her heels clicked on the tile floor as she walked to the reservation counter. Susan looked up at her and picked up the large box on the counter.

"Here, I'll take that," Hawk said, grinning at her.

Susan blushed and handed it over.

Abby turned to the men. "Just one more meeting and then we're done," she told them.

"Yes, Ma'am," said Shooter, grinning.

Abby headed straight up the large staircase and entered the double doors, leading to the large ballroom where everyone who was currently employed at the Custer Hotel was assembled, sitting at the tables.

Abby breezed into the middle of the room and stopped. She held up the signed paperwork. "As of now, I own the Custer Hotel," she told the audience. There were some murmurs through the crowd. "It's been a long and eventful morning, and I really don't have time for bullshit," she announced. "You all know what's been going on here. It stops today. I'm sure some of you have become accustomed to management looking the other way while you get paid for essentially doing nothing. That also stops now. If you don't like it, get the fuck out."

She nodded to Susan who directed Hawk to set the box down. Susan took off the lid and grabbed stack after stack of spiral bound business plans and set a stack down on each table as Abby continued.

"I have plans for this hotel," she announced. "We'll be doing a systematic renovation that, finishing on schedule, should take less than year and turn the Custer into a four star, luxury hotel which is the highest star rating we can achieve while still complying with the guidelines for obtaining and maintaining historic status, which I'm also applying for at the end of the year.

"What this means for you is more work, more attention to detail, and no excuses regarding job performance. It also means more guests and more money. *A lot more money. For all of us.* I'm inviting all of you to stay on and help me turn the Custer into the best hotel in the Black Hills. If you're not interested, get the fuck out. I'll replace you.

"If any of you think you'll stay and try and start up your own sidebusiness like Mr. Kessler, I will ask one of these men-" She jerked her thumb at the large bikers standing a few feet away, "to break your fucking legs. And then they will *throw* you the fuck out. I hope you're sensing a theme there. No more pussy for sale, no more bullshit.

"So take these home with you when your shift ends tonight," she encouraged. "Look them over. I'm going to need a lot of help making this place shine. You need to think about whether or not you want to be a part of it."

The employees filed out of the ballroom, eyeing the rangers warily, and keeping their distance. As Susan left the large assembly room, she shut the double doors. Abby, exhausted from the morning's events, collapsed into an empty chair.

Each of the men picked up an extra prospectus and looked them over.

"Abby," Mark said. "Where did you get that money?"

She sighed. "The Dugans."

Mark's jaw twitched. "You did not borrow millions of dollars from the mob."

She scoffed. "Of course not. It was a gift."

Mark narrowed his eyes. "How much did they give you?"

Abby could see no way around telling him the truth or any reason to keep it from him. "Ten million dollars."

Hawk let out a low whistle.

"Why would the mob *give* you ten million dollars?" Mark demanded.

Abby looked up at him. "I told you my mother was cheating on my father. But I didn't tell you with whom. With the old man. Mick Dugan. They'd been seeing each other for years. Even before my mother married my father. She actually started out as the old man's mistress. When he wouldn't divorce his wife to marry her, she married my father instead. She was pregnant with me at the time."

"So Slick Mick Dugan the mob guy was your real father?"

Shooter asked.

Abby shrugged. "Maybe. Maybe not. I don't really know. I never opened the DNA test results. My mother thinks he was. If it's true and I had filed a claim, I could have eventually ended up with a third of the Canyon."

"How much is that worth?" Easy asked.

Abby shrugged again. "Hard to estimate exactly, since a large chunk of its worth is based on the action at the casinos at any given moment. But say roughly, I don't know, two, three hundred."

"*Two hundred million dollars?!*" Easy cried.

Abby nodded. "Pretty conservative, but something like that. I signed away any future claim on the Canyon in exchange for a cashier's check for ten million. I bought the Custer for five and the extra five should more than cover operating costs until I get the place back in the black."

Easy scoffed. "You should have asked for more."

Abby shook her head. "Well, I didn't want to go for a ride in the desert."

"This is what you were talking about," Mark finally said. "When you were fighting with your mother and you said our relationship wasn't for sale."

Abby nodded. "It's not like the Dugans would just hand over the money to buy me out. And they sure as fuck wouldn't just give me shared control of operations, either. It'd be a court fight. I'd win. There's no doubt. But it'd take a few years at least. I'd have to stay in Vegas to sort it all out. My life is here. With you. With our friends."

Easy stared at her and then turned to Mark. "She gave up sixty million dollars for you."

Abby shook her head. "It doesn't feel like I gave up anything."

CHAPTER THIRTY-EIGHT

Six weeks later.....

It was Friday evening and Abby found herself yet again stuck in her office. Granted it was a bigger office, now that she'd thrown Kessler out on his ass and taken over his. But since she'd bought the Custer, she rarely seemed to actually leave it. She was determined, though, to get out at a semi-decent hour. She shut down her computer and opened her bottom desk drawer to get her purse. She had nearly made it out the door when the phone's intercom buzzed.

She considered it. Briefly. But then decided that she'd had enough for one day and just kept walking. She didn't make it far, though. Susan snagged her before she even set foot in the lobby.

"Complaint," the other woman said.

Abby groaned.

"They want to talk to someone 'more senior'," Susan said, making airquotes.

"Give them free champagne."

"Already did."

"What's the problem?" Abby asked, because to her way of thinking, all her problems could be solved with a few strong martinis.

"He's unhappy with the service."

Abby stowed her purse behind the check-in counter. "Which room?"

"Princess suite," Susan replied.

Abby frowned. "I didn't know we had that room booked this weekend."

"We didn't," Susan said. "We upgraded him. But he's still not happy."

Abby fastened the buttons on her blazer and tucked her hair behind her ears. "Thanks, Susan."

"Sorry," the other woman said, giving Abby a sympathetic look.

Abby took the elevator to the third floor and knocked on the door of second largest suite at the Custer. The door swung open and she nearly took a step back.

Mark grinned at her, wolfishly from the doorway.

She shook her head and he stepped aside, gesturing for her to enter the room. Abby went inside and he shut the door.

"Seems like this is the only way I can actually see you," he told her.

"I'm sorry," she sighed. And she really was. The Custer needed so much work and she put in ridiculous hours trying to drag the hotel back into the black.

"Don't be sorry," Mark told her, unbuttoning her jacket and peeling it from her shoulders. "Owning a place like this is takes a huge amount of effort."

"But still," she said. "I'm not around. I really miss you, though. I promise I'll try harder to make you a priority. It's just-"

"Abby," he interrupted. "I understand completely. Believe me."

"Do you, though?" Because sometimes, to her, it really did feel as though she was choosing the hotel over Mark. And she knew it was selfish of her to do it, but there just wasn't enough of her to go around.

His hands slid down her shoulders to the buttons on her blouse and he began undoing them, one by one, reminding her of all the ways she'd told herself she would make it up to him.

"Do I?" he asked her, sliding the blouse off and letting it drop to the floor. "Do I know what it's like to see something that's been neglected, uncared for?" He reached around her, his fingers finding the clasp of her bra. As it slipped down her arms, it rasped over her nipples which were already hardening.

"Something that you know in your heart could be beautiful and unique, with charm and style all its own? If only someone could see past the facade, into the heart of it, and bring out its best qualities? What would I know about that?" He unzipped her skirt and pushed it, along with her thong panties down to the floor.

Abby stood before Mark in only her stockings, garter belt, and heels. He left her there and crossed the room to the table and chairs nestled into the corner. Apparently he *had* ordered champagne, because it was already chilling.

He took a seat at one of the chairs. His eyes were dark and lazy, seductive smile played over his lips as he gazed at her.

"On your knees, pet," he ordered and still, after all this time, Abby's stomach flip-flopped. "Show me what a good girl you are," he demanded. "Crawl to me."

A similar smile played on Abby's lips as she slowly sank to the floor.

"Yes, Sir."

THE END

ABOUT THE AUTHOR

I live in North Carolina with so many pets that every time it rains I consider building an ark. I majored in English Education, though most of my jobs have involved using my hands: framing art, grooming dogs, stocking shelves. I started writing about seven years ago to avoid going back to a real job.

I've recently taken up roller derby just to test my health insurance coverage.

DahliaMWest@gmail.com

www.dahliawest.com

Made in the USA
San Bernardino, CA
27 December 2015